SHAKE!

If you weren't part of the sixties, read this. If you were, remind yourself.

January 1967: Lily Tempest, seventeen, dreams of university, joining the middle classes, looking like Jane Asher. She and her three sisters have drifted into the seaside town of Fairport, along with their parents Doug and Melody. Melody's ambitions for her daughters are summed up in one word: marriage. Lily would rather die. Instead she goads her sisters into reaching for far more than they want for themselves – with comic but also dark and dangerous results. Lily begins to realise that within her family, honesty and duty, love and sex, fidelity and loyalty, are not what they seem.

Please note: *This book contains material which may not be suitable to all our readers.*

SHAKE!

SHAKE!

by

Yvonne Roberts

Magna Large Print Books
Long Preston, North Yorkshire,
BD23 4ND, England.

British Library Cataloguing in Publication Data.

Roberts, Yvonne
    Shake!.

    A catalogue record of this book is
    available from the British Library

    ISBN   0-7505-2295-X

First published in Great Britain 2004 by Review
An imprint of Headline Book Publishing

Copyright © 2004 Yvonne Roberts

Cover illustration © Richard Haughton by arrangement with
Headline Book Publishing Ltd.

Published in Large Print 2005 by arrangement with
Headline Book Publishing Ltd.

Magna Large Print is an imprint of Library Magna Books Ltd.

Printed and bound in Great Britain by
T.J. (International) Ltd., Cornwall, PL28 8RW

To Stephen

Chapter One

'Isn't she gorgeous? Give us a quick spin, love. My, haven't you got a lovely pair of...What? I was going to say a lovely pair of green eyes. Now, Daisy, is it? How old are you, sweetheart? Nineteen? My, what a big girl you are. Now, Daisy, tell us what you want most in the whole wide world? Come on, don't be shy...'

My sister bends towards the microphone, trying to stop her teeth chattering. She stands, semi-naked, in the icy ballroom of the Grand Metropolitan Hotel, Cwmland, on a Saturday morning at the beginning of January. Her bare legs have turned a Paisley-patterned blue and red with cold. She hasn't been press-ganged into doing this. She has volunteered.

'What I want most in the whole wide world is to win the title, Miss Ross & Baker Assorted Biscuits 1967,' she whispers. Even more depressing than hearing her say it, in public, is the knowledge that she means it.

I have been forced to witness my sister's humiliation because I work part-time at the hotel as a waitress. My job this morning is to attend to the needs of the VIPs, otherwise known as Very Irritating People. The judges are Fatty Edwards, the mayor of Cwmland; Randall Thomas, the managing director of Ross & Baker Assorted Biscuits, Daisy's boss and the boss of two-thirds of the other contestants too. And, finally, Daniel 'Mr Big Ballad' Bright, recording artist *extraordinaire*, whose rendition of 'Ave Maria' had stayed at number one for eight solid weeks in 1961.

Six years on, he is starring as Prince Charming in the Christmas pantomime, *Cinderella*, at the Astoria. According to our local paper, Mr Bright, resident in Jersey, twice divorced and presently single, has especially chosen this pantomime engagement from the many international offers pressed upon him over the festive period. Yeh.

'Good for you, love. That's what I like, a girl with a bit of ambition,' says Oily Ian, the compère, who has two other incarnations. One, as the hotel's food and beverages manager, and second, as in-house dirty old man. He winks at the audience. He is at least fifty, and has orange streaks of fake tan, which stripe his face and ring his short fat neck. That, plus the beer belly and his hair Brylcreemed so it shines like black satin, gives him the look of a tropical beetle. 'Well, Daisy,' he's breathing so hard down the microphone, he sounds like a thunderstorm, 'well, Daisy, you've certainly got all the right assets. Hasn't she, lads?' he says, and bares his yellow teeth.

Oily Ian gives Daisy an unceremonious shove towards the side of the stage. That piece of meat has been poked and prodded. On to the next. 'Now, ladies and gentlemen, can we have a big hand for Samantha ... and Samantha certainly needs a big hand.'

Samantha lurches on to the stage in a leopard-skin one-piece. She is a mammary miracle: a pair of breasts on legs. My heart sinks. How can

10

anyone normal win against a 44D? I watch as Daisy joins the other contestants, who wait to hear the judges' verdict. She is fourteen months older than I am but, reluctantly, I've always looked out for her since she is the least capable of my three sisters. Now she has her eyes clamped on Daniel Bright as if he is her personal angel descended from on high.

Daisy is addicted to the stars. *Oh Boy!*, *Ready Steady Go!*, *Six Five Special!*, *Sunday Night at the London Palladium*, Cliff Richard, Elvis Presley, Billy Fury, Adam Faith, even Val Doonican and Jim Reeves. Young or old, fat or thin, hip or crap, on stage, screen and television, she laps them up. It's her one fatal flaw, not quite as catastrophic as in *Hamlet*, but close.

She gazes in disbelief at the most Famous Human Being she has ever met. And I can't say I blame her. Daniel Bright has wavy blond hair. He wears a heavy gold chain and bracelet, pale blue shirt and slacks, and a pink and blue diamond-patterned V-necked jumper. It is a combination that, on anyone else in Cwmland, would have him labelled a pansy. His teeth are very white, as are his shoes; neither is a common occurrence around here.

Samantha speaks: 'I would really like to do some good in the world. And that.' And *that*? I reluctantly accept that, since Daisy is set on winning this title, I have to intervene, not least to prevent her degrading the family name by entering any more contests in future. She swore to me that if she wins today, she'll retire while she's still at the top.

Discreetly, I ask Daniel Bright if he'd like his

11

usual whisky and soda. Over the past few weeks I've come to know quite a bit about him because he's been staying in a suite at the Grand Metropolitan. For instance, he always has a couple of doubles mid-morning on a Saturday so he can face the matinée. I also know he spends hours every day driving his maroon Rolls-Royce with cream leather interior (registration number DB 1) up and down the Esplanades, showing off.

I return with the drink and whisper again in Mr Bright's ear. He has his eyes on Samantha's nipples, which are protruding from her bathing-suit like a couple of table-tennis balls. 'Is that right?' He looks at me quizzically, and glances at Daisy. 'Without a word of a lie.' I nod.

'How tragic,' he murmurs and beckons Tony, the hotel's assistant manager. Tony organises not only this event but also, in the summer, Miss Cwmland Carnival. He makes a bit on the side from the snaps he flogs of the contestants to family, friends and the local newspaper.

Daniel Bright gives Tony an instruction and Daisy, alone among the contestants, is rapidly offered a chair. Sitting down in the blue and white polka-dot one-piece, she somehow looks even more undressed. She puts one leg over the other and her white slingback shoe falls off with a clunk. Daisy's naturally blonde hair is back-combed into a beehive and welded into place with a tin of hair lacquer. A hairpin breaks free, slides down her neck and into her cleavage like an amorous leech. She begins to retrieve it before, hand half-way down her chest, she's aware of the sniggers and flushes a deep red. How could she

12

do this to herself?

It's no surprise to me when, half an hour later, Daisy Tempest of Rydol Crescent, Fairport, vital statistics 34–24–34, is crowned Miss Ross & Baker Assorted Biscuits 1967. She wins five guineas, a signed photograph of Daniel Bright, two tickets to *Cinderella* and a large tin of Premier chocolate biscuits.

As Tony snaps away, Daniel Bright bends to kiss her cheek. Daisy tells me, when it's all much too late, that the blend of whisky and aftershave, gold and chest hair make him the most exotic peacock of a man she has ever encountered. 'This young lady is not only beautiful she is very, very brave too, take my word for it...' he tells the audience.

'Wait until Mam finds out about this. She'll create blue bloody murder. I bet it was you who put her up to it,' snaps my oldest sister Rose, who has crept up behind me. She works full time at the hotel as a chambermaid. She's twenty-three, and the prettiest of us all – she's got my dad's curly black hair. It's a waste because she isn't at all bothered about her appearance.

Rose has a six-year-old son, Billy, and had to get married. She was my heroine when we were growing up because she was wild and always in trouble. Now, she's just moody. Perhaps it was the breast-feeding that did it. Nobody can hate as well as Rose can. Once, during a fight, she knocked me out cold on the bedstead. 'What about Mam?' she says again.

'Oh, piss off,' I tell her.

'Bloody hell, Lily,' Daisy says, as she changes in

13

the ladies' toilet, ignoring the dirty looks of the runners-up. 'You've told Daniel Bright something, haven't you? I can tell by the way he was looking at me. What did you say? And why did I end up sitting on a chair like Queen bloody Victoria? You've stuck your nose in again. Why did y–'

A girl from up the valley in a silver lamé bathing-suit butts in. 'You've humped him, haven't you, you dirty little cow? That's why he–'

I push Daisy out of the room before she throws a punch. I can vouch from personal experience that she, like Rose, is also capable of physical violence.

'See what you've done!' she rounds on me. 'Why can't you let things be?'

'If I had you'd've lost, that's why,' I tell her. 'And then you'd've entered every beauty contest from one end of the coast to the other. I was saving you from yourself.'

'Tell me what you said,' Daisy insists, red in the face, showing no gratitude at all.

I could lie but I decide to tell the truth since that will annoy her even more. 'I told him you were suffering from a brain tumour and you didn't want anyone to know. I told him it was our little family secret.'

Chapter Two

Five hours into Daisy's reign as Miss Ross & Baker 1967, I am laying tables. Each afternoon four of the waiting staff on the day shift have to set the Grand Metropolitan's tables for dinner. Everyone has to hunt for supplies because so much cutlery and china is pinched from one meal to the next.

Pete 'The Mercenary' Wells creeps up on me and whips out a dozen silver knives and forks from inside his white jacket. 'Ain't I good to you?' He smiles, revealing more gaps than teeth, as he dumps his booty on the table.

Pete has DEATH tattooed across the knuckles of one hand and HATE on the other. His stomach, which he is fond of displaying, has so many scars it looks like the map of a maze. He claims they were acquired when he was fighting in the Belgian Congo, or maybe it was Malaya. Pete is a dedicated fantasist. He's the kind of bloke who claims Paul McCartney's cousin as his best friend.

His wife, Marie, resembles a whippet and weighs even less. She looks after their two-year-old, Hayley, while Pete stays out late every Saturday night, after work, using his alleged exploits as a hero (since Pete's looks aren't up to much) to get his end away. Pete's hobby is murder – committed by other people, of course. He knows off by heart the entire contents of *The Murderers' Who's Who, A*

15

Centenary of Bloodshed.

Recall the Bloody Benders? Pete can. I've spent many an hour polishing silver in the Grand's kitchen, listening to how in the 1870s the Benders of Kansas, father, mother, son and daughter, offered hospitality to passers-by. As soon as the guest sat down to eat, father or son would crush their skull. Then the family would rob the body and bury it in the cellar. Eventually eleven graves were found; the Benders went on the run and were never seen again. Pete's version is that a posse did find them and dispensed with them so brutally they took an oath of secrecy. One, however, that doesn't prevent Pete providing lurid anatomical details including gouged eyes and castration.

Unsurprisingly, I find a thirty-two-year-old married man with halitosis and a passion for the macabre easy to resist – particularly as he also exudes a strong smell of violence. Pete is the kind who's prone to taking without asking. He works as a barman – a job which, for some reason, girls find glamorous. At weekends he's constantly sur-rounded by sixteen-year-olds, nibbling away at his maraschino cocktail cherries and giving him the eye.

'Fancy a drink later?' he asks now. 'Before my shift starts?'

'You've got a wife.'

'She doesn't mind,' he says, breathing on a soup spoon, then giving it a polish with the tablecloth.

'What you mean is, she doesn't know.'

'Of course she fuckin' knows,' he says, instantly angry. 'She likes me to be happy.'

'So what makes her happy?'

He looks at me blankly. 'She won't be very happy if you leave her, will she?' I say, while he picks dried egg off a fork with his fingernail.

'Of course I won't leave her,' Pete replies, apparently appalled at the idea. 'I wouldn't have married her if I'd wanted to leave, would I? Where's the sense in that? I've got a thing about you,' he continues seamlessly. 'You know that, don't you? You're...' He searches for the right word, which doesn't take long since there are probably only ten at any one time in his head. But he surprises me. 'You're a fighter. A bolshie bastard, like me,' he adds, as if this is the supreme compliment. 'I reckon that must mean you're all right in bed. You wouldn't just lie there like a plank. We could have a really good time,' he adds.

'Then what?'

Pete is baffled. 'Then what, what?'

'What would happen after that?'

Pete shrugs. 'I dunno. I'd probably have a fag. That's what I usually do.'

'I mean in the long run.' I'm not remotely interested in getting between the sheets with Pete – or any other man, come to that. I don't care if the rest of the country is copulating itself silly. In my family, sex conjures up all the worst words in the dictionary that begin with M – Mistake, Maternity, Marriage, Misery and a Mother eternally saying, 'You make your bed you lie on it.'

Pete gives an exploratory poke at a scab on one of his tattoos.

'If you really fancy me,' I say, using him shamelessly, 'go and make us a nice cup of tea.'

For all his faults, I like Pete. Bullshit and

17

blackened teeth, thin and nervy, he is different from the average local man. For a start, he knows what it is to escape. He left home at fifteen and, if you believe his version, he only returns to his brother Robert, and now Marie and Hayley, when the killing business takes a dip. More likely he turns up when he's released from jail, short of cash and in need of a roof over his head.

I know he's been to jail because Daisy's boy-friend, Carl, has also been inside, and they both make roll-ups in the same miserly way. Escape isn't a trait in our family. I bet I'll be like my dad. I'll flap down life's runway, again and again, never quite having the courage to take off. Doing well for yourself, in the Tempest household, means earning a couple of quid more than the nextdoor neighbour, finding a husband and sticking together – which is not the same as staying put. We move often. Sometimes after a matter of months; occasionally we've managed a couple of years.

Once I reached my teens I realised we moved because my dad has big ideas. He's always wanted to be a man of means – seafood stall holder, painter and decorator, salesman. Then, somehow, each time it begins to gel it's as if he loses his nerve. As if he's allergic to doing well. The money melts away and off we go again.

I blame my mother. She's never pushed him hard enough. And when he has made a bit of money, she's spent it twice as fast – fluffy pink bath mats, cocktail glasses painted with French poodles, lemon squeezers. She thinks none of us knows but you've only got to look at the back of the kitchen cupboards to see if she's out of control

18

again. Occasionally, in the past, when the debts have got so bad even Dad couldn't pretend otherwise, we've upped sticks at midnight, bills unpaid, goodbyes never said, bits and bobs left behind, family photographs and memorabilia abandoned. And then we start all over again. That's us as a family – Douglas, Melody and the four girls, Rose, Iris, Daisy and me. We start but we never finish.

I walk into the laundry to dump my apron. Pete comes in with two mugs of tea and we sit side by side on one of the large hampers full of dirty linen. He sings 'Sweets for My Sweet' through his nose in a reedy fake-American accent. Suddenly he breaks off. 'I've a present for you,' he says.

'I don't want it. Spend your money on your wife.' Pete's conscience may be in a permanent coma but mine isn't.

'You'll like this – all seventeen inches of it.' He smiles.

'And I bet it's black and white.'

He looks crestfallen. 'How do you know it's a telly?'

I shrug. 'Thanks, but we've got a telly already. Still, if you're really keen, my aunties are desperate for one. They'd be happy to have it. Dulcie especially would love it.'

Pete frowns. 'I'm not giving it to no other bugger. I paid a tenner for it, good as new,' he says, then pauses. 'This Dulcie, how old is she?'

'Thirty-seven and never been kissed.'

'Fuck.' Pete is genuinely impressed. 'Is she close to you, like?'

'Yeah, really close. She lives next door.'

'No, you daft bugger. Do you like her a lot?'

19

'What difference does that make?'

'Well, if you and she are really close, I'll give it her as a favour to you. And when I come round to see if it's working all right, I could pop in and have a cup of tea with you.' Pete sometimes has a nervous tic, which makes you think he's winking at you when he's not. I imagine it must have got him into a lot of trouble as a mercenary. Still pursuing his own unique line in seduction, he suddenly adds, 'If you ever want anyone seen to, you know, you've only got to ask.'

I take a swig of tea. 'Seen to? What do you mean?'

Pete puts his hands around an imaginary neck and squeezes. I notice that, for a hard man, his nails are bitten raw. 'You know what I mean.'

'Do you think you could "see to" my whole rotten family?' I ask.

'Why? What have they done?' Pete takes the question seriously. Irony is not in his blood.

'Absolutely nothing,' I answer. 'That's the problem.'

Half an hour later, Pete insists on walking me to the bus stop. As we leave, Randall Thomas, his wife and someone I guess must be their daughter are in the lounge taking afternoon tea. Randall Thomas pays Daisy just over six pounds a week to work in his factory, removing the broken biscuits as they come down the conveyor belt. It takes great skill to spot an imperfect custard cream among a thousand others. Or so Daisy says.

Mrs Thomas is dressed in a black coat with a white fur collar. She has a patent leather handbag, shoes to match and she talks posh. Lots of darlings and sweethearts. And, unlike all the male relatives I know, her husband is pretending to listen. She must be at least forty-five but looks ten years younger. Lipstick on her teeth is all that stands between her and perfection.

The daughter is my age and resembles Jane Asher. She has long reddish hair with a fringe. She wears a pink, black and white woollen op-art shift, mini-length, white knee-length boots, PanStik on her lips and a black PVC mac. She might have stepped out of the pages of *Honey* magazine. 'Clemmie darling' is what her mother calls her. I'm sick with envy. I want a family like that. One day, I'm going to have a family like that.

'Bloody bunch of wankers,' Pete says, under his breath, as we pass.

I wait at the bus stop with Rose, both of us still dressed in our uniforms of black skirt and jumper and white apron. For the past couple of years, we have lived in Fairport, two miles away. We drifted there because a house to rent had become vacant next door to my father's two sisters, Kath and Dulcie. Fairport is on an inlet. It's home to a battered caravan site, the biscuit factory, a bra factory called Amore, Stimper's, the iron works, and Lawson's, the fish-filleting and dyeing plant. The combined effect of the last two means that the sea air is permanently permeated with a strong stink not unlike that of cat food when the tin is first opened. That, and the sight of the boiling wastage from the iron works routinely being spilled, hissing and steaming, into the bay, doesn't give anyone from outside – except us –

much reason to linger.

The quay, adjoining Coronation Park, is pretty, with a line of cottages, a small mussel-washing factory, fishing-boats and pleasure-craft of all shapes and sizes. Quite a few have been left to rot, as if the owners forgot that they had a hobby. Fairport is also distinguished by a branch of Woolworth's, and Ravelli's, a milk bar that calls itself a soda fountain and serves frothy coffee in glass cups and saucers. Ravelli's also has a juke-box.

I'm seventeen and still in education – if you can call it that. This is in defiance of my mam and dad. They would much prefer that I bring in a proper wage. I am the first member of my family to stay at school past fifteen. This means I have postponed the momentous decision as to how best I can exploit Fairport's extensive career opportunities. What will it be? Iron smelting, sewing brassières, packing biscuits or dyeing fish? Whichever it is, my mother insists that I take shorthand and typing since that always comes in handy for a girl.

I've read in the magazines and seen on television that everywhere else in the entire world the young are Happening. They are having the best time of their lives: drugs, sex and rock 'n' roll. Fairport, however, is in the back row of history. Here, people skip youth and move straight from short socks to middle age. It saves on the disappointment.

'Are you and Billy coming for tea?' I ask Rose. They always come for tea when Chalkie White, Rose's husband, is away. He is a long-distance lorry driver. When we came to Fairport, Chalkie,

Rose and Billy came too and rented a place up the road. We're that kind of family. Nobody ever makes the break.

Rose nods, which is a surprise. Normally she's away in her head somewhere and it takes several attempts at communication before she responds.

'Don't you dare tell Dad or Mam about Daisy,' I warn. She shrugs, which means she probably will.

'If Iris starts on again, I swear I'll throw the teapot at her head.' Rose flags down our bus.

Iris is twenty-one, two years younger than Rose and a wages clerk in Lawson's. She has a face like a crumpled crisps packet, and is not at all like her three gorgeous sisters. Iris is dead old-fashioned. She wears her skirts on the knee and thinks a pale pink twinset shows outrageously daring sartorial taste. Since she was seven she has been quietly confident that she will marry young. Last year, at Lawson's Christmas dinner and dance, she found another girl's boyfriend who was too weak to resist. Howard is in the RAF and wears a blazer. That should say it all.

Howard is in Cyprus, due back next month, and the two have been saving so they can marry and rent a flat. They plan to become man and wife in 1969. Nobody sane plans that far ahead. Iris is keeping herself for her wedding night, or so she claims. On reflection, if Howard was going to be my husband, I'd probably postpone doing it for as long as possible too. All Iris talks about is brides and bottom drawers and pots and pans. She is like a human catalogue. The only language she speaks is price, colour and size.

23

What is truly irritating about her is her optimism. She inherited it from our mam. If the house was on fire and we'd all retreated to the roof, Iris and Mam would be telling everyone how lucky they were to have such a brilliant view of the town.

'So where's Chalkie this week?' I ask Rose, as we board the bus.

'Are you trying to be funny?' she replies, even more sharp than usual. 'Why should I care?'

I don't think she does.

Chapter Three

In Fairport, we get off the bus and walk across the square towards home. We stop outside the two large windows of Bunting's, which offers 'High Class General Provisions, dried goods, cold meats, dairy produce, continental confectionery and alcoholic beverages'. Most of the items are cut, weighed and packed to order – sugar, tea, flour, butter, lard, ham, bacon. The money and a receipt are placed in a little brass canister, which, when a lever is pulled, zips across the ceiling to the cashier, who provides the change and zips it back again.

The shop has a staff of four: one cashier, two female assistants and the manager. We can see him now, carving a hunk of cheese with a wire cutter, twirling the paper bags over and over, pencil stuck behind his ear, giving the little boy at the front of

24

the queue a toffee from the pocket of his white coat.

He is late-middle-aged, tall, with a quiff, dark as coal, positioned in the middle of his forehead like a question mark. He is that world-famous star of stage, screen and television, the crooner who can crack a joke, Mr Dean Martin. As he serves and flirts, he has the relaxed, half-sozzled look that Dino does so well.

I wave and he waves back. In truth, he's not Dino, he's our dad. Douglas Tempest. He's made a living on the side for as long as I can remember singing in pubs as a counterfeit Dean Martin, performing for women who long ago got used to settling for second best. He's performing now, he's always performing, always smiling.

'See that woman?' Rose says. 'It's disgusting. She's thirty-five if she's a day. Talk about mutton dressed as lamb. It's bloody pathetic. They're both bloody pathetic.'

'Dad says it's only a bit of fun. It's good for business.'

'Good for his business, you mean,' Rose replies darkly, as we walk on. God, she's sour.

Inside Bunting's, Mrs Betty Procter, whose husband Dai owns eight caravans on the caravan site, sucks a child's dummy for several seconds smiling at Doug Tempest as she does so. Then she bends down and sticks it into the open mouth of her little boy, strapped squealing into his push-chair. Everybody knows that Dai Procter has tinker's blood in his veins. He and his large family live in three luxury caravans that have had their wheels

25

removed and stand on bricks. He works non-stop, scrap metal, demolition, industrial cleaning, and in spite of not having a proper roof over his head, he definitely has money. Otherwise, how could Betty Procter, with five kids, afford to go to Chester once a month to have her roots done?

Now she leans over the counter. As she does so, her duster coat falls open. She wears a pale blue thick ribbed cardigan with large whalebone buttons, the top two of which are undone. Doug Tempest concentrates on the cardboard stork dangling in the window, over her left shoulder, advertising margarine. It bounces and swings disconcertingly above the display of tinned corned beef and bottles of pale ales. It's not the first time he's had to struggle to ignore the swell of Betty Procter's breasts cradled in a variety of richly embroidered brassières, the colours of the Crown Jewels – deep turquoise, maroon and emerald green. She licks her pink lips, painted the colour of candy-floss.

'I've got something special for you, Doug.' She smiles. He smiles back. He tells himself he will not wander into the valley of misinterpretation, not so close to home. She puts her hand into her coat pocket and pulls out half a dozen empty Player's cigarette packets. She lines them up on the counter in front of him like a squadron of cardboard soldiers. 'I'm smoking myself to death for you ... and what do I get in the way of thanks?'

'How about half a pound of streaky bacon on the house?' Doug says, with a wink at his other customers, waiting patiently. He gathers the packets into a drawer and gives the silver wheel of the slicer a theatrical twirl. 'Then you can think of me at breakfast,' he adds.

'It's not bacon I want, Dougie.' Mrs Procter pouts in mock-petulance. 'I've got plenty of bacon at home...'

Two days after Doug Tempest and his family had first arrived in Fairport, Gerry Jackson, who had been employed as manager of Bunting's for years, dropped dead at lunch-time in the Duck and Fox. It had been a Wednesday, half-day closing. Doug had seen the ambulance in the square, made a few enquiries and, trusting that his face would act as his best reference, he had chosen his time to offer his services to the widowed Mrs Edina Bunting. She hired him immediately because she liked the look of the man.

Lots of women like the look of Doug, which is ironic since, for much of his early adult life, he hadn't liked himself. He had behaved as if he had no conscience while wishing that he had. On a whim one morning, after leaving the army, he'd bought a trilby, grey with a small brim and a wide band. On that day, instead of his father's face reflecting back at him, eyes black with fury, mouth lined by malice, he saw a much more amiable visage – none other than that of the great, the unmatchable, the one and only Mr Dean Martin!

He'd enthusiastically seized the chance to be someone other than himself, working for modest rewards in pubs and workingmen's clubs, pretending to like the booze, sliding in a couple of anecdotes, adding a slight American drawl to his Welsh-Mancunian accent. But he never gave up his day job. He saw Dino as a crutch not a career.

27

Doug sings softly now, 'Three Coins in a Fountain', as he begins the ritual of closing the shop for the night. Jenny Chapman, his assistant, waves goodbye. Helen Jones, the cashier, finishes adding up the takings, and deposits them in the safe, ready to be banked on Monday morning.

'Don't write songs like they used to, do they, Doug?' she says, producing a red chiffon scarf from her plastic shopping bag. She ties it in a bow at the back of her neck like Princess Grace of Monaco. 'Any of your girls take after you, singing and all that?'

Doug leans against the counter and folds his arms. He wants Helen to go so he can have the shop to himself. Then he'll check the shelves are restocked, the freezer doors closed, the mousetraps laid and fresh window displays arranged. He enjoys this job. He has replaced the chaos that marked his predecessor's reign with a system that works. The girls like him as a boss and he keeps the customers happy.

'None of the girls like singing, not in public like me, at any rate,' Doug tells her, over the jangle of the bell as he opens the door. 'Especially the one who's really got a voice. She can't abide my sort of stuff, doesn't even like the Beatles. She's a contrary madam. She goes for black music. Soul, rhythm 'n' blues.' Doug gives an impromptu performance, growling out the words: 'Hoochie coochie baby...'

'Oh dear,' says Mrs Jones, who has never seen a black man in her life.

Later, Doug smokes a cigarette and stands in the shop doorway looking out over Fairport's square. Just after six p.m. on a Saturday night, it's deserted. Christmas lights twinkle in the off-licence illuminating cardboard advertisements for Babycham and Wincamis Fortified Wine. An old man in flat cap and donkey jacket, a rolled up *Daily Mirror* sticking out of his pocket, walks past pulling his bedraggled dog in the sludge and slurry of the January snow and disappears up the road where the only sign of life is the fish 'n' chip shop, the Contented Sole.

In the window of Bon Marché the ladies' outfitters, a small mechanical Father Christmas, dwarfed by the Crimplene dresses and wrap-over aprons, waves at Doug rhythmically again and again, as if determined to hold on to his festive role. Charlton's, the hardware shop, always closes early on a Saturday, as if to spite all the weekend do-it-yourselfers. As Doug watches, lost in thought, a curly-headed small boy suddenly appears round the corner. He is coatless, his eyes are dark pools. He stands on the outer edge of the street lamp's halo of light. And then he is gone.

Doug Tempest shivers. He knows the boy will reappear. He always does.

Chapter Four

'Three egg and chips, please, love,' Veronica Turner shouts through the service hatch separating the Olde Tudor Tea Rooms (actually one room, built long after the Tudors, carpeted in

29

tartan with an overlay of stains, many pre-war). Veronica is very large and in her late twenties. She is a waitress who consumes gossip as hungrily as she devours pastries.

'Last order, pet,' she adds, as if an incentive is required. An open-air market – a dozen or so stalls – is held in Fairport's town square on Friday and Saturday mornings, during which time customers pour in. They are also plentiful in July and August – if the sun shines. Otherwise trade is only a steady trickle.

Melody Tempest rises up from the single chair at the large kitchen table. She is tall and statuesque and wouldn't look amiss on the prow of a ship. Pale blonde hair is piled haphazardly on top of her head, like a cottage loaf. She has smooth, clear skin and faint freckles. At almost fifty she is far more striking than she was when she was young and pretty and unweathered. She wears large gold hoop ear-rings, no makeup and a white overall over a jumper and skirt.

'Sorry,' Veronica's plump voice floats through the hatch again, 'can you make that one cheese omelette, two egg and chips?' The volume of the radio in the café is turned up. Alma Cogan sings a song about twenty tiny fingers and twenty tiny toes. Melody joins in as she separates the yolks from the whites and beats each vigorously in two separate bowls before folding one into the other. 'Have you heard?' says Veronica, from the hatch, her cigarette sending through smoke signals. 'May Jenkins's girl, Sally, is going around with Trevor Renshaw. She can't be more'n twenty and he's well past forty if he's a day. Men. They never bloody give up, do they?'

Melody transfers an omelette swollen with tangerine-coloured grated cheese on to a blue Wedgwood plate. She licks the corner of her tea-cloth and gives the rim a rub, then sticks a bit of green parsley on the side. The tea rooms are a step above a milk bar or a cafe so chips come separately in a silver dish. 'Sometimes,' Melody says, through the hatch, pinching a chip, 'I reckon it's these young girls who throw themselves at the men.'

'Well, you should know about that,' Veronica responds tartly, as two hands come through the hatch for the order. Then, she's gone. Melody shuts out the remark by reminding herself of the nice liver and bacon casserole cooking slowly in the oven at home for the family. Serve that with mashed potatoes, brown sauce, tinned peas followed by treacle tart and custard.

What more could anyone want?

The bedroom is freezing. Iris Tempest wraps a blanket around her shoulders and takes her dress-ing-gown off the hook behind the door. Carefully she inserts a knitting needle along its hem and gradually pulls out three sheets of lined notepaper, rolled up tightly Iris decided long ago that it was almost impossible in the Tempest household to have any secrets. This has been her most successful attempt yet to keep a little of herself to herself. She unrolls her latest love letter from Howard Cross. Once read, she'll take it to work and add it to the others in her locked desk drawer.

'Love letter' is stretching it slightly, since Howard writes as if he expects his mother to read what he has written. He tells Iris about his working day as a mechanic, the motorbike he is doing up, and the Bible-study classes he has begun to attend. Iris can see a positive side to this new development. Reading the Bible doesn't cost money, so their savings are bound to benefit. Howard signs off formally, 'Yours ever'. Then adds SWALK. Sealed With A Loving Kiss. Iris rolls up the letter and returns it to its hiding place, confident that it is secure. She is, she knows, much luckier than her sisters. Unlike, say, Lily, who sees herself as different from the rest of the family; always wanting to be somewhere else, doing something different, Iris's aspirations exactly match her abilities.

'You're only twenty-one and you're already stuck in a rut,' Lily often tells her contemptuously. What she doesn't understand is that is exactly where Iris is happiest.

As Iris lies on her bed, savouring the idea of becoming Mrs Howard Cross, her mother, still at work, fills one paper bag with freshly made scones and another with half a dozen sausage rolls. 'Night, Melody,' Veronica shouts through the hatch.

'Here, lovey,' Melody replies, passing her the sausage rolls, 'cheer up your old man with these. Freshly made today.'

It only takes a couple of minutes to walk from the tea rooms to Rydol Crescent, a line of two-up and two-down terraced houses, identical except for the customised front doors and decorated house names.

Melody stops outside number two, which has two brass cupids for a knocker; at each thump, they kiss. She savours the mix of excitement and worry that always comes just before a purchase. Later, she'll spend hours adding up the figures in her head as if repetition will deliver the magic of solvency. Number two is the home of Edith and Phil Stevens. Mr Stevens retired long ago from the iron works. Edith is happy to take in Melody's parcels in return for a little company. Edith's memory is so poor that she never remembers whether it's the first parcel the postman has delivered that week or the fifth. Her husband considers the postman's comings and goings women's business.

Now Edith watches as Melody excitedly rips away the layers of brown paper. 'What do you think of this, then?' the younger woman asks. 'Isn't she a beauty?'

Edith looks at the contraption blankly. 'Is it a frying-pan?'

Melody's face is pink with delight, as she flicks through the instruction book. She beams at Edith. 'This is a Sunbeam Electric Gourmet Frying-pan, which comes with an egg-poaching attachment. Heat control has settings up to four hundred and twenty degrees. Imagine that! And it's only ten pounds fourteen shillings and a penny!'

The price, said out loud, twists at her throat and makes her heart beat faster. This is her revenge, she reminds herself. Enjoy it.

'Haven't you got a frying-pan, then, love?' Edith asks.

'Of course I have,' Melody replies. 'I've got four

33

indoors but that's not the point, is it?'

Once in her own house, she puts the electric frying-pan at the back of the kitchen cupboard and dumps the packaging in the dustbin. 'Is that you, Iris?' she calls up the stairs. 'Fancy a nice scone?'

Iris declines. Melody picks up four letters from the mat in front of the door. She assumes they are bills and shoves them into the disused tea caddy in the kitchen cabinet. Doug hands her his wage packet each week, keeping back a couple of pounds. He then expects her to sort out the family's commitments. Melody tries to reward this misplaced trust with gratitude and devotion – and, when that fails to alleviate her guilt, plentiful supplies of (unwanted) food. Now she generously butters a plate of scones.

She is hampered by two of Iris's net petticoats hung on a line strung across the kitchen. Soaked in a solution of sugar melted in water, they drip stickily on to the linoleum. Eventually, they will dry to a stiffness that scratches like barbed wire. The kitchen is tiny and, more accurately, a lean-to shed with a corrugated-iron roof. When it rains, it sounds like an army of clog-dancers. On Thursdays it also doubles as a bath-house. A tin tub is filled from saucepans and buckets boiled on the gas stove. Then, one by one, members of the family carry out their ablutions.

Melody relaxes and allows her anxieties to slip away as the house is filled with the aroma of liver and bacon. Soon the girls will be home, squeezed tight into the back room, fighting over who can get closest to the fire, preparing for a night out, waiting to be fed. From next door, she can hear the steady thump of Dulcie's record-player.

She has taken great care in the building of her world. Anyone who threatens it, she will cheerfully devour.

Daisy Tempest dreams of her mother's Saturday liver and bacon and takes another sip of champagne. Her third glass in less than half an hour. She is dressed in a tight white mini dress, with a fringe around the hem, that swings when she walks. She also wears a new Marks & Spencer bulky cardigan, both bought that morning with today's winnings. After the contest, Daniel Bright had taken her to one side and suggested that they meet for a drink and 'discussions' between the matinée and his evening performance.

He instructed her to come to the Churchill Suite at five p.m., 'if your health is up to it'. 'I've never felt better,' Daisy had told him truthfully. She had refused the invitation, then said yes, then no, and finally agreed to the assignation because, she told herself, she didn't want to go through life with regrets. Not at nineteen. 'Whatever happens, I've got to be on the six o'clock bus home,' she'd explained. 'If I'm not home for tea, my mam'll kill me.'

Now she waits in the sitting room of Daniel Bright's suite, as he changes in the bedroom. Gradually, she smells the sweet, sticky, almond aroma of newly baked macaroons. That's a puzzle. Unless, of course, horror of horrors, it's the stink of the biscuit factory seeping out of her pores. Chocolate wafers, orange creams, ginger

35

snaps, macaroons... Oh, the shame!

The door opens and, suddenly, there is Mr 'Big Ballad' Bright, perspiring heavily, half undressed, and working himself up to a state of some excitement. Once Daisy recovers from the shock of seeing that which she has never seen before in a man – at least, not in daylight – she realises that it's not the odour of macaroons she can smell, but something for which she has no appetite at all.

Kath Morgan, sister of Doug Tempest, aunt to Rose, Iris, Daisy and Lily, nervily checks her reflection in the window of the Contented Sole, the fish 'n' chip shop where she works six days a week. Once upon a time she was even better-looking than her brother, but worry has whittled away at her features, leaving them as sharp as folded paper.

Her black hair has received the standard iron-wave set dished out by the local hairdresser to all women who have crossed the threshold and moved into the wasteland that is middle age. She wears no makeup and a brown jacket over the white coat embroidered with a leaping fish. She smells of frying fat and the sea.

Kath lives on cigarettes, sweet tea and American murder magazines posted to her from a specialist shop in Liverpool. They are full of messy black-and-white photographs of headless bodies and legless torsos and killers who look like ordinary, everyday people. 'You can't trust anyone, these days,' is Kath's favourite remark. Fear is her hobby and, consequently, she lives in constant anticipation of disaster.

She and Dulcie came to Fairport by accident because she fancied living on the coast, and she'd been told that the place was cheap, both in and out of season, since it lacked a pier and a fun fair and it was on the route to nowhere. It was also small enough to suit Dulcie, who now walks to work at Amore, the bra factory, every day.

Now, as she does most evenings if she's not working the late shift, Kath stops in front of the Rediffusion shop, which rents and sells television sets. A television is a luxury that Kath believes she and Dulcie cannot afford. A dozen sets are in the window, each switched on to *Juke Box Jury*. Kath watches for several minutes as, soundlessly, three panelists vote on whether a recent record release will be a hit or a miss. The compère is in a dinner jacket and bowtie.

'You all right, missus?' enquires an old man in a flat cap, passing with his dog. Kath starts and blushes as if day-dreaming is an indelicate act. Then she hurries off to Rydol Crescent, fantasising about the day she, too, will appear on television in a green silk dress with diamanté earrings, just like Katie Boyle or Lady Isobel Barnett, beautiful, kind, clever. A grown-up daughter of whom a mother would be proud. The kind of daughter that no mother could possibly want to leave and never see again.

As Kath makes her way home, Dulcie Tempest, aged thirty-seven, gives a twirl in front of the bedroom mirror, giggling as she slides in her stockinged feet, dancing in the cold to the music blaring out from a red and cream Dansette

37

record-player. She is short and round, with a flat, almost concave face, wispy brown hair and a complexion that chaps easily. She has always been cruelly teased. 'Pancake Patsy', they still call her. But Kath tells Dulcie to take no notice: when she smiles, she almost looks right. Since Kath never tells lies, Dulcie smiles as often as she can.

Each day at work, Dulcie sits at a large wooden trestle table. Her job is to cut stray threads off brassières and panties. The more boxes she gets through, a dozen garments to each box, the bigger the bonus. Dulcie tries hard, but most weeks she only achieves the basic wage.

Dulcie puts the Monkees' 'I'm a Believer' on her record-player and goes into her sister's bedroom. It is almost identically furnished except that there are several piles of second-hand murder magazines and paperback thrillers. Behind the curtain is the bucket used at night to avoid the outside toilet. Dulcie goes down on her hands and knees by the bed and struggles to reach a small cardboard suitcase, pushed to the back. From time to time, Kath hunts for evidence of her sister's 'funny ideas' but she never thinks to peek under her own bed. Dulcie smiles. Lily had suggested the hiding place – she's clever like that.

She opens the case and pulls out a pile of battered magazines. She spreads them out on the bed, taking her time to select one. Then, she pores over each page, studying the detail, touching the creamy flesh. Suddenly there is a loud knocking on the door. Dulcie gives a small scream. If it's Kath, she'll really, really be in trouble. Magazines slip out of her grasp, sliding away as she struggles

38

clumsily to gather them together and deposit them back in their hiding-place.

'Coming, Kath,' she shouts, her heart thumping. Please, don't let Kath be in a temper. When she opens the door, the street is deserted. Dulcie looks either way, then something draws her gaze downwards. On the doorstep is a television set. A large black television set with big cream plastic knobs. She looks up and down the street again, and sees no one.

Dulcie has only ever had two wishes. And now, miraculously, one of them has been fulfilled.

Chapter Five

Fairport station closed down soon after we arrived in the town – not that there was much to shut: two platforms, one waiting room, one ticket office and a car park the size of a baby's nappy. I walk past it every Saturday after work to reach the railwaymen's club, which continues to thrive in spite of the lack of any railwaymen. It's a custom-built two-storey building covered in grey pebbledash, which has as much charm, I imagine, as a Serbian prison camp. During the week the club attracts a trickle of customers but at weekends it overflows with teenagers (since the beer, which they're not supposed to drink, is the cheapest in the area) and married couples. They arrive together and immediately separate, the women to play bingo and jive and twist and shake together on the dance-floor, the men to drink and play darts.

My connection with the club is through the Berries, a group of lads who rehearse every Saturday afternoon and Thursday evening in the function room on the first floor. The Berries pride themselves on being able to replicate the exact sound of whatever is currently in the top ten. As a result, dressed in identical electric blue Beatle suits, they have regular bookings at engagement parties, weddings and, often, as a support band to the main attraction at local dances.

I've been going out with Bryn Taylor, who plays rhythm guitar and is the lead singer, for three months. He has a faint whiff of haddock about him and pale yellow hands but he's quite good-looking in a Paul Anka sort of way. His hands are due to his job. He is a dyer at Lawson's, the fish factory. The first date we had was in the back row of the cinema in Cwmland ('Meet you inside' – i.e. pay for yourself) which went exactly as expected. Bryn relentlessly rubbed each of my breasts as if he really believed a genie might appear.

I stopped him trying to get a hand down my knickers mainly out of fear of toxic poisoning from the dye on his fingers but also because his attempts were about as exciting as listening to my dad's rendition of 'Two Sleepy People'. Bryn is wary of conversation, unless it's to talk about his Ford Capri. Then he never stops. Of course, when he sings and performs you'd think he was a completely different person: American and extrovert, or Liverpudlian and extrovert, or

40

Mancunian and extrovert. As I said, it depends what's in the top ten.

I often wonder why Bryn continues to ask me out. He once said, 'Lily, you're different from the others.' Then I discovered he'd said exactly the same to Fay Price, who was his previous girlfriend. More to the point, why do I stay with him? It's partly because I don't want Fay Price to have him and partly because I hate the way everyone treats you as a deviant if you're not 'courting'. Once you've got a boyfriend, they shut up. Also, if I'm honest, a lot of Bryn's attraction comes in the shape of his dad, Barry.

Barry Taylor is a shop steward at Lawson's. Most of the time he's banging on about Marx and Harold Wilson and the Labour Party's betrayal of the working class. I don't fancy him, I just think he's the most interesting man I've ever met. He talks music as well as class war and plays the mouth organ.

He was a ship's steward in the Merchant Navy in the fifties. He worked the east coast of the States for two years, buying records all the time, Muddy Waters, T-Bone Walker, B. B. King, Etta James, Bo Diddley, John Jackson, Bessie Smith. He still gets them sent over. Barry calls the Berries counterfeit. It's his worst insult. He prefers Authentic. Every now and then, he lends me some of his rhythm and blues records. Bryn hates it all and so does my dad. 'Voodoo music,' he calls it. That's another good reason for me to love it.

Also in the Berries is Mick Dawson, who plays lead guitar and grew up on the same council estate as Bryn. He's a labourer (he was previously

41

a butcher's boy, an apprentice in the iron works and a municipal park attendant – and he only left school last July). He wears extra high Cuban heels because he's five foot two. Or, as Mick puts it, 'close to average'. His ambition is to become a lorry driver.

On drums we have Bryn's cousin, Matthew Harris, known to all as Podge. Podge is an apprentice plumber in the iron works. He's six foot four, bowed like a boomerang, and so thin it's difficult to judge where his arms end and the drumsticks begin. He also has raging acne and a face like a lunar plain.

Finally, there is Fred 'Bulbie' Williams, who plays bass and is an apprentice electrician in the biscuit factory. He's quite good-looking as long as he's in sunglasses because he has a lazy eye. He wears his electric blue suit on sufferance since he regards himself as a Mod. He has a suit and a parka and a pork-pie hat; he owns a Vespa scooter, swallows a lot of amphetamines and likes the Who. Most teenagers in Fairport still live in the teddy-boy era on the basis that 'If it were good enough for our dad, it's good enough for me.' So much for rebellious youth.

'Wotcher, Lily,' Mick says, as I walk into the rehearsal. Podge waves a drumstick. Bulbie ignores me. Bryn hunches his shoulders self-consciously and reddens in a way I find deeply irritating. Bulbie, Podge and Mick all joined the group for the same reason: to attract the birds. So far they have met with a spectacular lack of success. Then I notice the two girls. They are sitting in their coats hugging one of the cold radiators,

42

gazing at the Berries with adoration. They can't be fans. The Berries don't have any.

One girl is tiny. I've seen her around. She has dyed blonde hair backcombed so much it looks as if she's just had a couple of volts shot through her body. She wears elaborate glasses with frames that sweep upwards like a bird's wings and masses of eye makeup, including false eyelashes painted in black spikes on her lower lid and white eye-shadow. She resembles one of those dolls that never blink. Or a troll-like version of Dusty Springfield. She is in a short, black skirt, no stockings, black patent stilettos and a big, baggy pale blue V-necked jumper, which signals very clearly that she has a cleavage. She's chewing gum and smoking a fag, flicking the ash on the floor. She's common as muck but quite pretty.

The other girl has long hair parted in the middle like Joan Baez and tied back, no makeup, and is dressed in a below-the-knee boring dark green coat with a fur collar, a pleated tartan skirt, slip-ons and tights.

'Hiya,' they say in unison. I am not happy I am the only female associated with the Berries and have been for several weeks. 'Who are you with?' I ask, since Fairport girls rarely go anywhere under their own volition. They grow up trotting after their mam, then graduate to trailing after the boyfriend. Except for one night a week when they stay in and wash their hair. Bulbie gives me an answer by putting on his dark glasses, stumbling over Podge's cymbals, and walking over to put an arm around Joan Baez. He stands there looking daft, his arm draped awkwardly because Joan is sitting and he's standing.

I look at him and say, although it's none of my business, 'You told me you'd never go out with a girl unless she's a Mod... She's not even wearing Hush Puppies.'

'I'm going to buy some on Saturday and a suede coat with my Christmas money,' Joan Baez volunteers. It makes me despise her even more. 'They're fab, aren't they?' she adds, looking at Bulbie.

How much more embarrassing can she be? It's now the turn of Podge, the walking pimple, to claim possession. The girl with blonde hair stands up and reaches his ribcage. The two couples resemble one of those children's games where you muddle up all the pieces of the body, head, trunk, legs and arms, to create a composite monster. The blonde speaks. 'You know what? I think Matthew looks just like George Harrison. Especially when he smiles, smile for me, Matthew.'

Podge puts a lot of effort into doing as he's told, which can't be easy because he has a boil on his cheek. It stretches painfully as he flashes his teeth. He looks at her, and his gaze is full of such tenderness that I am deeply envious. I want to be in love too.

'We think they're the best group we've heard in ages, don't you?' Joan Baez says to me, in a wispy voice. She giggles after every few words. I hope for her sake that it's nerves. It would be a shame for her if it turned out that she was not only plain but silly in the head as well. 'We're going to start a fan club.'

'You can be the secretary, if you like,' the blonde suggests.

What a bloody nerve.

Fifteen minutes later, the newcomers are still trying to thaw me out. The blonde tells me her name is Kit, as in Caitlin Renshaw, and she works in Collins's, a fruit and veg shop in Cwmland. She's the oldest of six brothers and sisters; her mother died two years ago so she looks after the family and she loves her dad, who's a corporation dustman except he's been on the sick ever since her mother passed away. 'Broken heart,' she says. 'Won't let it mend.'

The other girl says she's called Penny Wilson, and she goes to St Winifred of the Cross. She goes pink when she tells me because St Winifred's is a private school and that makes her well off.

'What'll you do when you leave?' I ask.

She looks surprised. 'My parents want me to go to university, of course. What about you?'

The 'of course' hurts. Nobody has gone to university in our family. Nobody expects anybody to want to go. Just before Christmas, I had a 'careers consultation' with the morose Miss Wallace, who has front teeth that veer upwards and outwards, like the legs of a wayward can-can dancer. She has a double first from Cambridge – but that's hardly compensation for being so ugly. Now she's stuck in a third-rate comprehensive in the back of beyond. I suppose it could be worse. She could be teaching in the kind of fourth-rate secondary moderns my sisters attended.

'Ah, Lily,' she'd said, 'and what do you have in mind, young lady? I'll be frank, you probably haven't quite got what it takes to go to university, have you, dear? And only taking two A levels?' She

45

noisily sucked in her breath through her teeth. 'Most universities expect three A levels, these days. Three good grades too. So, what on earth are we going to do with you, Miss Tempest?'

We both looked at each other blankly. 'I suppose you could always try the civil service,' she sounded doubtful, then cheered up, 'or how about secretarial work? That would certainly tide you over until you settle down and the children come along. Clerical work would be well within your capabilities.'

So much for the inspirational teacher.

I realise that Kit and Penny are looking at me expectantly. 'I'm doing A levels too,' I answer, annoyed that Penny should think herself the only member of the trio with a brain. Then I improvise:

'But I'm modelling in Manchester, so I'll probably go to London and do that full time once I leave school.'

The two stare at me, making no attempt to conceal that they are impressed. 'Fab,' says Kit enthusiastically. 'I bet that's why you're so skinny. Have you met anybody famous?'

It upsets me sometimes how easy it is to fabricate a life. Where's the challenge in that? 'Have you got pots of money, then?' Kit presses. This is trickier territory. Elaborating on reality is one thing: supplying material evidence is very much another.

'I'm just starting, so you don't get much,' I reply, looking nonchalant. 'You get things instead – clothes, makeup...'

'She's got loads of money,' Kit volunteers, cocking her head in Penny's direction. 'We've only

46

known each other a year or so. That's when her parents moved here. We met at the bus stop and got chatting... She's got a huge house, haven't you, Penny? A lovely house,' Kit adds, looking smug.

'What does your dad do, then?' I ask.

Penny shrugs. 'Nothing much, really.'

Kit expresses disapproval. 'Go on, tell her. He's a university lecturer and he writes books. And he's got a Rover with leather seats. And her mam has her hair done twice a week and–'

'So,' I say, trying to keep the envy out of my voice, 'it's quite the perfect little family, is it?'

'Don't be daft,' Penny answers shortly. 'Everybody knows there's no such thing.'

At six, Bryn gives me a lift home. 'Fancy that,' he says, his entire contribution to the phenomenon of Podge and Bulbie finally acquiring girlfriends.

'Yes,' I say. 'Fancy that.'

At the bottom of our road he pulls the car over and switches off the engine. The windows immediately steam up. Bryn has tried it on several times and recently, predictably, accused me of being frigid. I tense, preparing myself for another wrestling match. Instead, he says, 'I want to ask you something.' In the gloom, his big yellow hands look as if they have a life of their own, like two floating blobs of custard. 'Only say yes, if you really want to. I mean, you don't have to if you don't, you know...' His voice has suddenly shifted several octaves higher so the words come out as a series of squeaks. 'But if you really love me, I know you'll say yes.'

Love? Love has never been mentioned before.

This is alarming. Here, in the dark, does Bryn Taylor seriously expect more of me than I am prepared to commit to any man – at least for the next ten years? 'Why don't we get married?' Bryn says. And only then does he try to get his leg over.

Chapter Six

Seven empty Player's cigarette packets lie flattened on the work bench like an exotic deck of cards. Doug Tempest carefully cuts them into strips. On the windowsill of his shed stand three identical life-size dachshunds, made of woven Player's cigarette packets, their bodies tattooed with endlessly repeating images of life-belts and hairy sailors. A constant draught makes their string tails occasionally wag as if in pleasure. Doug sings softly to himself.

He has already prepared a cast, a long balloon now covered in torn newspaper, cemented into place with flour and water. He begins carefully to weave the strips across the cast creating a second skin; one strip holding firm the next. Later, when the torso is complete, he will burst the balloon, then glue on the head and legs, made separately. The dog will finally stand alone.

Melody calls his name and waits for him to open the shed door. In her hands she has a mug of tea and a plate of scones. 'I thought you might be peckish, love,' she says. As she does almost every evening at the same time. In the early years,

Melody's obsession with food, roasted, baked, fried, sliced or boiled, almost drove Doug mad. She'd serve him with an overloaded plate and even before the last swallow she'd be making suggestions for the next meal, and the meal after that, and the meal after that too.

Straight from the butcher's, she'd offer him a bleeding pile of offal for inspection, as if she expected him to admire it like a work of art. Fresh from the baker's, she'd command that he smell the fragrance oozing from warm white bread. If he refused, if he dared to utter the ultimate insult, 'I'm not hungry,' it would be one of the rare times that a storm would erupt, awesome in its intensity and bewildering in its anguish. Doug could have understood if he'd said he was leaving her for another woman, but in reaction to his rejection of a plate of stew? It made no sense.

So, Melody would sob herself to sleep and he would be starved of her comfort. He hated to be cast out by her because it returned him to the darkness of his father's world. In the time she'd known him, she'd dragged him on to her own raft of optimism. Eventually the solution came to him. The way to this woman's heart was through his stomach. So he began to simulate satisfaction, fake interest, show willing and lie after the event. He did this so successfully that Melody either didn't notice or chose to ignore how little, in fact, he ate. Doug preferred a cigarette any day.

Of course, this degree of domestic capitulation had its consequences. No man can allow himself to be completely controlled. Over the years, Doug had had the occasional liaison, mostly lasting a single evening, always away from home, driven not primarily by lust but because it was on offer and he was flattered, and he liked to believe he was still his own man.

Now he smiles, kisses Melody's cheek and invites her into his shed. 'Lovely,' he says. And it is lovely: him and her and their girls. He loves the fact that when she looks at him he sees none of the contempt he witnesses daily in the eyes of other men's wives in the shop. He slices and weighs, packs and jokes, but it jars when the women refer dismissively to their husbands.

A few minutes later, he sees Melody, framed in the kitchen window, as she dishes up tea. Hair flying, kettle boiling, steam swirling around her until she almost evaporates, absorbed in her own cooking. Doug smiles. Every love affair is different. He knows from his own experience that the elements which initially draw two people together can mutate, alarmingly quickly, into a monstrous sense of resentment and disappointment that eats away at mutual respect, courtesy and desire. It isn't Melody's fault that, no matter how strong their bond, Doug still doesn't enjoy the freedom that only true love brings.

Iris looks with distaste at the piles of clothes that dot the other side of the bedroom like giant molehills. She takes off her office skirt and twin set, folds them meticulously, and carefully puts them away in the drawer. She shares the room with Daisy and Lily but while her half is neat and tidy, their half is a tip. They share half because as soon as Iris had become a fiancée, accepting

Howard's proposal of marriage, she had behaved totally out of character and pulled rank.

The bedroom contains a double and a single bed, a chest of drawers, a wardrobe and a dressing-table. The girls used to rotate so that every three weeks someone had the privilege of sleeping alone and not being kicked to near death by a sibling. Iris had put a stop to that. It wasn't right for an almost-married woman to be sharing her bed, she'd announced.

'Not even with horrible Howard?' Lily had teased.

'Don't be disgusting!' Iris had reddened.

Daisy immediately pounced. 'Go on, I bet you've done it. Everybody does it once they're engaged.'

Caught off-guard Iris had spoken the truth: 'He won't.'

'A bloke who won't? I don't believe it!' Daisy had fallen back on the double bed in a mock faint.

'What's the matter with him?' Lily had asked, more brutally. 'I told you not to trust that bloody blazer.'

'Nothing is the matter with him,' Iris had replied, cross with herself for revealing too much. Placid by temperament, she had grown up accustomed to all three sisters constantly trying to torment and provoke her. 'Talking to you is like shoving a stick into a pink blancmange. You give too much all the time. Stand up for yourself,' Lily would tell her often. 'Howard believes we should save ourselves until we're married,' Iris had reluctantly explained. 'That's what it says in the Bible.'

'Oh, my God.' Lily had groaned. 'I'm not going

51

to do it because I know, with my luck, I'd fall for a baby first time – but you're not doing it because you think it's a sin?'

Now Iris picks up Daisy's pink nylon baby-doll pyjamas from under the bed and places them on her sister's pillow. In his latest letter, Howard had said that his father had offered to pay for them to have a week's holiday in a boarding-house in Blackpool when he came home on leave next month. What could that mean?

Iris's stomach gives a small lurch of excitement and, alarmed, because she's not that sort of girl, she shoots out of the room, and closes the door firmly on her darker side.

Next door, at number seven Rydol Crescent, Kath arrives home from work to find Dulcie, down in the mouth, sitting in front of the fire, the table laid for tea as usual. But there is something odd about the otherwise familiar tableau. Then Kath spots it. A television set is balanced precariously on top of the sugar pink fluffy stool Dulcie won at bingo. Now she sits staring forlornly at the fuzzy blur on the screen. Kath is rarely physically demonstrative to the younger woman. 'Where on earth did that come from?'

'It won't work,' Dulcie replies mournfully. 'It's mine and it won't work. I've plugged it in and I've been waiting and waiting and the picture never comes on properly.'

Kath inspects the set. 'It won't work because it hasn't got an aerial. Whose is it? Where did it come from?'

Dulcie stands up and places herself between

Kath and the set, as if prepared to defend it with her life. 'It's mine. You're not going to take it back, are you? You can't. I don't know where it came from. It came down from the sky. Please let us keep it, Kath. Please.'

When Dulcie was young she used to help herself in shops, slow to understand that cash was supposed to be part of the transaction. Now, Kath reasons, it's unlikely that she could have stolen a television set. If it's been delivered to the wrong address, someone will come to claim it sooner or later.

'Fetch a coat-hanger from the wardrobe,' she instructs. Dulcie does as she's told. Ten minutes later, a makeshift aerial is delivering an image that might or might not be a quiz show. Dulcie sits enraptured. Kath goes upstairs to change. Briefly, she lies on her bed exhausted. As her head touches the pillow, a corner of a magazine, semi-concealed, digs into her neck. She shoots up, her face red with fury. 'Dulcie!' she yells at the top of her voice, her rage beyond reason. 'I thought you promised you'd never go near this disgusting rubbish again.'

Dulcie hears and refuses to avert her gaze from the screen, but her bottom lip begins to tremble.

'Grub's up,' shouts Doug, as he has done at tea-time every day of the week, three times on Sundays, in every flat, caravan, prefab and house in every town that the family has lived. He takes his place at the top of the table. Melody has the seat of power, next to the kitchen door, in charge of fresh supplies and the teapot. Billy, aged six, is

53

the miniature of his father, Big Billy, always known as Chalkie. The boy is pugnacious, mercurial and never still. He squeezes in happily between his grandfather and his mother. Rose.

Iris takes her seat looking miserable. She has vowed not to go out on a Saturday night but finds the self-imposed curfew exceedingly depressing. Melody carries in four plates, stacked high and brimming over with liver and bacon, gravy and mash, and realises that there are still three empty chairs. 'Where's Daisy? And Carl?' she asks nobody in particular. 'And Lily?'

'Maybe Daisy's gone to Carl's for tea,' Iris suggests.

'Mam says that Daisy's won a prize in a competition as a beauty queen,' young Billy announces, helping himself from the plate of thinly cut white bread and butter on the table.

'What competition?' Melody asks frostily.

'If she's won, the others must have been real dogs,' Rose replies brusquely, as if she has no knowledge of that morning's coronation.

Melody panics: 'Is it true? Is it really true? Oh, my God. You'll have to have a word with her, Doug. She'll be off to Morocco next. I've read about it in the papers. They offer these girls a wonderful contract and then when they–'

Before she can complete her sentence, the front door is thrown open with a crash, rattling the prancing china cats on the melamine coffee-table in the adjoining room. It is followed by terrible wailing. Kath storms in, pursued by Dulcie. The older woman slams a bundle of magazines on to the table.

54

'Where's your Lily?' she shouts, relishing the drama. 'Look at the rubbish she's been giving my Dulcie. Putting ideas in her head. It's cruel, that's what it is. It's leading her up the garden path. I won't have it, do you hear me? I won't have it. Fill her head with all this nonsense and next thing you know–' She glances at young Billy. 'Well, you know what men are like. They're all after one thing and they don't mind where they find it, thank you very much. And then where will our Dulcie be? You tell me. And who do you think will be picking up the pieces?'

Little Billy steals a glance at the pile of periodicals. What can they contain to trigger such alarm and commotion? He looks but all he spies on the cover of one is a woman smiling in a churchyard. 'It's only a picture of a lady getting married,' he says, disappointedly. 'What's wrong in that?'

Daisy's Carl is twenty. He works partly as a knocker man under the tutelage of his dad, Tanner Hicks. The two choose an area, then go from door to door, offering to clear unwanted furniture and bric-à-brac. The knack, Carl has explained often to Daisy, is to choose the right house, spot the piece with potential – Clarice Cliff china, an Arts and Crafts chair – and offer a few bob to clear the lot on the grounds that it's all a load of rubbish. The key is to act casual, show no interest, walk away if the customer starts to bargain because that means she (and it's invariably a she, old and alone) knows more about the history of her possessions than is good for a knocker man's profit.

Carl and his dad also run a market stall in Fairport and a couple of other towns in the vicinity. They flog whatever comes to hand. A lot of the time it's fake – fake 'French' perfume, fake Mary Quant tights. Most often, it's ladies' underwear, since both men have the gift of the gab. 'Come on, my lovely, I wouldn't want to see these knickers on anybody else...'

Carl and his parents live in a council house on a bleak estate on the outskirts of Fairport. Designed as a better alternative to the comfortable if small two-up and two-down terraced houses that were flattened to build a bypass, which has further drained the life out of the town, the estate is without shops, post office, youth club or a regular bus service.

The exterior of the Hickses' house is exactly the same as that of the others. Inside, however, it is a palace, even if Elaine, Carl's mother, says so herself – frequently. It has a wrought-iron winding staircase, like a corkscrew, through the middle of the sitting room, a giant gold fish tank set in a simulated-leather bar, from which Tanner serves drinks after the pubs close on a Saturday night.

The bar stools are rigged up like saddles. A steer's horns hang on one wall opposite mock Civil War rifles. The room has a deep apricot shag-pile carpet and a beige simulated-leather three-piece suite. Upstairs, Elaine is proud of her bathroom suite in rose pink.

Now Elaine, Tanner, Carl and Daisy sit in the kitchen at the table while Elaine dishes up enormous portions of steak, onions and chips. Elaine has a heart-shaped face, jet black hair swept up in a French pleat with two kiss curls that lie, like fat commas, on her forehead. She paints her lips fuller than their natural line and favours turquoise eye shadow, even at six thirty a.m., when she leaves the house for Ross & Baker, where she is section head of Packaging.

Soon after she and Daisy met, Elaine confided that, years ago, she'd had terrible trouble 'down there' so she'd had 'it' all taken away. That's why Carl is her only child and very, very precious. She also made it clear to Daisy that, first, she wanted only the best for him. And second, in her eyes, Daisy fell far short of the required standard. Daisy, determined that Carl will save her the indignity of turning twenty without an engagement ring on her finger, has used every opportunity since to ingratiate herself with his mother. She consoles herself with the knowledge that this is a humiliation for which she will make Elaine pay dearly once she is Mrs Carl Hicks.

'Salt, Mam,' Carl says, at the table, emulating his father's habit of treating Elaine as a domestic robot. No 'please' or 'thank you'. Elaine obeys, then pours her son's tea and stirs in the sugar. Daisy fully expects her to raise the cup to his lips, but she stops short. The food is eaten quickly. The men talk football. Tanner only refers to his wife once. 'Christ, woman, what are you trying to do? Poison us?' he says, when he tastes the rice pudding. Carl doesn't give Daisy a single glance. 'Was that all right, dear?' Elaine asks, when Carl has finished cleaning his plate with a slice of white bread so spongy it has a life of its own.

'Not bad,' Carl replies.

Daisy shivers. This glimpse of her future is scary. Later, in the kitchen, she and Elaine wash up while the men relax and wait for the football results on the television. 'I thought the meal was lovely, Mrs Hicks,' Daisy says insincerely. 'I don't know why Carl moans so much.'

'Moans? Oh, he wasn't moaning, love, that's just his way,' Elaine says, smiling brightly. 'He really loves his mam's cooking. That's why he always says he can't see the point in getting married. No wife will spoil him like I do.'

Chapter Seven

I know as soon as I walk into our house that something is not quite right. It's not just the look of panic in Dulcie's eyes or the set of Kath's jaw that signals trouble, it's the fact that it's tea-time, the food is on the table, *but nobody is eating.* Admittedly, my mam and dad rarely eat. In contrast, nothing can stop my sisters clearing their plates. Nothing, that is, except A Crisis.

'Ah!' says Kath. 'Here she is, and not before time, young lady. And what do you call these?' For years, Dulcie has cherished the dream of a white wedding with the entire rigmarole of orange blossom and bridesmaids, something old, something new, something borrowed, something blue. All she lacks is any understanding that getting married isn't the problem, it's living together afterwards that brings grief. She is also missing another essential: a groom.

Instead of treating this as harmless day-dreaming, Kath has always overreacted. In her view, any man who wants a woman of what she calls 'limited intelligence' is only out for one thing. But, then, Kath believes all men are Only Out for One Thing. I've come to realise that, like many women of her generation, Kath is simultaneously repelled and obsessed by sex. She loves nothing better than to see an enthusiastic Casanova throttled and dismembered.

Everyone says she's protective for Dulcie's own good. I'm not so sure. I think Kath is frightened to give her sister any freedom in case it leads to Kath finding herself all alone with only her corpses and copies of *True Crime* for company.

'Have you had your tea, pet?' my mother asks Dulcie. 'I'll get a little plate of something. Fancy a bit of liver and bacon, Kath? It'll make you feel a lot better.'

My dad lights a cigarette, forgetting that he already has one burning in a china ashtray shaped like a miniature bedpan with the legend 'A Present From Sunny Bognor Regis' written on it.

'Kath hates liver,' I say, irritated by the way my mother reduces every situation to the shape of a dish and its bloody contents. I have the strongest urge to hurl a plate at the three flying ducks and the brass horseshoes on our floral wall.

'Give it to me, if you don't want it,' Iris offers. She is slim but, like all the Tempest women, she'll swell out sooner or later; a physical tribute to our mother's influence. I sit down and Dulcie immediately sits next to me, as if we're in the dock together. Kath points her finger at her sister. 'She says that all this muck belongs to you. That you've lent them to her. You're trying to put ideas in her head, that's what you're trying to do...'

Dulcie gives me a gentle pinch. 'Of course they belong to me,' I lie unconvincingly. 'I asked Dulcie to look after them because–'

Before I can continue, Rose snorts. 'I don't believe a word of it,' she says. 'What about all that stuff you're always spouting about how you're never going to be tied down, you're off first chance you get? What happened to all that?'

'Yeah, what happened to all that?' Iris prompts.

Dulcie looks at me with an air of desperation. If I tell the truth and say these stupid magazines belong to her, Kath (none of us calls her auntie because she doesn't act like one) will be at her for weeks, sulking, not speaking, telling her she's bad and wicked. My reputation is a small price to pay. 'If you must know,' I say, 'Bryn has asked me to marry him.'

Dead silence.

'And?' Rose eventually prompts.

'And?' Iris repeats, annoying as always.

'You're having us on,' Rose adds charitably. 'He can't be that desperate.'

'You couldn't have changed just like that,' Iris persists. 'She's in the club, Mam, it's got to be that.' Iris is supposed to be so sweet- natured but she's not averse to stirring up the family pond just to see what debris floats to the surface.

My mother beams. 'Oh, how lovely,' she says.

'Isn't that lovely, Doug?'

Briefly, I shut my eyes and pretend I'm in the parlour of a nice middle-class family with an inside lavatory and lots of aspirations. A family in which somebody by now would be telling me that I'm far too young to marry, that I have my whole future ahead of me, that Bryn isn't good enough, that I should be sensible and wait, that I should acquire some qualifications first. That I'm making a monumental mistake.

Instead I open my eyes and my mother is still saying, 'Lovely, isn't it, Kath? How lovely. You did say yes, didn't you, Lily? How lovely.'

My mother's main problem, among many, is that she's besotted with my dad and not in a healthy way. She wants no life unless he's in it, under her thumb. She assumes that every other female shares the same goal and wants a man on the same terms. My mam is the conqueror and Dad is the colonised: his habits, routines, interests are all controlled by her. He's got a life of tiny lies and buried hopes. If that's love, you can keep it.

'So,' she says, hugging the teapot to her chest with delight, 'when's the big day? Has he bought you a ring? When's he going to come and see your father? I know you'll make a lovely couple. Won't they, Doug? Now, I know what–'

My dad interrupts mildly: 'The lad's dad is a shop steward at Lawson's, isn't he? A bit of a red, so I've heard.'

'Don't be daft.' My mother is rarely dismissive of my dad. The only time she is is when he's in danger of deflating one of her dreams. 'I've seen Bryn's mam in the butcher's. She looks perfectly

61

respectable... Lovely dog-tooth-check coat she wears. Must be all right. Well, love,' she addresses herself to me again, 'not much point in staying on at school now, is there? Might as well leave, get yourself a decent job so you can start saving ... and...'

As the words float by, alarmingly, my mother's face disintegrates into a thousand million swirling pieces of pink and blue and white confetti. And her voice is gradually drowned by the cheerful peal of wedding bells.

To me, they sound exactly like a death knell.

Saturday evening, Rose and Billy walk home past the pubs slowly filling with customers. A gang of teenagers hang around the market-place in spite of the cold because they've nowhere else to go and the weekend money all went on Friday. Rose and her family live five minutes away from the Tempests in a rented terraced house. It smells of damp and disinfectant and rotting linoleum. In the six years since they married, she and her husband Chalkie White have moved several times, always in step with Melody and Doug.

Once home, while Rose lights the fire, Billy slides up and down the lino in the passage. 'Look, Mam,' he says, 'look.' He glances at her anxiously. Rose comes to the hall and frowns, then cuddles him in compensation. 'I love you, Billy White, I really do,' she says, kissing his forehead.

Later, while the boy is watching television, she goes out to the coalshed in the yard. Hanging from a hook is a disused birdcage. She slides out the tray at the bottom of the cage and adds several smoothed-down pound notes to the thin pile already there. She returns the tray and covers it with a layer of newspaper. One day, Rose has promised herself, when she has enough money saved to begin again, she will go, alone. And when she goes, she will leave no note. A million words, no matter how well crafted, will never stop her son blaming himself for her departure, Rose knows that, but nothing can bring her to abandon her plan.

'Mammy, where are you?' Billy's voice holds a note of panic. She closes the door of the coalshed and returns to the kitchen. The boy, thin and wiry, limbs like pipe-cleaners, twists himself around her, as if to keep her rooted. 'Tell me a story, Mam, please.'

Rose smiles. She knows that as a mother she does many things wrong, but this particular private transaction between herself and her son she performs as well as she can. 'What's it to be, Billy?' she says softly.

He shuts his eyes tight and, suddenly, she is overcome by the way his long lashes curl on his freckled cheeks. This is the only real power a child possesses, Rose tells herself, the ability to steal his parent's heart at the most unexpected times, if only for a moment.

'A black dog and a one-legged monkey in Sherwood Forest in olden days!' he improvises excitedly.

She pulls him on to her knee and begins to weave a tale. He settles in, thumb in his mouth. After a little while, spontaneously, he reaches out and gently strokes her cheek. 'You tell the best stories, Mam' he says.

'Well, don't tell anyone, sweetheart,' Rose whispers in his ear. 'Not Daddy or Gran or anyone. OK?'

The boy nods gravely. 'Not a word, I promise. Cross my heart and hope to die.'

Rose has grown up believing that, unlike her sisters, she is not anything that counts for much. Daisy is the pretty one, Lily is contrary and clever, Iris is, well, dim but good-natured, while she, Rose, the secondary-modern sulk with ideas above her station, has grown against the grain: she is not a good wife, not a good mother, just not.

Treacherous thoughts and dark fantasies Rose pours into her poetry and stories – the wife who kills, the mother who flees, the lover who wants what she's not supposed to have. She keeps them hidden to avoid mockery and ridicule. But also because Rose fears, like all story-tellers, that they may reveal too much.

'And they all lived happily ever after,' she concludes, ten minutes later, as her son slides gently into sleep.

I wake very early on Sunday morning. Directly opposite our bedroom window, the church clock tells me that it's two twelve a.m. Daisy is in bed, fully dressed, face streaked with yesterday's makeup. Last night, Bryn and I had gone to the pictures, then come back to my house where he ate four of my mother's ham sandwiches and six pickled onions. One of Bryn's faults is that he doesn't plan ahead. On the doorstep I didn't know which was worse, his breath or the cold wind blowing up my skirt.

The light is on in my dad's shed. I pick up Daisy's coat left on the floor by the door, find my slippers, go downstairs and out into the yard. It's marginally warmer outside than in. I watch my dad through the shed window for a few minutes. He sits cutting and weaving and plaiting a paper dachshund's stubby leg, with intense concentration, fag hanging out of his mouth.

My father was a hero in the war. My mam told me that he was taught to make paper dogs in hospital after he was injured. That's what they gave grown men to do, said it might turn into a useful little job in Civvy Street, since they'd be too disabled to earn a proper wage. My dad says nothing about the war, almost as if he's ashamed. He never even goes on about the younger generation having it too easy, showing no respect, taking it all for granted, not knowing the value of anything. The only time he acts big, ironically, is when he sings. And even then it's not him but a copy-cat Dean Martin who's up on stage, down to the last embarrassing detail. Rose says we should be grateful for small mercies. He could've chosen Frankie Vaughan.

Now he opens the door, wreathed in cigarette smoke, as if he's at the gateway to heaven – or hell.

'Can't sleep?' he says. 'Nor me. Got up half an hour ago. Your mam had nodded off in the chair waiting for Daisy, so I steered her up to bed and came out here for a bit.'

I sit on one of the two kitchen stools, warming myself by the paraffin stove. He resumes working in silence. Wherever we've lived, I've always done this: come and sat while he worked. None of the others could stay quiet for long enough. People say my dad is happy-go-lucky. I think it's more as if, a long time ago, he swept all his untidy fears, worries and anxieties together and, like a houseproud woman, emptied them into a big tin dustbin and clanged the lid down fast. Other times, I think he hates to talk about his emotions, because he doesn't have any, not real ones. He can be hard. I told him about Rhys, a boy I knew, who was killed on his motorbike, two days after his seventeenth birthday. 'Bloody stupid to be on a bike,' my dad said.

Perhaps he's hard; or perhaps he's just trained himself not to go too near anybody else's pain. I suppose that's what war does to you.

He begins to sing. 'Volare'.

'Come on, girl,' he coaxes, 'sing...' Eventually, since he repeats the chorus again and again, I relent, if only so the bloody song will come to an end. We sing louder and louder, until something thuds on the roof – probably a cat or the next-door neighbour's boot. We laugh, like children making mischief, and fall silent again.

After a couple of minutes, Dad lights up another fag and says casually, 'We should do more of that, maybe get a bit of an act together. What do you say?'

Alarm bells ring. If I wasn't so cold already, I'd say I froze. 'Who'd want us?' He shrugs. Anxious to change the subject, I ask, 'Don't you ever fancy making something different? Like a cat or a rabbit? Why do you keep making the same dog over and over again?'

'They're not the same. That's the whole point. Every one is different.'

He lines up four dogs on his workbench. 'See?' he says. 'See how different they are.'

Gently, almost lovingly, he picks up the nearest to him and shows me that one ear is longer than the other. Another has a slightly fatter snout. The third has a stubbier torso.

'But if you hadn't shown me, I wouldn't have known. They might as well have come from a factory,' I persist, pleased to be invited, well, more or less, to say what I've thought privately for years. 'Except for that one...'

On the shelf, standing in isolation like a canine sentry, staring at the door, is an altogether much more roughly crafted model.

'That's Scrubs. He was the first,' my dad says. 'I've kept him. I look at him and I can see how much I've improved. He's my sort of watchdog.' He gives a strange chuckle and, unusually, his face grows sombre. 'You're wrong, you know. No conveyor belt can do this, only the human hand. It's a craft. I'll show you how, one day, if you like...'

'You've got to be joking,' I say, without thought. 'What I mean is–' He waves his hand, dismissing whatever it is I am about to say, the smile already back on his face.

Chapter Eight

Sundays: the smell of roast beef and Yorkshire pudding and cabbage boiled to the point of least resistance. *Two-way Family Favourites* on the radios in the kitchen, the back room and upstairs in our bedroom, messages of lust and longing from outposts of the empire delivered to council houses across the land by Jean Metcalfe and her jolly husband Cliff Michelmore in posh tones bleached of all passion. 'Harry in Akrotiri says to Sandra in Stockport, it won't be long now until he's home with you, so put the kettle on, love! Harry says the message is in the song – it's Brian Hyland's "Sealed With A Kiss".'

We girls, each in a different part of the house, join in and sing at the top of our voices, almost drowning the hymns from the chapel across the road. While we sing, we're supposed to clean. Mam works on the downstairs, except for the brass which is Daisy's job, and the windows, which are Iris's. I'm in charge of the two bedrooms. Dad's a man, and men in our family have only two tasks, to clean the oven after Sunday dinner and bring in the coal.

Usually, I squirt lavender polish liberally in the air; switch on the Hoover then lie on the bed. If Iris has had a letter from Howard, she hides it in the hem of her dressing-gown. Occasionally I have a read, but in all honesty, his lack of imagination is

68

hardly a spur to curiosity. Howard should join Acronyms Anonymous since his letters are plastered with them – and not much else. SWALK is his favourite. His alphabet of muted desire is always followed by 'I trust this finds you as well as it leaves me. Yours ever, Howard'.

I'm about to switch on the Hoover and retire to the bed as usual, when my mother arrives with a cup of tea. She is also carrying a yellow tablecloth covered with gypsy girls and tambourines. 'I got it in the sale,' she lies (I've seen it in the catalogue she keeps under her bed). 'I want you to have it – for your bottom drawer.'

I look at it, mesmerised not just by its awfulness but also by the realisation that she actually believes I need a bottom drawer. *A bottom drawer?* 'Go on, take it,' she says. Then she opens the wardrobe and starts tipping out neatly wrapped items, jumpers, blouses and scarves that she has been given over the years by us as Christmas and birthday presents. My mother is odd: she acquires at a sometimes terrifying rate but she doesn't personally consume much. 'Have this space in the wardrobe,' she says. 'You can put all your sheets and stuff in here. How about pillowcases?'

'Pillowcases?' I repeat, as if I'm learning English. She nods at me, the acquiescent bride-to-be. She smiles and I only just manage to duck her warm embrace. God, my mother can be so irritating. 'Look, Mam...' I am about to tell her that I have no intention of marrying Bryn or anyone else but I can't quite bring myself to do it. I've grown up with the knowledge that my mother has a happy disposition. If the smile goes, it's usually because of something I've done. So, now when I spy approval in her eyes, it's hard to tell the truth. 'Look, Mam,' I begin again. And fail again.

'Look, Mam,' I hear myself say instead, 'tell me about when you and Dad got together.'

She sits on the bed, and says, as she has done dozens of times before, 'We had no money in those days. The first time I saw him he was wearing a brown double-breasted suit and I had on a cherry red coat, black shoes and handbag. Very smart, even if I say so myself. I was queuing with a girlfriend to go into the pictures and he and his chum were just behind. They followed us home. Then, a few years later, all the photographs went up in smoke. Your dad and I had only been in the lodging-house two days, and it landed a direct hit. When we went back the following morning...'

Irritation rises again. I parrot the words along with her: '...there was nothing but a hole in the ground and your dad's trousers, still hanging on the bedpost, twenty yards down the road. Everything gone, everything except what we stood up in...' My mother pauses.

So I end the sentence for her: 'In my day, we had nothing. And, often, what little we did have, we lost. That's what the war was like. You young ones don't know how lucky you are...'

My mother chuckles. 'Am I that bad?'

Daisy sits on the floor surrounded by thirty-seven brass objects – miniature shire-horses, wheelbarrows, watering-cans and ashtrays. The smell of Brasso makes her retch. Her mascara has run and an excess of alcohol has further inflamed the boil that erupted on her temple some time last night.

She has little to show now for her elevation to royalty. The portrait of Daniel Bright was mislaid during yesterday's excitement and the sash and crown had been immediately retrieved for next year's competition. The fiver she spent. So all that remained was the tin of biscuits and the confidential information that she, Daisy Tempest, has bedded Fame.

After her encounter with Mr Bright, she had returned for tea at Carl's, then complained that she felt poorly. Carl had dropped her at the bottom of Rydol Crescent. She had waited until he and his motorbike had disappeared from view, then took a bus into Cwmland for a second rendezvous with Mr Bright. He had received three encores from the Saturday-evening crowd, so when she told him that her sister Lily had lied, she did not have a brain tumour, and she was definitely not a terminal case, he hadn't been cross at all. In fact, he'd appeared pleased to see her.

Mam had been asleep in the chair, waiting for her, when Daisy had let herself in, just after one. At breakfast, Melody had asked suspiciously, 'What time did you get home?'

'Not late,' Iris and Lily had chorused together. Her sisters were good like that.

Suddenly Daisy realises that what she hears isn't the banging in her head but the clatter of the door knocker. She flies up the stairs discarding curlers as she goes, since only family is permitted to see her without her face on.

Melody also hears the door, and sticks her head

out of her bedroom window, which overlooks the street. She sees the tops of two heads she fails to recognise. Her mouth dries – then common sense takes over. Her debts, so far, she reminds herself, are only small anxieties, not yet floating icebergs. The strangers can't be bailiffs.

'Can I help?' she shouts down, rounding out her vowels to appear posher than she is, since this is Sunday. Lily joins her just as the two faces below peer upwards.

'Oh, Jesus,' Lily says in panic.

Kath wears black slacks and a crimson shirt with the collar turned up, black velvet pumps, a pearl choker, a striped woollen stole, and her hair is swept up. Her aim is a mature version of Audrey Hepburn. 'So,' she says, 'have you actually ever killed anybody? I mean with your bare hands.'

Pete the Mercenary tries to settle himself more comfortably on the dining-room chair and glances at Lily, sitting opposite. It was he and his brother, Robert, who had called by that morning to see how the gift of a television set had been received. Lily had redirected them to Kath and Dulcie's next door and made the introductions. Pete runs his fingers through his hair and instantly regrets it. He wipes the excess grease on his trousers. 'I suppose you've heard of the Belgian Congo?' he asks casually.

Kath nods enthusiastically, her face animated. 'Terrible massacres, awful tortures...'

Dulcie puts her hands over her ears. 'Don't, Kath, don't talk about it. I hate it. Anyway,' she adds, suddenly coy, 'I'm going upstairs.'

Pete notices that Kath's eyes have narrowed alarmingly. He shifts his chair back a little. 'How's it going, Robert?' he asks, over his shoulder, addressing a large, shambling figure, dressed in corduroy trousers and an olive green cardigan with buttons shaped like footballs sliced in half, poking about at the back of the television set.

'Give us another five minutes,' says a muffled voice.

'Does Robert do this for a living?' Lily asks, feeling responsible for allowing Pete to cross the family threshold and further inflame her aunt's lust for blood. Pete gives a strained smile. 'No, he's a car-park attendant. He works on the sea-front. This is his slack time. Lucky if he gets a car a week, ain't you, mate? And then it's usually a couple out for a quick f–' Lily shakes her head furiously.

'Out for a quick fag... like,' he says. 'But this is our Robert's hobby. He's a divvy. Ain't you, mate? Went to special school, can't barely read nor write but show him a radio or a TV or a record-player and he's a bloody miracle worker.'

Robert withdraws his head from the back of the set to reveal that he is a fuller, fatter version of Pete but without any of his brother's bravado and minus the tattoos. He also has better teeth. 'It's a pity.' Pete opens up his tin of tobacco and begins rolling a cigarette. 'It's a pity because our Robert could make a packet but he can't hold down a proper job, needs the freedom to walk about a bit. Still, nothing wrong in that, is there? Everybody needs to feel their own man.' Pete gives a crude chuckle and winks at Kath. He sticks the roll-up

73

his ear and prepares another to smoke
/hat I meant to say is, everybody needs to
: own man, know what I'm saying, missus?'
Pete winks.

Lily looks at Kath. She sits straight-backed, head high, neck long, eyes glittering, like a boa constrictor who's just seen the mouse it's about to swallow as a snack.

'Mrs Morgan. My name is Mrs Morgan, young man, and in this house, we don't smoke and we don't–' She is interrupted by Dulcie's reappearance. It is the first time Lily has ever seen Dulcie in lipstick. It is the colour of raspberries, painted unevenly, so she looks as if she's just consumed a punnet of the fruit with her hands tied. She also has a new, bright blue slide in her hair and her face is aglow with anticipation. The smell of lavender suffuses the small room.

'Dulcie,' Kath barks, sniffing suspiciously, 'you look a sight.'

'No, you don't, you look fab,' Lily contradicts fiercely. 'Really gorgeous.'

Dulcie ignores them both and advances determinedly across the room until she stands in front of Robert, who is oblivious, still sorting out the television set. 'Excuse me,' she begins earnestly. He turns obediently. 'Do you think I'm all right?' The remainder of her words tumble out in a rush, as if she will lose her nerve if her message isn't delivered speedily: 'Would you like to take me to the pictures? Would you take me, please? Would you do that?'

Robert stands up, turns around and looks down with a baffled expression at this small female who is looking at him so anxiously. Pete fills the silence. 'Well, would you bloody well believe it? Go on, get in there, my son!' He chuckles.

Kath grimaces. 'Over my dead body,' she says flatly.

Every Sunday evening, for the past eighteen months, Doug Tempest has sung in the Cow and Fiddle, a forty-minute bus ride away from Fairport across the English border. Unlike its Welsh counterparts, the Cow and Fiddle remains open on the Sabbath. Doug offers the same repertoire each week, backed by the pub's resident pianist, Albie Walters, a retired butcher. The pair offer a small dose of Dino, a mix of standards and a sprinkling of requests, 'Come On Baby Light My Fire', 'My Way', 'Moon River', 'Fly Me To The Moon', 'You've Lost That Lovin' Feelin',' 'A Hard Day's Night'. It earns Doug a few bob and a few beers, although he's never been much of a drinking man.

Doug has his own routine, pre-performance. Melody brings up the electric fire to the bedroom, polishes his shoes, lays out his frilled white shirt, bow-tie, clean underpants and dinner jacket, shiny now with age but passable in the permanent twilight of pub land, and leaves the choice of cufflinks to him. A small red tin, previously used for Oxo cubes, holds his collection, a dozen pairs, each a different shape – beer barrels, skittles, teddy bears, a miniature version of the Eiffel Tower. Tonight Doug opts for silver cufflinks shaped like dice, each studded with six fake rubies.

He opens the wardrobe and swings into view in

the mirror on the inside of the door, cut off from the calves. He adjusts his jacket. He tells himself, wryly, that to everyone else he probably looks a lucky geezer.

The Cow and Fiddle, once a bare-boards-and-lino establishment, has been redecorated to look like a Victorian parlour, with maroon wallpaper with a brocade effect, artificial gas lamps and large engraved mirrors. Only the public bar retains its original Spartan appeal. At one end of the lounge bar a small stage holds an upright piano, a set of drums, a couple of speakers and a backcloth of purple satin to which gold foil stars have been pinned.

Opposite the stage, its illuminated lights changing colour according to the tempo, stands a huge juke-box. Like a malevolent robot, it eats up coins and spews out the latest top-ten hits, as well as country and western and 'Swinging Standards' – Sinatra, Andy Williams, Perry Como.

Tommy Aster, the publican, is a tall thin man with a face that looks as if it has spent a lifetime in mourning. He extends and retracts his neck alarmingly, so he resembles an agitated tortoise. Now it lengthens by a foot and he nods at Mattie the barmaid. She dutifully flicks off the juke-box, terminating 'What Becomes Of The Broken-hearted?' mid-chorus, to roars of disapproval.

'Ladies and gentlemen,' Tommy shouts above the din, 'ladies and gentlemen, I have great pleasure in introducing to you a star of stage, screen and television, brought to you at enormous expense, and a couple of bottles of Newcastle Brown, Mr Doug "Dino" Tempest, accompanied

76

by his boy wonder, Albie "Mr Piano" Walters. Give them a big hand, everybody, show your appreciation, *puu-leease...*'

Albie, the resident pianist for years, plays the first notes of Doug's standard opening, a medley of 'Mac The Knife', 'The Lady Is A Tramp' and 'It Had To Be You'. Doug begins to sing, clicking his fingers, taking a hop and skip over the notes that age now make difficult, smiling into the eyes of those females who cast admiring glances, watching out for men with resentment written on their faces and too much beer in their bellies.

'That's why...' he sings, taking in lungfuls of blue-grey cigarette smoke, 'that's why...' Out of the corner of his eye, he sees something small flying towards him. He sidesteps neatly and a pickled egg splatters against the side of Albie's piano, releasing a stink like a cabbage-fuelled fart.

'Christ, mate,' Albie mouths accusingly, his nose twitching, fingers still flying over the keys. Doug keeps smiling as a lad in his late teens sways towards him, spilling beer, inadvertently baptising sections of the audience.

'Hey, Grandad,' the drunk shouts, 'hey, Grandad, we want rock 'n' roll. We want bloody "Jumpin' Jack Flash".' He breaks into song, performing a little jig, beer splashing. Albie steadfastly plays on. Someone at the back shouts, 'Sod off.' Doug, singing louder, directs his smile towards his ally and realises that it is he who is the target of the abuse.

'You there, you in the pouf's frilly shirt, why don't you piss off?' the man shouts again at the stage. Doug is aware that a nerve is jumping in his cheek. He smiles all the harder.

'You're dressed up like a bloody ventriloquist's dummy. Who pulls your strings, mate, that's what I want to know? Give the young bloke a go. Go on, son, you get up there and sing for your supper. You've got to be bloody better than him.'

A woman in a bright pink coat, her hair back-combed to such a terrifying height she resembles a strawberry missile, gets to her feet. 'Sit down and bloody well behave yourself,' she bellows at the heckler, a couple of tables away. Meekly, the man does as he's told amid laughter. Another lad, only marginally more sober, links his arm through the young drunk's. Doug sings on, clicking his fingers resolutely, click, click, click, and watches cautiously as the rescuer leads his friend away, weaving through tables and knocking over stools.

'Sorry, sorry about this. No hard feelings? He was given his cards today,' the lad tells anyone who will listen. 'Him and five others laid off. Pissed off, they are. No hard feelings...'

Doug waves acknowledgement as the couple reach the door. The sound of retching outside fills the silence after the initial burst of applause. Briefly, Doug looks down at the ruffles on his shirt. Suddenly they seem grotesque and pathetic. The boy's right. He is too bloody old. Too bloody out of date. Albie plays the first few rolling bars of 'The House Of The Rising Sun'. The audience always join in, whether they know the words or not. Doug misses his cue.

'Sing it to me, Dougie boy,' Albie shouts robustly, above his own fortissimo piano-playing. 'Sing it to me like no other bugger here can.'

Doug obediently does as he's told. Stung, he sings as he hasn't sung in months.

This time when he looks out at his audience he sees only his father's face, again and again and again.

Later, during the interval, Doug spots her in the corner of the lounge. She is wearing a crimson jacket and several layers of makeup. She sits with a boy who looks about sixteen. He nurses a pint, she has a glass of orange – probably with a large gin in it, Doug guesses. She waggles her fingers in greeting. He smiles. She crooks her finger, beckoning.

Doug holds up his hand like a traffic policeman, partly in greeting, partly as if to stop physically whatever it is that Betty Procter has in mind. Then Tommy Aster intercedes. He puts his arm around Dougie's shoulders, his neck jerking nervously. 'Got a minute, mate?' Doug nods. Tommy propels him to the quiet end of the bar. 'Look,' he says, 'it's not you.' Doug senses what's coming next. 'We've got a younger crowd now. You know what it's like. They want a group, maybe a girl singer... So I reckon we'll knock your Sunday slot on the head. OK, mate? From this week? Know what I'm saying?'

Doug shrugs. 'Funnily enough,' he says, 'I had an offer only a couple of days ago. Pub in Hampton wants me regularly on a Sunday.'

They both know he's lying. 'Well, I was going to offer you something else,' Tommy says, 'but, then, it's probably not your style...'

Doug tries to look uninterested.

Tommy stares at the picture of a pelican

advertising Guinness above Doug's head. 'I'm looking for a duo. Sort of Peters and Lee. Young girl, older fellow, all pop stuff, no standards unless requested. Sonny and Cher with a few grey hairs. Bridge the gap between the oldsters and the youngsters. Interested? You and one of your girls, maybe? They're not bad looking, are they?' Tommy gives a strangled laugh, his neck jerking in and out as he avoids the other man's eyes.

Doug smiles, waiting for the surge of anger to abate. In the past, he never had the capacity to bide his time and that was when trouble came. Now, instead, he briefly closes his eyes and imagines smashing his fist into the nearest wall, then pulverising the fat bastard next to him, eavesdropping on his humiliation before tying Tommy Aster's neck into a large reef knot.

Of course, he'd always known it would come one day – relegation to the ranks of ghostly nobodies who wander up and down the streets of Fairport – but not so soon. And not without some preparation. Out of the limelight, away from the admiration, however synthetic, Doug fears that the shadow of his father will creep over him again, blotting him up, a dark, polluting stain. Tommy jerks again spasmodically, as if Doug's hands are already round his neck.

'Mind you, if you do pair up,' Tommy is saying, 'I'm not paying any extra for the girl. Just the usual rate. It'll be a Monday night. Oh, and do yourself a favour,' he adds, 'leave the dinner jacket at home – and the bloody awful blouse. OK, mate?'

Chapter Nine

Sunday evening, and I try to clear a space on the table in the back room, moving aside empty crisps packets, a basket of hair curlers, three bottles of nail varnish, tweezers, a sachet of mud face pack, a bottle of TCP and a hand mirror. Iris has been doing her face. Whatever maintenance is required she carries out in front of whoever happens to be in the back room. Squeezing, plucking, painting, there is no mystery to womanhood in a family without a bathroom, all is on public display – except what Mam calls the 'private bits'. Nobody sees them, not even their owners, as we pull panties off under skirts and draw bras out of the sleeve of a jumper. Underwear illusionists, that's us four girls.

'Sausage roll?' Mam asks, wafting a hot plate in front of me. 'Or a piece of pork pie?' I shake my head. Daisy and Iris accept, as they always do. I, in contrast, have scaled the mountainous heights of my mother's mashed potato, swum through platefuls of stew and successfully navigated the quicksands of semolina and mixed-fruit jam from Bulgaria but, and this is the trick learned from my father, I have done so with barely a swallow. My sisters have yet to realise that no matter how many plates they clear, or how many suet puddings they devour, they'll never eat enough to prove to our mother how much they really, really love her.

I return to my homework, *The Duchess of Malfi*, a tragedy written in 1614 by John Webster: '"Cover her face. Mine eyes dazzle: She died young;" What does this tell us about Ferdinand's changed state of mind before and after the killing of his sister?'

Sunday Night at the London Palladium is on the telly. Daisy, Carl, Iris and the man who comes every week to collect the pools money and has a shine for our mam are all transfixed by three Chinese acrobats standing on each other's shoulders, spinning plates. 'Pass the dandelion-and-burdock,' Daisy says. She looks terrible. She's got a boil that looks ready to erupt. Normally her skin is as smooth and unblemished as the suede coat I fancy in Chelsea Girl. She's also red-eyed and yet, in spite of it all, she's looking rather pleased with herself.

'Dandelion-and-burdock, *please*,' I tell her, passing her the bottle. Down our way, the Corona man drives round the houses every Friday morning and leaves whatever you order on the doorstep. For us, it's dandelion-and-burdock, limeade and ginger beer.

'Shift over, love,' my mother says, moving my books to lay out her best china for the benefit of the pools man. He's a nobody but he wears a suit and tie to disguise the fact. My mother is easily taken in. 'This can't be good for your health,' she says disapprovingly at me. 'Not on a Sunday.'

As far as I'm concerned, studying leads to exams, which result in qualifications, which, hopefully, equal freedom. Freedom to do what? I

82

haven't yet decided, but at least I'll have the opportunity to choose. My mother sees choice as the younger generation's H-bomb, bound to destroy all life as she's known it. She's probably right.

Mam is an optimist who is extraordinarily negative about any interests outside the narrow remit she has given herself – so politics, foreign travel (which includes London), theatre (except for Lionel Bart's *Oliver!* and *The Sound of Music)*, novels and my entire A-level syllabus she regards as the cause of great harm, second only to venereal disease.

It makes sense, in the circumstances, for me to hide that I enjoy a lot of my history and English. I like the quirky bits – like discovering Henry VIII had bedsores. I like the way that when you dig around for yourself, the past can suddenly spring out at you, like a page in a child's pop-up book. In class, it usually has the life flattened out of it by the weight of the teacher's boredom.

Mr Whitehaven, our history master, who's not a day over thirty, bald and has a face like a foetus, read out to the class the first five paragraphs of my essay on the causes of the Reformation. Then he turned to me and lisped, 'So, Miss Tempest, whose eloquent words are these because they're certainly not yours?'

My mother re-emerges from the kitchen. 'I met a girl called Kit Renshaw yesterday,' I say. 'Do you know her? She works in the fruit-and-veg shop. She's going out with Podge.'

My mother looks interested. 'Is that Trefor Renshaw's girl? Lots of brothers and sisters?'

I nod. Unusually for us, the conversation is going quite well. 'Kit says her dad's been off sick for ages. Her mam died and he's suffering from a broken heart.'

Mam chuckles. 'His heart might be broken but from what I've heard the other bits of his body are in good working order.'

'What do you mean?'

'Never you mind,' she says, then adds, in a more serious tone, 'I want you to stay away from her, do you hear? You never know what might happen.' This is typical. I resolve privately to overturn my previous prejudice and make Kit Renshaw a close friend as soon as possible.

Carl, bored with the acrobats on the telly, picks up my copy of *The Duchess of Malfi*. 'What's this, then?' he says.

'It's got writing and pages and a cover, so I'd hazard a guess that it's a book,' I reply.

Carl and I have a strong relationship – strongly antagonistic. He calls me lippy, which means I refuse to show him the blind admiration Daisy always displays. Carl cannot understand how any female can resist his double bill – he is, he thinks, not only good-looking but he knows how to make money. When he's not annoying me intensely, he's offering me makeup, talcum powder and knickers from the market at a special price. 'It's a play, innit?' he observes intelligently. 'You know, doing what I do, working the markets, well, it's like reading a dozen books. In my time on my dad's stall, I must've come across a cast of thousands. Makes up for any of the stuff they dole out at school, I tell you. I've learned a lot and it's all up here.' He points to where his brain is supposed to be.

Having established his intellectual superiority over me – at least to his satisfaction – Carl decides to wander even further into enemy territory for reasons best known to himself. 'So what's this about? Tell us. See if I can stay awake.' He clicks his fingers at Daisy and, without looking at her, orders, 'Sugar, girl.' The newly crowned queen of biscuits trots obediently into the kitchen to fetch the sugar bowl and puts three teaspoons into her boyfriend's tea.

'Why don't you say "please"?' I suggest.

'What for, when she'll do it anyway?' Carl replies cockily 'Go on, then,' he adds, pushing the book at me.

'Well,' I say, 'this is about incest.' He looks blank. 'It's about a brother who fancies his sister.'

'What?' Daisy comes awake. 'He fancies her? I think that's absolutely disgusting. I don't know how anyone could do that and–'

'Don't be so bloody daft,' Carl interrupts abruptly. 'Happens all the time. Dads doing it with their daughters and that – and–' Daisy gives a theatrical shudder. 'Go on,' he orders.

'Well, she secretly marries a working-class bloke, her steward, Antonio. She has his children, and then her twin brother has him and her babies murdered before tormenting and killing her. The man who does all the killing, Bosola, is into survival. We're told he's already served seven years in the galley for a notorious killing.'

Carl's eyes widen and, for once, I appear to have his full attention.

'Every person in the play is in one form of

prison or another. The Duchess says, "The robin redbreast and the nightingale never live long in cages..." She's broken the rules. Women had to marry who they were told to marry... Men were the boss. Of course, it's different now... I don't think,' I add, but, for once, Carl lets the dig pass by.

'Then what happens?' he says.

'Her spirit is never broken. Even at the end, she says, "I am Duchess of Malfi still." Then men thought powerful women were dangerous and unnatural.'

'Too bloody right.' Carl grins. 'What happens to her brother?'

'He goes mad. He says, "Cover her face; mine eyes dazzle: she died young." And even Bosola, the baddie, is moved. He says, "Other sins only speak, murder shrieks out."'

'"Murder shrieks out,"' Carl repeats. Then he remembers he's a hard man and the written word is for pansies. His face shuts down. 'I was right in the first place,' he says, swaggering as he reaches for the comb in his back pocket. 'It is boring. She should've done as she was bloody told. Shouldn't she, Daisy?' My sister nods agreement, smiles adoringly.

'Oh, you stupid little cow,' I tell her crossly, angry with myself for believing that Carl might really have been interested.

Out of the blue, my mother says, 'I like the Duchess of Malfi. She does what her heart tells her to do, no matter what society says. That's brave. Cup of tea, lovey?'

Betty Procter wedges herself between Albie and Doug at the bar and orders a drink. 'Can I give you a lift home, Doug?' she says. 'I've got my old man's van. He's babysitting tonight.' She indicates with her head the teenager looking lonely at her table. 'Don't worry about him. He's on his way out the door now. It's past his bedtime. He's my second one down. I was supposed to meet a mate but she didn't turn up so I said he could stay for a bit to keep me company.'

Doug looks at his watch. 'Thanks, Betty,' he smiles, 'I'm all right. I've got to sort out a couple of things with Tommy. Don't you hang around.'

The weight of her body, pressing up against his, shifts as if in physical reproof. She sighs heavily. 'Oh dear,' she says. 'You are a naughty boy.'

An hour or so later, when Doug does leave the pub, the car park is deserted. He hears Tommy lock and bolt the door behind him, turning off the pub lights, until only a string of fairy-lights remains, decorating the entrance. Normally Tommy pays for a taxi since the last bus leaves a little after nine. He hadn't seen the need tonight, so Doug had called one himself and, twenty minutes late, it is still to appear. Suddenly, three lads emerge from the shadow of the men's lavatory.

One is the drunk who barracked him earlier in the evening, the other two are strangers. Three against one, Doug tells himself. Three young men against one past middle age – but he has the advantage of being sober. He's known worse odds. Give them a gentle pasting or, better still, for their sakes and his own, run so no damage is done. Before he can make a decision, the three

87

rush him, arms flailing like aeroplane propellers, slipping and sliding in the slush. One lad lands a punch on the side of Doug's head. The other two collide with each other, swearing and cursing.

'Ow!' one says, like a child, as he stumbles and grazes his palm on the gravel. Doug stamps hard on the lad's hand, then punches him with far greater force than is required, full in the face, flecking the front of his ruffled shirt with polka dots of blood. Then he turns to the heckler, who has been clumsily attempting a head butt, and calmly, almost unhurriedly, he pinches the flesh under his arms until the teenager squeals with pain. The third throws himself on to Doug's back. The boy smells of fried onions and vomit. Doug reaches behind for his head, and holds him close, as if in endearment, before jabbing him hard in each eye with his thumb. Then he kicks back with the heel of his shoe at the boy's shin.

Two reassemble, looking uncertainly at each other; all snot and blood and bruises. The third, on his back, attempts to stand up. Doug lifts his hand to check if his own lip has been cut. 'Don't hit me, mister,' says the one trying to get to his feet and, in panic, scrambling sideways like a crab. 'Please, don't hit me.'

'Fuck off, just fuck off, you!' his mate yells in frustration at Doug, warily keeping his distance as he does so. 'I'm going to fucking kill you next time I see you. Hear me, you fucking twat? You're a dead bloody man.' Then, the three, as if responding to a silent command, make a running retreat, mouthing obscenities as if trying to convince each other that they have come out on top.

Doug bends double to ease his breathing, and watches as a drop of blood splashes on to the toe of his shoe. A wave of shame and disgust sweeps over him, as it does every time he behaves like his father's child.

Five minutes later, still waiting for his taxi, his mac buttoned up to conceal the clues to the fracas that has gone before, Doug sees a battered white van, a pair of ladders strapped to its roof, drive slowly down the lane towards him. Tensing, suspecting that his assailants have returned with the intention of mowing him down, he steps back from the kerb. The van pulls up and, out of the darkness, Betty Procter leans over and winds down the passenger window. 'Your lip's bleeding,' she says. 'Get in. I'll take you home.'

Doug hesitates, then does as he is told. As his eyes adjust to the gloom, he realises that her skirt is hitched up around her waist. Her white thighs remind him of two large loaves of unbaked dimpled dough. Forbidden food. Betty Procter laughs softly and places in his lap what appears to be a red carnation, flowering even as he watches. Then he sees it's a pair of crimson nylon knickers. The woman shifts gears and says, in a low voice, 'I took 'em off, see, while you were scrapping.'

Defeat, like a cast-iron blanket, wraps itself around Doug's shoulders. If he can't win redemption, he tells himself, then respite will have to do.

'Always smiling, aren't you, boy?' Betty Procter says. 'But, then, from where I'm sitting, I'd say you've got plenty to smile about.'

On Sunday evenings Rose leaves Billy with his

grandmother, and earns time and a half on the late shift at the hotel. Cleaning up the debris from the lives of strangers provides her with a writer's raw material. This evening, she folds down the beds of a businessman with a suitcase full of women's wigs and a vicar who keeps a pair of binoculars in the hollowed-out Bible by his bed.

At the end of her shift, one of the porters gives her a lift back on his scooter. He drops her off at the bus station and Rose takes a short-cut, running fast down an alleyway. As she emerges, she sees a solitary white van with two ladders strapped to its roof like an insect's antennae, parked on the far side of the road. She draws level and glances over, then quickly looks away again, shaking her head furiously, as if erasing the moment before a memory has time to form.

Rose soon arrives at her mother's house to pick up a sleeping Billy. She is followed, shortly after, by her father. Melody fusses over Doug and his cut lip, and searches his scalp for non-existent wounds, while he sits and surrenders to her attention. Rose watches and waits. 'Everybody must've thought you looked a right sight,' Melody says. 'Those stupid lads. I'll give 'em what for if I ever lay eyes on them. It's jealousy, nothing more, nothing less.'

Doug says nothing. Impulsively, he puts his arms around Melody and rests his head on her stomach. She kisses the top of his head. Rose turns away so intensely intimate is this scene. As she does so, it dawns on her. *Her mother knows.* Just as she herself always knows when Chalkie

90

has strayed. *Her mother knows.* Anger rises in Rose. Anger at the hypocrisy that seems an inescapable part of what passes for romance once it's aged. Anger at her own inertia and her mother's docility. Anger at her father's betrayal of trust. 'Dad,' she says, 'that–'

Doug stands up, stretches, and makes his way to the kitchen. 'Got to clean myself up.'

Behind her husband's back, Melody puts a finger to her puckered lips and, looking at Rose, softly, as if calming a baby, she says, 'Sssh…'

Chapter Ten

Monday morning at the end of January. Seven a.m.: radio blaring, fingers blue with cold and brown with the mud of unwashed carrots and potatoes and swede, Kit Renshaw stacks leeks and tomatoes, apples and oranges into neat pyramids, each with its own 'Please Do Not Touch' sign. She wears a green overall, a purple mini-skirt and black and mauve patterned tights.

She sings along to the Troggs' 'Wild Thing', pushing her glasses back up her nose and shifting her weight from hip to hip in time with the radio, occasionally using a carrot as a microphone. The bright, burning interest she briefly experienced in Podge – not least because he had the kudos of being in a group, however crap – is fast fizzling out, nineteen days after their first date. A long stretch in Kit's calendar.

Mid-morning, Marion Procter from the caravan site comes in when she should be at school. She is in her early teens and has one of her little brothers in tow. She asks for a pound of onions, half a pound of tomatoes and a swede. She tells Kit she wants to become a shop girl like Kit when she leaves school in the summer. 'Have you heard that Lily Tempest is getting engaged?' Marion adds.

Envy pierces Kit's heart so sharply she has to pause with her right hand round a large turnip.

The younger girl gives a satisfied smile at the response her news has triggered. A natural gossip, she elaborates on the basis of no facts at all. 'They say she's in the club. Who'd've thought it? My mam says she's got the figure of a hairpin. It probably won't show until she's due. Serve her right, always acting like she's better than everybody else. Stuck-up cow, she is. Do you know her?'

'Of course I know her. Our boyfriends are in the same group.'

Silently, Kit vows that she will make Podge propose to her within a fortnight or she will die. 'Lily's one of my best friends.'

'That'll be two, then,' Marion says, grabbing her brother by the back of his jacket as he makes a bolt for the door.

Kit adds up the bill, then sticks a pencil behind her ear. 'That'll be two what?' she asks.

Marion smirks. 'That'll be two Tempests in the club before they got married, my mam says. First Rose and now your Lily. It must–'

'It must be your mouth running away with

92

itself, Marion Procter,' Kit says. 'What's your mam so interested for?'

'That's what my dad's always asking,' the other girl replies slyly. 'Ta-ra for now.'

In winter, Robert Wells has no cause to be in work on a Monday but he still comes. His cabin, not much bigger than a garden shed, is set at the front of Fairport's municipal car park, on a rise overlooking the sea, a short walk from the town square. In the summer, he sets up his table and chair outside and dispenses tickets to a thin stream of visitors, most of whom picnic by the side of their cars, setting up tables and chairs very similar to his own, munching away on the Tarmac, as if the car is an unreliable family member who can't be trusted to be left while they seek a more pleasant setting.

This puzzles Robert since Coronation Park, a very pretty area of landscaped greenery with an aviary full of budgerigars, is only a few minutes' walk away. In the winter, when visitors only have to pay at weekends, the wind whips around the site, poking its long draughty fingers through the cracks in the cabin's wobbly walls, and pushing aside the multicoloured scraps of carpet Robert has hung, like a poor man's tapestries, to give some insulation.

Inside, he has a smelly paraffin stove, a couple of chairs, a transistor radio and a flask. Robert can look out from one window over the car park, or across the bay from the other. If he steps outside, he has a view of Fairport's high street, taking in the fish 'n' chip shop and the Rising

Sun on the corner. On the left is the television shop, and the bend in the road leads to the quay. Pete has given him binoculars, which he uses often. This is the world Robert has made small enough to manage. Change would spoil it, introduce risk, make the familiar turn threatening again, as it used to be when he was young and bothered by people all the time.

Robert lives just beyond the park, in the terraced house in which he was born. When he was five his father, a fisherman, died in an accident at sea. Robert's mam, Edie, passed on, on 26 October 1965. Everybody else remembers it because it was the day the Beatles received their medals from the Queen.

Pete, Robert's brother, had been in prison at the time of her death, so they buried her in a cardboard coffin. Robert knew she'd wanted her ashes scattered in the park, but nobody listened to him. He lives alone now but he's never lonely, he reminds himself. Too much to do.

At midday, he always goes to Bunting's for a bread roll and a couple of ounces of something to put in it, happy to be teased by Jenny behind the counter. 'I bet you'd fancy a nice piece of sausage?' is the sort of thing she says. Robert blushes beetroot, trying not to think about what she means in case it gets him into trouble. Then, he goes into the Rising Sun, orders a lemonade and sits in the window-seat next to the door for half an hour or so.

Afternoons, in winter, he potters about the town, home for tea at five – always tinned tomato soup followed by tinned rice pudding – then he works on the wirelesses and television sets that the neighbours ask him to fix, promising to buy him a lemonade next time they see him in the pub. Sometimes they leave a couple of bob on the mantelpiece. At nine Robert goes to bed.

So he has good reason to be disturbed when the woman appears, uninvited, upsetting his routine, knocking on the door. At first, he fails to recognise her because she is wearing a huge fur bonnet with pom-poms. 'My sister says can you come tonight to fix our telly, please? It's broken again,' she says. 'You can bring your brother too, if you like.'

Robert stands at the door and shakes his head vigorously. If he knows one thing about Pete it's that you can't tell him to do anything. He'd given Robert a pasting a couple of times and he wouldn't want to risk that again. Once, Pete hit him because Robert had told a neighbour they would give her a hand moving her sofa. The second time was when a girl, a holidaymaker, had said that Robert had touched her in a private place. He'd seen her go to the park with a boy but he hadn't been anywhere near her. Pete had hit him so hard he had to go to hospital. What had really hurt Robert was that his brother hadn't asked him first if what the girl had said was true.

'He won't come,' Robert replies. 'And I can't. I'm busy.' To his alarm, two of the largest tears he's ever seen roll down the woman's cheeks. Followed by two more, and then another two. 'Don't cry,' he says agitatedly, afraid she'll cause him mischief. 'Please don't cry. I'll come. I'll come. I don't know when but I'll come.'

Instantly the tears stop and a huge smile lights

up the woman's face. What surprises Robert isn't the speed with which her emotions switch, but how her smile makes it almost feel like summer in the hut.

'See you later, alligator,' Dulcie says, a bit too cheekily for Robert's liking. 'Toodle-oo, kangaroo.'

Half an hour later, he shuts up the cabin, pad-locking it (once, kids had broken in, peed every-where and chucked his paraffin stove through the window). Then he walks the five minutes to his brother's council house, its garden marked by a broken gate and a rusty toy pram, buried in a flower-bed as if it's expected to bloom.

Robert doesn't like visiting because he finds the combination of the chaos inside the house and the unpredictability of his brother's moods des-perately unsettling. 'My two best friends,' Pete tells anyone who will listen, 'are peace and quiet.' Robert knows he's telling fibs about that, like he tells fibs about everything.

His brother is in the sitting room; a coal fire throws out a small amount of heat. The room is uncarpeted, save for pages of the *Daily Mirror* strewn about. It has one lumpy armchair, a sofa with a couple of springs showing, an upturned orange box for a table while a television perches on a bucket. A plate shows the congealed remains of a fry-up, now being polished off by a black and white cat.

'Where's my fucking cup of tea?' Pete, barefoot and dressed in a vest and trousers, roars into the air. Robert knows that isn't polite. Their mam had been strict about minding your manners and not making a mess and saying 'please' and 'thank you'. And nobody had ever shouted indoors. Nobody, for that matter, had said anything very much except 'Hurry up, will you?'

'Fancy a cuppa?' Pete asks his brother. 'All right are you, mate?' he asks, his eyes glued to the horse-racing on the television screen. 'Tell that cow out there to make you a cup. And if she doesn't hurry up, I'll give her a bloody good smacking.'

Robert draws breath sharply in alarm. His brother winks. 'They love it when you're tough, my old son...' Pete slumps back in his chair, fag drooping, as if exhausted by the effort at conversation.

Robert follows his nose to the kitchen. The smell is a mixture of wet newspapers and sour milk, and something else unpleasant that he can't quite identify. 'Hello, Marie,' he says. The woman sitting at the kitchen table, holding a grubby toddler, jumps. She has the face of a permanently fright-ened underfed boy. That's not Pete's doing, she came looking like that – but he hasn't helped. All the rings on the gas cooker are lit and the oven door is open to provide warmth. 'He wants a cup of tea, please,' Robert says. For one awful moment, he believes she's going to be daft enough to refuse.

Instead Marie gives him a tired smile and says, 'Here,' plonking the little girl, who immediately begins to cry, in Robert's arms. 'Pete'll go mad if she doesn't shut it. You,' she suddenly points an accusing finger at the child, 'you belt up, or else.'

Robert gently places a protective arm around the child. 'Oh, don't do that. It's not her fault. She's only small. Perhaps she's hungry or something...'

His voice trails off, silenced by inexperience.

Marie's face softens. She opens the biscuit tin and gives the man and the child a chocolate finger each, gently kissing the man's cheek. 'Sorry, Robert. It's my nerves. It all gets to me, sometimes.' Robert returns the child to her. 'I'll make the tea, shall I?' he offers. 'And then if Pete doesn't like it, he can have a go at me. I'll show him who's boss,' he adds, in mock-defiance.

Marie lights a cigarette. 'I'm sick of it, you know,' she says, as Robert fills the kettle and searches for tea and sugar. 'He blames me all the time. But he's never home. He talks to me like I'm shit. In the letters he wrote when he was inside, he said he loved me so much he'd give me his last breath. He said he'd change. He'd go straight. He'd stay away from the girls. Now it's like he's angry with me because he wants me here and he's angry with me because he doesn't want me here... And I don't know what to do any more. Still, what am I telling you for? You wouldn't understand...'

Robert leaves her words trailing in the air as he takes the tea to his brother. On his return, he sits with her, cup in both hands for warmth. 'Mam always used to say that Trouble is Pete's middle name, just like our dad,' he says. 'Mam said that some men can change their ways, and others can't. And in our family we can't. But,' he adds, in a clumsy effort to raise Marie's spirits, 'Mam also used to tell me that miracles do happen.'

'Christ, Bobby,' Marie says wryly, 'and how often do you think miracles are likely to happen in this bloody house?'

On Mondays the customers are in Bunting's shop only for bread and company. 'Home is where the heart is, isn't that right, Mr Tempest?' says Betty Procter, standing at the head of a small queue. 'My boy's in the army and that's all he writes home and says. "Home is where the heart is, Mam, come and buy me out." His dad says it's good for him. Toughen him up a bit. Give him a trade. Keep him out of trouble.'

'Absolutely right,' says Mrs Hester Arndale, who runs the bed-and-breakfast next to the post office and who always shops in winter in a plum velour hat. 'Don't know they're born, youngsters today.'

'Was it half a pound, Mrs Procter?' Doug asks coolly. 'Under or over?' He waits, holding a slice of luminous-pink luncheon meat over the mound already on the scales.

'Always under,' Betty Procter says boldly, winking.

He wraps the meat and takes the pencil from behind his ear to write the price on the package. 'Will that be all?' he asks, busying himself, removing a side of bacon from the other slicer, avoiding her eye.

Betty Procter smiles. 'Lovely big brown eggs. Give us a dozen, please, love. Will you be at the pub on Sunday?' she asks casually.

Two women behind her in the queue, immediately stop chatting, their radars tuned. Doug wipes his hands on his white coat, aware of the silence. 'Dunno, really,' he answers evenly. 'I'm beginning to think it's too far for too little when it's too damn cold. That'll be one and thruppence, please, Mrs Procter,' he adds, adjusting the yellow and cream blocks of cheese on display. Betty Procter says nothing. Instead she lays the package of luncheon meat on the counter, opens it, and greedily tears a small strip from a slice. She dangles the sliver on her tongue, then, *zip!*, the meat is gone.

Her audience of shoppers shuffle their feet with embarrassment as if they have been caught watching an erotic fire-eater. 'Tut,' says Mrs Arndale.

Betty Procter gives a triumphant smile but her eyes are cold. Doug Tempest ought to show more appreciation. She places her money on the counter. 'I know I've forgotten something but I can't for the life of me think what it is,' she says, turning her smile on the other women in the queue. 'Take care of that cold, Mrs Arndale, I know how awful it is when you have to go sniffing around people all day...'

'Well!' blusters Hester Arndale, as the jangle of the shop door announces the woman's departure. 'Still, you know what they say, not that I'm one to gossip of course.' She adjusts her hat. 'I'm told she had an affair with a doctor in Cwmland. He left his wife and kiddies, then she didn't want to know. The wife tried to commit suicide but not before telling Dai Procter, who gave his wife a helluva pasting. Betty Procter's been good as gold ever since but she's a mischief-maker. You can see it in the way she walks. I swear she's a pyromaniac–'

Hester Arndale's words are interrupted by the jangle of the bell again. Betty Procter stands in the doorway, a mocking smile on her face. 'It's just a wild guess, Mrs Arndale, and do forgive me if I'm wrong,' she says, her voice steeped in sarcasm, 'but if you've been recounting the details of my so-called affair, can I assure you that it's a lie? A woman whom Dai had to evict from a caravan last summer for not paying her rent decided to spread a bit of poison. And you know poison, there's always a couple of rats happy to eat it when it's laid down. I couldn't give a damn what you ladies think of me, but I feel sorry for you Hester Arndale. You live in a mean little world. And, by the way, the word you're looking for is "nymphomaniac", not "pyromaniac". That means a woman who enjoys sex – and in that, you are absolutely right. By God, I do, but with my husband as it happens. Good morning, ladies!'

Madge Hill, the owner of the Contented Sole and Kath Morgan's boss, looks unimpressed. She shakes the chip fryer with one hand while generously sprinkling salt and vinegar on a portion of chips and cod for a customer with the other. 'Nobody's in here long enough to make it worth my while,' she says, popping a chip into her mouth and licking the grease from her fingers. She is small and thin with a leathery complexion the colour of a saveloy, the result of a lifetime sitting outside the shop, taking the sun when it shines, no matter the season.

'It'll work. I know it will,' Kath persists, straightening the jars of pickled onions. 'Customers will come because they'll know they can watch the telly while they're waiting for their orders.'

'Well, they wait now without complaint. Why should I fork out for rental every week?' Madge

101

gives her a shrewd look. 'Fancy yourself on the telly, do you?' she asks jokingly.

Kath turns to check her hair in the mirror, which runs the length of one wall. She is perfectly framed by a starfish and an octopus and a sign that reads, 'Fishing For Compliments? Eat More Cod.' 'Don't be daft,' she answers lightly. 'I've got far too much to hide.' And both women laugh.

Bunting's closes every day at twelve thirty for an hour. Doug Tempest normally catches up with paperwork and has a sandwich in the shop. Today is different. He has been summoned to see Edina Bunting, his employer. Now he sits uneasily in her large, dark front parlour and waits. Elaborate stained-glass windowpanes throw paint splashes of colour across the carpeted floor. A grandfather clock ticks loudly. Two large china Alsatian dogs stand guard on a table. Life left the house a long time ago.

'Mr Tempest, thank you so much for coming to visit.' Mrs Bunting, a woman in her seventies, appears at the door. Doug smells something in the air – and it isn't hope. 'I'll get straight to the point,' she says, sitting opposite him, a small neat woman with blue-rinsed hair and a large cameo brooch at her throat. 'I've decided to close the shop. The Co-op has been given planning permission to build a self-service store. We can't hope to compete with its prices – and you know as well as I do that business isn't as good as it once was. It's not you, really it isn't,' she adds, 'it's just ... people.' She waves a hand in the air, as if to spirit away a generation. 'You know how they are. They

102

change... They don't want the personal touch any more. They want Green Shield stamps and gimmicks and...' She shudders. 'I'm sorry.'

Doug clears his throat. Something draws his eye to the darkened corner of the room. Next to an elaborately carved wooden screen, sitting on a straight-backed chair, is the boy, bare legs swinging, a finger pointing, bright red blood on his cheek. Doug starts.

His employer misreads his response as a reaction to her news. 'Yes, I know, I can't tell you how sad I am,' she says. 'We're going to have to close quite soon, I'm afraid. We've had an offer for the property. Terrible thought, isn't it? All those years of service. If Mr Bunting were alive today, he would be distraught.'

'How long have we got?' Doug asks.

'Until the spring,' she replies. 'I'm afraid there's not much in the way of redundancy because you haven't been with us all that long. But I'll give you an excellent reference and perhaps we could organise a hamper of provisions by way of a gift for you and your family.'

'Thanks,' Doug answers, and gives her one of his best smiles. He would hate to give the impression that he was resorting to sarcasm.

Later, instead of returning to work, Doug walks along Fairport's quay. He is alone except for a woman hurrying in the opposite direction with a shopping bag full of groceries. In the distance, the howl of the hooter of the iron works signals that the dinner break is over. For a period when Doug was young, the sound of the dockyard hooter, early morning, midday and afternoon, summoning the men and disgorging them again, was the metronome of his and Kath's lives. It divided time into zones of peace and persecution. He shakes his head to rid himself of the single abiding memory of his father – a man rancid with hate, belting him, telling him as he did so that he was useless and stupid and ugly and unwanted by a mother who'd gone, and left him behind.

On the beach, a fresh layer of snow has settled on the boats, so they loom like pale and stately craft, rust and battered hulls painted white by nature. At the end of the wooden pier used by the pleasure-cruisers in summer, Doug stands and looks out as he has done many times before. Today the January sea and sky are welded seamlessly together, a grey cast-iron horizon, claustrophobic and brooding. Doug stretches his arms out to shoulder height, his palms turned out, as if holding back the steel walls that threaten to close in on him, squeezing out life.

Only now, in late middle age, has he finally begun to acknowledge that the constant uprooting, the serial fresh starts, the endless new beginnings had been less an exercise in resilience than a permanent act of cowardice. But could he learn to stop running now?

He throws his cigarette butt high out to sea. It drops like a miniature falling star. He hated the person he once was, he tells himself, but what has he allowed himself to become?

In Rydol Crescent, Melody Tempest carefully sets aside one pound and five shillings and passes it over the table to Annie Gilbert, sitting opposite.

'Thanks, Mrs Tempest,' the woman says, ticking off several columns in a small accounts book. 'You've cleared enough of the backlog so you can start shopping again, if you like.'

'Backlog' doesn't sound nearly so frightening as 'debt', Melody tells herself. Still, she shakes her head firmly. 'No more until it's all clear. The house is overflowing with stuff.'

'You know best.' Annie gives a tight, disappointed smile. 'Shall I leave the spring catalogue just in case?'

Chapter Eleven

Rose finishes her Monday shift at two thirty, in time to pick up Billy from school.

'All right, Rose?'

'Hiya, Rose.'

'Fancy a cup of tea later, Rose?'

The other mothers, mostly in their early twenties like her, some with two and three children, exchange banalities, moan about the weather, recount in detail what they've seen on the telly the night before and the old man's most recent misdemeanours. The conversations rarely change. For Rose, each repetition is another bar in the cage.

She can remember, from the age of eight or perhaps even younger, girls talking about the day they would become a bride. Half-heartedly, she'd enter into discussions about the wedding dress and the presents the bridesmaids would receive and where the honeymoon might be. Of course, what she could not have foreseen was how three minutes in the cab of Chalkie's lorry would lead to a register office and a size sixteen pastel tent, seven months pregnant. Rose looks around the gathering of women. They'd made the adjustment; a few of them were even happy. So why couldn't she accept her lot?

'Mam, over here, Mam,' Billy shouts excitedly. He runs out of the school gate, followed slowly by his best friend, Buster Jones. Buster watches her warily and Rose knows why. The previous week he'd come for tea and Billy had accidentally spilled custard on the table. Rose had instantly, ferociously, lost her temper. She'd whacked him with a rolled-up newspaper as if he was a puppy she was trying to house-train. She'd known it was an accident but she couldn't contain her rage. She'd shouted at Billy again and again, 'You're just like your father, absolutely bloody useless. What are you? Useless!' Thump, thump with the newspaper. Buster had looked at her as if he thought she was about to commit murder.

'Hiya, boys,' Rose says, sweeping both up in her arms. Buster tenses. 'Something really nice happened to me today, so why don't we go and have a cup of hot chocolate in Ravelli's to celebrate? What do you think?'

'Is Dad back? Is that it?' Billy asks, skipping along beside her.

Rose shakes her head. 'Not until later this week.'

'What's happened that's nice, then?' Buster asks gingerly.

'I've finished a story that I've been writing for a

106

very long time.' Rose smiles.

'Do you write stories? Real stories?' Buster asks, trepidation erased by his natural inquisitiveness. 'What kind of stories?'

Billy looks at his mother with surprise and disappointment. Stories are their secret. A secret he has kept. 'What happens?' Buster persists, growing bolder.

Rose laughs and the boy flushes with delight that he has pleased her. 'You'll find out soon enough,' she answers, her voice almost drowned by the hissing of the coffee machine as she opens the door of the milk bar.

'What's it about, Mam?' Billy asks.

'It's about a little boy and a mother who...' Rose looks at the boy's face, at the eyes he has inherited from her, and changes her mind. 'It's about a little boy and a mother who learn to fly like birds,' she says. 'It's just for you, Billy. I've written it especially for you ... so that you can read even if I'm not around.'

'Why? Where are you going?' Buster asks sharply.

'Nowhere.' Rose smiles. 'I'm going nowhere.'

As Rose and the boys sit at Ravelli's window table overlooking the square, a woman comes in with a toddler on her hip. Rose has seen her around before but she takes little notice now.

'Mind if I join you?' the woman asks, a few minutes later, with frothy coffee in a glass cup and saucer in her hand. The child, aged three or four, hangs on to his mother's coat. Rose pointedly glances around the almost empty room, then shrugs agreement.

'Only it keeps the little one happy to look out and see what's going on. Not that much goes on here at all,' the woman says, with the confidence of those who are accustomed to attention. The boys are intrigued, they sense drama. The woman sits down, pulling the child affectionately on to her lap, nuzzling his neck and making him giggle. 'Look,' she says, kissing the top of his head, 'one day soon you'll be a big boy like these two. Aren't they gorgeous?' Then she reaches over and pinches Billy's cheek.

Doug Tempest stands in Bunting's doorway and surveys the to-ing and fro-ing in the town square. On the previous night, as he had each Sunday for the past fortnight, he'd dressed as usual, left the house at the customary time, and then, instead of making for the pub, he'd taken a couple of bus rides, his scarf wrapped high around his neck so nobody could see his bloody stupid frilled shirt and ridiculous bow-tie. Eventually he'd walked and walked, blanking it out, keeping it all at bay. He couldn't remember where he'd gone or what he'd done.

He had learned the skill of blanking out as a child. Only later, when Melody had come along, had he recognised that this was a form of slow suicide. The more he had numbed himself, the more he had lost the capacity to put himself in another's shoes. 'An inability to empathise,' the court report had said.

Now he looks across the square, his gaze drawn to Ravelli's window. It is decorated with extra-vagantly coloured plastic replicas of ice-cream sundaes festooned with bananas and cherries, alongside slices of mock chocolate cake sinking under clouds of greyish fake cream. As he watches, he sees Betty Procter lean across to his grandson, Billy, then turn to his daughter and whisper in her ear.

Iris gazes at Dulcie in amazement. She has popped next door after work because Kath has asked to borrow the *Radio Times*. Although the fog is thick outside, Dulcie is wearing a favourite floral summer cotton dress and a pink cardigan. She is watching with intense concentration while a man fiddles with the television set and Kath Morgan sits brooding and watchful in the corner. 'This is Robert,' Dulcie announces with pride. Kath's frown deepens. 'He's good with tellies.'

'Should you be messing about with it?' Iris asks. 'I mean, you don't even know if you can keep it, do you?'

'It's all right, missus,' Robert replies. 'My brother's given it to her.'

'Has he?' Kath squawks. 'Why? And where is he?'

'He says he's in bed with flu,' Robert reports accurately. 'I don't know why he wants to give her a present. He didn't tell me.'

He turns on the switch. The television gives a little ping, a black-and-white image comes briefly into view – and then the screen goes blank.

'It's the tube,' he pronounces. 'It's an old set. It needs a new tube. I'll take it home with me.'

'Will it be expensive?' Kath asks suspiciously.

Robert shakes his head. 'I don't ask for money.'

The woman makes him unhappy.

Dulcie shows him to the door. 'Have you got a girlfriend?' she asks.

Robert, alarmed, says, 'I've got a sort of girlfriend, more a lucky mascot, really.' Then he retreats down the street as rapidly as his bulk and the television set in his arms will permit.

'Do you like him, Dulcie?' Iris asks gently, standing behind her on the doorstep.

'Yes, I do. I really do,' she replies. 'But promise you won't tell Kath.'

'I don't think I have to.' Iris sighs.

Chapter Twelve

Howling Wolf wails scratchily from Barry Taylor's gramophone as he lies on an ancient sofa with such a pronounced sag that he bends alarmingly. He beckons for me to sit on the only other chair in the room. Briefly, he turns the volume down. 'Not speaking?' he asks.

I nod. 'I am but he isn't.'

'Take a look,' he answers, thrusting a seventy-eight vinyl record into my hand. Barry always does this. I mean, one black vinyl record looks much like another but he always presents them as if they are individual works of art. 'Got it Friday. Lovely stuff. Lightnin' Slim, Louisiana swamp blues man. Discovered by Jay Miller. He records all the best, Lonesome Sundown, Sleepy John Estes but Lightnin' Slim, he's the king. Listen to him, and you know what it means to cry in the dark, what it really means.

'That's the trouble with a lot of the crap that Bryn plays, it's too much moon-in-June. Listen to the blues and it's the history of the people. The history that no middle-class bastard's ever going to write. Listen to Slim Harpo, Blind Willie McTell, and you hear it all, sex, money, unemployment, poverty, booze, the triumph of the human spirit, the joy of–' Barry stops, embarrassed, then adds, brusquely, 'You should visit the South – it's different from the rest of the States. Louisiana, Mississippi... Memphis... Lovely stuff.' He turns up the volume again.

Barry is tall and stringy and bald with a tangerine-coloured moustache and tobacco-stained teeth from a diet of roll-ups. He has a perfectly round pot belly that looks as if he's about to give birth to a beach ball. Barry is at war with what he calls the System. He also believes that he and the Comrades are winning. His main handicap as a Marxist is that he's never read Marx but he talks about the Dialectic a lot and invents the rest. At forty-five, he's the closest Fairport has got to a rebellious youth.

Barry's room was once the garage, until he boarded up the doors. It's here he plots the revolution and listens to his music. He has several posters on the wall. One is of Fidel Castro. Barry spent his last summer holidays building prefabs for the People outside Havana instead of redecorating the bathroom as Pamela, his wife, had wanted. Also in his gallery are Ho Chi Minh and Harold Wilson, except that the latter has 'Class

111

Traitor' written in red across his face.

Books, pamphlets, leaflets and old newspapers are piled everywhere, as are racks of records, each carefully labelled with the date it was purchased. Barry also has a workman's bench along one wall and a battered dining-room table that doubles as a desk on which there are a couple of mouth-organs. The garage is like a tropical jungle, since it's heated by four three-bar electric fires. It also houses a camp bed, a candle stuck in an empty Hirondelle wine bottle and the biggest radiogram I've ever seen, twice the size of a coffin, on elaborately carved legs. Barry also has a kettle, Camp coffee, milk, sugar and biscuits, bread and several tins of baked beans – emergency supplies for when the domestic scene becomes too turbulent and he has to retreat.

Today I'm in retreat too. Bryn believes that I am being unnecessarily obstructive about the idea of setting up a fan club. He's right, I am being obstructive but not unnecessarily so. It just seems a daft idea, and I don't think Kit is all that keen either. I've told him if he wants one he should get his mother to organise it, since she's his biggest fan. So now Bryn isn't speaking.

Since he says next to nothing anyway, so far it hasn't proved too gruelling an ordeal. As he always does on a Tuesday, he picked me up from home and drove me to his house for tea – silently. And they say girls are moody. When the record ends, Barry rolls up a ciggie. 'I hear you and Bryn are engaged?' The fact that my possible future father-in-law is so rapidly in possession of what was originally my own lie is not at all surprising

112

in Fairport. He pauses. 'Shame,' he says. 'Great shame.'

I flush. He clearly doesn't think I'm good enough.

'You shouldn't be even thinking about marriage, not at your age,' he continues. 'Not at any bloody age, if you've got any sense. That's how I got caught. Saw the missus for the first time after I'd had a couple of drinks, asked her out. Next thing I know I'm married. It's a trap. For women it's a worse bloody trap and that's saying something. Do this, do that, fetch, carry, not a minute to yourself...'

I try to hide a smile. Pam Taylor is the diva of do-it-yourself. What she wants, Barry carves, welds and sticks together. He's only allowed time off after the chores are done. She expects his wages on the table every Friday night. Then she doles out his subs for fags and beer and revolutionary literature and he accepts it, quiet as a Marxist mouse. The worker in this house has already been well and truly defeated.

'You want to go to university, you do,' Barry persists. 'Bryn's all right with his apprenticeship and he's the settling sort. You're not, I can tell. Get your arse out of here, girl. Women can do anything now, anything they want... See the world. Change it. Do something with your life.'

Simultaneously, I'm flattered and frightened. Flattered that Barry thinks I should go to university and frightened at the thought of what that might mean. I shake my head. 'I haven't got the brains. Anyway, we haven't got the money. And my mam and dad would be dead against it.'

'No, they wouldn't. They'd be proud,' Barry says, polishing a record with a duster before slipping it back into its sleeve.

'I'd hate it. I wouldn't fit in.'

'That's the whole bloody point.' Barry snorts. 'You're not meant to fit in. You're a proud representative of the working class. You're meant to change the bloody system, not join it.'

'And if I did go, what then?' I ask.

'What do you mean, what then?'

'What do I do after I've been to university?' I repeat. 'I mean, I wouldn't be one thing or the other then, would I? I wouldn't be posh and I wouldn't be a worker either. Well, not a factory worker.'

'That's a deeply pessimistic view of the path of human progress, if I may say so,' Barry says, plugging in the kettle. 'You're saying the only way to have a future is to bury your past, am I right? Well, that's very sad, young lady. What about your glorious heritage? We're building on the foundations – the blood, sweat and tears, the honest toil of all our working-class ancestors – that's the history of the ordinary people. You're putting your arse on solid oak, so to speak, not some flimsy bit of French royal gilt. Make a difference, girl, get the forgotten voice of the people down the ages heard in universities instead of all the bloody family sagas of the toffs. Be proud, I–'

When Barry talks like this, I'm never sure whether he's pulling my leg or speaking from the heart – but either way it riles me. 'Proud?' I say incredulously, helping myself to one of his chocolate wafers. 'Proud? Proud of what? Proud of the outside lavvy, no peace and quiet, no money, three in a bed, no books, no conversation, no rocking the boat, fifty years in the same dead-end job and not a chance in hell of seeing the world except, if you're lucky, for once in your life, on honeymoon. A fortnight in Lloret Del Mar, thirty quid for two – except that you have to go by coach so it takes you six days to get there and another six to get back. Some pride. Some bloody heritage.'

We look at each other, he clearly appalled at my denigration of much of what he holds dear, the sentimental old fool, and me, well, me just surprised. I didn't realise I hated it quite as much.

'I'd have a look at *Das Kapital,* if I were you, girl,' Barry says, after a long pause – which is a cheek, considering he never has. 'It holds many truths.'

He puts Lightnin' Slim on the turntable.

'Barreee!' Pam Taylor's high-pitched voice cuts through the wall.

'Stuff that,' Barry says, rolling up another fag.

'Barreee!' Mrs Taylor yells again. 'The spuds won't peel themselves, you know.'

'Coming, dear.' He sighs.

It takes Kath all evening to complete her first application. She takes ten years off her age, elaborates slightly and says she has recently won a trophy for producing the best batter in the North West (she knows from what she's seen on the television that they like people with a novelty angle or, better still, Proof of Personality). She adds that she can play 'Land of Hope and Glory' on a Jew's harp. She can't but she'll learn fast

115

enough if the call comes.

She then sends it to a programme called *Take Your Pick*. All she'll have to do, if selected, is answer questions of increasing difficulty, then face the compère, who asks a series of questions to which the contestant must refrain from answering, 'Yes' or 'No.'

'Ask me some questions,' Kath demands of Dulcie.

'It looks funny, doesn't it?' Dulcie says, ignoring her sister's request.

'What does?'

'The corner where the telly used to be ... I mean, we've only had it a little while but it looks funny now it's not there any more. Do you think he'll bring it back soon? He's a nice man, isn't he?' she adds slyly.

'He's soft in the head, like you,' Kath answers brutally. 'Go on, ask me some questions, ordinary questions. Like "Do you live near the sea?"'

Dulcie looks puzzled. 'Of course you live near the sea. Why would I want to ask you that? I know we live near the sea.'

Kath makes an exasperated noise. 'It's practice. If I get asked to go on the telly, the compare will ask me questions and I can't say "yes" and "no". If I win I'll bring home enough money to buy a new telly – and take us to Margate for a week.'

'You'll be on the telly, just like famous people?' Dulcie asks.

Kath nods enthusiastically. 'Yes, I will,' she says.

Dulcie claps her hands as she dances around the room. 'You're out. I got you,' she says. 'I'm cleverer than you. I asked a question and you

116

said, "Yes". You said, "Yes, I will".'

Barry's wife, Pamela, is glamorous. She wears nail polish and dyes her hair blonde. She wears a frilly pinafore in the kitchen and she is so houseproud she whips away your plate before you've finished, all the quicker to wash the dirty dishes. Mrs Taylor, I wouldn't dream of calling her Pamela, likes frills. She has frilly covers on the jam pots and the lavatory rolls, frilly curtains, and she even has a frilly tablecloth she places over the brand new washing-machine and spin-dryer when it's not in use, as if it's too brazen to leave it bare. Men, she believes, are cleverer, more important and altogether better than females. But, strangely, she treats them like babies.

The Taylors are doing all right. All three work at Lawson's, the fish factory, so they have a good wage coming into the house. Mrs Taylor is a senior progress chaser. A daft name, which means she goes from department to department – Sorting, Weighing, Cleaning, Dyeing, Packing, Dispatching – to ensure that production is maintained at what Barry says is an inhuman pace. His goal, as shop steward, is to slow it all down as often as possible.

Now, she gives us cream of tomato soup, then dishes up roast chicken. 'So,' she says, when she finally sits down, her face shiny from the heat of the stove, 'are you going to the dance on Saturday, dear?'

Bryn says nothing.

'I think so,' I reply brightly.

'Got a couple of vacancies coming up in the

factory. Know anybody looking for a job?' Barry asks me. I shake my head. 'It's bloody scandalous,' he continues, leaning forward conspiratorially. 'Blokes on the line are getting good bloody gear, fifteen quid or more a week if they do overtime. Do you know what the women get?'

Mrs Taylor tuts loudly. Three tuts and Barry will be out on his ear, dining alone in the garage. Still, he seems happy to push his luck. 'Have a guess. Go on, have a guess, Bryn.' Bryn shrugs. 'Have a guess,' Barry says to me.

'I don't know. You'd know, wouldn't you, Mrs Taylor?'

She picks at her teeth delicately with an orange nail. Her lipstick has faded and run into little lines around her mouth; her mascara has smudged. Tiredness makes her melt. Barry bangs on the table. 'I'll tell you. Eight bloody quid. She'll get eight pounds and the fella will get fifteen. And do you know what? That's the way a lot of the union blokes like it. Bloody scandalous.'

Barry has made the mistake of laying down his knife and fork to make his point. Mrs Taylor whisks away his half-full plate, dumps the contents in the bin, and puts the plate in the bowl in the sink. He opens his mouth to protest but Mrs T gets in first. 'Don't be ridiculous,' she tells him. 'Eight pounds is perfectly fair. Most of the girls live at home, and if they're married they've got their hubby's wage as well. I don't hear any of them complaining, only silly old men like you, Barry Taylor. We've got no complaints, have we, Lily?'

Barry, Bryn, Mrs Taylor and Kevin, Bryn's

118

younger brother, aged twelve, all turn to look at me. 'I'll ask my dad if he knows anyone who's after a job.' I avoid the question. 'I know he'd hate to work in a factory, with the boss always on his shoulder, but you don't seem to mind it, do you?'

'Of course we mind, you silly little girl,' Mrs Taylor replies curtly. 'We hate every single minute. But needs must...'

Suddenly Bryn comes to life. 'Leave her alone, Mam,' he says.

After tea Bryn gives me a lift to Penny Wilson's house. To mollify him, I said we were going to discuss the fan club. In truth, I'm visiting out of curiosity.

'She'll show you her heated rollers if you come, won't you, Penny?' Kit had tried to tempt me.

I wanted to say no. I've already got a best friend called Mary Johnson. I don't need any more. Especially not now that the future is tapping at my door. Mary is in Bury, which is the last place we Tempests lived. Mary and I used to write to each other every week. We made a pact that neither of us would ever marry. Mary was going to become a doctor and work in South America. Then she met her boyfriend who's doing chemistry, physics and maths A levels and belongs to the Territorial Army. Now she writes less and less frequently.

'Penny's got masses of records,' Kit persisted, as if she was on a commission or something.

'OK, then, I'll come,' I said, 'but I can't stay long.'

The house is detached with mock-Tudor cladding and a large front garden. It's far from

119

public transport, which is a sure sign that someone is posh. Two cars, a Mini and a Riley, are parked in the drive. 'Christ,' Bryn says, impressed.

The door opens immediately I ring the bell. 'Hello, I'm Adele, Penny's mother. You must be Lily. Penny's told me so much about you. Do come in.'

She doesn't look like a mother. She wears a black polo-neck, a long black checked skirt, heavy silver and turquoise ear-rings and rings on every finger. Her hair is black and in a bob with a fringe, and she is wearing eye pencil like Elizabeth Taylor in *Cleopatra*. She wears bright red lipstick and smells foreign.

'Hi, Lily,' Penny shouts, from the landing at the top of the stairs.

Adele smiles. 'I'll pop up later. Have fun!' She disappears into a room from which I can hear a woman singing in French. The walls have lots of framed film posters from the Continent and the stairs have piles of books stacked higgledy-piggledy. I spot a paperback of *The Duchess of Malfi* – and Penny isn't even doing English A level.

Her bedroom is bigger than our entire ground floor. Everything matches. It has a blue fitted carpet, a kidney-shaped pine dressing-table, lots of bookshelves, a chest of drawers, a desk, a table with a record-player, a radio and lots of records. One wall is covered with rosettes, mostly yellow, won at pony events.

The bed has a white counterpane covered with blue forget-me-nots in the same pattern as the curtains, and several teddies, one of which is in the arms of Kit who has draped herself across the

120

bed like Marilyn Monroe, except that Marilyn doesn't have cricket bat legs.

'Lovely, isn't it?' Kit says, propping herself up on her elbow. 'Wish I had a room like this.'

I nod. It's not to my taste: it's too much like a window display. Penny's mother knocks and comes in with a tray that holds three mugs of cocoa and a plate of chocolate biscuits. She puts it on the carpet and then, alarmingly, sits down alongside it, crossing her legs as if she's an Apache. 'Mummy.' Penny sounds exasperated.

'Lily,' Adele pats the space next to her, 'come and sit here and tell me all about yourself. We know a bit about Kit, and a little sweetie she is too, but you're still a bit of a closed book, isn't that right, Penny? I hear you're modelling, how exciting... I did a bit of photographic modelling myself when I was younger. Do you remember the Drink-a-pinta-milk-a-day ads?'

Kit and I shake our heads, mesmerised by this strange creature who clearly expects to be treated as if she's one of us.

'Well, it was a really big campaign – huge hoarding, lots of publicity. I tried for that – didn't get it, of course, because they wanted a white Anglo-Saxon blonde. And that certainly isn't me.' She shakes her head, so her hair swirls out shiny and black. If she was younger I'd say she was showing off.

'We've got private things to talk about. Couldn't you just go away and leave us alone?' Penny snaps.

I wait for Adele to erupt. Instead she gives her daughter a look as if she's just done something

121

rather wonderful. 'I know exactly how Penny feels,' she says. 'I was the same when I was her age, except that in my day we had to hold it all in, repress our anger. It was all so very damaging ... I'm glad your generation has so much freedom. Freedom to think, freedom to breathe, freedom to be who you really are, freedom to–'

'Adele? Are you there, darling?' A man invites himself in. He wears a polo-neck jumper tucked into dark green corduroy trousers, suede moccasins and no socks. My dad wouldn't be seen dead without socks, he even wears them in bed. The man has a floppy fringe, longish brown hair and a gold ring on his little finger. He glances at himself in Penny's mirror as he walks in. You can tell he's pleased with what he sees. My dad hates himself. I think that's much healthier.

'Wow,' Penny's dad says, in a voice that has a slight drawl but no accent that I can identify. 'What a roomful of beauties.'

Kit simpers, and attempts to pull her mini-skirt down over her knees, a fruitless exercise. 'Mr Wilson...'

'Don. Remember, it's Don. And who may this be, Cuddle Bear?' he asks Penny, turning to me. It's odd: Penny looks really old-fashioned in comparison with her parents. Perhaps that explains the folk-singer look. Perhaps she does it on purpose to annoy them both. They seem the sort who would find it annoying.

'I'm Lily,' I say. 'I'm doing A levels.' To my annoyance, I hear myself trying to plump up my vowels, like my mother always does when she talks to a teacher or the vicar. Why mention A

122

levels? Why isn't Lily good enough on its own?

'Aah!' says Don. 'Off to university soon. Another recruit to the red-brick revolution – what did I tell you, Adele? They'll soon be pouring through our doors. And not before time. I remember saying to–'

'No!' I stop his flow. 'I mean, I don't know what I'm going to do yet... I want to travel, go – well, go somewhere away from here. I'm not sure about university for lots of reasons,' I finish lamely.

Don smiles at me, patronisingly. 'Is this another member of the beat generation I see before me?' he says, looking at his wife. 'Jack Kerouac, where art thou?'

I say nothing. Kit sits bolt upright with her mouth hanging open. 'You know Kerouac?' Don Wilson asks me. 'Let's see, can I remember it?' He runs his fingers through his hair, and tosses his head back. 'It's *On the Road*, and one character says to another – Have I got this right, Adele? "We gotta go."' He adopts a fake American accent without embarrassment.' "We gotta go and never stop going till we get there." Strike a chord?' he asks me, in his normal voice. 'Is that how you feel, Lily? Don't know where you're going but you gotta go?' He looks at me as if we're the only two people in the room. I open my mouth and shut it again, aware that a deep red flush is spreading from my face down my neck.

Penny picks up a record and puts it on the record-player. 'Well,' she says glaring at both parents, yelling over the music, 'not only am I not going anywhere, I'm very specifically not going to any bloody university. I don't care what either of

123

you says. I'm sick of school. I can't wait to leave. I'm going to be a hairdresser or something and I'm going to get married as soon as Bulbie asks me, so there!'

Adele grimaces. 'Bulbie? Who or what is Bulbie? He sounds like a Turkish guru.'

Penny glares at her mother. Instantly the mystery is solved. I understand precisely why Penny is attracted to Bulbie. He's exactly the kind of boy that her mother would loathe. 'Bulbie is into voltages,' she says. We giggle. 'He's an apprentice electrician, if you must know.'

'Is that right, Persephone?' Adele grimaces. She turns to me. 'Aha! I see from Lily's face she didn't know your real name is Persephone. Do you know why we called her that? Persephone is Spring, the goddess of creativity. What's creative about working in a hairdresser's, giving doltish women permanent waves all day, my darling? Tell me that,' she suddenly snaps at her daughter. 'You've got a future ahead of you – and certainly not as some idiot boy's domestic doormat. Not if I have anything to do with it, young lady, and make no mistake.'

Strange words, really, considering she's just been telling us how many freedoms our generation is supposed to enjoy.

In the end, Penny evacuates us from her bedroom, leaving her parents to stare at the pony rosettes on the wall alone. The three of us set up a new camp in the den in the basement. She tells us a den is an American thing. Her parents used to lecture at a college near New York. They lived in a house with a den, and brought the idea back.

Basically it's a sitting room – except darker and damper with a table-tennis table.

'Where's the telly?' Kit asks.

'We don't have one,' Penny replies, pulling a face. 'It atrophies the mind.'

I don't say anything, but I wonder whether words like 'atrophies' are sprinkled through her conversations with Bulbie, who takes two weeks to read the back page of the *New Musical Express*.

'We've got a radio,' Penny volunteers. 'Over there.' She switches it on, then off again quickly as classical music pours out. 'And a gramophone.' We all sit down and stare at each other. 'Do you like *The Duchess of Malfi?*' I ask eventually, to fill the silence. 'I saw a copy on the stairs.'

'No, it's my mum's,' Penny answers. 'She loves it. It's one of her favourite plays.'

'God. What's that like?' I ask, recognising the stupidity of the question even as I speak. How would Penny know what it's like to have a mother who reads seventeenth-century plays for pleasure if she'd never had any other kind of mother with whom to compare her own? To cover myself, I nod in the direction of the upright piano. 'The piano, what's it like?'

'Oh, nobody bothers with that.' Penny shrugs. 'It's only for show.'

I play a few bars of the chorus of the Ronettes' 'Be My Baby' because it's dead simple. 'Can you sing?' Kit asks.

'Our whole family sings, except my mam. She shops,' I tell her.

'Why don't you sing with Bryn on stage, then?' Penny asks.

125

'He'd hate it. And I'd hate it even more.'

'I can play the cornet,' Kit offers. 'I used to play for the Girls' Brigade. I can read music too and–'

Penny interrupts, addressing herself to me: 'Can your whole family really sing? How fab. You must all be ever so close.'

It's the von Trapp syndrome again. It happens all the time. People who've seen *The Sound of Music* mistakenly assume that any family that contains a couple of musicians and sings together are also extremely nice to each other and spend hours around the piano every night, dressed in pinafores and leather shorts. Before I can answer, Penny embarks in a flat soprano on 'Be My Baby' except that she enunciates the words as if she's in the church choir.

Kit joins in, and she's a revelation. She has the deepest bass I've ever heard coming from a girl. '"Be my baby..."'

After an hour or so of practice and a lot of laughs, we agree that we're not bad. We're absolutely diabolical.

Chapter Thirteen

The following Saturday, we arrive early at the Rialto in Cwmland. It's a run-down cinema that has been converted into a dance-hall. The seats in the balcony double up as the unofficial heavy-petting parlour. It's patrolled by overweight, middle-aged bouncers who can barely see in daylight never mind in the semi-dark, and are too fat to squeeze between the rows. Groups perform crammed on to a tiny platform that passes for a stage within arm's length of the audience if, that is, there is an audience. The Rialto has a cafe and a bar upstairs. The men's lavatory on the left of the stage has been converted into a stars' dressing room, but the pong of wee lingers on, only occasionally obscured by the smell of dope and sex and pale ale and Old Spice aftershave.

At night the dance-hall looks a treat: silver glitter balls throw out dancing lights, and psychedelic slide shows create a world of multi-coloured splodges floating around the walls and ceilings and floor. People mostly dance looking at their feet or stand in the shadows so imperfections are hidden. Under this system, even the ugly stand a chance. Along the corridor opposite the cloakroom there is a gallery of black-and-white photographs of the groups who have appeared. Most are unknown, but occasionally a booking has happily coincided with an unexpected appearance in the top twenty. The faces in the publicity shots – the Hollies, Spencer Davies, the Troggs, Manfred Mann, Them – look as surprised to find themselves in Cwmland as those who gaze at them.

In daylight the Rialto is shabby and faded: the wallpaper is peeling and the bars have that desperate unloved look of railway station waiting rooms – cold linoleum, ripped plastic 'leather' banquettes and more graffiti covering the walls than hieroglyphics in an Egyptian burial chamber. But I don't mind. It makes the nocturnal transformation that much more enchanting. A couple of hours to dress, a couple of glasses of cider, a couple of beltingly loud chords, recognised instantly by all of us, and everybody's out there, including me, pumped full of possibilities, propelled three feet off the ground by alcohol and the determination, since it's Saturday, to have a bloody good time. Unless, of course, you're depressed or newly dumped or spotty and sober.

Bryn and the Berries play most Saturdays as a support act. The top of the bill is usually a group with a dance-hall reputation if not a hit record, like the Undertakers or Brian Auger's Steam Packet. Occasionally a roadie will be sent out to whisper an invitation in someone's ear. Later, sometimes after midnight, when we're loading up equipment in the car park, a girl will be unceremoniously pitched out of the other group's van, dishevelled, distressed, occasionally followed by the words, 'Fuck off, you cunt,' because she's refused to deliver. Or because she has and 'the romance', begun two hours earlier, has reached its accelerated climax, and already come to an end.

The Berries set up their equipment and carry out a sound-check. They're always on first, at eight when most people are still in the pub, tanking it up on lower prices. Kit and Penny are also in attendance, twittering like skylarks on speed. Penny has turned herself into a passable Mod. She's ironed her hair and it's dead straight with a fringe like Cathy McGowan's on *Ready, Steady, Go!* She's wearing a long, olive green suede coat and lace-up shoes from Mansfield that I know for a fact cost fifty-nine shillings and elevenpence.

Bulbie is jittery. He's clearly not told Penny

about his taste in pills because she keeps telling me he's suffering from stage-fright. As if. The only time Bulbie has shown any emotion of any sort on stage was when his cousin passed a message to him while he was playing to say his uncle had dropped dead from a heart-attack. Bulbie rubbed his eyes and continued.

'Coming to the lav?' Kit asks, while the boys set up on stage. 'Are you in it?' she asks, referring to the magazine that I've brought to flick through for the next boring hour or so.

'In what?' I ask, temporarily forgetting that I'm supposed to be enjoying a flowering modelling career.

'In that. Go on, let's have a look. Penny, come and see Lily in the magazine.' I grab it back and give her a filthy look. Something about her tone makes me suspect that she's taking the mickey. She's wearing a white polo-neck and a navy blue hipster skirt with a chain belt. She's also painted the rims of her glasses emerald green and stuck a pearl on the corner of each frame. If she took off her glasses, and lost a couple of floors from the three storey construction that passes for a hair-do, Kit might appear quite attractive.

'You and Penny go,' I answer.

Kit ignores what I say and sits down companionably next to me as Penny joins us. Both girls break off the conversation every few minutes to flutter their fingers like butterflies at their boyfriends, as if their love will die from neglect if they don't constantly semaphore their affection. The boys act as if we girls don't exist.

'Is it true, then?' Kit suddenly asks, giving a sly

129

glance at Penny. 'Are you engaged? Are you getting married? Have you got the ring?'

Penny joins in, lowering her voice to a whisper: 'Have you done it yet? If you let on, then I'll tell you something in return. Fair play...'

'What will you tell us?' Kit and I say simultaneously.

Penny looks across at Bulbie, who is stumbling about the poorly lit stage in his dark glasses. She takes a deep breath, then announces, 'I'm on the Pill.'

'Christ,' I say. 'Does your mam know?'

'Of course she knows,' Penny replies scornfully. 'She's the one who told me to take it.'

The Berries are half-way through their first set of the night and the dance-floor is slowly filling. Several circles of girls dance together, watching their handbags in the centre as beadily as cannibals surveying the contents of their pot. At the sides, the lads hover, hands in pockets, swaying out of step to the music, deciding whether to try their luck on the girls they really fancy or go for the dogs who are too grateful to say no.

'Do you wanna...?' A gangly teddy-boy with a quiff and a black shoestring tie held in place with a silver dollar indicates the dance-floor with his head.

'He's a spaz,' whispers Kit generously. 'Don't do it.'

But I do. I'll dance with anyone who asks. I love dancing. I'm wearing a mulberry-coloured mini-dress with a Peter Pan collar, empire line, beige tights and maroon patent shoes with a buckle.

After a couple of ciders, I think I look all right. But it always takes a couple of ciders first.

I bought the shoes with my hotel tips. Kath says they look like a pair she had in the 1940s. She doesn't mean it as a compliment, she's not that sort. Kit and Penny are standing close to the stage, all the better to bathe in the reflected glory of their loved ones (and, more to the point, to keep the resident groupies, all two of them, at bay). Suddenly a girl I've never seen before, with blonde hair, suede boots and a floaty skirt, appears at my side and pokes me hard on the shoulder. 'And who the bloody hell are you looking at?' she says, in what I recognise as a Scottish accent, although the music is so loud she's barely audible. 'You keep your eyes off my fella, do you hear me, you gobshite?' She gives me another prod. She's probably a head taller than I am.

In the shadows behind Kit and Penny, I can see the cause of this trouble. Two of the Curators, a Glasgow band who model themselves on the Animals and who are the main booking tonight, are drinking with a group of girls. They – the Curators – have the kind of naturally curly hair that does not look its best worn shoulder length. One has an extremely beaky nose.

'Are you listening to me?' says the girl with the Lady Guinevere look. I am, by instinct, a coward. 'Don't you bloody give ma man the eye.' She pushes me again. 'You!' she says.

This time I shove back, hard. She loses her footing and falls against one of the circles of girls, who immediately cave inwards, like a row of paper dolls, sending handbags skidding. A lot of squealing takes place. Two of Guinevere's friends immediately come rushing out of the shadows, heels clattering. One slaps me around the face. A bouncer comes running over from the direction of the bar. Thank God, rescue is nigh. Instead he runs straight past me and shouts to Bryn, 'Whatever happens, keep fucking playing!'

The Berries, faltering, pick up pace again. Someone pulls my hair. The squealing girls have converted into spectators, hungry for blood. The bouncer doesn't appear too averse to it either. 'Go on, girls,' he says. 'Give it your best.'

It's me against three, and I don't even want a fight. Out of the corner of my eye, I can see that Bryn is taking off his guitar while the group plays on. I'm about to take the sensible option and turn tail and run when suddenly Kit and Penny are at my side, just like in the films. Kit has taken off her glasses and holds one of her stiletto shoes in each hand, a demented dwarf. Suddenly she rushes forward, pummelling anyone in her path, sliding about in stockinged feet. Penny is doing a lot of dancing up and down, her hair bouncing like a shampoo ad, feigning punches, growling as she does so. One of the girls kicks her shin. For a second, it looks as if she's going to burst into tears but then she puts her head down and runs straight at the girl's stomach, winding her.

Another bouncer arrives. 'Girls, girls,' he says, trying to disentangle as many of us as he can while avoiding accusations of indecent assault. 'Please, ladies, any more trouble and you'll all be out.'

This stops Penny in her tracks. 'What? You mean ejected?' she shouts, in tones of complete shock, as if he's just passed a life sentence. 'You can't possibly! I'm with the group.'

'I don't care if you're with the Virgin Mary. If you don't behave yourself, you're out. Understood?'

Half an hour later, Kit, Penny and I are drinking in the bar. They were prepared to save my skin at some expense to their own, so I should at least treat them as confederates. But this far and no further. They're just not my type. Penny is too posh and Kit is too much of everything – too loud, too brash, too ready, I bet, to put it about. Possibly too thick, although I'm not entirely sure about the latter: she has a kind of cunning.

'Did you see Podge's face?' Kit says. 'I swear he was about to throw his drum kit at that stupid cow.' I say nothing. The drum kit is Podge's world. I doubt he would sacrifice it for something as minor as his girlfriend's health.

'See you Tuesday as usual at my house?' Penny asks me, at the end of the evening.

'Course,' Kit replies on my behalf.

Chapter Fourteen

On Sunday evening Melody, helped by Iris, lays out Doug's clothes as usual: frilled shirt, bow-tie, shiny suit. She empties out the box of cufflinks, and sorts them into pairs. She picks up one shaped like a dice and returns it to the box. 'Why don't we go with him tonight?' Iris suggests. 'Howard won't

133

mind if I'm out, not if I'm with you.'

'When's he back?' Melody asks.

'Eight days.'

'Then it's off to Blackpool in February, you lucky girl.' Melody smiles.

'Are you being funny?' Iris asks suspiciously.

'Course not. He's a lovely lad. I like a man in a blazer myself.' Melody switches on the electric fire.

'Shall we, then? Shall we go?' Iris persists, desperate to leave the house but knowing that, without a suitable chaperone, she'd be bound to meet one of Howard's extended family who would immediately report back.

Melody shakes her head. 'That's your father's world,' she says firmly. 'This one and that don't mix. I learned that a long time ago. Pass his shoes, love, and I'll give them a polish downstairs.'

Pam and Barry Taylor have a telephone. Mrs Taylor likes to keep it quiet – otherwise, she says, half the people in the street will be knocking on her door to avail themselves of her private little luxury. At eight thirty in the evening, the phone rings. It rarely rings on a Sunday. Come to that, it rarely rings on any day of the week. She picks up the receiver suspiciously.

A slurred male voice asks to speak to her son. 'Bryn!' she calls up to his bedroom. 'Somebody on the phone for you.'

Ten minutes later Bryn pokes his head round the sitting-room door to tell his parents he is going out for an hour or so. 'You be in by ten at the latest,' his mother instructs. 'You've got work

134

in the morning.'

Half an hour later, Bryn drives into the car park of the Labour Club in Stockbridge. Inside Carl Hicks sits slumped at a corner table, gazing at an almost full glass of Newcastle Brown. 'Fuckin' marvellous!' he says, once his eyes focus on Bryn. 'Fucking wonderful, thass what you are. Did I tell you that?'

The two boys attended the same primary school and secondary modern, played in the same football team on Sunday mornings and occasionally go out together for a pint. But Carl has called on Bryn tonight not as a sign of their closeness but because he is the only one in their circle with a car.

Carl tries to smile, a process that takes for ever, as if he's only just mastered the mechanics. 'You know me,' he says. 'All front. Make 'em feel special, make 'em believe that you only want what's best for them. Good luck, madam, and may your God go with you. I got that from that Irish comedian on the telly. Good luck, and may your God go with you. The punters love it.

'Back they come the next week, good as gold. Only been nicked twice. Did I ever tell you that? Nicked once for receiving – four thousand pair of women's panties, seconds they were. Bought 'em when we were on holiday in Margate and passed them down the line the same week. Went like hot cakes. Then the bloke who nicked 'em got caught and the rozzers were on my door. Never knew that, did ya? My mam kept it quiet. It was in the Margate papers but not up here. Got six months in Borstal. Good boy I was until I got nicked in

135

the nick. Can you beat that?' Carl spends several minutes consumed with laughter. 'Nicked in the bloody nick, can you beat that? I helped myself to a few of the governor's carrots and apples and got caught red-handed. Ten days' solitary and three days' bread and water. When I came out, I thought, Right. That's it. Fiddling, yes, but no more nicking.'

Carl clumsily knocks his empty bottle of beer off the table with a clatter. 'Oops,' he says, like a small boy.

Bryn hauls him to his feet. 'Come on, mate, I'll take you home.'

'We've got to take the stuff as well,' Carl insists, sitting down heavily again. 'I've got two dozen tins of assorted biscuits in the boot of my car and a bloody big bag of broken custard creams. Met a bloke from the factory here who let me have the lot for a fiver. I'll sell 'em for four times that on the market.

'You know how it is, mate, we had a couple of drinks to celebrate. Then he went home. I bought a couple of rounds for my friend at the bar. Then he went home. Next thing I know, I'm pissed as a fart. It's that twat, Daisy,' he adds, suddenly morose. 'She's done this to me.'

Bryn helps Carl up again and begins to steer him towards the door. 'You two fallen out?' he asks.

'No, mate,' Carl replies. 'She's found herself another fella. She says she hasn't but I know she has. And it's really got to me. It really has. And I don't know why.' Carl's bottom lip begins to tremble.

136

'Perhaps it's you-know-what, mate,' Bryn suggests.

'You-know-what?' Carl smiles inanely.

'Christ, you know,' Bryn repeats, his face flushing crimson with both embarrassment and strain, as he tries to half carry Carl to the door. He drops his voice: 'Perhaps you've fallen for her. Love and all that.'

Carl stops short. 'Love? Love? Don't be bloody mad, lad. I just can't stand the thought of someone else giving her one. Not before I bloody do.'

'I thought you said you had.'

Ten minutes later, with the biscuit booty loaded into his car, Bryn is driving back to Fairport. 'Hey, mate, slow down, slow down a minute, will you?' Carl suddenly commands. 'Stop, for Chrissakes!' he instructs again.

Bryn drives faster. 'If you're bloody sick in this car, I'll kill you,' he says.

'Do you know who that was?' Carl slurs. 'Walking down that road? It was Daisy's old man. I know it was. I'd know his frilly bloody shirt anywhere.'

'Don't be daft,' Bryn chides. 'He sings on a Sunday night. Why would he be out here in the middle of bloody nowhere? You're seeing things.'

'It was him, it bloody was,' he says, sinking back into his seat. Then, he falls blissfully asleep.

Late Sunday night Lily is at the table writing an essay. Melody sits opposite with her breadboard, sliced loaf, corned beef and butter. She watches television as she makes sandwiches for Doug and the other two girls when they come home. 'You and Bryn decide on a day yet?' Melody asks.

Lily doesn't bother to look up. All day she has found her mother profoundly irritating: her mannerisms – scratching her head with the pencil she has stuck over her ear; her habits – saying as soon as she crosses her front door, 'Who'd like a nice cup of tea?'; her endless interrogation, as if the only conversation she can have with her daughter is one splattered with question marks. It has driven Lily into a surlier and surlier and more evasive mood. 'Mam, I've got to get this done,' she says.

'You've not had a row, have you?' Melody probes. Common sense tells her to keep quiet, but anxiety won't allow it. 'I mean, it's silly to let small things get in the way. Your father and I–'

'We haven't had a row. It's nothing. Don't worry about it,' Lily interrupts curtly. 'I've got to get this finished. Do we have to have the television on so loud?'

Melody turns the volume down to the point where it is inaudible. She has another try. 'It's normal to have a few butterflies before you make a big commitment like this. I mean, with your father, I can't pretend it's all been easy but–' She stops mid-sentence, aware that her daughter has finally looked up from her books. 'What?' Melody asks defensively.

'I'm trying to work, Mam. I've got to get this finished. It's always the same, as soon as I get my books out, you're there. Chat, chat, chat – like as if it's a personal challenge to you to make sure I can't concentrate. And no,' Lily adds, seeing Melody move towards the plate holding a leaning tower of sandwiches, 'having something to eat will not make me feel better. If you must know, I'm not getting engaged or married to Bryn or anyone else. I just had a funny five minutes. I'm not marrying. Not now, probably not ever. For God's sake, why don't you let them make their own bloody sandwiches?' she adds crossly. 'Why do you always want to do everything for everybody? It's – it's suffocating. Why don't you go out and live your own life? Go to bingo or something, like normal people your age. Have an interest. Penny's mam has books and music and she goes to films and she isn't breathing down her daughter's neck all the time about engagement rings and courting and that kind of rubbish. Why can't you be like her?'

Melody, usually slow to anger, bangs her hands down on the table, making the breadboard leap into the air. 'Do you know why I do it?' she yells. 'Do you really want to know? Because I like it. I like it! Do you hear me? I like to cook and make sandwiches and fuss over your dad. I like it! No matter what you think, that doesn't make me simple or stupid or any less of a person than you, Lily Tempest. That's my choice. You're born of me, and what I am you are too, like it or not. You think you know so much but, by God, there's a lot you've yet to learn, not just about the big wide world but things much closer to home.'

Melody stamps out into the kitchen. Lily snaps her book shut and is about to march off in the opposite direction, to the frozen zone of the bedroom, satisfied to have levered a reaction from her mother, when the doorbell rings. Only strangers ring the doorbell.

139

When she opens the door, a middle-aged woman whose face is vaguely familiar is standing on the doorstep.

'Hello, love, is your mam in?' Betty Procter smiles. 'Sorry to call so late, but it's urgent. Can I come in?'

'She's the spitting image, isn't she?' Betty Procter comments, cup of tea in hand, sitting gingerly on the edge of the sofa in the front room. The electric fire is on but the atmosphere is icy.

Melody smiles tightly in response. She's seen the woman around town, usually with several children in tow. Now she wears an expensive-looking coat and black boots, as if she's been out somewhere special. Or wants to make whoever she is visiting feel inferior. Melody straightens her back and lifts her chin. When she'd handed the visitor a cup of tea, she had caught a whiff of whisky.

'I'm sorry to call so late,' Betty Procter says again, 'but Doug promised me one of his dogs for our raffle. It's for the old people in the centre – we raise a bit to take them on a couple of outings in the summer. Bon Marché's in the square said we could have a little display in the window for publicity – and the dog will attract attention. They said they'd do the display tomorrow,' she adds, as if to reinforce her case. 'So I thought I'd pop round now. I couldn't come earlier, because I was waiting for my hubby to come home. Works seven days a week, he does. Bless him. Can't complain, though, makes good money. Doug in, is he?'

'Would you like a sandwich, love?' Melody asks,

140

giving herself time to collect her thoughts.

'How do you know my dad then, Mrs Procter? Through Bunting's?' Lily asks bluntly, irritated by the woman's condescending air. Only she is allowed to patronise her mother, not strangers.

'Don't interfere, there's a good girl,' Melody says evenly, smiling as usual, but Lily is surprised to see that her mother's eyes are as cold as a wolf's. 'Doug works on a Sunday night. He's singing in the Cow and Fiddle up Bilton way. Shouldn't be long now.' She glances at the clock.

'Is that where he is?'

Even to Lily's unpractised ear, Betty Procter's words sound more like a taunt than a question.

'Only I gave him a lift back the other day – I'm sure he told you – and he dropped this.' She tosses the cufflink, shaped like a dice, on to the coffee table, like a lifelong gambler.

Just after eleven p.m., Rose turns off the gas fire and goes upstairs to hide her notebook and pencils under the sheets in the airing-cupboard on the landing – a safe place since her husband regards domesticity as a desert that no sane man need enter. Then she checks on a sleeping Billy, takes her old coat from the back of the door and slips out.

She knows she shouldn't leave the child alone but sometimes the urge to walk away, for however brief a time, is too strong. Besides, Rose reasons with herself, she never goes far. She walks past several houses up the steep hill to the brow where a large nest of boulders marks the site of the old town wall. A bench has been carefully positioned to catch the most of the sun.

Now she looks down on the dark frieze of the town. The church clock bongs out the quarter-hour. On the roof of the Contented Sole, where Kath works, a large, illuminated neon pink trout winks on and off, mid-leap. Further in the distance, where the high street slopes down towards the quay, a man walks his dog, the only two figures to be seen. She watches as he stops for what seems several minutes in front of the TV rental shop, as if urging the blank screens to come to life just for him.

Ahead, Rose can see the giant knickerbocker glory attached to the wall of Ravelli's, and close to it, Bunting's, its two windows softly lit. A lone side of ham hangs like a giant's severed thumb. A couple of tom cats screech in the dark; the clink of milk bottles nearby indicates that not everyone is in bed. Rose watches as, incongruously, a Rolls-Royce drives into the square and turns left, moving out of sight into the deserted railway-station car park.

It is a twenty-minute walk to the main road that would take her, in a couple of hours or so, to half a dozen cities. She could go now. She could flag down one of the long-distance lorries making their way to Liverpool or Manchester, get a job, begin again – single, free, a different name, a fresh history. She would sign up to night school, acquire qualifications. In her pocket, she has a folded pound note. Tips. Less than average for the week but this is the post-New Year gloom. Soon, Rose tells herself, she'll have enough to make the break. Very soon.

142

On her way home, at the bottom of the hill, a flush of rouge in the sky above the rooftops catches her eye. As if the seasons have grown confused and a summer dawn has come, prematurely, in midwinter.

She is several steps away from her own front door when she hears the sobbing. Billy is sitting at the top of the stairs, rocking to and fro, in tears. 'I thought you'd gone away,' he says again and again, holding on to his mother with all his young strength. 'I thought I was on my own. I thought you'd gone away...'

Chapter Fifteen

At the same time as Billy – with a child's intuition – clings to his mother, Daisy Tempest glances over to Daniel Bright. Up close, his evenly tanned skin has a rough, sandpaper quality, as if his features are slowly crumbling to dust. One of the men at work suffers from a similar complaint. Drinker's eczema, Lily calls it.

Bright had picked her up at one thirty p.m. from the bus station in Cwmland. She hadn't wanted him to drive to Fairport for fear of being spotted by Carl, who was normally with his dad having a pint in the railwaymen's club, the only drinking place open on a Sunday and packed.

They had eaten a late lunch in a hotel twenty miles away: prawn cocktail, well-done steak and chips and Black Forest gateau. Daniel had ordered

143

wine. Daisy had had two sips and that was enough. She prefers something sweet. He'd got quite cross when she refused to drink any more.

He had talked and talked about his successes, his fame, his favourite bookings, the celebrities he'd known. When he wasn't talking about himself, there had been long awkward silences that Daisy didn't know how to fill because what do you say to a Prince Charming when everything about you is so ordinary? Reluctant to let go of a dream, she had ignored the signs.

'Look at the tits on that girl,' he'd remarked crudely, in a very loud voice, about a girl old enough to be – well, Daisy's age. Then, after lunch, they had 'motored', as he put it, aimlessly around. At one point, Bright had lifted one buttock off his leather seat and farted fruitily. Farting is not a part of romance as Daisy knows it.

It was as if the fart was the cue for a different character to emerge. As the afternoon stretched into evening, and he drank steadily from his hip flask, a coarser, more belligerent and crueller man had emerged. Daisy, more and more upset, politely and repeatedly requested that he drive her back to Fairport, no longer caring whether she was seen. He had ignored her – until now.

In the dark, in the creepiness of the deserted station car park, Daisy reaches for the car-door handle. 'I've got to go. My mam will be worried sick. I've got to get back before my dad's in from work or he'll murder me. I said I was at a girl-friend's. My mam knows the time of the last bus – and–'

Daniel Bright reaches out and grabs her by the

144

hair, pulling her head back forcefully and pushing his flask into her mouth, so hard it cracks against her teeth. She almost gags on the brandy as she fights for breath. It drips down her coat.

'Why did you do that?' Her voice quavers with uncertainty and trepidation. She is frightened and he knows it. And that has its own effect. Wordlessly Bright unzips his fly and pulls out something Daisy has no wish to see. Bile rises in her throat.

'You know what you are?' Daniel Bright says, playing with himself with one hand, and drinking from his flask with the other. 'You know what you are?' He is panting and sweating. 'You're a fucking little cock-teaser – all tits and arse and no bloody delivery. But I know a slag when I see one. I'm going to teach you a fucking lesson that you will never forget. Now, come here.'

'Please don't hurt me,' Daisy hears herself whimper, hating herself for begging. 'Please don't hurt me.'

'Please don't hurt me,' he mimics. He drops the flask, reaches for another fistful of Daisy's hair and pulls her down hard into his lap as he rams his other hand up her skirt, scratching her skin and tearing at her suspender belt. She bites hard. He releases her hair yelping, and she bangs her head on the steering-wheel as she jerks back. He hits her across the face with the back of his hand. Her skin tears, as it catches his ring. Her nose is running, she is bleeding and, to her mortification, she wets herself in terror. 'You cunt! Look what you've done to my leather. You cunt!' he screams, and slaps her once, twice, three times, masturbating as he does so.

'Why me?' she hears herself say, certain that she is about to die. 'Why me?' Then he punches her hard in the stomach. And as she bends double she realises, surreally, that her blond-haired Prince Charming has a penis surrounded by ginger hair.

Seconds later, the car park is swept by headlights and the night is filled with the noise of clanging bells. 'Christ!' Daniel Bright says, his face caught fleetingly in the glare. Daisy seizes her chance. She jumps out, skirt around her waist, blouse torn, bra strap broken, blood smeared on her thighs. Remembering her shoes she turns back, foolishly, opens the door again, searches desperately, retrieves them and runs. She hears him swearing at her fleeing back. In the opposite corner of the car park, in the darkness again, she takes off her ripped nylons, hanging in shreds like sunburnt skin, and throws them away. As she does so, the Rolls reverses, turns with a squeal of tyres and disappears.

Daisy, her hand shaking, smooths down her hair, puts her scarf over her head and tries to cover her face. Her bottom lip is swollen and she has bitten her tongue. Only now does she taste the blood. The cold stings her urine-soaked legs. All she has to do is walk up the slip-road to the square, cross it, and five minutes later, she'll be safely at home. That's all she has to do, but her legs have turned into lead weights and, no matter how hard she wills them to move, they disobey.

She will never tell a living soul what has happened to her, she silently swears. Never. She will never go to Cwmland again, not as long as he

146

is there. She will never even wear a mini-skirt again. She is filthy, dirty, a whore. He chose her because he knew she was easy. What if he comes back? What if he tells everyone what happened? Daisy blushes in the dark. What if the whole hotel finds out? And Lily and Rose and–

Terror now succeeds where will-power previously failed.

Enveloped in shame and humiliation, Daisy begins to walk across the square, head down. Only then does she realise that the air is filled, bizarrely, with the rich scent of a fry-up, eggs and bacon and sausages, especially bacon.

A fire engine pulls up close to her and a handful of people in their night clothes gather. Briefly, she steps back into the gloom of a shop doorway. As she does so, opposite, one of Bunting's two windows shatters, spraying shards of glass out on to the slush of the pavement. From where Daisy is standing, she can see that the rear is a-dance with flames. Flames lick a side of ham hanging in the remaining window.

To her left, Daisy sees her father walking up the high street from the direction of the quay. His coat collar is turned up and his hands deep in his pockets. It's early for him. The pub normally sends him home in a taxi, long after the last bus. He stops when he reaches the mayhem of the square. Then, instead of running towards the flames, as Daisy expects, he steps back into the porch of the hardware store, and watches as if, like the growing group of spectators, he is a disinterested observer.

At nine Rydol Crescent, the front door slams. Lily and her mother, their unexpected visitor only gone an hour before, look at each other.

'It's only me,' Daisy shouts, running up the stairs, torn between revealing the scandalous news of Bunting's fire and terrified that a member of the family will see her and know. 'I'm tired. I'm going to bed. Night.'

'Fancy a sandwich, love?' Melody shouts after her, plate already in hand. 'And where do you think you've been?' she adds, as the bedroom door closes. 'You've had me worried half to death.'

Doug comes home shortly after, at his customary time. Melody gives him a hug. 'How did it go tonight, love?' she asks. 'Usual crowd?'

Doug smiles wryly. 'They stayed awake. Even asked for an encore.' She pours him a mug of tea. He takes off his coat.

'A woman came here when you were out. Says you–' Lily begins, but she's interrupted by loud knocking on the door. Harry Shelton, who runs the off-licence on the square, bursts in, eyes bulging with excitement. 'It's bloody Bunting's, mate, there's been a fire. It's almost gone,' he says. 'You'd better come quick, Doug.'

Daisy opens the bedroom door in time to overhear her father affecting surprise. 'A fire? Christ almighty. How did that bloody happen? Come on, man, let's go.'

And she weeps – for herself, and for her father.

Senior police officers come from Cwmland and insurance investigators from Manchester to investigate the fire. While they wait for reports on

148

the forensic tests, both expect PC Hywel Roberts, 'the man on the ground', as they keep calling him, to point a finger at who the culprit might be if, indeed, a crime has taken place. The investigators have already agreed among themselves, perhaps foolishly, that if the fire proves to be non-accidental, the culprit is male, since women don't 'do' arson.

So Mrs Bunting is ruled out, as are the female members of staff. That leaves Doug Tempest. Relations between him and his employer have been good, the books are in order, and it seems unlikely that he would resort to arson simply because he'd been told he is about to lose his job. PC Roberts speedily rules out him too. Except that on the day after the fire he receives a phone call from a woman who refuses to identify herself (although PC Roberts has a very good idea who she is) and she has a lot to say on the subject of Mr Tempest's whereabouts on the night in question.

At ten thirty a.m. on the Tuesday after the fire PC Roberts, helmet under his arm, stands in Doug's shed and watches while his suspect weaves and moulds strips of cardboard. 'You should do that for a living, boy,' Hywel Roberts says. 'Bloody marvellous it is. One minute it's twenty Player's, next it's as good as cocking its leg. Nothing's what it seems, these days, is it, mate?'

Then, embarrassed that Doug might think he's making a more pointed remark than he intends, Hywel Roberts noisily drinks from the mug of tea in his hand and has another sly look at his interviewee. PC Roberts was born with less than average looks, further undermined by his passion

149

for rugby, a hobby that, in his teens, ensured that his nose is now spread across his face, like a chicken split and splayed ready for the grill. The policeman muses to himself that if he looked like this bloke he'd never run short of the other.

Doug looks up and smiles. 'If I were to give you this when I've finished, you'd be the only man in the world with one like it.' The policeman flushes with pleasure. 'Can't say that about much, these days, can you?' Doug continues. 'My girls would rather have it cheap and plentiful, but what's the point in that? Too much – of not a lot that counts? That's no food for the heart, is it, mate?'

PC Roberts nods gravely 'You're right there,' he says, which is what he always says if someone seeks his opinion. He clears his throat to signal that he is moving on to official business. 'About Sunday,' he says ponderously 'Mrs ... a lady has been on the phone to us to say that you weren't singing at the pub as usual. The publican confirms that you are no longer one of his artists, and my informant says that to her certain knowledge you were not at your own abode on Sunday evening, so you could have been ... anywhere. Even here in Fairport. Even in the town square. So, what exactly were your movements on the aforementioned evening, Dougie lad?'

Doug, a cigarette hanging from his bottom lip, says drily, 'I confess. I did it. I set fire to my one chance of continuing to pick up a wage packet for the next few weeks. You know the old woman's sold it, don't you? Co-op's taking it over. Look, Hywel, you know what this is really about?' He stubs out his cigarette and lights a replacement,

150

relaxed, taking his time. 'What this is about, Hywel, is pride. Pride, that's at the root of this.'

'Whose pride? Your pride?'

'No, Hywel, a woman's pride. I wouldn't want Melody to know, but the lady who phoned you, she comes into the shop all the time. She's a bit of a liability if you know what I mean. I've told her I'm a married man, but you know how it is, don't you, Hywel? Women and trouble.' PC Roberts doesn't know at all. His wife is eight years older than him, and when he proposed, the one subject upon which they both agreed was that each was the best the other was likely to hook. Hywel reflects morosely on the fact that he's never had trouble from women in his entire forty-one years. Once would have been nice.

'And now,' Doug shrugs, 'she's finally got the message, and I think she's out to cause a bit of mischief. Pride, that's what it is, mate, because she's been spurned. That's how her kind of women behave. You're a man of the world, you'd know all about that anyway wouldn't you?'

PC Roberts leaves shortly after, deeply flattered.

Only in the police station, when writing up his report, does he admit to himself that his brief conversation has yielded very little. He duly returns. 'Have you forgotten something, man?' Doug asks.

PC Roberts steps into the hall. 'It's only a formality but I wonder if you could give me the details of your address previous to Fairport – oh, and the name and address of your employer before Mrs Bunting. Nothing to worry about, it's all routine.'

'I'll tell you what,' Doug says, 'I'll dig 'em out and bring them down to the station later on. Is that OK?' And he gives the broadest of smiles.

Chapter Sixteen

For the last couple of Tuesdays I've called at the veg shop for Kit and waited while she locks up. Then we both walk to Rydol Crescent for tea before going on to Penny's. Today on the way home, Kit talks about whether Egyptian spuds are better than Guernseys and why no wholesaler in their right mind would look at mushrooms from Holland at the price they are now.

'You know so much about it, why don't you have your own shop?' I suggest.

'Don't be daft,' she answers, lighting up a ciggie in the street. My mam hates smoking in public and wearing white high heels in winter. Kit does both. 'I'm not a boss,' she smiles, 'I'm a grafter.'

On the night of the fire, Daisy says, she slipped getting off the bus and ricked her back. Now she keeps taking the odd sickie. I think she's a hypochondriac. She's been home again twice this week. I make the three of us hot chocolate and we sit round the table, dunking KitKats as we listen to the radio. Cilla Black's 'Love of the Loved' comes on, and Kit gets up and sings in that big fat bass, then dances about the room. Even Daisy laughs.

I get my history books out. I am so sick of

school, homework, teachers' attitudes, uniform and ridiculous rules – I mean, is it really necessary for a seventeen-year-old to wear white socks in summer and brown socks in winter? Once the exams are over, I'll never pick up a textbook again in my entire life. Maybe I'll follow Penny and become a hairdresser. Crop and crimp and wave and perm, smile at the clients and earn so much I won't have to be like Mam and borrow from here to pay there. I'll become famous like Vidal Sassoon.

'Is it true that Sally Jenkins is going to move in with your dad?' Daisy asks Kit. I give her a jab in the ribs for tactlessness. 'Blimey she's even younger than you, isn't she?'

Kit reddens. 'It's not like that,' she says defensively. 'He's paying her a bit, not much, but a bit. She's going to be the housekeeper so he can go back to work. I'm glad,' she adds, not very convincingly. 'I'm sick to death of all the housework and ironing and shopping and cleaning. Let her do it – so long as she's all right with the little ones.' Kit shrugs. 'Who knows? I might move out soon, marry Podge if he asks. Then I'll have somewhere to live.'

'Don't you mind his ... you know?' Daisy asks.

Kit laughs. 'His spots? Course not. He hasn't got any on his backside which gives me hope for the future.' She sticks her finger into the mug and licks off the residue of chocolate. 'To be honest, he gets on my nerves a bit. But that's me. Two weeks and I'm bored.'

'You can't marry someone just because you want a roof over your head,' I protest.

'Why not?' Kit replies flippantly. 'People get hitched for less. Go on, then,' she presses Daisy 'how did you slip off the bus? Were you pissed?'

Daisy shakes her head. Then, without warning, she breaks down in tears.

'Oh, God...' Kit says. 'Have I said something?'

'What is it? Has somebody hurt you? Tell me, Daisy tell me what it is.' I give my sister a cuddle, sensing she isn't so much sick as scared. Dead scared.

However much we coax, she won't say a word.

Melody Tempest loathes the smell of kidneys cooking. They give the kitchen of the Olde Tudor Tea Rooms the aroma of a public urinal. Now she pulls a tray of steak and kidney pies out of the oven and leaves them to cool in the pantry for tomorrow's lunches. Then she scrubs down the industrial oven and the small domestic cooker, washes the kitchen floor, places six blackcurrant fruit tarts in an empty biscuit tin, switches off the lights, shouts goodbye to Veronica on the other side of the hatch and lets herself out.

Doug makes her jump. He is waiting, leaning against the wall, a cigarette drooping from his bottom lip, hands in pockets, coat unbuttoned, apparently oblivious to the cold. No matter what has happened between them over the years, the pleasure his presence in her life gives her has yet to wane. Looking at him now, she senses he is afraid, like a man looking into the future, bereft of his dreams.

'You gave me a scare, love,' Melody says. She draws him into her arms.

He kisses her cheek, then half buries his head in her neck, more like a child than one lover with another. He lingers for a few seconds, as if drawing on her strength, then says, 'Fancy a walk down to the quay?'

Melody nods. The house will be full: outdoors, at the cost of becoming semi-frozen, they will have privacy She slips her arm through his and, silently they walk down the alley that leads to the high street. They cross the road and turn left, walking behind the police station and parallel to the square to avoid the half-shell that is Bunting's.

'What did she say?' Doug knows he doesn't have to elaborate.

Melody gives his arm a squeeze. 'She said you'd told her she could have one of the dogs for a raffle. I asked her to come by when you were home because I didn't know which of them to give her. I told her she was very welcome, any time at all.' She gives a satisfied chuckle.

'I never...' he begins. But she shakes her head, so they walk on in silence. Eventually Doug tells her, 'Hywel Roberts said she'd more or less told him that I'd done it.'

Melody makes no response.

'Hywel wants me to bring the details of my previous employer and my last address to the station. I said I'd do it this afternoon. You know what'll happen once I do. They'll trace the debts. There'll be one helluva lot to pay. You haven't spent more, have you?' he asks, breaking his rule of never questioning her because he believes he doesn't have the right, not in the circumstances. He doesn't wait for her reply. 'What if they

155

decide to go further back? What then?'

'I like it here,' Melody says. 'I really like it here. Lily's got her exams coming up. She won't want to go. Rose won't uproot again, not now Billy's older and settled at school. Iris has Howard. Daisy and Carl are courting strong. They've all got their own roots now, Dougie. It's not like before. This time let's stay. Let's stay and see what happens.'

'We can't stay.' Doug shouts the words into the wind, as if the elements have dared to question his judgement. 'Don't you understand? We haven't got a choice.'

'You're wrong, Doug,' Melody replies. 'There's always a choice.'

'Howard!' Iris throws her arms around his neck. He has come by train to Cwmland and then bus to Fairport. She has waited, hanging out of the bedroom window, oblivious to the cold. As soon as she saw the blue of his RAF coat, she was down the stairs and out the door, flying down the street.

She drags him into the house as Melody bustles around in the kitchen, buttering bread. 'Corned beef or potted paste?' she calls out. 'You're looking ever so well, Howard. And our Iris has been as good as gold...'

'Nothing, thanks, Mrs Tempest,' Howard says. 'I promised my mam I'd be home for a late tea with them. I just wanted to pop in and say hello.'

An ice cube of doubt slides down Iris's back. 'Can Howard come upstairs and see what I've got in my bottom drawer, Mam?' she asks, pushing aside negative thoughts.

Minutes later, Iris has pulled out from under her bed a vast quantity of household goods. 'I've gone for lime-green handles. I thought that would look nice and cheerful. I've bought something every week and I've put money in the post-office account. I'm so excited,' she says, producing more and more utensils, pots, pans and casserole dishes while Howard stands by, mute. 'Only another twenty months and eleven days to go. I told Mam they needn't worry if they couldn't help much with the wedding. Dad's going to be out of work at the end of the month and ... Howard, are you all right?'

Her fiancé gives a strained smile. 'I didn't realise there was so much...' He searches for words that won't pull the pin on the hand grenade, which he could swear is nestling on the eiderdown among the egg whisk with the lime-green handle and the lime-green egg cups, so nervous does this ritual make him. 'So many things, so much preparation. When you're away from it all... I don't know, you forget what's involved. It's just a bit of a shock. A nice shock,' he adds lamely.

'Anyway,' Iris smiles, determined as always only to see the best in the situation, 'we're off on holiday next week.'

'Oh, yes,' Howard says weakly.

Chalkie White has been home on overnights three times in three weeks, but now he is due to stay for a five-day break. On the way to school, Rose can tell Billy is excited and distracted by the

157

imminent arrival of his father. She, too, has made preparations, restoring the chaos in which she and Billy live to the order maintained by a reasonably dutiful wife. She has resentfully cleaned and swept and washed and tidied. She dreads the process of adjustment. Chalkie questions her decisions, challenges the choices she has made in his absence. While Rose admits that she is the first to bicker and criticise.

Eventually, without fail, there is an explosion. That is the rhythm of their union, strife, fuelled by mutual disappointment, punctuated by temporary peace. On occasions, when Chalkie has fallen asleep in the chair, mouth open, Rose looks at him with contempt, railing to herself about his lack of curiosity, the predictability of his views, the narrowness of his pleasures.

What he values, she doesn't: his lorry, the countryside, the dream of a small farm, fishing, walking for hours in the mountains, imparting to his son what he knows about nature. She shuns these enthusiasms for fear that, otherwise, her own resolve to leave might weaken. How can you break free if half of you yearns to take your gaoler with you? On other occasions, Chalkie reaches out for her in the night, gentle and considerate, as if only in the dark can he afford to show a softer side. And then, to her surprise, a part of her wants never to let him go.

''Bye, Mam,' Billy shouts, as he runs through the school gates.

'Old man back yet?' asks one of the mothers.

Rose shakes her head. 'Tomorrow.'

The woman winks.

158

Rose walks towards Rydol Crescent to check how her father is faring, now work at Bunting's is limited. The house has a light on in the bedroom. She calls up and Daisy shouts back, 'I'm off sick.'

'What's the matter with you?'

'Nothing. I'm going back tomorrow.'

The fire is laid and Melody has left the table set for tea. Rose lets herself into the yard. 'Dad, it's me,' she says.

Doug sighs when he hears her call. From a small child, she had been fiercely independent, showing more thorns than sweetness to all adults in her path. Rose had only one way to do things – her way. In that, she shared her mother's single-mindedness but lacked Melody's flexibility and optimism.

Rose pokes her head around the door of the shed and invites herself in. He believes she is the prettiest of all his girls but not conventionally so. Jet black curly hair pinned up any old way, green eyes, heavy eyebrows, a face that reveals fine cheekbones now she has escaped from her mother's cooking. She wears no makeup and smells of Lifebuoy soap. Rose kisses his cheek. He detected early in her life that she shared his capacity for profound selfishness. As she grew older and recognised it in herself, too, he knew she despised him for the curse of this legacy.

'Any news about the fire?' she asks, opening the packet of chocolate waffles she has in her shopping bag.

Doug shakes his head. 'We had the police up here making enquiries,' he replies.

Rose studies her half-eaten biscuit. 'Why?

159

Wouldn't be much point in any of you lot setting fire to it, would there? Christ, it's cold in here.'

Doug moves the paraffin stove closer to her and lights a cigarette. 'What will you do? Sign on?' she asks.

Her father studies the end of his cigarette. He senses there is something else she wants to ask. 'Your mam and I have been talking about upping sticks.'

She recognises the voice he always uses when upheaval is imminent, except this time it comes with an edge of weariness. 'What do you think? We could go somewhere where there's plenty of jobs. Perhaps down south.'

Rose's heart contracts as if squeezed in a vice. Chalkie will never cope alone with Billy if her family aren't around to help. If they go, she'll have to go with them, see Billy settled again, and only then will she be able to slip away. How long will that take? A year? Two years? 'Bloody hell, Dad,' she says angrily. 'When is it going to stop? When are you going to start thinking about everybody else instead of just me, me, me all the time? Lily's got A levels in May. She can't go anywhere until they're done. Billy's happy in school. Daisy isn't about to leave Carl. Iris has Howard. This time, if you go, you know you'll leave half of us behind, don't you? You and Mam do realise that, don't you? We can't be forever trailing behind you, in search of God knows what. Why can't you get a job in the iron works – or go to Lawson's like everybody else?' She stops, then adds, 'Is it Mam? Is she piling up the bills again? What? Why can't you ever stay longer than

160

five minutes? Why?'

Doug takes a drag of his cigarette and contemplates the consequences of telling the truth. 'You know your mother.' He gives a strained smile. 'It's not cash she spends, it's credit, so I never really know until it's too late. She does what she has to do. Anyway, it's not her. It's just...' He looks around the shed.

'It's just what, Dad?' Rose presses.

'I don't know. I haven't told your mother yet but...' he struggles as if his lips are welded together '....I've been sacked by the pub too. Tommy Aster says he's after someone younger. He says he's after a duo. He says he might give me a regular booking if I can find a younger girl. I thought of asking Lily but you know what she's likely to say. And I don't blame her. Singing to half a dozen pensioners on a Monday night...'

Doug stubs out his cigarette and rubs his eyes with his fists. Rose, often fiercely critical of what she sees as his vanities, is filled with sadness. She experiences one of those moments when the grown-up child realises the parent is ageing and mortal, and nothing can be done to stop the course of time.

'Something will–' She stops as Daisy bursts in, her face flushed.

'Quick, Dad,' she says. 'It's the police. Not just Hywel, it's two other men as well. They want you. They're not going to put you away are they? Dad, what have you done?'

Hywel Roberts and two men in suits, strangers to Doug, stand awkwardly filling the front room.

161

'Would you like a cup of tea?' Rose asks politely, alarmed by the greyness of her father's face.

'What can I do for you, lads?' Doug asks, smiling, shaking hands. 'I know I haven't brought those details down you asked for, Hywel. Clean forgot, to be honest, lad. I'll do it today. That OK?'

Rose watches a nerve jumping in her father's left temple. He smiles even more. PC Roberts waves. 'It's not that we've come about, Doug,' he says.

'Oh?'

One of the strangers opens his mouth to speak, but Hywel Roberts, milking the theatricality of the situation, rushes in: 'We'd begun to make a few checks on you, like, only a formality, of course...'

Doug sits down, and everyone else follows suit. The room is unheated but Rose sees beads of perspiration on her father's upper lip. PC Roberts is speaking again, looking into the upturned helmet in his hands, as if there is some strange object at the bottom that he can't identify. 'Look,' he glances around, to establish that he has the full attention of his audience, 'I'm pleased to say that the cloud of suspicion is lifted. The forensic boys have sorted it.'

Doug, visibly relieved, falls back in his armchair as if an unseen hand has pushed him hard in the chest. The policemen also relax, their knees almost reaching their chins as the sofa sucks them in. 'What do you mean?' Doug asks, eyes bright. 'Sorted?'

'It's not arson,' Hywel Roberts says. 'Mind you, personally I never thought it was, not for a moment. But you know how it is, we got the phone call and we're duty-bound to follow it up.

162

Still, it gave me a nasty five minutes, boyo, I can tell you. So, just thought we'd pop by and put your mind at rest. The forensic lads say there was a wiring problem on one of the deep freezes. If it had happened during the week you'd have spotted it, and the damage wouldn't have been nearly so bad. I hear old Mrs Bunting's calling it a day anyway Great shame, that.'

Immediately the policemen have gone, Rose turns on her father. 'What the hell is going on? What phone call? I saw you the other night in that white van. I can find out easily enough who she is, you know. Just because Mam turns a blind eye doesn't mean I've got to. It's bloody shameful the way you treat her. Shameful. If you've got a new woman, I swear to God I'll kill you with my bare hands, I really will.'

'A new woman?' Doug says.

Rose is even more infuriated as her father turns on the charm in a way that she has seen him do to her mother so many times before.

'Don't be bloody daft. I wasn't doing anything. Nothing at all, that's the problem. I swear to God. She won't leave me alone. It's an obsession, that's what it is. You know I wouldn't do anything to hurt your mam. Not intentionally She means the world to me. Anyway, now this little problem has worked itself out, let's see how we go and think again maybe in May or June. What do you say to that, Rosie? Chalkie will be up for it. Move down south maybe...You know what your mother will be like if we leave any of you behind.'

Then he starts humming to himself as he takes a cigarette from his packet. Rose knows that

163

whatever her father was on the verge of revealing has once again been returned to his personal vault, padlocked in smiles and camouflaged with song.

Chapter Seventeen

Wednesday is half-day closing for Kit. *So* Penny and I skive off school. We go to Penny's house and spend the afternoon, drinking warm port and lemonade because that's what there's most of in the drinks cabinet, chatting and singing *a capella* or trying to. We've expanded our repertoire. We've moved on from 'Be My Baby' to 'Da Doo Ron Ron', 'The Chapel of Love', 'Baby I Love You' and Dusty Springfield's 'I Only Want to Be With You'. Penny has a couple of Marvin Gaye and Smokey Robinson LPs too so we sing and dance to them for a while in her bedroom. An activity again made possible by the magic of central heating. In our house we'd be human icicles within ten minutes.

Half-way through the afternoon Penny, port talking, starts to weep and says she misses Bulbie every minute of the day when they're not together and if I don't feel like that about Bryn it can't possibly be love. Who's arguing? 'Come on, then,' Kit says to Penny. 'Out with it. Is he any good?'

'What do you mean, good?'

Kit licks port off her fingers. 'You know...' Penny buries her head in her pillow. 'I thought you said you were on the Pill?' Kit adds accusingly.

Penny emerges. 'I am. I take it to keep my

164

mother quiet. She says intelligent girls use contraception. But that doesn't mean I have to have sex as well,' she adds fiercely.

'The best sex I've ever had was with a postman,' Kit volunteers, keen to establish her superiority. 'I babysat for him and his wife. They had twin boys of eighteen months. The two of them would go out to the pub and then he'd nip back and finger me on the sofa.'

Penny dives into the pillow again. Kit doesn't appear in the least embarrassed. In my head is a message that plays again and again: it says, in my mother's voice, any sexual activity is depraved, corrupt, messy and nasty – until you are a wife. At which point, miraculously, it changes. Your partner is no longer a walking health hazard to women, he is A Husband. Now, as I listen to Kit, half of me is titillated while the other half feels slightly queasy. How can she be so shameless? How, too, has she escaped from the curse of caring what others think?

'I didn't go all the way with him, mind,' she adds, backcombing her hair in the mirror so it stands up like a guardsman's busby.

'Why not?' Penny's muffled voice comes from the pillow.

'Because he could've been arrested,' Kit answers calmly. 'I was only thirteen at the time.'

Penny sits bolt upright with the pillow held in front of her like a shield, as if whatever it is that makes Kit so happily promiscuous, might somehow leap across the room, sink its teeth into her neck and leave her infected with the same craziness.

'How old was he?' she asks breathlessly. Kit shrugs. 'I dunno. Probably forty, maybe forty-five. His wife's about twenty years younger. I think he'd been married before. Anyway, he was good at what he did. Bloody good,' she adds reflectively. 'Poor old Podge doesn't have a clue. But if I try and help him a bit, he gets all upset and says he wishes I wouldn't act like the town bike.'

'Forty-five? That's the same age as my dad,' Penny says.

'So? Don't you think your dad's interested in sex?'

'Kit,' she says nervously, 'if I ask you something, do you promise to answer honestly?'

'I promise.'

'Do you fancy my dad?' Penny asks gravely. 'Personally, I can't stand him. But I've got to know because my mother has asked if you and Lily want to stay for supper. If you're going to...' Penny hunts for the appropriate phrase '... if he's not safe,' she finally says, looking at Kit as if she's a cross between Diana Dors and a black widow spider, 'you can't.'

Kit giggles. 'Don't be daft. I don't fancy him at all,' she says. 'But I'm bloody sure he's got his eye on Lily.'

'I failed my driving test five times. Now, what do you think that says about me, girls?' Don Wilson looks around his supper table expectantly.

'Could I have a glass of wine, please?' Penny asks a little too loudly.

'It's Wednesday, darling,' Adele replies, as if that offers sufficient explanation. Before her parents arrived home, Penny had poured several cups of coffee into us. Now we are giving a reasonable impression of sobriety.

'Well?' Don Wilson asks again.

Kit smiles. 'That you don't know how to drive, Mr Wilson?'

He looks slightly miffed. 'Don, Kit, Don. No, I think it says just a little something about my determination. On the sixth attempt I passed. I never give up. That's what we say in this house, isn't it, darling? Persevere, give it that extra mile...'

Adele keeps her eye on Kit and me, presumably watching for whether we eat peas off the knife, talk with our mouths full, drink and masticate at the same time, that sort of working-class thing.

'Pass the condiments, please,' Adele says, when she wants the pepper and salt. She had appeared ten minutes earlier pushing a heated hostess trolley. It contains potatoes and peas and rissoles in separate serving dishes. The Wilsons help themselves to very little and leave a lot of it untouched on their plates. Kit and I copy.

'Don, darling,' Adele says.

He obediently removes the plates and brings in dessert. This is something brown and fluffy in a glass bowl, the taste of which is somewhere between Marmite and cocoa. 'Lovely,' everyone says.

The hostess trolley rattles out and Adele returns with tiny cups and a pot of coffee. Don lights a cigar. 'Lovely, darling,' he says again to his wife.

So we all join in. 'Lovely, Mrs ... Adele, lovely, thanks...' I can tell by the look on Kit's face that

167

she's still so hungry she'd happily eat the host's cigar if she had a knife and fork.

'So,' Adele turns to me, 'tell me what you think of *The Duchess of Malfi*. Penny says you're doing it for–'

Penny has sat stony faced throughout the meal, blanking both parents. 'So, Lily, tell me what you think about *The Duchess of Malfi*,' she mimics. 'Oh, for God's sake, give us a break,' she adds sourly.

Adele beams. 'Sorry, darling,' she coos.

Don exhales and disappears behind a cloud of cigar smoke. 'We've got high hopes for Penny here,' he says. 'University, here we come... What's it to be for you Lily? English maybe? A little crack at Oxbridge?' He looks at us. 'Penny's got three interviews for university places coming up. The world's your oyster once you've got a degree under your belt. Isn't that right, Adele?' He appears cruelly oblivious to the effect his words are having on Kit, who is shrinking in her seat.

'I've told you, I'm not going to university,' Penny says, in a monotone. She has kept a close eye on me ever since Kit's remark this afternoon. I'm sure her old man doesn't fancy me, he's just creepy around women. A knicker-sniffer without doubt.

'I'm not going to Oxbridge,' Penny continues. 'I'm not going anywhere. I'm a free person, I can do what I like. That's what you've always told me. That's what I'm going to be. Free. All you really care about is what your friends and neighbours say anyway, not what makes me happy. For all your talk, you two are more bourgeois than

168

anyone I know. God, look around you, how many more *things* can you cram into a bloody suburban house?' Penny steams on. 'Well, I'm going to live my life the way I want to. I've got a job lined up. I'm going to be an apprentice in Cut Above the Rest, working for Gwendolyn, when I leave school.'

'Gwendolyn?' Kit and I say simultaneously. *'Gwendolyn?'* What Penny decides to do with her life is her own business, but *Gwendolyn's!* Ask Gwendolyn about Vidal Sassoon and she'd tell you he was a German general in the First World War. Adele's bracelets rattle a protest as she flicks her hair back. Disapproval has flattened her features as if she's squashed her face up against a window.

'Lily?' she says, looking at me, as if she expects me to conjure up Aspiration, like a rabbit out of a hat, for her daughter.

'Yes, Mrs ... Adele.'

'I'm sure you've discussed the issue of universities and your future plans in a much more grown-up way with your parents than Persephone appears to be able to manage.'

I am in awe of Adele Wilson's level of ignorance. Our kind of family doesn't 'discuss' anything, let alone universities and the 'future'. They don't think like that; the day-to-day carries enough risk. Ahead in the next twenty-four hours lies possible disaster: the clap, the bun in the oven, the horse that ought to win but doesn't, the sack, the unexpected expense. Why, in addition, torment yourself by considering what may or may not happen in 'the future'?

The Tempests don't discuss, they know by

169

osmosis what's expected. So they 'know' that university is a waste of time and out of the question since it adds up to three years without a wage. It's even more of a waste for a female, who is bound to stop work as soon as she has babies.

Adele is speaking again: 'Which universities have you applied to, Lily? You should have heard by now if you've got any interviews.'

'Should I?' I say, sounding as stupid as the Wilsons clearly think I look.

Chalkie White stands on his doorstep, an arm's length from his wife. To him the distance is as vast as the length of a football pitch. Next door, on the radio, Gerry and the Pacemakers are belting out 'How Do You Do What You Do To Me?'. The cheery determination of the song temporarily gives his spirits a lift. Chalkie is a man who is easily boosted: all it takes is a tune or a laugh or a pint or a game of football with the lads or the sight of his son's smile – or Rose at peace with herself and him.

Now he hovers uncertainly. He has handed in his cards, tired of always being somewhere other than where he wants to be, at home with his family. Now, in greeting, Rose kisses him perfunctorily on the cheek. All thoughts of telling her tonight that he is back for good evaporate.

Rose sees the change in his face and misreads its meaning. She chastises herself for punishing him again and again for a single encounter to which she'd willingly, enthusiastically, agreed. On that one night she had gloriously discovered that everything her mother had drummed into her about sex before marriage was a lie. So, of course, she had returned for more. Recklessly.

Now conscience makes her reach out again and kiss her husband's lips, moulding her body to his, the breadwinner's reward. Young Billy rushes into the hall, spots them together and claps his hands in pleasure, before leaping on to his father's back.

'House looks nice,' Chalkie says tactfully, putting down his bag of dirty washing. 'Shall I take it out the back?' he asks quickly.

Rose stops him, each playing out their role. 'It's OK, I'll do it.' She picks up his clothes and makes her way to the kitchen. She puts his underwear in a bucket of water to soak. She leans against the wall briefly, listening to the jubilant sounds from father and son. Chalkie had bought a twin-tub Hoovermatic washing-machine and spin-dryer for seventy-nine pounds nineteen shillings and fivepence on the hire purchase for her Christmas present. It makes her life as a housewife easier, just like the advert says, but Rose doesn't want it easier, she doesn't want it at all. Each time she sets eyes on the infernal machine, she kicks it – hard.

She realises that Chalkie has come into the kitchen, Billy hanging on to his leg, like a human anchor. 'I've brought you something. It's not much. If you don't like it, I can always get you something else,' her husband says awkwardly. He always brings Billy a gift but never before has he brought one for her. He holds it behind his back. 'It doesn't matter if you don't like it,' he says again. Rose is drawn to his eyes, yet again, a

171

beautiful sea-green, the reason why she had climbed into the cab of his lorry in the first place.

He hands her a paper bag. She opens it and pulls out a paperback, disguising her surprise. *The Penguin Book of Contemporary Verse.*

'Is it all right?' he asks anxiously. 'It's second-hand,' he adds, as if she might shy away if he has committed too much of himself to the gift.

'Thank you,' she says formally, wondering how he knows, when she gives so little away. Then, Rose sees the disappointment at her response, in his seductive sea-green eyes – and she is glad.

On the way home on the last bus, Kit and I decide that while we envy Penny's mod cons, her parents are weird. For a start, the entire family barely eats. They bring out food at regular intervals, only to put it all away again on their hostess trolley. I don't eat much in my house either but I have a reason: my mother.

Second, although they are darling this, and angel-heart that, they show as much genuine interest in each other as strangers who chat while waiting for the same train.

Third, why have the Wilsons chosen to live over an hour's drive from the university where they both work? The few attractions the town has have been largely unchanged since the 1850s. The closest it comes to French cinema, radical intellectuals, love-ins, speakouts, flower power, cannabis, the Beatles, union militancy, student revolt and patchouli oil is watching it all on the telly.

We fall silent, contemplating the strangeness of the middle classes.

'So, how's your dad's new ... housekeeper?' I ask eventually.

Kit is unusually curt. 'Dad's been unhappy and now he isn't. If she's the cause, well, I'll have to put up with things being a bit different, that's all. I've told the others they've got to get used to sharing our dad now. Do things her way...' She stares out of the bus window, her shoulders hunched. I think she may be crying.

After a minute or so, Kit clears her throat and says, 'They've given me a rise in the shop. I'm the acting manager now. If I stay they'll make me a proper manager in a couple of years. I'll only be twenty-one or so – and the money's not bad. Not as good as a factory but at least I'll be my own boss.'

'That's brilliant.' I'm genuinely pleased. 'That's really brilliant. You're on your way.'

'What do you mean, "You're on your way"?'

'Well, what happens after they make you manager?'

Kit shrugs. 'I manage. That's it. It's better than a lot of people have,' she adds. 'We can't all be clever.'

'But you are clever,' I blurt out.

'Oh, for God's sake, Lily,' Kit mutters, and it's hard to tell whether she's pleased or cross. 'You sound like bloody Don and Adele.'

When I let myself into the house, smoked haddock perfumes the air and everyone is in bed. Rose, however, is visiting. She sits in the back room. 'I thought Chalkie came home today?' I ask, passing through to the kitchen to put the

173

kettle on.

'He did. He and Billy fell asleep early. I came over to have a word with you. Daisy and Iris have their heads permanently in the clouds, so it'll have to be you.'

Rose always talks to me antagonistically, these days, and I hate it. It's as if she believes I have something I don't deserve. She puts another two lumps of coal on the fire. 'What do you make of Betty Procter, then?' she asks.

I'm flattered. This is going to be a grown-up conversation after all. 'She came here, all dressed up, wanted one of dad's dogs. I thought there was something funny about her, but Mam treated her all right. Why?'

Rose raises her eyebrows.

'You're kidding,' I say. 'Our dad wouldn't, not so close to home. He's never ever done that. What would be the point? Mam's bound to find out.'

'Oh, and then what happens?' Rose asks sarcastically. 'I'll tell you what. Bugger-all – no rows, no recriminations, nothing. That's why their marriage is such a huge success. He does what he wants. And she lets him.'

I shake my head. 'No, I know there are rules. I don't know how it works, but I know there are rules.'

Rose sighs. 'God, you're naïve sometimes, Lily. He's middle-aged, for God's sake. He's vain, he thinks it's all slipping away. Mam knows. She's always known.' Rose continues to poke the fire ferociously. 'She probably knew before she married him that that's what he'd be like. Marriage is a trade-off, isn't it? Nothing's perfect. So

174

you settle for less. The question is, how much less?'

'I'd rather settle for a life on my own, thank you very much.'

'Oh, yeah? We'll see.' Rose grimaces. 'You're only seventeen. Come back in ten years' time and talk to me then. I promise that if he goes near Betty Procter or another woman again, I'll shove this poker where it hurts most. I swear to God I will.'

'Blimey, Rose, anybody would think it was you he's cheating on.' I stop as awareness dawns. 'That's it, isn't it? Chalkie plays the same game. Oh, Rose...' I throw my arms around her. 'Leave him, why don't you? I would if anybody did that to me.'

Rose shakes her head fiercely. 'Don't be so stupid, Lily. What do you know about anything?'

'OK, OK,' I say. 'At least we can be practical. Maybe Mam's been on the spend because he's got Betty. You take the kitchen, I'll have a look in here.'

Hunt the Bill is a traditional family game. When we were growing up, there were periods during which there were no apparent money problems, alternating with episodes in which, after school every Thursday, Mam would take all four of us to what she called the borrowing house.

She'd borrow, and return the following week to pay the interest, then borrow some more. 'Don't tell your father,' she'd say, making it sound like an act of benevolence. Even when we were older it never occurred to us to question what triggered these sporadic bouts of profligacy. We just accepted that that was the way it was.

175

Now, Rose moves into the kitchen, while I hunt through the cupboards in the back room. It doesn't take long. Within minutes, Rose returns with the old tea caddy. It contains several bills and letters demanding final payment. She calculates rapidly. 'The total amount is ninety-seven pounds five and eleven,' she says flatly. 'It's been worse. What are these?'

In her hand, my sister has two letters addressed to me. She reads over my shoulder. 'So, you're not as daft as you look,' she says. 'You're going to go, aren't you? Of course you've got to go.'

The two letters offer appointments in the first week of March for university interviews. I have to telephone or write to say whether I will attend. One interview is at Westfield College, part of the University of London; the other is the following day at the University of Warwick, a red-brick university near Coventry. The letters have been stuffed in the caddy for so long that the deadline on an application for travelling expenses has already passed.

Rose becomes bossy. 'Phone in the morning and say you're going. If you don't I will. We'll work out how to pay for you to get there later. Have you got anything saved?'

'Are you kidding?'

'Perhaps the school's got a special fund or something.'

'I'd die before I ask.'

'What about Kath?'

'She's always broke.'

Rose presses on: 'What about borrowing? If Mam can do it, so can you.'

176

I snort, still trying to make sense of what I've just read. 'Borrowing? Dad's out of work, Mam's in debt up to her neck, the house is rented and nobody round here has known us for longer than five minutes. Who do you think is going to lend me the cash, considering there's absolutely no prospect that they'll get a penny of it back?'

'Oh, suit yourself, then,' Rose snaps. 'If it was me, I'd do anything to go.'

'Well, that's the whole point. It's not you, it's me.' I take a step back out of her reach.

'Sod you,' she says. 'Sod bloody you. I'll tell you something for nothing, Miss Bloody Smug. Whether you like it or not, you've got to get off your backside and start putting something back into this family. Dad wants you to sing with him in the pub and you should bloody well do it. That money could go towards paying your way out of here – and it would help Dad.'

'Never!'

'You listen to me, you silly little cow. If you won't do it for yourself, do it for him. If you're with him, he stays away from women and he earns a couple of quid when he's got nothing else coming in. You owe him the chance of that little bit of self-respect.'

'What do you know about self-respect?' I say, taking a risk.

Suddenly, Rose grabs a chunk of my hair and pulls so hard I swear I've been scalped. I try to grab her throat and we both knock against the table, rattling cups. Small flakes of plaster fall from above as Daisy, upstairs, bangs furiously on the bedroom floor.

'I hate you, Lily Tempest. I really, really hate you,' Rose hisses. And then she is gone, slamming the front door.

I sink down in a chair and stare at the nearly dead fire for several minutes, trying to sort out my thoughts and contain a growing sense of excitement. It had never seriously occurred to me that university might be a possibility. But why not? Why shouldn't I go? Alex Baxter in my class is going and he's thick as a brick. But then again, his dad is a bank manager. He has a sense of entitlement that I entirely lack.

The pub job with my dad and the hotel work wouldn't earn me nearly enough in the time to meet my travelling expenses to London but perhaps I could hitch. Perhaps Rose was right. Perhaps I should do something to help my dad. On the other hand, I've never known him to be out of a job for long. Something will turn up to keep him occupied.

On a whim, I climb the stairs to the attic. The bridesmaid's dress that Iris wore to her best friend's wedding hangs in its plastic cover. It is lavender, the colour of honeymoon négligés. It is made of satin and organdie, empire line with floaty nylon sleeves. It is monumentally hideous. It is the kind of dress 'cabaret' singers wear at the railwaymen's club. Shivering, I hold it up against me in the moonlight, and look at myself in the old, cracked mirror, propped against a packing case.

Dad and me in a duo. What kind of a fate is that? How will we be billed? Two of a Kind? Sweet and Sour? Coffee and Cream? Today is supposed to belong to the young, and what am I expected to do? Step back into the flaming fifties and sing like Doris Day.

That is truly too much to ask.

Chapter Eighteen

Dulcie Tempest clocks into work at seven thirty a.m. as usual. Later in the morning, she complains of a headache and a sore throat so the supervisor tells her to go home. At lunch-times in January the Rising Sun attracts a reasonable number of customers – clerks and bank employees from the high street, men off the building site constructing new council offices and white-collar workers from the iron works who have just long enough to make the fifteen-minute walk there and back and swallow a pint and a pie.

Dulcie has never been into a pub on her own before. In truth, Dulcie has rarely done anything of her own volition. Kath has always been very firmly in charge. Now, when she opens the door to the public bar, everybody turns to stare. She glances at the window-seats on either side of the entrance but Robert hasn't arrived yet. She goes to the bar, head down, and shyly asks for an orange squash. Then she sits alone in one of the window-seats and waits.

Robert arrives, as she knows he will, at twenty past twelve. He buys a lemonade, pretends he hasn't seen her and sits on the other side of the door. Dulcie is nonplussed. She expects him to say hello. She stares at her glass, her heart is breaking, she can feel the pain like a stitch in her side, except higher.

'Oi, dozy.' A man's voice makes her start. 'Shift along there, pudding, there's a good girl.' Dulcie looks up to see three men in their early twenties, dressed in jeans and lumber jackets, each holding a pint. One has a moustache and he speaks to her again. 'C'mon, sweetheart, you don't mind sharing with me and my mates, d'ya?' He bends down and pinches Dulcie's cheek. She half smiles, uncertain how to behave but embarrassed because she's aware that others in the bar are watching.

'You're a bloody big handful and that's no mistake,' says the man with the moustache, almost falling on top of her, accidentally on purpose. Dulcie lets out a little squeak of alarm.

'The spaz speaks!' says another in the trio. 'She's not as bloody daft as she looks.' He gives Dulcie a dig with his elbow, too hard to be matey. She reddens. People are laughing; others appear unsure how to react. Dulcie herself is confused. She wants Kath. She wants to go home. She knows her lip is quivering but she will not cry. Please, Kath, come now.

The man picks himself off her and casually gives one of her breasts a poke. Another man, in a suit and tie by the bar, laughs. Dulcie, pinned in on either side by the unwanted strangers at her table, struggles to extricate herself. 'I want to go home,' she says. 'I want to go home.' Each move she makes, one or other of the men blocks her, smiling. It's just a bit of fun. The kind of 'fun' Dulcie has had imposed on her for most of her

180

life. Spaz, spazzy, spastic. 'The bird's a divvy,' says one of the men.

She can't stop herself. She bursts into tears – out of humiliation and fear, frustration, rage and powerlessness.

'Let go of her! Go on, leave her. She's not hurting you. Let her go!' The anger in the words shakes some of the spectators free of their own ambivalence about what they are witnessing. A few voices murmur disapproval.

The publican says belatedly, 'Leave it out, lads.'

Dulcie looks up and Robert stands before her. 'I'm telling you, leave her alone,' he says again to her tormenters, red-faced. He holds out his hand, to give her help, only to realise that it's clutching a glass of lemonade.

He rapidly switches hands. One of the trio stands up, menacingly, but his friend pulls him back. 'I don't know what's the matter with people,' he says loudly. 'Got no bloody sense of humour.'

The third man in the group clears a space to allow Dulcie out from her human prison. 'Sorry, miss,' he says. 'Didn't mean no harm. We were just mucking about. Sorry. You all right? Good girl.'

Once they are out on the street, Robert says awkwardly, without looking at her, 'You can come for a cup of tea in my place if you like – but you can't stop long.'

Dulcie nods, her heart thudding. 'Thank you.' She tries to smile. 'You were ever so brave.'

Robert nods but says nothing.

'Is your girlfriend at your house?' Dulcie asks, as they turn the corner into Robert's street.

He stops dead. 'She's not a girlfriend, she's a

mascot. Sort of. Anyway, perhaps you'd better go home now,' he adds, changing his mind at the thought of the upset in his routine. Dulcie marches determinedly ahead. 'I don't think you'd better come,' he repeats. A few minutes later, he catches up with Dulcie who is standing outside his house. 'How do you know where I live?'

'I asked Mr Roberts, the policeman,' Dulcie replies. 'I wish I had a house that was all mine.'

Robert opens the door and, for the first time in his life, he is ashamed of the shabbiness of the place: the battered sofa with saggy seats, the rag rug, the old lino peeling at the edges and the radios and TVs, their insides hanging out, scattered around the room. Then he reminds himself fiercely that he never asked for any visitors.

Dulcie has moved, without invitation, from the sitting room through to the lean-to kitchen. He hears a squeal of surprise. She reappears standing in the doorway, holding a large cardboard cut-out of a woman in a swimming-costume, one leg posed seductively in front of the other, a Kodak camera in her hands, smiling broadly with shiny white teeth and wavy brown hair. The girl towers above her head, but Dulcie is twice as wide. 'She used to be outside the chemist, next to Woolie's, didn't she?' Dulcie asks.

'Put her back where you found her,' Robert replies crossly.

'Is she your girlfriend?' Dulcie persists.

'Don't be so silly,' he answers, blushing crimson.

Dulcie is incapable of concealing her delight: she can handle a cardboard rival. She obediently does as he's requested.

When she returns to the sitting room, shyness suddenly overwhelms her again. She hovers awkwardly beside the sofa, looking down at her hands.

'Your sister'll kill you, when she finds out you've been here,' Robert mutters morosely.

Dulcie looks up. 'I know,' she says happily.

Doug Tempest listens to the wind whistling through the teeth of the young woman in the labour exchange when he signs on and tells her his age. She looks at him expectantly as if this might prompt him to slice twenty years off his life. 'Have you ever thought of ancillary sanitation?' she asks. Doug admits that he has not. 'What's that involve?'

'Well, basically,' she shuffles papers officiously, 'sweeping the streets. But there's ever such a nice uniform that goes with it. Apple green.' He politely refuses.

At dinner-time, he takes a bus ride, anything to be outdoors. Houses in the day-time are a female domain. He puts it off as long as he can, then walks into the Cow and Fiddle. He swallows his pride and seeks out Tommy Aster. Circumstances have changed. When Tommy gave him the boot, he still had Bunting's. Now he has nothing: a regular gig is the toehold that will keep him from joining the permanently unemployable. Lose that, and he's lost all.

Tommy Aster delivers his terms. 'I'd like the girl in something sparkly, nothing scruffy, and you in a V-neck jumper. Like the Irish fella, Val

Doonican, or Andy Williams, easy-listening gear,' he says, neck jerking in and out like a piston. 'What do you call yourselves? How about Twice As Nice? The wife thought of that. Twice As Nice. Quite like it myself. Twice As Nice. Start in a couple of weeks. Give you time to get your act together. I've got a bit of a plan. Monday, Tuesday, we get the oldies in, forty-plus, OAPs, middle-of-the-road. End of the week, bit of psychedelia, pop what-not, know what I mean? That's where the real money is, mate. Kids. Who'd've thought it? When I was sixteen I didn't have two pennies to rub together. Now they're millionaires. Tell you what, if you're any good, I might even give you a Tuesday.' He smiles at his own munificence.

Just after four Lily comes home from school. Doug, sitting in the back room reading the *Daily Express*, hears her half-way down the street. She and a couple of friends are bellowing out a medley of Beatles songs.

The door slams. He rarely notices what Lily's wearing but this afternoon, he wonders briefly why she doesn't come down with chronic pneumonia, skirt hitched up to her thighs, thin blazer wet from snow.

'Been in all day, Dad?' she asks, as she warms herself at the fire.

Doug shakes his head. 'Signed on, then went for a drink at the Cow and Fiddle.'

'Oh, yeah,' Lily says.

Silence falls.

'You should come some time. It's not a bad

little place. A bit off the beaten track. But not bad.'

'No, Dad,' Lily says firmly. 'I hate pubs. I especially hate pubs off the beaten track that have bingo ... and chicken-in-a-basket. I'm saving that for when I'm old and thirty.'

Doug slumps like a man who has had his backbone extracted. 'Fair enough. I'm off to the shed, give us a shout when Mam's back.'

Lily watches her father walk across the yard, head down. 'Dad,' she bangs on the window with her fist, 'Dad.' She runs out. 'Look, if you want me to, I'll sing but only for a few weeks, just till you get sorted and I–'

Her father sweeps her off her feet and spins her round. 'Fantastico!' He lifts his head back and shouts, snow sticking to his eyebrows and hair. 'Bloody fantastico! You know he wants you in fancy gear, no mini-skirts?' Lily nods. Then she blurts out, turning beetroot, 'Are you having it off with Betty Procter?'

Her father says nothing. Instead he leads her into the shed. He lights the paraffin stove, sits in the chair opposite hers, then reaches for her hands, which he clasps in his, rubbing warmth into them. He looks straight into his daughter's eyes.

'I swear to you,' he says slowly, 'whatever I might or might not have done in the past, I have no intention of repeating it now. I've grown up since those days ... not much but a bit. If anyone tells you they've seen me with a woman, they're lying. I promise you that.' He studies her face. 'OK, sweetheart?' he asks softly.

185

Lily has so many questions she wants to ask but she knows that on offer now is trust, not information. One lesson childhood has already taught her is that the continual small deceptions do as much damage as the large, life-changing lies. Maybe – or maybe not – the truth is buried in what her father has just said. 'OK,' she says.

Chapter Nineteen

On St Valentine's Day Howard Jones-Davies, the local Conservative MP, visits the Ross & Baker factory in Fairport, accompanied by the crew from the regional television news programme. Daisy is duly presented to him as the company's reigning beauty queen. Mr Jones-Davies watches her at work for several minutes, picking out broken ginger nuts on the conveyor belt, then shouts, over the roar of the radio and the racket made by the machinery, 'So, what exactly do you do, my dear?'

'What do I do?' Daisy yells back incredulously, as if the evidence isn't all around her. She wraps her overall around her a little more tightly to accentuate her best points and bellows, 'I work a forty-hour week for six pounds and seven shillings, before tax and national insurance. Here, sir, why don't you have a go?'

Helpfully, one girl places a nylon cap on the MP's thinning head while another offers him a white coat and translucent pair of rubber gloves.

'Don't look up, don't look from side to side,' Daisy shouts. 'Or–'

Mr Jones-Davies rejects her advice, and repeatedly bobs his head up to smile at the camera, only to keel over in a dead faint, crushing a few dozen ginger nuts in the process, and being propelled several yards down the conveyor belt with Daisy, giggling, hanging on to his legs.

'What happened?' he asks, when he comes round on the floor of the factory, staring up at the anxious face of Randall Thomas, the biscuit boss.

'You're not a woman,' Randall Thomas explains, helping his visitor to his feet. 'It's not your fault, Mr Jones-Davies. You see, women are used to looking down. They're not interested in the job, they just let their hands do it for them, they don't look to the left or the right. They just look down and chat. We men are more *engaged*. We think... Girls here haven't got that curiosity. They don't want to know where something is coming from and where it's going to or why.'

Daisy and Howard Jones-Davies make the second page of the local paper. They are holding a huge heart-shaped piece of gingerbread, engraved with the words 'Happy Valentine's Day'. The headline reads, 'Crumbs! Look who's taking the biscuit.' After Daisy reads it, she makes it to the lavatory just before she vomits copiously.

Kath Morgan celebrates Valentine's Day by sending a postal order to *Woman's Own* for its Valentine Special Offer: two Tea V Trays for the price of one. Instead of standing in the high street, watching twelve sets through the window of Rediffusion, she now watches her own box, eating from a tray on her lap. She also uses it as a desk since she spends much of her time writing applications to a range of television game shows in the hope of being selected as a contestant.

Even the rejections are exciting since they bear the logo of the television company and the stationery is always expensive. One letter suggests that if she can find a suitable partner – husband, sister, friend, priest of the parish – they can apply as a couple for a new show, *Double or Quit*, imported from the USA.

It is a quiz on a subject of the applicants' choice, the wackier and weirder the better. Each couple takes it in turns to double or quit. The winning duo receive a holiday for two and fifty pounds' spending money.

Kath knows that nobody matches her on dates, details and knowledge of acts of homicide since the last world war. Only one other person she has met can equal her contemporary knowledge with an historical appreciation of the same subject: Pete the Mercenary. However unsavoury she finds him personally, she is sure he will co-operate. After all, only a madman would turn down the chance of being on the telly.

Dulcie takes advantage of her sister's pre-occupation to sneak an entire week off work. She hadn't realised how easy it could be. She rises at the same time and leaves with her sandwiches. As soon as she turns the corner, she changes direction and makes her way to Taff's, a transport café in a lay-by a quarter of a mile outside town.

She buys a cup of tea and a slice of toast and, unhindered, watches the people come and go. Occasionally she helps Alice who works behind the counter.

If the cafe is relatively empty Alice, a vast quantity of woman of indeterminate age, puts on an impromptu performance. She picks up the big sugar shakers on each table and shakes them like Mick Jagger with his maracas, twirling round, in a snowstorm of sugar, singing whatever comes to mind and urging the truanting Dulcie to join in.

On Monday and Tuesday, Dulcie positions herself in the afternoon outside Robert's house, having avoided the high street where she might bump into Kath. He barely acknowledges her presence. On Wednesday, Thursday and Friday, he grudgingly asks her in. He makes her a cup of tea, then fiddles with his television sets and radios and acts as if she isn't there. After an hour or so, she washes up the cups and saucers and says goodbye. He pretends he hasn't heard. 'I've got a boyfriend,' Dulcie announces proudly to the lady in the newsagent's on Friday afternoon. 'We see each other every day.'

On Fridays Amore, the bra factory where Dulcie works, finishes an hour early at four. Usually she comes home, hands over her wage packet to her sister, waits for her pound pocket money, then goes with Lily to Ravelli's for a knickerbocker glory, two shillings and sixpence worth of vanilla, strawberry and chocolate ice cream, fruit cocktail, raspberry syrup, whipped cream, chocolate sauce, nuts, wafers and jelly. Lily pays; Dulcie eats.

Sometimes Lily and Dulcie buy a record. Dulcie contributes a shilling, and Lily makes up the remaining five shillings and elevenpence. This Friday, Dulcie's wage packet bears witness to the number of days she has failed to clock in.

Kath is incandescent. 'If you don't do as you're told, I'll put you in a home, do you hear? A home,' she shouts at Dulcie, pushing her violently against the wall. 'You'll be locked away and you'll damn well stay there for the rest of your life. And do you know what happens in there if you misbehave? They whip you with wet towels and leave you locked up in the dark where there's rats and spiders. That's what happens to you. DO YOU HEAR ME?'

Dulcie nods, too terrified even to cry. What distresses her even more than the threats is the hatred she is sure she sees on her sister's face.

'Where have you been? Have you been with him? We'll see.' As Kath is about to launch another verbal assault, Lily opens the front door. 'Oh dear, what's Dulcie done now? Gone out and bought the *Radio Times* all by herself?' she says sarcastically.

Kath's anger is immediately redirected. 'I don't need any of your backchat either, young lady. It's all your fault I've got this on my hands. She's not been at work all week. Left here as brazen as brass and then gone God knows where.'

'Have you actually asked her where she's been?' Lily suggests.

'What?'

'I said, have you asked Dulcie why she hasn't been in work?' Lily repeats, wondering whether possessiveness always, eventually, squeezes the life out of love.

'Of course I haven't asked her. What's the point? She'll only tell lies.'

'How do you know?'

'Because she's a Tempest,' Kath replies. 'They all tell lies. I'll have to take her to the doctor.'

'Whatever for?'

'If she's been interfered with I'll hold you responsible. I bet it's that simpleton you brought here. They should all be done when they're daft like that. Have their willies put in a mincer. They're a menace, that's what they are. A bloody menace, preying on women like Dulcie. She just doesn't know how to say no. I've told her if this goes on, I'll put her in a home,' Kath adds flatly.

'That's terrible.' Lily is aghast. 'You wouldn't. You couldn't. We wouldn't let you.'

'Nobody can stop me.'

'Well, why shouldn't she have a boyfriend? Come to that, why can't she get married, if that's what she wants? It's not much to ask, is it? A bit of fun?'

'Fun, you call it?' Kath is tight-lipped. 'We'll see about that. I know what you call fun, these days. Don't think I haven't seen those flower-power hippies on the television, smoking marijuana with their bare bottoms bouncing up and down in the open air.'

'What's Dulcie got to do with hippies?' Lily asks, exasperated, not for the first time, by her aunt's peculiar leaps in logic. 'She wants to settle down with a nice, gentle bloke. That's all. What's wrong in that?'

Dulcie turns her face to the wall, as if to make herself invisible, and puts her hands over her ears. 'Everything,' Kath snaps. 'It's not healthy. She's not normal, is she? Once she's had the taste of one fellow, there'll be no stopping her. Who knows what she's capable of? She's not like us. She's not even like a child. At least they can be made to understand right from wrong. Next thing you know, she'll have been with every Tom, Dick and Harry. It's not just that she's simple. I knew her father, you didn't. He was a wicked man and she'd have gone the same way if it wasn't for me.'

Lily sees a disturbing coldness in Kath's eyes but, still, she keeps a lightness in her tone. 'Honestly, Kath, all that bunkum about the bad seed. I saw a film about that when I was nine. I swore that was me. The bad seed. But do you know what? It's horrible. It's that kind of rubbish that used to send women to the stake for witchcraft. Dulcie's as good as anybody else and probably a lot better than most in our family – aren't you, Dulcie?'

Dulcie remains mum and Kath defiant. 'It's all very well you saying let Dulcie do this and let her do that but I'm the one responsible for the messes she makes.' Her voice rises in anger again. 'I'm the one who's kept her out of trouble all these years. Let her be herself, you say. But do you know what that would mean?' She shudders theatrically. 'I'll take her down to Dr Davis to have her looked at tomorrow. He'll tell me if there's been any dirty business. He's a good man like that.'

'"Dirty business"? What do you mean, "dirty

business"? I think you're frightened that Dulcie might have a better time than you've ever had. If Dr Davis had sense, which he hasn't,' Lily replies recklessly, 'he'd prescribe contraception and a little bit of freedom. That's what Dulcie really needs.'

'Aagh!' Kath makes a strange guttural sound. Then, she takes three strides across the room and grabs the younger girl by the shoulders, shaking her in frustration. 'What do you know about freedom?' she screams in Lily's face. 'Freedom doesn't mean forgetting your duties and your obligations, doing what you like when you like and ignoring the consequences. That's not freedom, that's stupidity. You do your own thing.' She savagely mimics an American accent. 'You do your own thing. You throw out all the rules and see how you'll end up – nobody giving a damn about anyone else. I promise you this, Lily Tempest, if you grow up in a world in which nobody depends upon you and you depend on no one, then you'll have "freedom" all right, but what will it be worth? You tell me that.'

In answer, Lily picks up Dulcie's coat, wraps it around her shoulders and steers her to the front door.

'Don't you dare leave this house!' Kath screams, aware that it is too late. She has already lost what matters most in her life – control of Dulcie.

'Don't you dare leave this house,' she says again, to the closing door. This time, it sounds more like a plea than a command.

Half an hour later a superficially composed Kath leaves the house on an errand. She has established that Dulcie is with Lily next door. She treats her bewildered sister as if nothing has happened but refuses to say where she is going – for Dulcie's own good, Kath tells herself.

When Robert sees the older woman standing on his doorstep, he blinks so hard he gives himself a headache.

'Is it your television, missus?' he asks timidly.

Kath pokes a finger in his chest. His body is soft and spongy like a baby's. She is both surprised and repulsed. 'Listen, you,' she says, savouring the sudden surge of power to which all bullies are addicted, 'Dulcie doesn't want to see you ever again. Do you understand? If I discover that you've been so much as in the same street at the same time, I'll get the law on to you, is that clear? I'll get a policeman to take you away and lock you up for a very long time so you won't be able to bother anybody else like you've been bothering my Dulcie.'

Words fail Robert. He wants to say he's not a bad person, he's a good person. He wants to say that he's never bothered anybody – but his tongue is locked by fear. Stuttering, he finally manages to say, 'I don't think you're right, missus. Your sister doesn't like me because I'm nice to her. She thinks I haven't been nice enough.'

Kath lifts her hand and strikes Robert hard across the face. It is the first time that she's struck a man, and a lifetime's grievance goes into the blow.

Chapter Twenty

Clothes, shoes and underwear bulge out of the sides of the small blue canvas case on the uncarpeted floor in the narrow space between the two beds. 'God, Iris, you're only going for a week. And that's my bloody suspender belt in there,' Daisy says amiably.

'You don't mind, do you?' Iris asks. 'And I've borrowed your pink cardigan, Lily. The one you never wear. I reckon if I put it on back to front with a jacket, it'll look all right. Sit here, both of you, stop mucking about!'

Lily and Daisy flop theatrically on the suitcase, endeavouring to squash it flat, and dissolving into laughter as they do so. 'I bags the single bed on my own when you're away,' Daisy says.

'No, you stay in the double bed, I'll have the single. You're so damn fat these days, you need the extra space,' Lily teases. Daisy tips her off the case.

'It looks nice, doesn't it?' Iris says, showing her sisters a postcard of a grim and forbidding-looking semi-detached house, its garden awash with painted gnomes. 'It's a B-and-B. Howard's mum and dad go there for a week every June. Howard says he's got a room on the first floor, and I'm on the second. What?' she adds defensively, as Daisy and Lily exchange a glance. 'I wouldn't dream of staying in the same room. Howard's parents would

195

go mad. So would Mam and Dad, you know they would.'

'You can still get rooms on the same corridor or something, can't–' Daisy begins but Lily, determined to avoid a time-consuming squabble, intervenes.

'Look, Iris, let's perk you up a bit,' she suggests. Without waiting to see if her offer has been accepted, she grabs her sister and rolls over the waistband of Iris's sensible, pleated skirt, lifting the hem to mid-thigh. 'Throw us your waspie belt, Daisy,' Lily instructs. She snaps it around Iris and, picking up a comb, begins to comb her hair vigorously. 'Shed ten years, girl. Go on, be a devil. Think Cathy McGowan, not Vera Lynn. Give Howard a treat!'

Iris breaks away and looks at herself in the mirror. 'Ugh!' she says, pulling a face. 'I look like a common little tart.'

Daisy throws a pillow at her head and, playfully, Lily follows suit. 'The Mother Superior's saying that's what we are, Lily. The cheeky little bitch.'

An hour or so later, Lily and Daisy hang out of their parents' bedroom window, waving goodbye as Howard, in his blazer, whisks Iris away by taxi and coach to Blackpool.

Daisy, whose spirit has revived slightly since Daniel Bright's pantomime closed and he moved on, shouts at the elderly neighbour opposite, who is pretending to fuss over her empty milk bottles, 'It's all right, Mrs Hillyard. They're booked in separate bedrooms!'

Four days later, Iris is back. She was homesick. She couldn't sleep on her own. She missed her mother. Howard said he was quite pleased to come back too.

Once Rose knows that Chalkie has resigned and isn't driving long distances again, she takes on extra shifts at the hotel, her desire to leave even more powerful. As a result, the wad of notes at the bottom of the birdcage thickens. The mixture of anticipation and fear for the future makes her hungry for her son's affection, as if she wants to store up sufficient hugs and kisses to last him a lifetime. The boy, in turn, responds instinctively, generously.

'You two are as thick as thieves,' Chalkie says, smiling, a few days after his return as he watches his wife helping Billy with his homework.

'No,' says Rose sharply, as if he has said something deeply offensive. 'You're the one he worships. You're the one he always misses.' Then she turns away, leaving Chalkie mystified yet again by the ways of his wife.

'Shift it back, mate,' Carl Hicks shouts, as he and Chalkie dismantle the Friday market stall. It has been one of those days when winter is determined to run through its entire repertoire – rain, hail and bright, luminous sunshine, adding a gloss to the ice-clad streets. Chalkie often helps Carl when he's home in return for cash in hand and the chance to get out from under Rose's feet. Now he offers Carl a cigarette and lights one himself. The crowd had been slow to materialise, deterred by the unpredictability of the weather.

'Do you reckon Doug might be glad of a bit of work?' Chalkie asks.

Carl shakes his head. 'My old man offered him some in a roundabout way. He turned it down. Says he's got a couple of things on the go. But all he's doing is making those bloody stupid dogs. I said I'd try and sell a few but they're like his babies. He'll only give 'em away if he knows they're going to a good home.'

'Poor bastard,' Chalkie says reflectively.

Later, running across the square to buy a fresh supply of ciggies, he hits an ice patch and slips heavily. Even Carl, twenty yards away, can hear the crack of bone.

Rose waits until five, then she and Billy go to look for Chalkie. He is supposed to have been home at four thirty, so that she can go to work. He is rarely late. He is also dependable. As the minutes go by, anxiety alternates with a blinding anger. As she rushes Billy into his coat, to take him to her mother's, Rose asks herself, How is it possible to love and hate simultaneously in equal measures?

'Can you imagine what they must feel like?' Kath says. 'Salt and vinegar?' she adds. The woman nods. Kath sprinkles liberally, then deftly wraps a portion of fish and chips in newspaper. Both women look up at the television now installed in the Contented Sole on a small ledge on the wall. It shows scenes of a police hunt for a seven-year-old, missing for over a fortnight. Daniel Andrews had left his house in Ashby Newton, seventeen miles from Fairport, on the last Sunday in January, in the early afternoon, to play with his cousin, who lived a five-minute walk away. He had never

198

arrived. Several sightings have turned out not to be Daniel. The boy had wandered off twice before, his parents told the police, because he was obsessed with buses. Once, he had even taken a long ride into Cwmland. But he had always returned within hours.

'Those poor parents,' Kath says. 'I expect he's dead and buried by now. What do you reckon? Definitely assaulted, I'd say. Or maybe it's a hit-and-run. Mind, the most respectable-looking fellows turn out to have a thing for little boys. It's not your obvious perverts you've got to look out for. Poor little beggar.'

'What are his mam and dad thinking of – letting him roam about? That's asking for trouble, that is,' the woman says, handing over coins. 'They want their heads examined.'

'And what can I do for you, young lady?' Kath asks coldly, as Lily appears at the door.

'Two lots of chips for me and Dulcie, please. I've asked her to come round to our house and she says I've got to ask you first. She's sitting in your place all on her own in the dark, staring at the wall. Hasn't even got the telly on. You should let her go and see him, Kath. What harm can it do?'

Kath pointedly ignores her request and nods up at the television. 'Boy missing. Have you heard? Child murder, I'll bet. It's a terrible business. Do you remember – no, you won't, it was long before you were born. A good few years back, three or four kids went missing, different parts of the country. All small boys. They never did find the killer but they reckoned it was a lorry driver. Evil bastard.'

She dumps a wire basket of uncooked chips into the boiling fat and smiles with satisfaction as the fat sizzles and seethes. 'If they get hold of this one they should burn him alive,' she says, with relish. 'Monsters, that's what they are. Evil monsters ... Salt and vinegar?'

Chapter Twenty-one

Melody sits in the kitchen of the Olde Tudor Tea Rooms, one eye on the oven where four egg and bacon pies are baking, while her daughter tries to extract an apology from her that is grovelling enough to meet a seventeen-year-old's standard of contrition. So far, Melody has failed miserably. She tries again. 'Look, I'm really sorry, Lily, love, I really am. I didn't even bother to look at the letters. I just assumed they were bills. No harm done, though, is there? You know your father and I aren't keen on the idea, not really.'

Lily bangs her hand down on the table. 'What do you mean, "no harm done"? No harm done? They were interviews that could've changed my life. Of course there's harm done. If I'd had the letters in time, I could have applied for travel expenses and at least given the interviews a go. Now I'm stuck. Stuck here because we can't afford the fares and nobody trusts us enough to lend us a penny.

'I'm sick of this family. I'm sick of us never having any money. I'm sick of everybody telling me to be grateful for what I've got. Just because you and Dad are happy with next to bloody nothing, that doesn't mean I've got to want it too, does it?' Lily shouts, ignoring her mother's fluttering hands, signalling to her to keep the sound down so the customers can't hear.

'Why do you make me feel as if I'm committing a great big bloody betrayal by even thinking about university? Education isn't a disease, you know, Mam. But then again, given that you can barely read and write...' Lily pushes the knife in with no regrets.

Melody's face is impassive but something in her middle-aged head bursts. In the distance she hears the voice of her daughter telling her, as she has for too long now, that she is stupid, inert, too cowed to demand more of her husband, more of life, more of anything... She rises to her feet majestic in her anger. 'You may despise us – me, young lady,' she says, her voice shaking with emotion, 'you may wish we were better and posher and smarter, but what you should ask yourself is what you mean by "better". Better at what? Making money? Buying big cars? Impressing the neighbours? Do you know the best lesson you can learn, Lily Tempest? It doesn't come from schoolbooks. It's learning how to trust your own instincts, even when, at times, that may mean going against what your so-called "betters" say is the right and proper thing to do. I'm proud that I've grasped that lesson as well as I am able. And I am able. Very able.

'Let me tell you this, madam, where I am now, I am by choice. So stuff your silly little ideas that

201

I am some put-upon pudding with a mind like a sponge. Stuff them. Do you hear me? And don't you ever talk to me again with such contempt in your voice.

'Now,' Melody continues, wiping her hands on her apron with some satisfaction, 'do you really want to go to these interviews? If you do I can try and find the money from somewhere. But that doesn't mean your father or I approve of this university thing.'

Taken aback by the force of her mother's feelings and fearful that this time, she may have pushed her just a little too far, Lily conceals her uncertainty with defiance. 'Don't bother. I wouldn't want to spend the rest of my life grateful for a couple of your favours, thank you very much.'

And then she is gone, slamming the door so hard that Veronica's inquisitive face appears at the hatch. 'Everything all right?'

Kath Morgan is ready. She wears a black two-piece suit with a black nylon fur collar; black patent-leather heels and a matching handbag complete the ensemble. She looks as if she is going to a funeral, which is precisely the occasion for which the outfit had first been bought.

'Are you going out?' Dulcie asks. Kath ignores her. She puts money, keys, compact, lipstick and comb into her handbag and snaps it shut. A heavy dose of Soir de Paris has drowned the faint aroma of fried fish. 'You, young lady,' she says to Dulcie, 'come with me.'

Next door, at number nine Rydol Crescent, Daisy is preparing to go out with Carl. She has been getting ready for an hour and a half, and she's still only a work in progress. Her entire wardrobe is tipped on to the bed, as is her sister Lily's. Lily buys from the Biba mail-order catalogue, which consists of half a dozen sheets of paper stapled together with sketches of girls with no eyes who resemble Martians. Her first purchase, last year, was a summer frock, puff sleeves, empire line, very short, which cost one pound nine and eleven. The big buy in November had been a corduroy coat in mauve with big lapels and a belt – four pounds nineteen and eleven.

No one in Fairport had ever seen a mauve coat before. Coats are meant to be brown, black, navy, grey, green or tweed. Lily had also bought a couple of shift dresses with round necks and long, tight sleeves. It is one of these, in plum corduroy, that Daisy had decided to wear without asking her sister's permission. As a result, Lily has Daisy on the floor by the hair when she is interrupted by Melody calling both of them from the bottom of the stairs.

When Daisy and Lily look over the banisters, they see their mother, Kath – dressed like a female psychopath from a 1950s B movie – and a miserable Dulcie. The two sisters know what Kath is about to ask so they each attempt to make a pre-emptive move. 'I'm going out. Bryn's playing tonight. Why don't you ask Daisy?' Lily speaks first.

'I can't. Carl's in the darts league.' Daisy smiles sweetly.

'Come down here, both of you,' Melody orders. 'I'm going out with your dad, so it's got to be one of you two. Toss for it,' she instructs. 'Heads or tails?'

Daisy wins. Lily calls Bryn from the telephone box on the corner of the crescent and tells him she'll meet him later. 'OK,' he says, in his usual expansive way. Kath says she'll be home in a couple of hours.

'Promise me, Lily, that you won't let Dulcie out of your sight. Your mother swears I can trust you.'

Lily nods.

Half an hour later, when the coast is clear, Dulcie and Lily walk to Robert's house. 'You broke your promise to Kath,' Dulcie says, a smile on her face.

Lily shakes her head. 'No, I haven't. I promised to keep you in sight, not lock you up indoors.'

Dulcie gives a chuckle of pleasure. Then she asks, 'What will we do about Kath?' as if she's already decided that Lily has assumed full responsibility for making her dreams come true.

'We'll think of something. She'll come round.'

'What if she puts me in a home?'

'Of course she won't do that,' Lily reassures her. 'She can't, not in this day and age.'

'She can,' Dulcie says glumly. 'I know she can.'

Dulcie knocks repeatedly before the door is opened a fraction. 'Go away,' Robert hisses. 'You've got to go away now.'

'Come on, let's go home,' Lily tells her. 'Robert doesn't want us here. Let's go.'

'What's wrong, Robert?' Dulcie persists.

His distress grows. 'You got me into trouble. The police will come. Your missus hit me. She said you didn't like me. You didn't want to see

204

me. So I don't want to see you. Go away. Go on. You're a bad person. I don't like you. Go away now. You're trouble.'

'Who said Dulcie didn't want to see you?' Lily questions gently.

'Her missus said that,' Robert replies. As he speaks, Dulcie inches her way into the front room, holding Lily's hand.

'Kath?' Lily asks.

Dulcie stamps her foot. 'It's not fair. She doesn't want me to do anything by myself. She just wants me to do what she says and I won't, I really won't. I'll run away and then she'll be sorry. Then she won't be able to put me away.'

Robert's face registers concern.

'Nobody is going anywhere,' Lily says, more confidently than she feels. 'I'm sure Dulcie would never say she didn't like you, Robert. She asked me to come with her to see you. Look, I'll talk to Kath, I promise I will. Do you mind if we sit down?'

The man slowly sinks into a seat, so his two unwanted guests follow suit.

Dulcie turns to Lily. 'He's made the place tidy since I last came here. He wouldn't do that if he didn't like me, would he? He's a nice man, isn't he, Lily?'

Suddenly, to Robert's obvious alarm, she gets up and sits next to him on the sofa. Very carefully, she puts her arms around his neck and clumsily kisses his cheek.

'Oh dear, oh dear, oh dear,' Robert says.

Lily takes in the room. 'My mam liked brown,' Robert says morosely, as if reading her mind.

'She's dead.'

'I'm sorry. Shall I make us all a cup of tea?' Lily suggests.

'I'll do it,' Robert offers, still acting warily. He soon emerges from the kitchen, bearing three new china cups and saucers and a plate of chocolate biscuits on a tray that still has the Woolworth's price tag stuck on it.

Lily asks if she can use the toilet. Robert indicates towards the back. Crossing the yard, she notices a bizarre sight. A pair of women's legs are sticking out of the dustbin. Lily lifts the lid and the cardboard face of a young woman smiles up at her, a Kodak camera at the ready.

Chapter Twenty-two

For the first time in his life, Pete 'The Mercenary' Wells is a hunted man. The experience is distinctly unsettling and nothing like the stuff of his own invented recollections repeated many times: no adrenaline charge, just panic and confusion. A door opens, music blasts out. Pete is aware that Kath Morgan, sitting at the other end of his bar, has him unnervingly in her sights. He endeavours, nevertheless, to keep up with an avalanche of Friday-night orders.

'Pete-y, Pete-y, can I have two gin and oranges?' A girl, obviously under-age, leans across the bar, parking her breasts under his nose.

'Gin and blackcurrant, please,' Kath says, 'and

have a drink yourself.'

Pete gives Kath a cautious once-over. She isn't bad, considering, and he'd take a bet that she even has her own teeth. During the week, Pete often has the sensation that he is surrounded by an army of dancing dentures, when the middle-aged fill the bar. At weekends the click-clack of conversation is far less noticeable because the young also pour in, as long as their money lasts, attracted by the live group playing in the basement. Kath offers a pound note. 'Remember me?' she asks. He nods.

Kath takes a sip and then, keeping her voice low, says, 'I've got a bone to pick with you, young man. Your brother, he's bothering my sister and I don't like it. If he carries on, if he so much as comes near my house again, I'll get the police on to him and have him arrested for sexual assault. Do you hear me?'

Pete, polishing the counter, anticipating pleasantries, reacts as if he's unexpectedly run the palm of his hand along a dozen razors embedded in the wood. 'Our Robert? Never. He's not interested in girls. Give him a dicky black-and-white telly and he's happy as Larry. But women, never. More like your lass has been bothering him. He's easily upset, he is. But harm somebody...'

For as long as Pete can remember, he has tried his best to look after his brother. The first time he'd been sent away at fifteen, he'd felt bad about the effect on his mother but it had been Robert he was most concerned about. Robert had had a rough time. 'He wouldn't harm a fly,' Pete repeats.

'I suggest that you come round to my house so

we can discuss this. Let's see if we can nip it in the bud before it turns nasty,' Kath says, picking up her change, leaving her drink and putting on her coat. 'I also have another small but potentially lucrative matter that I wish to discuss with you privately – something that the two of us might undertake together. We might even be able to kill the two birds with one stone.'

Pete goes pale. 'A business matter,' Kath snaps. 'Not anything of an indelicate nature.'

'Excuse me, Grandma,' giggles the girl with two empty glasses clasped to her breast. 'This man's got something I want. Two gin and oranges, please, love.'

The following morning, Pete has the scrubbed and over-groomed look of those who drink too much but wish to pretend otherwise. He knows exactly where to find his brother. In Woolworth's. He is standing by the sweet counter, chatting to one of the assistants. Robert has always loved the noise and excitement of the shop on a Saturday. Pop music blares; children come in from the farms and villages around, with their mothers, to spend their pocket money. They all know Robert. 'Hello, Uncle Robert. Would you like a sweetie, Uncle Robert?'

'All right, lad?' Pete says, by way of a greeting. Robert expresses no surprise at his presence. The two amble past Cosmetics, go round Hardware and move towards Records, Pete pondering all the time, how he is tactfully going to raise the issue of his brother's possible misbehaviour.

'What's all this, then, about you and a bird?'

Pete finally blurts out.

He is surprised at the smile that transforms his brother's face. 'Didn't like her at first. She got in the way. Then she didn't come any more. I was sad. She's all right. But her sister is bad. She says bad things about me. Am I coming to your house this afternoon?' Robert usually comes every Saturday for his tea.

'You can come but Marie isn't there. She's scarpered again. Taken the kid to her mother's. So it's just me on my tod and a tin of baked beans.' Pete studies the cigarette cupped in his hand.

'Are you sad?' Robert asks.

'Nah,' Pete lies. 'I was going to give her the old elbow anyway. Let's go and have a drink, shall we, mate?' He steers Robert out of the warmth of Woolworth's, and into the grey drizzle of Fairport's high street.

In Ravelli's, Pete orders a frothy coffee for himself and a hot chocolate with whipped cream for his brother. Then he speaks bluntly: 'That bird. You've got to stay away. Her sister says if you see her again, the police will come and take you away. I mean it. I've never said anything like this before, have I, mate?'

His brother shakes his head numbly.

'Believe me, stay away. Or you'll be in big trouble.'

Robert stares down into his mug of chocolate. Impulsively Pete reaches for his hand. Then he looks out of the window, to avoid witnessing his brother's distress.

Chalkie White sits up in bed, the blankets up to

his chin, smoking a cigarette, watching the rain wash against the windows. The radio is tuned to *Saturday Club* on the Light Programme. Brian Matthews is talking to Freddie of Freddie and the Dreamers. Chalkie has seen Freddie on the telly, in a shiny suit and Cuban heels, saying that he'd been a milkman once and success hadn't changed him one bit. What's the point in making thousands of pounds, Chalkie muses to himself, if you don't change the whole bloody lot?

He looks across at his wife. He knows she is pretending to be asleep because she is still. When Rose is genuinely asleep, she moves constantly, restlessly.

'You look like Snow White,' Chalkie says out loud, to no response. He pulls the covers back and lifts his right arm, then drops it again making a valley in the bedding. A couple of people have already signed their name on his plaster cast. Chalkie sticks his arm back under the cover, and levers up the counterpane. 'Look at this great stiffy,' he whispers, leaning over to dig his wife in the ribs with his other hand. 'Look at it, Rosie.' She moves away, saying nothing.

Chalkie had assumed that his marriage would follow the pattern set by his own parents. Dad got on with his life, Mam with hers, and they'd overlap at weekends. Once a year, the family would go to Butlins for a week's holiday. Chalkie had told Rose about those times, how happy he and his two brothers had been and how his Mam and Dad had seemed content too.

Now, he lies next to her, moving awkwardly because of the cast. Sometimes she treats him

210

with such contempt he feels like a clumsy half-wit. Other times, when she closes down, saying nothing, it triggers such fury he has to walk away to avoid harm being done. Now he shuts his eyes and makes a wish, just as he used to do when he was a lad. He wishes that Rose, just once, would turn and take him in her arms and hold him, and say she loves him from the bottom of her heart, as she used to do in their early months together when she was in love with love.

Chalkie opens his eyes to see if his wish will come true – but his wife remains as still as death.

Downstairs, Billy fills the kettle and lights the gas, using matches, which he is forbidden to do. He carefully puts four spoonfuls of tea in the pot and milk in the mugs. He stands by the stove patiently waiting for the kettle to boil, removing it just before the whistle blows. A few minutes later, he is wobbling up the stairs, tea and biscuits and two slices of bread and butter on a tray, thrilled that, for the first time, he is bringing his parents breakfast in bed.

He opens the bedroom door just as Chalkie digs Rose in the back, this time much more forcefully. 'Rose, Rose, wake up. I know you're not asleep, wake up will you, for Chrissakes. I'm in pain. I need help.'

'Get lost,' Rose says. 'I mean it, Chalkie, just get lost, will you?' As if in a dream, Chalkie holds up his arm encased in plaster and brings it down hard on the side of her head. Then watches, aghast, as the skin breaks open in pinpricks of blood like the flowering of a hundred tiny poppies.

'Mammy!' Billy screams in the doorway and drops the tray. Hot tea spills over his bare feet. 'Mammy!'

'Oh, Jesus,' says his father. 'Oh, sweet Jesus.'

Chapter Twenty-three

The wound is nasty but not deep. Chalkie has wept and pleaded and apologised and wept some more. Rose has said nothing – except to Billy. 'Why did Daddy do that?' Billy asked, distressed and bewildered.

'Nobody should hit anybody,' Rose replied, 'but sometimes, no matter how hard we try, we lose our tempers. Daddy has said he's sorry.'

'Daddy's sorry but what about you?' the boy had asked, in a flash of anger she hadn't expected. 'You weren't nice to Daddy. You're never nice to him. I hate you. I hate you. I wish you were dead.'

At Billy's football practice, she tells the others that she walked into the wardrobe door. They don't challenge her because they, too, one day, might also suffer the same unfortunate experience. Then she comes home and tells Chalkie that there is no point in them staying together any more. 'You know your bloody problem?' he retaliates. 'Whatever you have, you want something else. You despise anyone who's content with what they've got. You're mad, that's what you are. Even my mam reckons you're a loony,' he flounders, inventing fake allies.

Rose decides it's easier to take the blame. What has she to lose? She's leaving anyway. 'It's my fault,' she agrees. 'If we don't separate, I'll destroy you as well as myself and then neither of us will have a chance of redemption.'

She regrets the use of the word as soon as it's spoken. 'Redemption?' Chalkie mocks her. Then he adds savagely, 'Don't look at me like that. I know what it bloody means. It's the act of deliverance from sin. Sin? Is that how you see us? Our marriage? A fucking sin?'

Rose sits calmly. Chalkie in a rage is easy to handle. It's when he is subdued, upset, withdrawn, she finds it difficult to suppress her own guilt, remorse and regret.

'It also means the act of freeing,' she answers. Then she leaves the room.

'What are you doing? Where are you going? You're not leaving this house until I say so!' Chalkie shouts after her.

She hadn't expected her departure to be quite so hurried. Now Rose rushes around packing two shopping bags with one set of clothes, a nightdress and her toothbrush. She leaves the toothpaste for Billy. As she does so, she hears the front door slam. Chalkie is a proud man. She knows he would rather remove himself than witness her defying him and walking out of the house.

She collects the money from the birdcage, puts on her coat and stops in the passage. On the wall, there are three school photographs of Billy. In each, he has grown a little older, his smile a little more hesitant. I have done that to him, Rose tells herself. She kisses each image in turn, then takes a deep breath and steps out into the street.

Miraculously, one foot is placing itself in front of the other. Heart thumping, tears pouring down her face, she finds herself running as if every fairy-tale monster from her childhood is in pursuit.

Kit does not approve. Her father has taken Sally, the housekeeper, on a special away-day on the coach to see the waterfalls at Betws-y-coed. They have left the children, including the youngest, Harry, aged seven, who always comes home from school for his dinner, to their own devices. In her new capacity as shop manager since three other employees here handed in their resignations, Kit is entitled to a forty-five-minute lunch-break. So far she has preferred to stay open and keep the takings boosted. Not today. At eleven forty-five, she sticks the closed sign on the door, then scoots to the corner shop to buy two meat and potato pies, a bottle of pop and two Mars bars. She and Harry will have a bit of fun at dinner time. Maybe she'll let him come back to the shop and bunk off school.

Now, she runs for the station. If she's lucky and a train is in, she can do door to door in fifteen minutes. That leaves fifteen minutes for dinner. She gallops down the high street in her high heels and bare legs, immune to the cold. A window-cleaner gives her a wolfwhistle. She runs into the station in Cwmland and is first in the queue at the ticket office.

She pays for her ticket and turns to find Rose Tempest standing behind her.

'Oh, I didn't realise it was you, Kit,' Rose says,

alarmed. 'Are you off somewhere nice?'

'I wish.' Kit smiles, her eyes full of curiosity. 'I'm going to check on our Harry. He's only seven and no one's home today so he's all on his own at dinner time. He likes to think he's a big man but he's only a baby at heart. That's my train, see ya.'

'See ya. Bradford, please,' Rose asks the man in the ticket office.

'Single or return?'

'Single, please,' Rose requests firmly. 'A single to Bradford.' She glances around but Kit has already gone.

It hadn't taken Melody Tempest long to calculate where the best source of a loan to finance Lily's travel expenses lay. The only obstacle was pride – her own. That became less of a hindrance when the pawn shop in Cwmland refused to give her more than thirty bob for her new, unused pots and pans.

After work, she makes the fifteen-minute walk to the caravan site along a country lane that runs parallel to the sea. A fog rises from the sea and drapes itself around shrubs and trees, its long tendrils snaking out into the road, as if to trip her out of malice.

Round a bend, and suddenly lights lie ahead, dogs bark, a child screams; a strong smell of frying sausages wafts through the air, acting like a dose of smelling-salts on Melody's scattering senses.

To the left of the entrance to the caravan site is a gate that bears a wooden sign. It reads, 'Casa Procter'. The 'casa' is one large and two smaller caravans, linked by covered walkways. A garden has been created, using redundant lavatory pans and an old bath as flower-beds. The area is neat and tidy and illuminated by dozens of fairy-lights.

'All right?' says a boy who looks about twelve, as if the shorthand is sufficient to prompt a full explanation from this unexpected guest. Then, receiving no immediate response, he adds, 'Are you from the Education?'

Melody shakes her head. 'Is your mam around?' she asks.

The boy points to the largest caravan. 'She's feeding the little ones,' he says.

Melody walks up to the door and rings the bell, which plays the first few notes of 'Home Sweet Home'. Betty Procter opens the door, a young child on her hip and another in the room behind her seated at a table, eating a meal. Her hair is uncombed, her blouse half undone, but she gives the impression of a woman who has just been roused from a deep and invigorating sleep. Her movements are unhurried, her face is handsome.

'Is your husband home?' Melody asks politely.

Betty Procter gives a lazy smile. 'He's never home, that's why we get on so well. Brought the dog, have you?'

Melody looks blankly at her, then remembers the woman's request for one of Doug's cardboard dogs. 'Sorry, you'll have to see Doug about that.' Betty Procter says nothing. A teenage girl emerges sulkily to take the toddler from her. Then Betty beckons to Melody to follow. She opens the door of an old banger parked close by, switches on the engine and turns the heater up full blast. 'Get in.' She smiles. 'If you want peace

216

and quiet, get in and lock the door. They'll be all right for a bit.' Then, as if reading Melody's mind, she says, 'We like it here. It suits us. We could move into a house but that's a bit too ... permanent for me. Too flash. We've got money, no need to spread it around, is there?'

Melody flushes and is grateful for the darkness. 'I'd like to borrow some of that money,' she says quickly. 'Not for me ... for Lily. To get to London. I'll pay you back. It might take a little time, but I'll pay you back with interest... It's not much ... please.'

She expects the woman to ask precisely how much. Instead, Betty Procter takes her time, brushing her hair back with her hands and twisting it into a knot. Then she turns to look at Melody. 'What is this, then?' she says softly. 'Are you asking me to pay for the pleasure of having enjoyed the company of your husband?'

Melody's instinct is to hit out or leap from the car, slam the door and turn her back on the woman for ever. Instead she shuts her eyes and forces herself to focus on what she had seen on Lily's face, an appetite for life that had once gnawed at her, a very long time ago.

'As a matter of fact,' Betty Procter is speaking again sounding as if she is enjoying herself hugely, 'and I mean, as a matter of fact. We didn't. Me and your husband. We didn't. You know why? Because he refused. Turned me down, right at the last fence, as it were. To be frank, it made me ever so annoyed. It still makes me cross. I'm not used to being turned down. Not used to that at all. Course, it's up to you whether you believe me or not,' she adds slyly.

She leans forward and switches off both the engine and the heater. Melody says nothing. The silence grows.

'About the money,' Betty Procter says eventually, 'I've always had a rule in life never to lend money to strangers. So, until the day we become friends, Mrs Tempest, I'm afraid there'll be no lending between us. I'm sure you'll understand?'

'Yes, Mrs Procter,' Melody says with dignity. 'Yes, I understand that. There'll never be any lending between us.'

'Cod and chips and mushy peas, no salt and vinegar. And a pickled egg,' Pete the Mercenary says. Kath raises one eyebrow. 'Please,' he adds. He had hung across the road, waiting until the shop was empty.

'You'd better mind your Ps and Qs when you're around me, young man,' she says, 'or I'll have you in there and battered better than this piece of cod.' She dangles the white uncooked fish, dripping in a creamy coating and then drops it theatrically into the fat with a hiss. Pete watches as it bronzes and bloats to twice its size, and he gives an involuntary shudder.

'You said you wanted to see me,' he says, anxiety for his brother, and the need for a drink, making him even twitchier than usual.

Kath watches as he rotates each shoulder, then starts mindlessly singing along to the radio. Seeing the expression on her face, he stops. She leans towards him. 'Have you ever thought of television?' she asks.

'What?' Pete looks at her, uncomprehending. 'Have you ever thought of television? You, on television. On the box.' Kath enunciates her words very carefully as if she is talking to a moron.

'Don't be stupid.' Pete laughs, his whole body jiggling alarmingly, like a puppet in the hands of an amateur.

A boy of eight or nine comes into the shop. 'We're closed. Go away,' Kath barks.

The boy looks at her mouth open. 'But it's only five o'clock. What about our tea? My mam'll kill us if I go home without our tea. I only want six fish 'n' chips,' he adds wistfully.

'Fuck off.' Pete glowers at him. The boy does as he's told. Kath turns the sign on the door to 'Closed'. Then she beckons to Pete to come into the back and take a seat at the small table. 'Read that.' She gives him the letter outlining the details of the new quiz show.

After a matter of seconds, she snatches it off him impatiently. 'Look,' she says, 'they want couples. They want couples who can answer questions. Do you know what you and I know a lot about?'

'Haven't got a bloody clue,' Pete says, by now totally flummoxed.

'Murder.' Kath stabs him in his bony chest with her finger. 'Murder. That's what we know a lot about.'

Five minutes later, she has elaborated on her plan. She tells him that her intention is to appear on television in a quiz show. She focuses on the material advantages in the form of the booty they may win. She – and the right partner – are only an audition away from appearing on the screen.

So, what does he say?

'Not fucking likely,' is Pete's immediate response.

Kath's features contract unpleasantly as if her flesh has suddenly shrunk. 'What do you mean? Do you think you're not bright enough? Is that it?'

'Do you mind?' Pete remonstrates, gyrating both shoulders. 'I'm as bright as a button. I just can't. It wouldn't be... It wouldn't be smart. I've got responsibilities,' he adds.

Having faced more rebellion in the past few weeks than she's encountered in years, Kath has had enough. She stands up abruptly, a move that coincides with furious banging on the shop door.

'I'd have a think about that, if I were you, young man,' she says threateningly. 'What with your brother acting like a pervert and all...'

'Come on, eat up. It'll go cold, there's a good boy,' Chalkie White says to his son, ruffling his hair. It is seven thirty p.m. Chalkie has endeavoured to follow Rose's routine exactly, lighting the fire, calling Billy in from the street where the lads are playing. He'd nipped out earlier to the chippy for their tea and left it, still wrapped, warming in the oven, so the slight smell of singed paper hangs in the air. Neither had felt like eating. He has set the table: three places because he couldn't yet bring himself to tell the boy. How could he put into words what he couldn't believe himself?

Now Billy sits morosely, toying with his fish 'n' chips. 'When's Mam coming back?' he asks for the third time. Father and son, simultaneously,

220

push away their plates, barely touched.

'She's been a bit poorly and now she's shopping. That's where she is,' Chalkie says wearily. 'Tell you what, lad, why don't we get the old dartboard out and have a game until she gets back?'

'Maybe later, Dad,' the boy says.

Chalkie pulls him on his knee. He'll tell him a half-truth tomorrow. As preparation, he says, 'You know women, Billy, they're a funny lot. Just when they're happy doing one thing, they want to be up doing another and...'

They tense and look at each other as they hear the front door open and close. Rose, shivering, comes into the room, her eyes red-rimmed. Chalkie stands up. Silence. 'I've got your fish 'n' chips in the oven,' he hears himself say. Then he walks into the kitchen before she has time to read his face.

Billy bolts from the table and rushes to his mother, locking her in his arms. Later, as Rose sits mute, he asks her the same question again and again: 'Where's your shopping, Mam? Dad said you'd gone shopping. Where's your shopping?'

Rose had watched the train to Bradford arrive and depart. Then she had walked up and down the platform, trying to keep warm, her thoughts a jumble. She had been so determined, so elated when she'd left home, and all of that had been punctured in a few minutes. What had Kit said? Poor little Harry, a year older than Billy, all on his own in the house. The phrase had taken on the drumming rhythm of the trains on the tracks. All on his own. All on his own.

221

'Can I have my money back, please?' Rose had asked the man in the ticket office abruptly. He'd made her fill out a form in triplicate and announced that the money would be sent to her in due course in the form of a postal order.

'Had a funny turn, have you?' he'd asked, more curious than concerned.

Then Rose had walked along the road that the lorry drivers use. She'd decided that if a lorry stopped when she stuck out her thumb, she would have her answer. She would go, without looking back. If she left the decision to fate, it somehow eased the sense of betrayal.

As the first lorry drew close, ferrying sheep, she flapped her hand ineffectually and then let it drop again. The second and third, she put her thumb out determinedly but kept her back to the oncoming traffic, so they couldn't tell in her long, black coat whether she was treat or trout. The fourth time, she faced the lorry, stuck out her thumb firmly, and felt her heart lurch when the man put his brakes on hard.

'I'm going Birmingham way. Any good, love?' he'd asked.

She'd nodded her thanks, put her hand on the door handle, then been unable to move, as if her boots had taken root in the Tarmac.

'Are you coming or what?' he'd asked. Waited a couple of seconds and then revved up and was gone. She'd walked and walked until the disappointment and anger and frustration at what she saw as her own lack of will had turned to numbness. Then she'd come home to Chalkie and Billy, sitting at the table as if nothing had happened. She'd put her money back into the birdcage and washed up the dishes that had accumulated during the day. Chalkie had asked nothing of her, not even how she'd spent the hours away. He didn't even ask her to promise to stay. As if he knew it was a promise that, sooner or later, she would be bound to break.

Chapter Twenty-four

Singing a medley, I gaze into my dad's eyes as if he is the only man in the world for me and he reciprocates. That's show business. It is Monday night, our début at the Cow and Fiddle. I refused to wear Iris's bridesmaid's dress. Instead I've borrowed a black skirt and jumper from Rose, who is two sizes larger than I am. To my chagrin, Tommy Aster has insisted that I 'add a bit of glamour', by which he means his wife's ridiculous diamanté earrings.

While I'm expected to dress like Shirley Bassey at the Talk of the Town, odorous Aster has insisted that my dad look as if he's lost on a golf course, open-neck shirt, pullover and slacks. The good news is that there is a God. Divine intervention has ensured that it is raining hard. We have half a dozen in the audience, three of whom are asleep.

'Any requests from you lovely people?' my dad says, in his fake American accent. 'How about "My Old Man Says Follow The Van"?' asks a lady in the front row in a pink chiffon scarf. I swear her teeth are wrapped in a hankie in her hand.

My dad takes one look at my face and knows it's an indignity too far. 'I know something that will warm the cockles of your heart, sweetheart,' he says, bending down to lift the woman's hand to his lips, gazing into her eyes while trying to avoid kissing the dentures. 'Memories are made of this...' my dad begins. I pick up the tune on the piano; Albie has switched to the drums. I harmonise on the chorus. The audience clap in time. The minutes drag by. I look at my dad and he's actually enjoying himself. Jim Reeves's 'Welcome To My World'; Perry Como's 'Catch A Falling Star'. This is entertainment for the embalmed.

'Can you sing *The Sound of Music* for me, miss?' says a man with a walking-stick and a blackhead the size of a lump of coal on his nose.

'How about that lovely favourite, "Three Coins In A Fountain"?' My dad tries a counter-suggestion.

The old boy persists. 'I'll have Julie Andrews.'

'"Moon River"?' my dad presses on.

The old bloke is adamant.

'"Autumn Leaves"?'

Albie looks at me and shrugs. '*The Sound of Music* it is, then,' my dad says.

At the end of our set, as we come off the stage, a man who rarely ventures out of his revolutionary cell on a Monday night asks if he can buy us a drink. It's Barry Taylor. 'Thought I'd give you a bit of moral support,' he says. 'You were very good. Twice As Nice, eh? Lovely outfit, Lily,' he adds, and winks.

'How's it going?' my dad asks.

'Not bad. How's yourself? Any luck with a job?'

He doesn't wait for an answer. 'Come up to the factory, lad,' Barry says. 'It's shite work but it pays the rent. We've got a couple of vacancies.'

'Yeh,' my dad says, noncommittally.

Barry jerks his head towards me. 'She'll be off to college soon, I bet. Bloody marvellous. I wish my Bryn had it in him.'

My dad shifts his chair noisily.

'She needs all the encouragement she can get, she does,' Barry persists, almost as if trying to provoke a reaction.

'I'm not stopping her,' Dad says, swirling his pint and looking at the brown liquid as if it's the most interesting thing he's seen all night.

I don't know what game Barry is playing but it's definitely not going to be one in which I emerge a winner. Still, he means well. 'Pint?' he asks.

'Half, ta,' my dad says. 'We're back on soon.'

'I'll have a double gin and orange,' I ask cheerfully.

'So that's another lemonade,' Barry responds drily.

One advantage of an empty pub is that the service is quick. He's soon back, drinks in hand, smile on his face, a lecture on his lips. 'Kids today don't know how lucky they are,' he says, ignoring my groans. 'At fourteen, I was a drayman's boy, lugging barrels, working day and night, and fortunate to have a job that kept me outdoors. Then there was the war. And, of course, the factory got me eventually. Money's too good to turn down. Even if you hate every breathing moment you're inside. How about you, Doug, how old

225

were you when you left school?'

I've never heard my dad talk about his childhood to anyone outside the family. He barely says anything to us in the family. So I'm surprised when he replies: 'Fifteen. Mam left my dad. Dad blamed us. I got away as soon as I could. That's it, really. No different from a million other kids. After the forces I always promised I'd be my own man – and I have, from that day to this.

'Don't like unions,' he adds pointedly, looking directly at Barry. 'My father was three months off his pension. Had a bad chest. Usual caper. Asbestosis, but the company would have none of it. And the union did bugger-all. He was sacked for having too much time off on the sick and he didn't get a penny of the money they owed him, not a penny. I've never wept tears for my father but it taught me a lesson. You're better standing alone. Look after me and my family, and let everyone else fend for themselves, that's my creed.' My dad gives one of his best professional smiles. Barry grins back. I can see each one thinks the other couldn't be more wrong. That's how men converse – with smiles, smacks and silences.

'That'll do for a start,' Barry replies amiably 'Many a revolution has begun as a result of men looking after their own – but there comes a time when everybody needs a bit of back-up. I'm sorry it didn't work out for your dad.'

A few minutes later, Barry says his goodbyes. Just before we're due to go on stage again, the words I've been trying to suppress ever since Barry raised the subject spill out. 'I'm going to university, Dad. If it kills me, I'm going. You know

226

that, don't you?'

He says nothing but I can see that a muscle in his cheek is beating as hard as the breast of a bird in distress. 'Come on, girl,' he says. 'It's time to sing for our supper.'

'What are you doing in the dark, pal?' Pete asks gently. He is visiting belatedly, having discovered that Robert has failed to follow his usual routine for several days. Now Pete steers his brother into the kitchen and sits him on a chair. Robert is wearing his duffel coat but his nose is blue and his hands are those of a dead man.

'I've got a chilblain,' Robert suddenly says, with a tinge of pride.

'Have you, mate?' Pete asks. He switches on the two-bar electric fire and lights the gas oven, opening the door to heat the room. In spite of the cold, the milk in the bottle is sour. 'How about a nice hot cup of cocoa?' Pete asks.

As he waits for the kettle to boil, he watches his brother, who sits as if in a cocoon of misery. Pete is at a loss to find the right words, hampered by the growing ball of anger in his gut. That stupid cunt of a woman brought this about, he tells himself. She's put the fear of God in Robert.

'It's not her fault,' Robert says slowly. 'It's not Dulcie.'

'I know, mate,' Pete says. 'It's her sister. I know. But, look, there are plenty more birds out there, queuing up for you.'

For the first time, Robert looks at him. 'She's not a bird,' he says fiercely. 'She's my friend. And now I can't see her any more or the missus will have me locked up.'

'What's so good about her?' Pete asks, with a wink.

Immediately Robert grows agitated. 'It's not like that. She's interested in radios, you know. She asks me things and I tell her. She says she's never met anybody like me, good at radios and things. She says I'm kind.'

Pete gives his brother the cocoa and a pat on the back. Then he sets about clearing out the ashes, laying and lighting a fire. As he does so, he contemplates the fact that, for the first time in his life, he feels envious of Robert. He's found companionship, something Pete has never had with a woman.

Later Pete sits, smoking a cigarette, while his brother gently rocks back and forth in the chair as he used to do when he was young, staring into space. It's then that Pete has an idea. One that involves a small but acceptable sacrifice on his part.

He leans forward and pats his brother's knee reassuringly. 'It's going to be all right, Robert, my old son,' he says. 'It's going to be all right.'

Once a week, every week, Bryn and I go to the pictures. It doesn't matter what's on, we go. You can always tell which couples have access to a car. Those who own a motor watch the film. The majority poke and prod and rub and wrestle in the fake privacy of the semi-dark, the lads aware that if they don't make their serious move in the first few minutes everyone's eyes will have adjusted to the dark. They should put sub-titles on every film because, in the back, the breathing is so noisy you can barely hear the dialogue.

Bryn and I arrive late, after the film starts. The back row is full so the usherette shows us to seats in the middle of the half-empty cinema. It takes several minutes before I realise that the four heads in front of me are familiar. In the interval, when the lights go up, I give the tense and bony shoulder-blades in front of me a gentle poke. Kath turns around, a frown on her face. Next to her is Dulcie; on Kath's other side is Pete the Mercenary and to the left of him is Robert, wearing a helmet made of patent leather – which turns out to be excessive Brylcreem.

'Don't ask,' Kath instructs sharply.

Dulcie gives me one of her big smiles. 'We're coming to the pictures every week, aren't we, Robert?' she says excitedly.

'We're all coming,' Kath adds pointedly.

'What's going on?' I ask. Dulcie opens her mouth, then shuts it again, probably because Kath has reached out and is holding her wrist so tightly it makes her wince. Then the lights go down again.

At work, Pete tells me the deal that he has struck on Robert's behalf. He has agreed with Kath to audition for a television quiz show. She has agreed that Robert and Dulcie are allowed to meet once a week, strictly chaperoned, a concession that will be immediately withdrawn if Robert makes any advances.

'So, you're going to be a famous star on telly?' I say, helping Pete to stack bottles in the bar.

Pete looks miserable. 'I bloody well hope not.

229

The last thing I need is my mug on the box for all the world to see.' He cheers up. 'Still, not much chance of that, is there? How many people do you know round here have ever been on the telly?'

'What's the problem with being seen?'

Pete squints at me as if deciding whether or not to take me into his confidence. This usually signals an intensive dose of bullshitting. 'They've got a warrant out for me down south,' he says. I smile. 'I swear on my Hayley's life,' he adds, annoyed. 'They really have. Me and a mate did a bookie's. The police have got descriptions of us so if I go on the box that's me done for a year or three.'

'So where's all this money now, then?' I ask, not believing a word.

'I've spent most of it, of course. I gave some to the wife so she could clear off back to her mother and buy a new coat and some gear for the kiddie. I bought myself a mohair suit, hand stitched 'n' all. Lovely indigo blue. Just like the one Gene Pitney wore on the telly. I gave Robert a fiver. I took a girl to Liverpool for a night. I bought your telly and I might have just a little bit left over for a box of Milk Tray for you, if you're nice. What's it to you, anyway?' he asks slyly.

I resist the temptation to ask for a loan. 'First, you shouldn't have taken it, and second, you shouldn't have spent it. Don't you ever think of saving?'

'Of course I do,' he retorts, blowing smoke-rings with his cigarette. 'I think about it all the time. But this is somebody else's money. It wouldn't be right to keep it.'

Daisy and I watch the telly together, eating ice-cream with chocolate sauce as thick as mud. Sometimes my sister can be all right. Halfway through *The Avengers*, she rushes off to the kitchen and I can hear her chucking up in the sink. Mam is down the street, helping Mrs Stevens with her husband, Phil. Old Mr Stevens hasn't spoken to his wife in years and now he can't stop. He's just had a stroke. So he talks gobbledegook, his words all jumbled up – they gush out of him like water from a broken pipe.

Mam says the first note he wrote to his wife, after the stroke, said, 'Thank you, Edith.' It's strange that you can fight for years and years and suddenly surrender, just like that. Mam says it isn't strange and it isn't surrendering. Falling in love sometimes makes people really cross with the people for whom they've fallen. So that's another pleasure in store for me.

Daisy comes back into the room, her face so bleached that even the shadows under her eyes are almost white. 'Are you all right?' She nods. She moves closer to the fire and stares at the TV screen without really watching. Nobody in our house takes any interest in events in the outside world – man on the moon, starvation in Africa, strikes on the docks. What's that got to do with us?

'Do you think you and Bryn are going to get engaged?' she asks.

'God, don't you ever think of anything else?' I say.

The blow-up comes a few days after Rose's return. On the way back from school, she and

231

Billy chat as they cross the market square. Rose casually glances down the high street towards the quay. She stops when she sees her husband, relaxed and laughing, as he rarely is with her these days, his hand on a young woman's elbow, guiding the two of them into the post office.

Anger engulfs Rose like a sheet of flame. Only Billy's tug on her sleeve prevents her racing down the high street and – and what? What would she do? Confront him, humiliate herself, expose herself to ridicule and pity from neighbours and bystanders who are always hungry for the fodder of domestic disputes? All that would be worth it, she decides, for the sheer pleasure of catching him in the act.

Shaking, she steps out into the road and her son pulls her back sharply, as a cyclist skids in the slush, brakes screeching, flat cap tumbling. 'Mam!' Billy shouts, then laughs as she skates and slithers, struggling to keep her balance. As mother and son walk home together, Rose plots how she will corner and confront her husband. She can box him stupid with words, any day.

An hour later, Billy is sitting at the table, doing his homework, one eye on the television. Rose is upstairs putting the ironing away. Chalkie opens the front door. 'Anyone home?' he calls cheerily.

'In here, Dad,' Billy shouts.

Rose comes to the top of the stairs, hands filled with folded towels. Chalkie, sensing her presence, looks up and, instantly, all the plans she had made to ease the truth out of him by stealth are burst apart by one look at the pleasure on his face. 'How could you?' she screams, raining towels down on him with every word. 'How could you humiliate me with a girl in my own backyard? Didn't you give a damn who saw you? Is that what it's about? Mr Bloody Big-time with a wife at home and slut on the street?' Chalkie ducks and weaves as towels flap through the air like multicoloured birds of prey.

Briefly stunned by the suddenness of her attack, he curses and climbs the stairs two at a time, face set. Just as he reaches Rose, he hears his son's voice behind him, screaming in distress: 'Don't hit her, Dad, please don't hit her again.'

Again? Again? As Chalkie struggles to make sense of his son's use of the word, Rose puts two hands on her husband's chest and pushes hard.

For a split second, both Rose and Chalkie wobble at the top of the stairs as Billy's pleadings fill their ears. Chalkie grabs hold of the banister and takes the full force of Rose as she falls against him, losing her footing. Her chin hits the banister, teeth slice into her tongue. Her grimace is suddenly bright, bright red, ear to ear, like the exaggerated smile of a clown. 'Christ, woman,' Chalkie sobs.

He holds her to him as best he can, bewildered at the way in which violence has invaded his family with such unpredictability and force, as if he and Rose no longer have a will of their own. 'Oh, Rose–' Then the door slams, and Billy is gone, driven out, in flight. Chalkie, in pursuit, reaches the street first. It is already empty, except for the mist creating dancing ghosts, whipped into movement by the wind. 'If something happens to Billy...' Chalkie says, tears pouring down his face.

But Rose, coatless, is already running down the road, shouting her son's name.

Chalkie, his thoughts scattered, leans against the wall. In the distance, he can hear the voice of a child, screaming, 'I hate you, I hate you ... I hate you all...'

Kath is taking out her curlers when I visit. She looks at me suspiciously. 'What's that?'

'It looks like a pile of magazines to me,' I reply.

'Don't you be so mouthy, my girl,' my aunt says, her jaws working agitatedly as if she's chewing the cud.

I take a seat, mischief in mind, and aimlessly flick through one of the magazines.

'Don't make yourself comfortable either. I've got to be in work in five minutes.'

I pretend I haven't heard. 'Come on, Kath. Tell us what you wore. Was it a ballerina-length white-lace number? Or a neat little two-piece in a register office?'

'You know your trouble,' Kath answers, 'you ask too many questions.'

'Seriously, though,' I persist. 'I thought now that Dulcie and Robert are... friends, it might be all right if she could borrow these again and perhaps even–'

'Never,' Kath interrupts flatly. She is always at her most comfortable when at her most dogmatic. She takes the ashes to the backyard, washes her hands in the kitchen and returns. Still without speaking, she picks up the *Daily Mirror*. 'Terrible this,' she says, pointing to the centre spread, which details the continuing search for the missing boy,

Daniel Andrews. 'Poor little mite,' Kath adds. 'The animals would've got him by now.'

Since the business with Dulcie, I've rapidly come to the conclusion that Kath hasn't a single saving grace. She is selfish, narrow, possessive, ignorant, bigoted, unfair and, given half a chance, probably violent. A Beatles song plays softly on the radio. Kath reaches out and snaps it off. I flick through one of the bridal magazines and succumb again to the desire to give her the needle – but with a constructive goal in mind: Dulcie's future.

'Kath, I think Robert's a good friend for Dulcie, don't you? Now that you've got to know him. I mean, he's not a maniac or anything, is he? He's harmless. I bet he'd make a better husband than most of the blokes around here. One day something might happen to you, and we might not be around, so Dulcie needs other people in her life. It's only right.'

'I'm not planning on going anywhere. Are you?' Kath asks sarcastically, looking at me over the top of her glasses. 'So as that's two of us not going anywhere, Dulcie doesn't need anybody else. You know my views on this subject. I made a promise when she was born that I would take care of her and that's what I intend to do. If I don't know what's best for her, who does?'

I open my mouth to reply but before I have a chance to speak, the metal flap on the letter-box bangs loudly. Kath reacts to it as if it's a starting pistol. She sprints to the front door and returns, holding a letter, hands shaking. She rips open the envelope and reads the brief note. Then, much to my surprise, she executes a jig. 'We're in!' she

235

shouts. 'We're in! We've got an audition. Two of us. Manchester. Oh, my God. Thank you, thank you, thank you. Oh, my God. I saw a programme last week and the woman won three lovely crocodile handbags. Oh, my God. Me. On the telly. Don't tell a soul,' she adds incongruously.

'Congratulations, Kath. What do you mean, don't tell a soul?'

'I don't want any of the nosy so–and–sos around here knowing. It's my business, thank you very much.'

'But if you get through, of course they'll see you. Millions will probably see you.'

'That's different,' Kath replies primly.

I get up to leave. 'Whoa!' Kath says. 'I told you, take all those magazines away with you, madam, or I'll put them straight in the bin. We'll have no silly ideas in this house, thank you very much.'

I retaliate. 'Silly ideas? What can be sillier than the most bloodthirsty widow ever to man a fish 'n' chip shop and Pete, Mr Dick Indecent, in person, answering questions from some third-rate comedian about garrotting, dismembering and stabbing to death in the hope that the pair of you might win a sodding Teasmaid? Dulcie walking up the aisle in a white dress is perfectly sane in comparison. So don't talk to me about silly ideas. And you asked me if I was planning on going somewhere. Well, as a matter of fact I am. I'm going to university a long way from here. In fact, as far as I can get.'

'We'll see what your father has to say about that,' Kath shouts, as I bang out of the house.

Chapter Twenty-five

Half an hour later, Dulcie is sitting in the corner of the Contented Sole, eating a bag of chips, when Lily comes flying in. Kath, filling the salt cellars, frowns at her disapprovingly. 'Have you seen our Billy?' Lily asks. 'Has he been in here? He left home over half an hour ago and nobody's seen him since.' The two women shake their heads.

'You don't know who's out there these days. Think of that other poor little lad, still out there, still not found. Oh, my God, do you think he's got our Billy?'

Lily ignores her. 'If Bryn comes in, will you tell him to go to Mam's house and bring the other lads – the more people looking the better. See you later.'

Then she is gone. Dulcie follows her to the door. 'And where do you think you're going?' Kath demands. Dulcie doesn't look back. 'I'm going to get Robert. We can look for Billy too. If he's hiding, he'll come out for me. He likes me. Don't say anything, Kath,' she shouts defiantly over her shoulder, 'because I'm not listening.'

In Rydol Crescent, Doug directs operations, anxiety deepening the lines on his face. He endeavours to give Chalkie and Rose reassurances. 'He'll come back when he's cold and hungry... He's probably in a friend's house, we'll soon find him... Probably gone on a bus ride.'

237

At each suggestion, Rose shakes her head, fear easily winning the battle against reason.

Melody comes up behind Doug as he stands in front of the fireplace, running his hand through his hair distractedly, and places her arms around his waist, pressing her face into his back, unable to speak of the guilt that she knows Billy's disappearance will have reawoken in her husband.

After some debate, Daisy is dispatched to inform the police. Iris volunteers to visit Billy's friends. 'Don't say he's gone missing,' Melody warns, mindful of the neighbours even in a crisis. 'Just say he's late home.'

Chalkie sets off to walk the road to Cwmland, silently making all kinds of pacts with God and the Devil, just so long as Billy is returned home safely. Billboards outside three newsagents along the way reflect his worst fears. 'Daniel: Hunt Continues for Lost Boy.'

As he walks, faster and faster, sometimes breaking into a trot, he sees a small figure ahead, a blur in the mist. As the child turns, alarmed at the sound of running footsteps, two long plaits swing out. Chalkie stops dead and doubles up as if disappointment has swung a heavy punch. Billy isn't missing, he tries to reassure himself, he hasn't been gone long enough. He's just away from home. And when he comes back things will be different. 'I promise you that, son,' Chalkie whispers into the creeping fog. 'I promise you that.'

Daisy pours pennies into the phone box outside the burnt, half-demolished building that is Bunting's. Carl cruises around the estate in his dad's van while Melody waits at Rose's. Doug dispatches himself to the quay and Lily volunteers to go with Rose to the park. First they walk in silence. Lily slips her arm through her sister's and is rewarded with a squeeze. 'He'll be fine,' Lily feels obliged to say.

'He'd better be,' Rose answers, in a voice that is partly pleading, partly defiant.

Dusk has begun to fall, so the park gates are already locked. Both women go to the gap in the mesh netting that the children use out of hours. It's a squeeze. Lily begins to laugh, then tries to stop. 'Sorry,' she says.

'It's OK,' her sister says. 'It's not a funeral.' Then she bites her lip.

Together they walk past the battered swings and a merry-go-round from which most of the slats have been removed, leaving only the iron skeleton. The seesaw is an informal noticeboard carved with dozens of messages, most of them crude. A single light near the tennis courts flickers on and off unsteadily, stirring up the shadows.

'Christ, this is spooky,' Lily says, as they quicken their pace. 'Do you really think he'd come here by himself?'

'Billy!' Rose shouts in answer, at the top of her voice. 'Billy, it's Mam. Billeee!' A cat flees from a nearby bush, making both women jump. 'Do you remember the time we got flashed at?' Rose whispers, as if the dark hides a thousand eavesdroppers.

Lily starts to laugh, then finds herself unable to stop. Soon Rose joins in, gasping between the giggles, eyes streaming.

'You got me a smack around the legs for that,' Rose says, when she has calmed down, and anxiety, briefly held at bay, floods back. 'You were always getting me smacks. We weren't supposed to be in the park – where was it? Doncaster? Southampton? Because it was late. And this little old man said he'd got sweeties for us, then he showed us his willy. I was nearly sick and absolutely petrified, but you were only four or five and didn't have a clue. You kept peering at it, like it was a caterpillar that you'd never seen before. And then he took fright because a bloke came out of the fog walking his dog. I made you swear not to tell, and what's the first thing you do when we get home? Tell the whole bloody lot to Mam, exaggerating as usual, saying this man in the park had shown us his great big wiggly snake that he could make do whatever he wanted.'

Lily gives her sister a hug. 'Do you think we could... I mean, we used to get on ... if you know what I mean ... a bit better than...' She runs out of steam.

Rose stops at the locked door of the cricket pavilion and tries to peer through its glass panels. 'Billy!' she shouts, then turns and yells into the gloom. 'Billy, are you there? Come on, love, nobody's cross.'

'I don't think he's here, Rose,' Lily says gently. 'I bet by the time we get back, he'll be home and watching the telly...'

'Do you think?' She begins to retrace her steps. Then her heart stops. Under a bush, a hundred yards away, she sees what looks like a foot in a white sock: Billy's white football socks.

As she runs, she can hear herself making an animal-like howl. 'Billy, Billy...'

Lily arrives at the spot first. Afraid, she drags at the leg, scratching her arms and face with the brambles. Then, she sinks to her knees, weak with relief. In her hands is a white paper bag with half an iced bun inside. 'Next time I see someone drop even the tiniest bit of litter, I'll strangle them on the spot,' she promises. 'Murder doesn't happen in places like this. He'll be fine. I know he will,' she adds fiercely.

They walk in silence for a time, until they reach the gap in the fence and the brightness of the street-lights. Rose leans against the park gates, exhausted by anxiety. 'What you said, about us getting on,' she says. 'It's not you. It's me. It's how I feel. Resentful, angry, stupid, really. You'll be all right, you're going to get qualifications.' She makes the word sound weighty. 'But what happens to people like me? I'm not thick enough not to care and not clever enough to find a way out.'

'If you hadn't had Billy, you could've done what I'm doing,' Lily says tentatively, anxious not to jeopardise this new rapprochement with her sister.

'There you go again,' Rose replies savagely. 'You make it sound like I had a choice. But what choice did I have? No bloody money for an abortion. Everybody acting as if I was committing murder by even thinking about it. I didn't make a choice. I just let things happen. Never have kids, Lily,' she adds bitterly. 'They work their way into your flesh like a thousand tiny hooks so whichever way you move, whatever you do, you bleed. Believe me, I'd give anything in the world, my own life, to see Billy walk towards me now,' Rose gives her sister a glance, 'but sometimes, just for a fraction of a second, I wish he wasn't in my life. Sometimes, I just want to run and run and run away from Chalkie and Billy and always having to do something for somebody else, never for myself. Do you think that's really terrible of me? Do you, Lily?'

'No, of course, I don't,' Lily lies. If the circumstances had been less fraught, she would have told her sister to stop moaning and look at the positive side of her life – aware that that would make her sound annoyingly like her mother. Instead, as they walk down the high street, Lily changes the subject, trying to distract her sister from the endless possibilities attached to her son's flight. 'Are you still writing, Rose?' she asks, as they turn into Rydol Crescent. 'I used to love the stories you told us when we were small. I remember you had them written in an exercise book with a bright red cover. It had "Do Not Enter" on the front. Me and Iris found it. We always found everything. I mean–'

'They were rubbish,' Rose interrupts.

'You won two prizes.'

'That doesn't mean it wasn't crap,' she corrects her sister fiercely. 'Do I write? Of course I don't bloody write. I've got something far more important to do. Haven't you noticed? I'm a wife! I'm a mother. When would I have time to write? To write you need a private income, a cleaner, a hysterectomy before you conceive your first child, and a husband who doesn't think you're nuts because you put squiggly lines on paper and who doesn't mind that his wife has interests other than him. How many women out there do you think that describes?'

Lily wraps her arm around her sister's shoulders. 'I'm so sorry, Rose,' she says, not quite sure for whom or what she is apologising.

It's then that Rose makes a silent promise. If Billy comes home safely, she will put herself and her own needs second, like a proper mother. She will stay. If she can.

'Hello, lovey.' Alice beams a welcome. Taff's is packed with lorry drivers, at different time zones in their working 'day', either eating cooked dinners of gargantuan proportions or swallowing massive breakfast fry-ups. 'And who's this, petal?'

Dulcie advances shyly towards the counter, pulling Robert by the hand, their first official unaccompanied outing. 'This is my friend, Robert.'

'Hello, Robert. Like a cup of tea?'

Robert lifts his eyes from the lino floor. He looks at Dulcie as if for guidance. 'Next time, please, Alice,' Dulcie says. 'We're looking for Billy. He's about this big.' She gestures with her hand. 'He's our Rose's boy and he's run away from home. Been gone a long time now. All afternoon. Nobody can find him and his mam and dad are ever so sad.'

'Leave it with me.' Alice smiles reassuringly. She steers them to an empty table and, disregarding their refusal, places two cups of tea in front of them with two Penguin biscuits. Then she grabs the pudding spoon of a customer to her right, who is just about to tuck into jam roly-poly

243

and custard. She whacks the Formica table several times with it, making Dulcie giggle.

Alice rapidly has the attention of all those in the room, the majority of whom lay down their forks and pick up their fags. Two dozen men draw tobacco heavily into their lungs and exhale like a squad of synchronised smokers.

'We've got a little boy missing here, lads,' Alice bellows. 'Been missing a couple of hours...' She repeats Dulcie's description, suggesting that they should give her a ring at the café, use their citizen's band radio or contact the police in Fairport if they spot him. 'Thanks, lads.' She smiles.

'Where are they all going?' Dulcie asks, as Alice joins her and Robert at their table.

'All over the country, pet. If Billy's out there on the road, one of them'll find him.'

'They haven't found the other boy. The one that's still missing,' Dulcie frets. 'I don't like to think of Billy out there by himself. What if the murderer finds him first?'

Bashfully, Robert places his arm around her and says, 'Don't worry, Dulcie, I'll look after you.'

Doug Tempest is too preoccupied to return the nods of acquaintances on the quay as they make their way home or carry out a final fleeting errand to purchase something for tea. The whole town operates on the same timetable: wake, work, eat, sleep. Now, drawing near to one of the boats docked on blocks for the winter, he hears scuffling, like steel wool scraped across wood. It comes from under a tarpaulin. 'Billy,' he whispers into the dark, pulling back the sheet. 'It's your grandad, come out, son.'

'Oh, God,' says a small female voice. 'It's Tempest, the grocer.

'Please don't tell my mam, Mr Tempest. Don't tell her.'

Doug glimpses a girl's shoe and the creamy face of the lad who works in the milk depot. 'Go home before you catch pneumonia,' he says, covering them again.

A few minutes later, fruitlessly walking from boat to boat, he hears the couple make their escape. He turns and the girl gives a little wave. 'Ta ever so, Mr Tempest,' she says, 'for not saying.'

He makes his way back up the high street, a man without religion who believes profoundly in retribution. An eye for an eye. He has lived with the constant fear that, one day, a price will be exacted not from him but from his family for the sin he had committed. Keep them close, guard them constantly – and then Billy slips away. If the boy is returned safe perhaps that will force him to face the ghosts of his past, end the dishonesty that has contaminated the years. Doug throws his cigarette butt into the gutter and stops as a bout of coughing rakes his ribs.

In the glow of the street-lamp, one half of Bunting's stands semi-intact, upstairs and downstairs, revealed to the street like a doll's house with the front removed. The other half is charred, blackened and under demolition. The whole has been encased in temporary metal fencing plastered with 'Keep Out!' signs. The demolition of the premises has proceeded slowly. Standing in front of the shop, impervious to the occasional passing bus that sprays him with mud, Doug notices that the weighing scales have gone.

Made of brass and polished daily, they stood in the centre of the main counter; a pyramid of weights parked alongside, symbols of unquestionable fairness. Now scales and weights have been spirited away. He knew they had survived the fire because he had seen them the following day, untarnished. Doug lights up another cigarette, draws in deeply, and takes comfort from the fact that whoever took them, unless he'd had a forklift truck handy, would have undoubtedly suffered a hernia in the process.

Then, it comes to him. He knows where Billy is hiding.

At five o'clock on the dot, Monday to Friday, the police station on the square shuts up shop. It is also closed on Saturday and Sunday. At five past five PC Roberts bikes home. He and colleagues from Cwmland work a shift rota so that there is emergency cover in the evenings and at weekends. Except that, in Fairport, emergencies rarely occur.

Now he lets himself in quietly at the back door of his house. Mrs Roberts claims she is suffering from flu and has remained in bed all day, much to her husband's joy. If she's upstairs, the usual rigorous regime – no shoes on the carpet, no pipe in the lounge, no newspaper in the lavatory, no chips except with fish on Fridays – is suspended. He makes himself a cup of tea and is just about to dunk the first of two chocolate fingers in it when the doorbell rings.

'Sorry to bother you,' says Daisy Tempest. PC Roberts has always thought her the prettiest of the sisters. Small snub nose, blonde hair like her mother and bright blue eyes. 'Who is it?' his wife shrieks down the stairs, not so ill that vigilance goes by the board.

PC Roberts ignores her query and ushers Daisy in, defiantly leading her through to the kitchen when usually Eluned Roberts places all guests in the lounge.

'I came to the station but it was closed,' Daisy begins again.

PC Roberts realises she is close to tears. 'Sit down, my dear,' he says, pouring her tea and pushing the mug towards her.

'It's our Billy. We've tried all his friends. All the usual places. Lily and his mam are in the park, his dad's walking the streets. My dad's down the quay. He's not been gone this long before. We've just got this feeling … what with that little boy missing.'

PC Roberts pats her hand and replies gently, 'He'll come back. They always do. Is he in a spot of trouble or–'

He stops and Daisy follows his gaze. Standing in the doorway is Mrs Roberts. She is dressed in a high-necked white nightgown and a blue candle-wick dressing-gown designed for warmth rather than glamour. Daisy takes one look at her and thinks, Poor PC Roberts. Then, before she can help herself, she vomits all over the pompoms on Mrs Roberts's sensible checked carpet slippers.

Chapter Twenty-six

'Wake up, son,' Doug says, pushing a slick of hair from the boy's forehead. 'It's time to go home.'

Billy is lying under the counter in the intact rear of the shop where sugar and flour used to be weighed and butter sliced and packed. He has made a bed of a couple of empty sacks. Flour has left its imprint on his face and clothes, like a layer of dust. 'You look like Rip van Winkle,' Doug gently chivvies. 'Remember him? Lazy so-and-so slept for a hundred years, woke up and wanted his tea.'

He blows warmth into the child's hands. Then he slips off his jacket and raises the boy so he can cover his shoulders. 'Billy,' Doug says again.

Billy opens his eyes, and smiles. He knew his grandad would come. 'Why did you run?' Doug asks, crouching under the counter, alongside him. 'We've all been worried.'

'Is Mam upset?' Billy asks, and appears satisfied when Doug nods. 'She's going to leave. I know she's going to leave. She hates me and my dad. I know she does. I heard her shouting at my dad. They're always shouting.' Billy's face reddens with anger and fear.

Doug does what he is unable to do with his own children. He reaches out, puts his arms around the boy and holds him fast, rocking him gently. 'Your mother loves you more than she can say.

248

And your dad. It's just a spot of trouble. That's part of growing up, learning how to live with a spot of trouble...'

'I thought if I ran away Mam would know what it was like to miss me. I was going to go far away. And then it got dark so I changed my mind. I thought I might as well wait here until you came and found me. I wasn't scared,' Billy adds, with bravado. 'And I'm not going back. Ever. Promise me, Grandad, that Mam won't leave us. Will you promise?'

Doug looks into his grandson's eyes. He opens his mouth but the words of reassurance fail to form. 'I can't do that, lad,' he says, holding the boy's face in his hands. 'I can't make a promise for somebody else. Nobody can.'

Two days after Billy's return, I am on my own at home at dinner time, having bunked off school. I am about to write cancelling my interviews 'for family reasons'. I refrain from adding, 'namely, that my family are both broke and buggered if they can see any point at all in further education'. Broke, I admit, is partly my fault. I have a Saturday job. I could have saved but it's not in my nature. I earn and spend. 'Earn and Spend' is the Tempest family motto.

'What are you doing?'

Rose's voice makes me jump. She has a tendency to creep about, like a ghost who hasn't yet found a satisfactory place to haunt. 'Nothing,' I lie. 'Are you all right? You look as if you've got TB or polio or something.' She seems to have shed two stone in forty-eight hours.

'Let's go out,' she says. 'I get sick of being indoors. If it's not this house, it's my house or it's the hotel. Let's go where there's a bit of life...' We both look at each other blankly. 'Life' is not to be had in Fairport. Not in broad daylight on a weekday.

'Ravelli's?' we say together. The milk bar is as good as it gets. It's hot and steamy and loud and the juke-box is always upbeat. Mr Ravelli banned all ballads after his wife died because they made him cry into his ice-cream sundaes.

Ten minutes later we order hot chocolate and, on Rose's insistence, we sit in one of the booths away from the windows. Lesley Gore is on the juke-box, singing 'It's My Party...' which, although miserable, is sufficiently bouncy to pass the management's test. Mr Ravelli is happily squirting whipped cream and joining in the chorus.

'Here,' Rose suddenly says, 'take this.' She pushes something covered in what looks like birdseed towards me. 'Christ, it's not a dead budgerigar, is it?' I ask facetiously.

'Take it,' she says again. 'Don't ask me any questions and don't tell anyone I gave it to you. I want you to use it to go to the interviews. I want you to do well in those interviews, do well in your exams, and then go to university. If you don't, you'll regret it for ever. I know you will. You go for it, Lily. Never mind Dad or Mam, you do this for yourself. Pick it up!' she orders.

I do as I'm told, and immediately realise that the package is a bundle of notes. I have never seen so many pound notes before in one go. 'How much is it?'

'Twenty-six pounds. You'd better buy a decent suit or something before you go too. Call it an investment,' she adds drily. 'One day you can pay me back with interest. Perhaps, when the time comes, you can encourage Billy to try for that little bit extra too.'

I open my mouth to ask her a stream of questions but Rose shakes her head. One minute, life's a brick wall and the next it's a fireworks display and you're certain that anything, absolutely anything, is possible. 'Oh, Rose!' The words come out as a scream and everybody in the milk bar turns to look. I don't give a damn. I pull Rose out and waltz her round and round in the aisle. 'Don't be daft, Lily,' she protests smiling. 'Just do your best. And bring a present back from London for our Billy.'

'Same time, same place!' Kath wipes her hands down her white coat. 'I'll put the books in the back.'

Pete the Mercenary looks down at his brothel-creepers, fake leopardskin, with large silver buckles – a memento of his teddyboy days.

'What you need to do,' says Kath, looking at him sternly, 'is find some decent clothes to wear and mug up on Jack the Ripper. They always ask about him.'

Pete has been coming into the fish 'n' chip shop late morning before the dinner rush starts for a half an hour or so of Kath's testing. Her behaviour towards him is still frosty, no matter how many questions he answers correctly. 'What about you? Got yourself something nice to wear, have you?' Pete asks nonchalantly, helping himself to a sweating saveloy.

'That'll be sixpence to you. My boss will be counting how many of those went out and how much money went in the till, and I don't see why I should subsidise your petty thieving. As it happens, I have got something to wear. It's a black two-piece.'

'How old?'

'What do you mean, how old?' Kath bridles.

'How old is the bloody suit?'

'I bought it for my father's funeral, if you must know. I wasn't going to go but then I did and...'

Pete raises an eyebrow.

'It's good enough for me. I'm not spending money on something that'll only ever get worn once.'

'What makes you say that?' Pete asks. 'At your age, you've probably got quite a few funerals ahead of you. Invest now for the future, is my advice. That wasn't a smile I saw then, was it, Mrs Morgan? Fuckin' hell...'

If it was a smile, it evaporates instantly at the profanity. 'That's the trouble with young men like you,' Kath says grumpily, cross that she has allowed herself to soften, however briefly. 'Give you an inch, and you'll take my whole backyard and the contents of the house with it. I know your sort.'

'I expect you do, sweetheart.' Pete winks to annoy her further. 'See you.' He slams the door with relish, so the jangle of the bell follows him up the street.

I take Rose at her word and the three of us, Kit, Penny and I, go shopping in Tolmeath an hour's bus ride away, further along the coast. It has a big Marks & Spencer and a Wimpy where we eat cheeseburgers and chips and an ice-cream on a stale doughnut, covered in chocolate sauce. I also have a strawberry milkshake.

'How can you eat so much and not get fat?' Penny asks. 'Or do you starve for days on end?'

'Why would I do that?' I ask, between mouthfuls.

'For the modelling, of course.' She knows. Of course they both know.

'I made it up,' I say bluntly. 'I don't know why. It just came out.'

'Oh, I am sorry.' Kit wraps her arms around me, as if she's personally responsible for my failure to get on the cover of *Honey*.

'Anything else about you that's a lie?' Penny sounds a touch condescending.

'Not that I know of,' I answer lightly.

In Chelsea Girl I shop with the sense of liberation that only those spending another person's money can know. I buy a plum-coloured suit. It has a double-breasted three-quarter jacket and a mini-skirt. I also buy a cream polo-neck and cream tights, a plum and pink suede belt with dangly bits, a cream beret and plum patent shoes with a stack heel, which are a wee bit tight but the pain is worth it.

Penny, annoyingly, buys an almost identical outfit except that her suit is brown. We persuade Kit to stay away from yet another pair of white high heels. Instead, we help her to choose an

253

olive green suede mini-skirt, black boots and a black polo-neck.

Apart from her headlamp glasses and the black roots on her blonde beehive, she looks good. Should we become single again, and we hunt in twos, I'll be stuck with the ugly one.

Kath fumes. Pete has disappeared for two days and failed to materialise for their final preparations for the television audition. She checks the Grand Metropolitan. He hasn't reported for work. She marches Robert to her house, as if he might act as a magnet, and cross-questions him about the whereabouts of his brother, anger mounting. 'He sometimes does this,' Robert says nervously.

'Does what?'

'He sometimes goes off without telling anyone.'

'How long for?'

Robert smiles helpfully. 'Oh, sometimes months and months. But he always comes back.'

'But he promised me!' Kath splutters. 'He said he'd come to the shop today and then he'd go with me to Manchester. We had an agreement. He as good as promised.'

'Oh dear,' Robert says, looking at Kath sympathetically Privately he is pleased. For the first time he has discovered something that he and this frightening woman have in common: Pete. Or, rather, Pete's inability to keep his word.

Later, much to Dulcie's surprise, Kath leaves her and Robert together when she retires, crushed, to bed. 'She's crying,' Robert says shortly after.

Dulcie nods. 'She often cries like that but it's usually in the night when she thinks I'm asleep.'

'What's she got to cry about?' Robert asks. 'I mean, besides Pete?'

Dulcie shrugs. 'Me, I expect,' she says sadly.

The following morning Kath, tight-lipped, looks into the mirror at the Contented Sole and sees nothing, a reflection of the vast emptiness that exists within her heart. Kath Morgan and Pete Wells will not be participating after all in the auditions for *Double or Quit.* Yet again she has been betrayed by a man.

That evening Pete arrives at Kath's front door, a new suitcase in hand, a handsome, expensive camel coat on his back and leather gloves on his hands. 'Don't let him in,' Kath bellows down the stairs. 'If I lay hands on him, I'll murder him.'

'That's the spirit.' Pete winks at Dulcie and squeezes past her. She dutifully follows him into the back room. 'Make us a cup of tea, there's a good girl,' he says, rubbing his hands together. 'It's so cold out there it'll freeze the fucking brass balls off a monkey.'

Dulcie blushes and retreats into the kitchen to do as she's told. Kath appears, hope battling with indignation. 'Where the hell have you been?' she demands. 'Just walking out like that! What have you got to say for yourself?'

'Good evening, my old sunshine,' Pete replies cheekily. 'I apologise but I was unexpectedly called away on business. Business in our mutual interest. Allow me, madam.'

Dulcie arrives with the tea. Pete places his suitcase on the table and opens it with a flourish. 'First, something for the little lady,' he says. 'If you don't mind me saying, you two need to loosen up a bit. Know what I mean? So, this is for stepping out, Dulcie my old love.'

Dulcie gasps with delight, as Pete pulls out a turquoise twopiece. 'I reckon you're a size sixteen, is that right? Get yourself a nice pair of black boots and you'll be our Robert's little darling. Do you for a honeymoon that would, wouldn't it, Kathleen, my *compadre*-in-arms?'

Kath looks at Pete suspiciously. 'Have you been smoking those cigarettes?' she asks, her waspishness tempered by her need for his co-operation.

'Of course I have, Kathleen, and washed them down with a couple of large whiskies,' he answers truthfully. 'Shut your eyes,' he instructs. 'Now, open them!'

Kathleen obeys. Pete stands in front of her holding in each hand a hanger. On one is a lilac wool suit with a co-ordinating patterned blouse; in the other is a dark grey swing-back coat. 'You'll have to get the shoes and bag but I'll give you a tenner for them,' Pete says, handing her the clothes and pulling a handful of notes out of his pocket.

'Oh, and this is for Robert,' he adds, clearly relishing his role. He gives Dulcie a bulky, multi-patterned dark blue cardigan.

'Thank you.' She kisses his cheek, wincing at the pungent taste of recently and copiously applied aftershave.

'Try them on,' Pete tells Kath. 'Then we'll have one last go at the old Jack the Ripper ding-dong and that should do us nicely.'

'Are these stolen goods?' Kath asks bluntly.

'Now, is that something to ask a gentleman?'

Pete replies amiably. 'I have been recompensed for several days' hard labour and a bit of a win on the old gee-gees. Besides, I don't want you alongside me in some bloody old suit smelling of the crematorium, if you don't mind. That'll depress me something rotten. Somebody around here has to have standards. Now, go and try on the bloody gear.'

Much to his surprise, Kath takes the clothes and walks towards the door, then stops. Pete sighs.

She turns, and stretches her lips in what might be a warming-up exercise, preparatory to a smile. 'Actually, I quite like lilac,' she says.

Chapter Twenty-seven

My conversation with Bryn goes like this.

Me: 'Our Billy ran away. We didn't find him for hours.'

Bryn: 'Yeh?'

Me: 'I'm going down to London for a couple of interviews.'

Bryn: 'London?'

Me: 'Yes.'

Bryn: 'Our dad went to London once. Hated it. He only likes ports.'

Me: 'London is a port.'

Bryn: 'Are you coming down the club tonight? We're practising.'

So much for a supportive discussion on my future prospects. I do go to the club, to get out of the house and to see Penny and Kit. I've got a pocketful of Rose's pound notes and a continuing urge to spend. We end up swigging cider from the bottle in the ladies' lav while the lads plonk away in the hall.

Only then do I realise that Kit has several carrier bags with her. 'I've left home,' she says, looking defiant. 'I'm going to stay with Podge and his mam. It'll be fab. I'll have my own bedroom, and they've got fitted carpets, even in the upstairs. Podge's mam is nice. She's only charging me thirty bob a week. Except she's told us we'll have to get engaged, keep it respectable, or the neighbours will talk.'

'Engaged? Are you mad?' I say.

'Engaged?' Penny also says, in a totally different tone. 'You lucky cow.'

'Is it Sally?' I ask. 'Has she told you to go?'

'I don't want to talk about it,' Kit says, her glasses misting up. 'My dad doesn't want me to go but I want him to be happy and...' She takes a big gulp of cider.

'I'll ask my mam,' I offer. 'See if you can stay with us. If you don't mind sharing a bedroom with Daisy and Iris and me.'

'I'll ask Mummy too, if you like,' Penny offers.

Kit doesn't appear over-keen at the idea of staying with the Wilsons. I wonder why, since she's paraded Penny, Don and Adele like a trio of trophies ever since we first met. 'I've packed in my job too,' she announces, clearly beginning to relish her role as the diva of doom. Her eyes seem as large as portholes behind her glasses.

'This is clearly a seismic moment in your postpubescent life,' Penny, who is doing sociology A level, announces.

'Or, to put it another way,' Kit responds drily, lighting up a fag, 'I'm fucked.'

To try to demonstrate her nonchalance, she saunters over to the mirror and begins to back-comb her hair, viciously spraying lacquer in all directions. A man could break his fingers trying to run them through her coiffure. 'Nice,' Penny says insincerely, to cheer her up. 'Really groovy.'

Kit ignores her and looks at me. 'I've got a job in the fish 'n' chip shop. Only occasional shifts, but it'll do for now.'

'What – with Kath?'

'She's all right.'

'Here,' I say, taking advantage of the fact that I am temporarily a woman of means. 'Have a quid.'

Kit is not one to ask about the source of such unexpected generosity. 'Thanks.' She takes it before I can think twice.

'Why did you leave the shop? I thought you liked fruit and veg.'

She waves a hand airily. 'The owner came on strong. Very strong. It's not the first time. He only has to see a couple of oranges and it sets him off. It's been going on a long time and I finally decided I'd had enough.'

'You can't work in a fish 'n' chip shop!' Penny remonstrates. 'That's a dead-end occupation. My mother thinks you've got a lot more going for you than you realise,' she adds patronisingly.

'Does she now?' Kit shows a rare flash of anger. Hand on hip, voice sweet, she says, 'Well, tell Mummy from me she can take her opinions

259

along with her heated hostess trolley and shove them both up her jacksy. OK?'

Half an hour or so later, the lads go for a break and a pint, which usually stretches to two, depending on whether one of them has the money to fork out for the rest. Women aren't allowed in the public bar of the railwaymen's club. So we stay upstairs and we do what we've been doing quite a bit recently. We sing and mess about on the group's equipment.

Later, Bryn and I give Podge, Kit and all her bags a lift to his mam's house. Podge sits bolt upright on the back seat, saying little, as if the electrifying consequences of having a girlfriend move in have only just hit him.

'Poor sod,' I remark to Bryn, as we drive away.

Bryn gives me one of those are-you-sure-you're-not-really-a-Martian looks. Then he becomes unusually loquacious. 'What do you mean "poor sod"? My dad was married at nineteen. Can't see anything wrong in that. Nothing wrong at all. They're dead happy. My mam worships the ground my dad treads on. She'd do anything for him – and he would for her.'

How can a boy be so deluded?

Billy's return results in an uneasy peace in the White household. This is further strained by Chalkie's frequent and unexplained absences. Rose assumes it's his 'other woman'. Still, she is determined that her son, angry and irritable, does not witness any further scenes of domestic upheaval. So, only the banal is discussed – and she and Chalkie sleep a foot apart in bed.

260

One afternoon, after collecting Billy from school, Chalkie tells Rose that he has a surprise for her. The three walk down the high street and stop outside the launderette, newly opened. 'Look at that,' he says. He points to an ad in the window for a job in the launderette, three hours a day, nine to twelve, five days a week. Duties include keeping the premises clean and undertaking service washes for the customers. 'Tips possible,' the ad reads.

'I want you to pack in the hotel and try for this,' Chalkie explains, and then, aware that he might sound too domineering, adds, 'If you think it's a good idea. It'll give you more time for ... other things.'

'And how are we going to manage for money?'

'We will,' Chalkie says, taking Billy's hand and steering Rose by the elbow, not homewards but towards the park. 'I've got a job. It's continental work, bloody good travel allowance and better paid than the last one. It means I'll be away for a couple of weeks at a time instead of a few days. Give you a longer break,' he adds, his eyes trying to deliver the message he can't articulate.

'This job, you've taken it already, have you?' Rose asks.

Chalkie nods. He turns left at the entrance of the park, walks a hundred yards or so down the road and stops in front of a terraced house, set back, with a small front garden. He walks up to the front door, takes out a key and opens it. Then turns, realising that his wife and son are still standing by the garden gate, watching him as if he is a trespasser.

'Come on,' he says. 'It's ours.'

Fifteen minutes later the tour of the premises is over. Billy is playing in the garden at the rear. Rose and Chalkie watch him from the kitchen window. The house is sparsely furnished, every room painted white. Rose notes that it has no signs of damp, a fitted carpet in the back room, an avocado green bathroom suite upstairs and three bedrooms.

'I liked the idea of the extra bedroom,' Chalkie begins awkwardly. Rose turns to look at him. He searches for signs of softness but her eyes are opaque, like the surface of a frozen pond.

'I'm not getting pregnant, again, if that's what you think.' She bridles.

'I thought you could use the bedroom,' he begins again, 'to do what you want to do in it. Like your dad has his shed and his dogs, you'll have your own room to do what you want to do in it.' Rose raises an eyebrow. Chalkie shuffles uncomfortably, looks out of the window at Billy and then back at his wife, uncertainly. 'Well, you know ... do your writing stuff or something...'

Rose follows Chalkie's gaze. So Billy has told his father. She quietly promises herself that if Chalkie has read any of her 'stuff', her private stuff, she will not only threaten to kill him, she will actually do it.

'I swear I haven't read a word,' he says, as if reading her thoughts. 'Billy mentioned that you tell him stories. He said it was all right to know because you'd broken your – well, you'd told Buster. Then I remembered when we were first

262

together, you talked a little bit about... Well, anyway, perhaps you won't want to ... I just thought–'
'The woman?' Rose asks, flushing. 'Who's the
woman?'
Chalkie looks at her, perplexed, then
understanding dawns and he laughs, a flush of
pleasure on his face. 'You're not jealous, are you?
She lives in Runcorn. This house belonged to her
grandmother. The old girl died. I saw the ad in
the paper. She's let me rent it for six months,
longer if we want it. When I saw it, it was brown
and black and filthy. The old lady hadn't cleaned
it in years. A few of the lads and your old man
came over. It didn't take us long. I told them it
was a surprise. For you.
'I did it white but you can have it any colour you
like. Carl and Tanner gave a hand with a few bits
and pieces of furniture. I'm away on Monday.
Then it'll just be you and Billy – for a while. I
wanted to do it and get you moved in before I left.
I don't want to go, leave Billy and that ... and you
... but...' He stops, defeated, realising she isn't
going to pick up on his cues.
Rose moves towards him. She takes his face in
her hands and gently pulls him towards her.
'Is it going to be all right?' Chalkie asks. 'Oh,
Rose, are we going to be all right?'

My dad and mam's lives intersect in three places:
the bed, the table and, much more rarely, the
Duck and Fox. As the only way to have any
privacy in our family is in a public place, I track
them down when they're out for a drink.
My dad buys me an orange squash. Even before

263

he's sat down again, I blurt it out: 'I've the money to go to London so I'm going... I'm going to university. I know you both think it's a bad idea and I know you can't give me any help, cash or anything, but–'

'Oh,' my mother says. She looks neither cross nor pleased, just neutral. As if I was the next-door neighbour discussing what to cook for tea. Then she gives me one of her repertoire of smiles, the one that shows just a little too much of her teeth, signalling criticism. 'I can't pretend that that isn't upsetting. I mean, I'd always hoped you'd meet a decent fellow and settle down, so I could see you every day. Look after the grandchildren. Like other mothers do. That's not too much for anyone to ask, is it? I can't pretend to understand, Lily, my pet. I mean, what's wrong with us that you want to go so far away?'

'You've got all that settling-down and kids and stuff with Rose and Iris and Daisy,' I point out, determined that they won't make me lose my way in a fog of guilt.

'But they aren't you, are they, Lily?' She smiles.

'I can't stop you,' is my dad's only remark. 'But I don't like it.'

The subject isn't raised again. They don't even ask how I managed to find the money.

On Monday, on my way home from school, I visit Rose in her new place, surrounded by bags and boxes. The house stinks of paint. She says she's given in her notice at the hotel and is hoping to start a part-time job in the launderette. Chalkie's on his way to Germany. Everything is changing, except Rose. She gives her usual impression of the Human Brillo Pad.

'You just don't get it, do you?' she says, poking furiously at the fire, which stubbornly refuses to burn, when I tell her how our parents responded to the news that I might go to university. 'You want Mam and Dad to say, "Well done," but why should they if they don't believe in it? What they want from you isn't A levels or degrees or a big fat wage packet. What they want are babies, a husband, a routine just like theirs. They want you to be the same, not different. To be the same as them in where you live, how you spend your time, what you expect from life.

'Why else do you think the sons and daughters of the middle class rise to rule the bloody place while us lot breed generations whose only ambition is to stay put? It's not that we haven't got the brains or talent or drive,' her voice grows more sarcastic, 'it's much simpler than that. It's that we don't want to do anything that will widen the gap between us and our mams and dads. Stupid, isn't it? We bury ourselves for fear of becoming someone they're not.

'All that teenage-rebellion stuff? It's bollocks,' she adds. 'It's not us, it's the posh kids who are rocking the boat, and that's because they know if they fall in the water Daddy'll be there to fish 'em out. Come back in thirty years and they'll be as bloody conservative as their fathers, except with a couple of pictures in the family album showing them with long hair and skinny arses and memories of a few free fucks before Mammy made sure they became engaged to Jemima

265

Ponsonby-Brown and put the announcement in *The Times.* Some bloody youth quake.

'Meanwhile what do we, the good old obedient working class, do? We do what we've done for years. We get an apprenticeship, get courting, get engaged, get pregnant, get married, get a husband who expects to be waited on hand and foot, get depressed then get resigned at twenty-something to the knowledge that the wedding was the first and last time anyone paid us any attention. The rest of life will be just one bloody long anticlimax – except for the few contrary ones, like me and you. I'll sit and stew but what'll you do?'

Rose throws coal on the weak flames of the fire, making the temperature plummet again. She's so overheated herself, she doesn't notice. 'Don't think exile from the family home is the only trial you'll face, my love. Shall I tell you the other problem you're going to have? It's whether in order to have a future, you're willing to forfeit your past. Wait!' She puts up her hands to stop me interrupting. 'Don't tell me you're proud of where you come from and all that crap. That's now. Wait until you're surrounded by girls and boys like that girl Penny, who talk ever so nicely and who have parents who assume that you have an indoor lavvy and a domestic who does, and you go to winter balls...'

Rose is both bitter and depressing but since she is now, officially, my benefactor, I moderate my words: 'God, you sound just like Barry. Of course I won't change,' I say. 'Barry always says what matters is to be true to yourself and your roots. Be authentic. That's what the blues men from the

266

Mississippi delta did. Some of them had done time for murder but they never hid their past, they sang about it and–'

'Oh, yeh,' Rose interrupts. 'Well, I don't notice too many of them in the upper echelons of white society, do you? Ripped off and leave it to the white boys to make the money. True to yourself, my arse. What, standing on the outside looking in, a living bloody black legend but with bugger-all in the bank? I wouldn't call that living happily ever after – would you?'

Rose works a pair of bellows with such fury that the coal flares brilliantly into flames. 'You've no idea how small they can make you feel,' she says. 'I know. It happens all the time in the hotel, and it makes my blood boil. Not because of the way they behave but because I allow myself to feel less good, less able, less ... well, less everything. Like a bird who's stunned itself flying up against a window-pane that's perfectly visible to everyone else. Stupid, stupid, stupid... Then, at other times, when I'm on my own and writing, I know I'm more than good enough – I'm bloody brilliant!' She shouts the last few words, and jumps up, poker in her hand, like a fencer on guard, laughing like a madwoman.

'So you lied. You are writing,' I say mildly.

Doug Tempest, out of work, imposes a strict routine upon himself. Up at six a.m., first fag of the day, clean and set the fire, wash and shave before the others rise, down to the newsagent's for the *Daily Express* and fresh supplies of cigarettes, then a walk around the town for an hour or so until the women have cleared out of the house. Back to the shed, a mug of tea, more ciggies, read the paper and out again to the labour exchange. Later, for fifteen minutes or so, he pours coppers into the phone-box out near the caravan site, where no one can see him, listening to one rejection after another – Vacancy already filled... How old did you say you were? ... Experience essential...

He walks again for another hour, to ease himself out of the anger. An anger rooted not in the lack of a job, or the prejudice against his age, but because, for the first time in his adult life, he has no escape. Love of his daughters has him in chains. Lily's exams, Daisy's love-life, Iris's engagement and Rose's fierce resistance mean that if he goes he knows he will go with only Melody by his side. Doug's anger is also directed at himself. He has never before been short of inspiration when it comes to making (and losing) money, but this time, confidence rotting away, he is bankrupt of ideas.

Three weeks is as long a gap as Doug can afford without earning a wage because he has commitments, unbreakable commitments that stretch beyond the immediate family. So, now he finds himself outside Lawson's fish factory, just as the dinner hooter wails. He watches as a troop of men, like an army of canaries in overalls stained bright yellow, comes out of the gate and crosses the road, heads down, hands in pockets, marching in step, like automatons, apparently oblivious to all around. Silently, they file into the ugly brown-tiled pub opposite. As the door swings back and forth, Doug catches a glimpse of the sawdust floor and the counter. On it, four deep, are lined pints and pints of bitter. Soon the place is full. Quietly, each man puts his coppers down, raises a glass and drinks until it is half empty. Then comes an enormous burst of noise, as if someone unseen has turned up the volume. Doug shudders. Ever since he'd left school at fifteen, he'd been told the factory would be his inevitable destination. And, so far, he'd proved the predictions wrong. So far.

Doug no longer even works on his dogs. Instead he sits mulling in his shed. He muses on the way lies, if they are told often enough, like magic, turn into a kind of truth. When his daughters had come along, he had promised himself he would view the world through their eyes, respect their choices. Instead, in recent weeks, Lily in particular has made him realise how, over the years, he has filed down their ambitions and limited their horizons.

Melody says that this is natural, every father thinks he knows best. It's love. Every morning Doug has woken vowing to give Lily a few words of support. By evening he has said nothing. Is that love? In his sleep, he dreams of decapitations and hangings. Sometimes he is the victim; sometimes it is Lily. Whoever it is, he laughs in the face of death.

Each morning, when he awakes, he is ashamed.

Melody has fallen into the habit of popping home from work for fifteen minutes or so in the early afternoon. She brings a pie or sandwiches as a distraction from Doug's regular diet of introspection, nicotine and tea. Experience tells her that the lower her husband's spirits, the more fixed is his mask of conviviality – and the more relentlessly he endeavours to entertain her, jokes, anecdotes, snatches of song.

Today he is different. Doug sits in the back room, a piece of paper filled with pencilled numbers on the table in front of him. 'I've not paid her for three weeks,' he says. 'That's the longest it's ever been. I thought I'd get a January bonus from Bunting's and that would see her right...'

'You've paid enough. You don't have to pay any more,' Melody replies. 'Stop. Don't send her any more. You've paid your dues.'

Melody gives Doug a long look. 'Why don't we finish this for good and tell the girls? They're old enough now...'

He shakes his head. 'Think what people will say. Think what people will say to the girls.'

Chapter Twenty-eight

'Battenberg cake, please.'

'I don't like marzipan,' Robert says mournfully

'A Battenberg cake, please,' Dulcie repeats firmly, to the girl in the Co-op in Cwmland. Iris has come with them on the bus and is waiting outside.

'It's self-service, love,' the girl replies, intent on manicuring her nails. 'We don't do anything. You do it for yourself.'

Dulcie looks at her blankly.

'Look!' The girl comes off her stool and out from behind the cash register. Dulcie's alarm diminishes once she realises the girl is as short as she is. She grabs hold of a wire basket from a pile near the door and places it in Dulcie's hand. 'You take this, you put things in it, and then you pay.'

'So what do you do?' Robert asks, genuinely curious.

The girl gives him a filthy look, then, checking first to see if the manager is around, says sourly, 'Believe you me, too flipping much.'

Dulcie and Robert have come into Cwmland to buy a celebration tea. Kath and Pete are in Manchester trying out for the television and due home around six. Dulcie is in charge. 'You get some boiled ham,' she instructs Robert. 'Don't ask the man. Just take it. It'll be all right. I'll get some pickle and tomatoes. Kath likes pickle and tomatoes. And a tin of fruit cocktail.'

'And a tin of cream, please,' Robert asks.

Dulcie smiles and gives his cheek a pat. Robert tries to return the smile but he continues to live in fear. Instinct tells him that one day soon Kath will stop being nice.

I skip the last hour of school and call in at Penny's. She's promised to lend me her dad's copy of *On The Road*. I can hear Johnny Mathis blaring out. Nobody answers when I ring the bell. I open the door and go in. 'Pen!' I call. No answer. Recently she's been bunking off more than I do but perhaps not today.

271

I'm about to go upstairs to see if she's in her room when there's a thud from the den. The door is ajar. I go down the stairs and into the gloom. Without thinking. I switch on the light. Half under the table, a man's bare bum is bobbing furiously up and down, trousers around his ankles. He is on top of a spreadeagled female form.

The eyes are wide open, staring, makeup like soot, smeared and smudged, the head thrown back, neck straining. It's Kit without her glasses. Stupidly I assume assault and battery. 'Let her go this minute, you bastard!' I scream. 'Let her go!'

The bum stops bobbing. Kit's eyes, independently of each other, swivel into focus. The man attempts to sit up and gives his head a whack on the table. As he turns, I recognise the polo-neck. Kit is shagging her best friend's dad. Worse still, she looks as if she's actually *enjoying* it.

Before either can speak, I flee. If they say nothing, I'll say nothing. I'll pretend it never happened. We'll all pretend it never happened. I run for the bus, unable to decide whether Kit is a slapper, a whore and a tart – or having the time of her life. And much to be envied.

As I walk into Rydol Crescent, she is already waiting for me outside our front door, coat buttoned up against the wind. He must have given her a lift, got her out of the house before the family returned. How could she be so disloyal? What if she destroys the marriage? I stoke up my indignation as much as I can as I walk, in part to distract me from my embarrassment.

'Your dad's home,' she says, without an ounce of shame. 'I didn't go in, in case you thought I'd

272

shagged him 'n' all.'

'Well, that's very considerate of you,' I reply, annoyed because every time I look at her I go pink.

Kit links her arm through mine and we walk on down the street towards the quay. The cold nips at our knees. Kit always has bare legs. My school tights have got a hole, which I've coloured in with black ink.

'Did he make you?' I eventually ask.

'Did he hell,' she answers, chuckling. 'He's been trying it on for ages. So this time I thought, Oh, sod it. I didn't expect much but he was all right, considering.'

'What if you get pregnant?' I ask. Fear at being caught out is the basis of all my moral decisions.

Kit shrugs. 'Don says Adele is in charge of the johnnies in their house, so we winged it. I often do. Nothing's happened so far.'

She jumps up and down on the spot, to keep warm, the pompoms on the tie of her hat bouncing merrily. 'I've been told this stops you getting pregnant,' she says deadpan, then bursts out laughing. Eventually, she says, 'Don's scared you're going to tell.'

'Of course I can't do that, can I? But it's not fair to Penny – or Adele. You can't just barge into people's lives and do what you want. It's not right.'

'What harm does it really do?' Kit says. 'It's a bit of fun, that's all. Nobody knows, so nobody's hurt.'

'It doesn't work like that. People do find out and it does hurt. What if he's just using you? As soon as he gets what he wants, you're out on your ear like some kind of ... prostitute?'

'God, you're a right little Puritan, Lily,' Kit says amiably. 'It's not an ordeal, you know. It can be nice. What if he is using me? It's a two-way thing. That's life, isn't it?'

'Don't you feel dirty?' I blurt out.

'Yeh,' Kit growls. 'Filthy.'

An hour or so later Robert, Dulcie, Lily, Iris, her eyes red-rimmed since Howard has failed to write for the second week in a row from his camp in Yorkshire, Daisy and Kit sit in the back room of Kath's house, while the cuckoo clock, which Robert had bought earlier for Dulcie in Cwmland, ticks loudly. Dulcie and the cuckoo parrot each other. 'Cuck-oo, cuck-oo, cuckoo, cuckoo, cuckoo, cuckoo...'

'Would you like a pale ale?' Robert asks Kit politely. A solitary bottle stands on the sideboard.

'No, thanks. I'm not much of a drinker,' she lies, aware that supplies are limited.

'What's that?' Robert asks. The others hear it too – the toot of a car horn. 'It's them, it's them. It's Kath and Pete!' Dulcie shouts excitedly and rushes for the front door. Several other neighbours have had the same impulse.

Kath and Pete are in the back of a Rover. The driver wears a smart grey suit and a peaked cap. 'They must have done OK,' Kit whispers to Lily. 'Otherwise they would have let them make their own way back. Bloody hell! Who'd've thought?'

Kath, however, is not smiling. Grim-faced, she sweeps past the group. Pete raises his hat to the neighbours, then gives his brother a slap on the back by way of a greeting and presents Dulcie with a bunch of artificial peonies. 'Whipped those from what they call the hospitality room, just for you, sunshine.' He winks.

Kath removes her coat and hat. She turns on Pete and says coldly, 'I told you, I don't want you in this house. You ruined it for us, you know you did. I believe you did it on purpose. Go on,' Kath glares at Lily as if she has contributed to her disappointment, 'ask him who Eugene Weidmann is. Go on.'

Pete makes himself comfortable in one of the two armchairs in the room, hands behind his head. Then he notices Kit.

He speaks as if she is the only person in the room. 'They were as nice as pie. Provided us with a lovely plate of sandwiches. In return, I gave Hughie Green a joke or two. Told him to feel free to make use of them. Then, how's your father, me and Kath shoot through the first three rounds faster than diarrhoea out of a cat's bum.'

'And?' Lily, Kit, Dulcie and Robert say almost simultaneously.

Kath frowns, then says angrily, 'In 1939 Eugene Weidmann was the last man to be executed publicly in France. He murdered six people.' She points an accusing finger at Pete. 'It was his question, he knew the answer and he got it wrong. *On purpose.*'

'It was nerves,' says Pete. 'Don't I have trouble with my nerves, Robert?'

His brother looks uncertain. Pete, unfazed, already has new interests in hand. 'So, where do you come from, sweetheart?' he asks Kit. Lily could swear she purrs in reply.

'Out that door. And you too,' Kath interrupts, glaring at Robert. 'I don't want to see either of you again.'

'You agreed that these two could be friends.' Pete brings his face closer to Kath's than any man has done in a very long time. 'If you try and stop that, I promise you'll be in the kind of trouble you only read about in your comic books. And I'm not joking.'

We leave Kath to simmer. I've been invited to Bryn's for tea. He announces shortly after I arrive that he's going to work on his car. Parts of the engine decorate his bedroom floor. 'My dad's just had some more of his records arrive, go and bother him,' he suggests, propelled by the belief that no woman knows what to do with herself left to her own devices.

Barry is in the garage, writing a pamphlet. He fills the kettle with water and, without asking, puts instant coffee in two cups. 'Hear that?' he says. 'That's "Walkin' The Dog" by Rufus Thomas, being sung as it should be sung, not like our Bryn's version. That's a travesty, that is.'

'I think he does all right,' I say loyally. 'It always gets people up on their feet.'

'Bryn makes it sound as if it's a song about taking the bloody poodle for its constitutional... How's your dad?' he adds, handing me a mug of coffee.

'All right. He keeps busy. He's tried for a few jobs but no luck so far. We're still singing on a Monday night and he's got a few weddings next month. Something'll turn up, it always does. Or he'll have a brainwave. Maybe he'll get a job in

276

the new Co-op when it opens.'

'I ask with a specific purpose in mind,' Barry says, in what sounds like his shop-steward voice. He rolls up a cigarette. 'We've got another job going at Lawson's. Not bad pay, white-coat job, supervising. Bugger-all to do, really. Turn a bit of a blind eye when the lads nip out for a drink, and that's it, really. Seventeen quid a week if you do overtime on a Saturday morning, a bit of fresh fish thrown in now and then...' Barry pauses for dramatic effect and inhales deeply. 'What do you reckon? Suit your dad? Why don't you mention it, in passing?'

'Thanks,' I reply. 'But he's got a thing about factories...'

Barry changes the subject. 'I've got you a little good-luck present for the interviews,' he adds casually. 'Bryn told me you liked Otis Redding. If your confidence drops just a little bit, when you're down in London, run through a few bars of this. Did I tell you that's what the slaves did under the lash? Sang their hearts out in their heads? Did I tell you that?'

I smile and refrain from saying, 'Many times.' I wish I could explain to Barry how much his enthusiasms and beliefs have meant to me. I wish I could tell him how much I've valued being able to listen to someone who never once mentions soap-powder bargains or the weather or what he saw on the telly the previous night. I wish I could, but instinct tells me that if I did we would never relax in each other's company again. So, gratitude will have to wait.

'When you off for the interviews? Next

Tuesday?' I nod. 'It's *Otis Blue*,' Barry says. 'Have you got it? Shall I play it? You listen to the horns... Bloody marvellous. I'm a steel guitar and harmonica man myself but I've got a bit of a soft spot for the horns. When you're away from home and a little bit down, you play this. You'll be back up punching, girl, I promise you.'

He takes the record ceremoniously out of its cover, polishes it with his sleeve and reverentially places it on the deck. He positions the pick-up, then turns the volume up loud.

'Shake the whole bloody system up, that's what we've got to do, girl. Shake!' Barry yells, as he bangs out the beat on the biscuit tin and bellows at the top of his voice, moustache reverberating, as he joins in the chorus, performing a kind of long, tall, skinny war-dance around his garage, oblivious as he barges into chairs and books and piles of rubbish. 'Shake!' He is one man who is absolutely confident he can change the world – with or without help.

Later, Bryn drives me home, his car in working order again. I sing all the way.

Chapter Twenty-nine

Daisy has always vowed that she would give herself to Carl only after he had proposed. Now, however, in early March, since he still shows no sign of going down on bended knee, circumstances dictate that a second plan of action is urgently required. So, on the same evening that Barry Taylor is attempting to fire up Lily's confidence with the help of Otis Redding, Daisy is bobbing up and down in the back of Tanner Hicks's van in an effort to provide some personal insurance.

They had driven to Cwmland to the pictures. On the way back, she had said abruptly, 'Do you fancy it?'

Carl had looked at her disbelievingly. After months of fierce resistance, he couldn't understand why she was surrendering with no swag in her bag, like an engagement ring. 'Don't mind if I do,' he'd replied.

Nine minutes later, five minutes of which had been taken up finding somewhere suitable to park, the deed was done. The couple sit wordless in the car, the heater on against the cold, the windows steamed up. 'That reminds me,' Carl says. 'I've got to get a new windscreen wiper.'

The garden of Rose's new house backs on to the park. The first week she and Billy were alone in the house she hardly slept. So when Kit, already bored with living in Podge's pocket, offers to move in until Chalkie's return, Rose agrees. Kit is a surprise to Rose. She had expected a shambolic, untidy, invasive, occasionally drunken presence. Instead her lodger is neat, industrious, careful not to intrude.

'Do you think you were a good girl in a previous life?' Rose asks her ironically one morning, as she watches Kit washing up the breakfast dishes and wiping every surface with a thoroughness bordering on obsessiveness.

'My mum was houseproud,' Kit replies. 'It's a curse.'

On the quay, late Sunday morning, Barry Taylor bumps into Doug Tempest, apparently by chance. They chat for five minutes or so, shake hands and part. 'I've got a job,' Doug tells Melody, on returning home. He smiles but she can see the defeat in his eyes. 'Start tomorrow. At Lawson's. I'll bring you home a nice piece of haddock for Friday's tea.'

He doesn't raise the subject again. Later, alone in the cold of her bedroom, Melody pulls out a new catalogue. 'Home shopping,' she reads silently. 'One shilling in the pound over twenty weeks or even less over thirty-eight weeks...'

On Sunday afternoon, two days before I go to London for my two interviews, Kit and Penny come round. Penny's house is warmer but I want to avoid her father. Kit acts as if nothing has happened. We sit under the quilt in my bedroom, listening to Otis Redding on Iris's record-player, occasionally having a dance to warm up, then retreating under the bedclothes again. Iris comes up to complain that the music is so loud it's giving her a headache.

'Where's your sense of fun, girl?' Kit teases.

'She was born without one,' I tell her.

'You're so mouthy,' Iris responds. 'I hope on Tuesday you get run over by a bloody great tram or whatever they have in London.' Then she retreats.

'She'll feel terrible if something really does

280

'happen to you,' Penny says helpfully.

'Nothing's going to happen,' Kit tells her firmly. 'Lily is going to look confident, walk proud and wipe the floor with the lot of them – then, like the good girl she is, she's going to bring us back a present each, aren't you?'

Penny asks if I'd like to borrow her fake-fur coat. 'My dad said he'll give you a lift to the station and he can bring the coat with him. He's always at the university early on Tuesdays and he goes right past the bottom of your street.'

'Look, I really don't need a lift,' I begin.

'Oh, he insists,' Penny replies. 'He's very fond of you. Not in the way that you mean,' she adds, glaring at Kit.

'I haven't said a word,' Kit protests. 'I was just thinking that I'd like to fly the coop too one day, be my own boss. No more working for dirty old men, no more handing the profits over each week, no more crap wages.'

'You didn't used to think like that,' Penny says, almost accusingly.

'I know I didn't. I used to think that love would sort me out. That I'd be bailed out by a handsome young man and do sweet sod-all for the rest of my life – but then I met Podge's mam.'

'Podge's mam?'

'I took one look at what a miserable bloody life she's had and that was it. She was dumped by Podge's dad after fifteen months of marriage and she's spent the last nineteen years waiting for the next white knight to come along. She gets by on a few quid a week, dishing up dinners at Lawson's.'

Penny looks thoroughly disapproving. It's

ironic. Her ambition is to switch from a four-bedroom double-fronted house in which she does not have to lift a finger to a two-up, two-down and Bulbie, who behaves as if he's a victim of narcolepsy.

'You're wrong,' Penny insists. 'Love is all that counts.'

Iris reappears and says she wants to go to bed, so it's the end of party-time. She has also been eavesdropping.

'Why are you two so sneery to Penny?' she demands. 'What's so bad about settling down and having a nice home? I think you're both jealous because you've never really been in love. Not like we have.'

Kit and I make gagging noises.

On the Monday that Doug Tempest clocks in for his first day's work at Lawson's, Dulcie is beginning her second week at Woolworth's. Without consulting her sister, she had handed in her notice at Amore's and, helped by Lily, found herself this new job. Kath is mollified because her sister's wages have increased slightly. The change of job also means that Robert is able to meet Dulcie out of work for her lunch-break since Kath is usually in the Contented Sole. Today Dulcie emerges from the store in the company of two fellow members of staff.

Kath has also popped out to buy a packet of aspirin so she spots Robert hovering. She immediately marches up to her sister. 'You come with me, young woman, I'll give you a bag of chips for your dinner,' she says, grabbing her by the arm. Surprisingly agile for her size, Dulcie slips out of her coat, leaving it in Kath's grasp, and runs, giggling, darting in and out of cyclists and pedestrians, her bright green Woolworth's overall making her look like a well-fed leprechaun out to cause mayhem in the street.

'Come back here, this minute!' Kath shrieks. 'Do you hear me?'

Robert, in a half-walk, half-run, gives chase hesitantly, unwilling to catch up with either of them.

'I don't care what people say, I think it's lovely that they've got each other. It's just like something you see in the pictures,' says Marlene Dickens, a senior supervisor at Woolworth's.

Kath, walking back empty-handed, overhears. 'Yes,' she snaps. 'It's called The End.'

In the first couple of hours that Doug spends at Lawson's, the response wherever he goes is variations on the same theme. The men break into song, amiably taking the mickey. It pleases him that they know who he is. Still, he avoids the canteen, the pub and the illicit poker game in the dinner-hour. Too many men in too close a space making the best of it reminds him of the army and the war.

'What's it like, Dad?' Iris asks that night.

'Not bad,' Doug replies. Later, he goes upstairs to dress in his Fair Isle jumper and beige corduroy slacks for that night's appearance at the Cow and Fiddle.

Lily meets him at the pub. She is wearing white boots, a hipster mini-skirt and a skinny-rib multi-striped jumper. 'It's Ruby Murray I want to see up there,' Tommy Aster says by way of greeting, neck jerking furiously. 'Not Ruby bloody Tuesday. Get your gear on.'

The ladies' lavatory at the rear of the pub is icy cold with a broken sink, a filthy towel, puddles of scummy water on the concrete floor and the stink of wee. As Lily changes, a woman introduces herself. 'Excuse me,' she says. 'My name is Edie Stewart. Mrs Edie Stewart. We're organising a nineteen forties supper as part of our fund-raising for the church, and me and Livvy, that's my friend, we don't normally go out much, but we came tonight to give her a bit of a break. She's been bereaved, you see. Tragic, he was only sixty-five, three weeks past retiring. Anyway, me and Livvy wondered if you might come and sing. We thought you could do us a lovely Vera Lynn. Would you do that for us? Do a Vera Lynn?'

In the lounge, Doug orders a pint for himself and a lemonade for Lily. Unusually, tonight, he has a strong desire to get drunk. Except that tomorrow he'll be clocking in at Lawson's at seven a.m.

'How have you been keeping, Dougie?' a woman's voice asks. Betty Procter stands by his table. She sits down without asking. She wears a red dress and big brass ear-rings that remind him of bedknobs. 'Singing better than ever, you are,' she says. 'Although I'd rather have the dinner jacket than that jumper. Best place for that is the cat's basket. It's not a proper man's garment, is it, Dougie? Not by any stretch of the imagination. Aren't you going to ask me if I'd like a drink? I'll

284

have a Dubonnet and lemonade, if you don't mind. And not too much lemonade, ta.'

'Dad?' Lily emerges from the ladies' and stops as Betty Procter gives her a broad smile. 'Hello,' the older woman says comfortably. 'How are you keeping? And your mam? Your dad's kindly offered to buy me a drink. Each time I see you round town, I think, Gosh, there's a good-looking girl for you, just like her father.' She smiles again, disingenuously, turning to Doug. 'Lovey, either sit down or go and get us a drink, there's a good lad.' Doug does as he's told.

'He's a one, isn't he, your dad?'

Lily, frozen-faced, makes little attempt to hide her animosity. Betty Procter prattles on, a gleam in her eye: 'Your mam came to see me the other day. About you, as a matter of fact.'

'About me?'

'Yes, didn't she mention it? Wanted to borrow a few quid to get you to London. Sadly, I couldn't help. Hope it's sorted, is it? Anyway, don't mention it to your dad. Shouldn't have told you, really. You've got no idea what slips out of my big mouth. Oops, here he comes.' She turns to greet Doug, who has returned empty-handed.

'Taxi's here, Lily, we've got to go,' he says abruptly. 'Sorry about that drink, Mrs Procter. Come on, now, quick.'

Outside, there is no taxi. 'Keep walking!' Doug instructs. 'Don't bloody look back.'

'Jesus!' Lily protests, struggling to keep up in her high-heeled boots. 'What happens if we do look back? Get turned to salt, do we? What was all that about in there? You promised me you hadn't laid a finger on her but up she pops, looking like she's drunk the cream.' Her father disappears ahead of her into the gloom. As far as Lily is concerned, he is a phoney, vain, self-obsessed, middle-aged man whom, too often now, she isn't even sure she likes.

'Dad.' Doug walks on. 'Wait. Rose says you've had lots of women. Is that true? How could you do that to Mam, you dirty old bastard?' Lily shouts after him, in fury and frustration, expecting the words to be blown away in the wind.

Unexpectedly he stops, spins around and runs towards her, arm raised, fist clenched, his face distorted. Instinctively she takes a step back, expecting to be struck. Instead her father lets his arm fall and shakes his head, as if in disbelief at his own behaviour. Then tears begin to stream down his cheeks but he makes no sound.

Lily has never seen her father cry before. She is afraid, aware that something has changed for ever. But she has no idea what.

'One egg, sausage and baked beans, please, two teas and a packet of Player's for my dad,' Lily asks Alice at Taff's all-night café. 'I didn't think you did the night shift.'

Alice shouts the order through to the kitchen and makes a fresh brew of tea in a giant silver kettle. 'I don't. But it's staff. Always off sick on a bloody Monday. Nobody likes Mondays, do they? Your Dulcie all right? She's got herself a fella, I see. Bless her. Lot of people don't like it but, in my opinion, they're only flesh and blood. Just like us, flesh and blood. She often comes in here. How's it going at the Cow and Fiddle?'

Lily shows no surprise that Alice knows where she and her father have been. Everyone knows everything in Fairport – or they think they do. What they don't know they make up. She returns to the table by the gas fire where her father sits.

Doug, composure restored, says, 'Order us a round of toast, there's a good girl. And see that *Daily Mirror* over there? Pick it up on your way back. Maybe that young boy's been found. Ever since Billy I can't get him out of my head.'

Lily does as she's told and returns again to the table, eating hungrily when her food arrives. 'Christ.' Doug looks at her plate stacked high. 'You never eat like that at home.'

'I'm never hungry at home,' Lily replies. 'What's happened?' she asks indicating the newspaper.

'Still not found. Arrested a bloke, let him go. Now, they've found the boy's shoe, eight miles this side of Cwmland. Must've come this way. It's a good few weeks now. I–'

'Dad,' Lily begins.

Her father deflects her as if anticipating an inquisition on what happened earlier. 'What do you reckon?' he asks, drawing deeply on his cigarette, ignoring his slice of toast. 'For all we know, this poor kiddie might have been run down, the bloke's panicked, hidden the body and now doesn't know what to do. Sometimes bad things happen by accident and, no matter how hard people try, there's no way to make amends.'

'"Life is merely a general mist of error,"' Lily murmurs, wishing her father would move back into his more familiar upbeat mode, irritating

287

though that is at times.

'What's that?' Doug says.

'"Life is merely a general mist of error." It comes from a play I'm doing at school for English. One of the people in it is a paid killer who throttles anything that moves and loves his work far too much to worry about making amends. A bit like Pete, except that with Pete it's all bullshit. To be fair,' she adds drily, aware that this is the first time her father has ever discussed any part of her curriculum, however indirectly, 'he did have a terrible time when he was younger and that's what turned him bad. Not Pete, the bloke in the play.'

'What happens to him?' Doug looks genuinely interested.

'He marries the girl next door, takes a mortgage out on a lovely three-bedroomed semi, acquires a job for life with the gas board and lives happily ever after.' She stops. 'No, I'm kidding. He's killed. But listen, he could've ended up with a lot worse. He could've been sentenced to spending every Monday night singing to the completely deaf at the Cow and Fiddle.'

'Do you really hate it?' Doug asks. 'If you do, we'll...'

Lily gives her father's hand a squeeze. 'It's a privilege to work with a real professional, Dad,' she says, in a fake American drawl, wishing she meant it.

They wait for the last bus outside Taff's, her father smoking and coughing and stamping his feet to keep warm. Neither refer to the night's events.

Silences that speak volumes and truths that hide a thousand lies, that's the mature way to create a happy family life, Lily thinks, on the bus ride home. She ponders on how Don and Adele Wilson prance about as if they have the perfect marriage while he's shagging young girls, Rose and Chalkie play house and spit blood, Kit and Podge and her and Bryn have absolutely nothing in common but hold on just in case love blooms. Howard isn't sure what he wants but proposes to Iris anyway. And Mam and Dad and Betty Procter? God knows.

Lily's thoughts scud and skim and bang into each other as the bus winds its way past fields and unlit houses, the interior steaming up like a Turkish bath. The real irony, she tells herself, is that poor old Robert and Dulcie, the only straightforward pair among the lot of us, aren't even allowed to sit next to each other in the pictures in case it all gets out of hand.

Doug sings 'Give Me The Moonlight' softly, tapping out the rhythm on the silver bar of the seat in front. Lily breathes on the bus window and draws the round face of a smiling baby with her finger, adding a solitary curl like a question mark. Betty Procter must be thirty-five if she's a day, she tells herself. She couldn't possibly be pregnant. Could she?

'You look bothered, Lily. What's the matter?' Melody asks her daughter, after the others have gone to bed and they are alone in the back room. 'Is it the interviews? Do you wish you weren't going?' she adds hopefully.

'No.'

289

'Are you going to wear that new suit? If it was a couple of inches longer, it would be ever so smart.' Melody pours two mugs of tea. 'Penny's dad called me at the café today and said he's happy to give you a lift to the station. Ever so surprised I was. Very thoughtful, don't you think?'

Lily looks from the mug to her mother. What is it about the middle-aged that they have the unending capacity to interfere in the worst possible way? 'I don't want a lift. I'll get the bus.'

'Why ever would you want to do that if a lift's on offer?'

Wearily, Lily surrenders. 'OK, OK, OK.'

'I've got something for you.' Melody kisses her cheek and produces a parcel from the sideboard. 'Open it.'

Lily does as she is told. The maroon patent leather satchel is exactly like the one owned by the local librarian with corrugated iron hair who bikes past the school bus queue every day. Lily privately resolves to die rather than be seen with it. 'It's gorgeous,' she says. 'Really lovely. Thanks, Mam.'

'It's not from a catalogue,' Melody asserts proudly. 'It's from Peacocks – and there's money inside too, just a couple of quid but it all helps. We don't always see eye to eye, and you can be difficult, but I do love you, Lily, you know that, don't you?'

Lily doesn't resist when her mother gives her a hug. Instead she pretends she is a child again and the world is black and white, instead of so many confusing shades of grey.

Chapter Thirty

I don't sleep. It's the combination of the interviews ahead and facing Don Wilson for the first time since I saw his bare bum. I'm up and dressed by five a.m. Mam comes down and reaches for the frying-pan, takes one look at my face and, wisely, puts it away again. She hands me a carrier bag. 'It's sandwiches, just one or two,' she says. 'You'll need them to keep your strength up.'

'It's an interview, Mam, a couple of fifteen-minute interviews. I'm not leading the Light Brigade.'

She gives a strange twangy laugh and I realise she's nervous on my behalf. I've only seen her like this once before, when Rose was getting ready for the register office. 'You'll be all right, petal,' Mam had said over and over again to her. 'You'll be all right.' Only now does it dawn on me that Mam was probably trying to reassure herself as much as Rose.

'I'll be fine,' I tell her. 'Don't worry. I'll be back tomorrow afternoon and Bryn's going to meet me at the station. If I'm late, I'll phone. Don't worry,' I repeat, because she's beginning to look stricken, as if she'll never set eyes on me again. 'I love you, Mam.'

I'm on the doorstep when she rushes after me. 'You've forgotten your new bag,' she says, handing me the maroon eyesore.

In the pitch black, Don Wilson is standing with his car door open, not too chummy, not too distant, just right for the father of a friend. He is dressed in a dark brown coat. He is also wearing what looks like a very large fedora. 'Morning, Mrs Tempest,' he says, raising his hat. The smell of cedarwood wafts around us. 'Is Lily ready for her big day?'

'It's very kind of you,' Mam says, a little too ingratiating for my liking.

'Nonsense. I've got to make an early start anyway. You know what it's like, one lecture after another.'

My mother has no idea what one lecture after another is like but she smiles as if she does.

'Right, let's be off,' he says.

Mam wipes away a tear.

Just as we're about to leave, Rose comes running up the road, hair flying, slippers still on. 'Wait,' she shouts. I open the window and she sticks her head in, oblivious to Don Wilson or his fedora. She kisses my cheek and presses something into my hand. 'It's my good-luck charm bracelet. Wear it. And, Lily,' she smiles, 'don't let me down.'

Over the next twenty-five minutes, as he drives, Don Wilson makes small-talk. He mentions in passing that Penny is to spend a day at Oxford, 'just looking around'. So, true love hasn't quite won the day. 'She seems pretty happy at the moment,' he adds, giving me a sideways glance. 'Well, not with us, of course, we're boring old farts. But in general.'

'Does she?' I reply, presuming that this is a

coded way of saying, Don't upset the applecart.

Apart from that, the man is so convincingly untroubled, so pleased with himself, so obviously guilt-free, that by the end of the journey, even I am beginning to wonder if perhaps I imagined the entire encounter. He drops me off at the station. *'Bonne chance,'* he says. As I watch his car disappearing into the mist, I realise I've just learned a lesson in how some people get away with it: they trust that you haven't got the guts to tell.

'Excuse me.' I stop a porter at Euston station. 'I'm looking for the Underground, please.'

'See that sign?' he answers, pointing to his right. 'What does it say?'

'Underground.' I flush.

'Well, that'll be it, then, darlin'.' As he walks on, tears well up in my eyes. I want my mam.

I button up Penny's coat, then wish I hadn't borrowed it since it appears to be attracting far too much attention. Something has to be wrong with it, with me, and definitely with the bloody maroon bag. I dive into a newsagent's and buy a *Daily Mirror*.

'Can I have a carrier bag, please?' The girl behind the counter stares at me blankly. She has meticulously drawn eyelashes on the lower part of her eye. They give a spooky effect as if a fat spider is sitting in each socket, trailing its legs.

'A bag – could I have a carrier bag, please?'

The girl reluctantly hands one over. I stuff my mother's gift inside it and make my way to the tube. Nothing is right. My skirt is too short, my shoes too tight, my hair too frizzy, my coat too ridiculous, my suit too sweaty. I give Rose's charm bracelet in my pocket a squeeze, waiting for the magic to work. Instead my mind goes blank. I can't even remember the answers I've rehearsed to the questions I'm bound to be asked.

'Why do you want to go to university?'

'What are your long-term plans?'

'Why study history?'

'Who is your favourite historical figure, and why?'

'The hedgehog or the fox? Do you believe in the great man or great movements?' Don Wilson had suggested that one.

The carriage is full. A man presses against me. I move slightly, he follows. The train stops at King's Cross, I move to the next carriage. I try to act as if I make this journey every day, as if London doesn't bother me at all. But it does. A couple take the seats opposite. The girl is wearing a skirt the width of an army belt, high silver boots and a long coat made of patchwork suede. Her boyfriend is dressed in purple velvet flared hipster trousers, a black astrakhan coat down to his ankles and a pink velour hat with a large floppy brim. He seems not to have eaten a square meal since he was a child. I'm the only one in the carriage to look twice.

At Liverpool Street, following the instructions sent to me, I walk out of the station and wait for a number fifty-four bus, final destination Mile End. Once on it, everyone pushing and shoving, I look out of the window but notice little except that the combination of Penny's fur coat and the heat generated by several dozen passengers, plus a recurring attack of the nerves, is making me perspire profusely.

'Next stop, miss,' the bus conductor bellows. My heart gives a lurch.

Ten minutes later I'm in the Whitworth Library at Westfield College, London University. It is furnished in dark oak, red brocade and green leather. A clock ticks. Hunting lithographs hang on the only wall bare of books. It is intimidating, alien, and instantly my various ambitions are conflated into one: I want to go home.

A door opens. A boy of my age, dressed like an undertaker in a black suit and dark blue tie, his hair carefully parted in a style probably unchanged since he was four, emerges, eyes down, shoulders stooped. He scurries out, as if glad to be released. I swallow hard. Too late, I remember the advice from school. Take the trouble to read a newspaper on the way to the interview. A 'decent' newspaper.

The door opens again. A woman in her thirties, in a grey jumper and green tweed skirt, beckons me. 'Miss Tempest?'

I follow her into a room, which is a smaller version of the library. It holds a very large desk in a bay window and three armchairs around a coffee-table in front of a coal fire. A male and a female are standing by the fire, drinking coffee. I only have to look at them to feel a large and probably immovable chip appearing on my shoulder.

'Good morning, Miss Tempest,' the woman says. 'Do give Miss Pringle your coat and make yourself comfortable. I am Miss Daynforth, head of history, and this is my deputy, Mr Stein, an

American.' She makes it sound as if an American is a highly commendable piece of gadgetry that no *contemporary* college should be without. 'You'll know our specialities, of course.'

Miss Daynforth reminds me of a photograph I've seen of Lawrence of Arabia. She shares the same thin face, high cheekbones and pointed nose. She is tall and dressed in numerous layers of brown and beige wool. Her brown hair is coiled at the back of her neck. She wears no makeup and a heavy gold ring on her little finger.

The man is sparrow-boned, bald, wearing a bow-tie and steel-rimmed glasses. He is the most colour-co-ordinated man I have ever seen. His entire wardrobe – suit, waistcoat, shirt, even shoes – is in various shades of green, as if he was Robin Hood in a previous life. I sit down.

'Only two A levels, Miss Tempest?' the woman says. 'That's giving yourself a bit of a challenge, isn't it? Why not three? Usually we expect three, and we have some very clever people anxious to join us.'

I bumble, umm and aah my way through an explanation. The truth is that I'm only taking two subjects because nobody at the school thought there was any good reason why I should attempt three. 'I am taking an S level,' I end lamely, irritated that my sporadic attempts to talk posh are producing extremely weird results, like trying to gargle and sing simultaneously. Yet the ache to impress, the desire to be just like Them is irresistible.

Miss Daynforth gives a pinched smile. 'It's so terribly confusing, isn't it? These new red-brick universities and all the polytechnics have thrown up all sorts of problems with standards. Once upon a time we knew exactly how to measure entrants. Still, I'm sure it will all settle eventually. Mr Stein?' she says.

'Miss, er...' He looks down at his notes. 'Miss Tempest? Do you think Mr Wilson and his cabinet have made a good fist of governing the country so far?'

I find my eye drawn to the man's pale green bow-tie: what look like yellow tadpoles chase each other, disappearing under his collar, wriggling around his size fifteen and reappearing again.

'Miss Tempest?'

'Harold Wilson?' I repeat, playing for time. I slip off one shoe to relieve my throbbing feet, look down and see that my foot has turned a mulberry colour where the dye on my shoe has run. An aroma that my mother would immediately identify as Welsh rarebit begins to fill the room. I try to force my swollen foot back into its instrument of torture and find myself chasing the elusive shoe around under the chair with my toes.

Miss Daynforth looks pointedly at her watch and gives the smallest of sighs. As she does so, something red and ripe and juicy bursts inside me; my ears pop and crimson heatwaves shimmer up from the Afghan carpet. For the first time that day, I no longer care about how I look, walk, speak or behave.

How dare they both be so unfriendly, so super-cilious, so bloody damn dismissive? I ask myself. I look my female interrogator straight in the eye and tell myself, this sanctimonious, unfriendly upper-class cow hasn't said one word to put me at my ease. Well, she can stuff her bloody educational opportunity.

'Harold Wilson?' I answer sweetly, suppressed anger making me bold, a sense of injustice giving me eloquence where before I was dumb. 'I'll tell you what I think of Harold Wilson and his government, Mr Stein.' I give him a condensed version of Barry Taylor's several dozen lectures on the iniquities of King Harold.

I come to a conclusion. Silence. Miss Daynforth and Mr Stein exchange glances. He clears his throat. 'If I may précis your impressively robust assault, young lady,' he says, and proceeds ostentatiously to tick off with his fingers each of my points, 'first, Harold Wilson has sold out to the bosses. Second, he hasn't done enough to redistribute wealth. Third, he's been blinded by technology. Fourth, he is too much in the pocket of the United States of America, and fifth, he has let down the working man by his obsession with a prices and incomes policy while the rich get richer. Have I got that about right?' I detect a sneer in his voice. 'May I ask if you support any particular political party or revolutionary group, Miss, er ... Miss Thomas?'

'Tempest,' I reply curtly. 'My name is Tempest. No, I don't, but I've begun to think about the reasons why I don't,' I continue, passionately. 'Part of why I've stayed away from politics is my dad. He's working class but he doesn't wear a cloth cap, he's never worked down the mine and he doesn't vote Labour. Or Tory, for that matter. He says he only believes in the family. For him, that comes before politics, before unions, before country, before anything else. He says he fought in the war not for Britain or Churchill or freedom but to protect his own.

'He was a hero. He's got a medal to prove it, although he won't talk about it much, but he says that when he reads what the historians write he doesn't recognise himself or anyone else he fought alongside.' I'm aware I'm rambling but I no longer care. I've something to say and I'll say it, however incoherently. 'I think it's really strange that so many of the people who are part of the making of history never feel they are important enough to be considered a witness, don't you?' I look challengingly at Miss Daynforth, who shuffles the papers on her lap. 'We never talk about that in our history lessons. We never talk about the fact that a lot of what we're being taught is only a partial truth. We never even begin to consider whose voices we might be leaving out, which could change the picture altogether. Do we, Miss ... er ... Miss…?'

'Daynforth,' the woman prompts icily. 'That's a very interesting observation,' she comments flatly. 'Now, have you any questions you would like to ask us? Anything at all?'

I finally succeed in shoving my swollen foot into my shoe, suffering silent agonies as I do so. 'What I could ask is why you even bothered to see me when it's obvious to me from the start that you'd already made up your minds that I'm really not your kind of university material, not with two A levels and an accent,' I say aggressively, cheeks flushing. 'I could ask that but I won't because, frankly, I'm not interested in the answer any more.' Then I walk out, relieved that it's over and that neither Stein nor Daynforth can see my tears of rage.

I'd been true to myself. Authentic, as Barry would say. But where the hell had it got me?

Chapter Thirty-one

How about a lovely bacon sandwich?' Melody asks Daisy, later that Tuesday morning, when her daughter comes down dressed for work. She shakes her head. Her face is the colour of putty. Melody looks at her. 'Sit down, petal,' she instructs.

'Not now, Mam, I'll be late for work.'

'Sit down.'

Daisy does as she's told, pouring herself a mug of tea from the pot, shovelling in sugar. 'Queasy, are you?' Melody asks lightly.

Her daughter avoids her gaze. 'It's a bug,' she says. 'Everybody's got it at work. It's going round.'

'Is it a bug that turns into a baby in, what, six or seven months' time?'

Daisy bursts into uncontrollable sobs. 'I'm not pregnant, I'm not,' she keeps repeating, as if concocting a magic spell that will render her barren.

'How late are you?' Melody asks calmly. 'Have you told Carl yet?'

'Carl?' Daisy repeats, bewildered at the speed with which her plight has been revealed.

300

'Yes, Carl. Have you told him yet you're pregnant?'

Daisy shakes her head miserably. 'What's going to happen to me, Mam? What if he won't marry me? What if he leaves me once he knows?'

'He won't,' Melody replies firmly. 'That's not how it works. He's had his bit of fun, now it's paying-up time. Listen, in your dinner-break you go and tell him the truth and say we'd like to see him here this evening to discuss things.'

'I don't have to have it,' Daisy says. 'I know a girl at work who got rid of hers and she's fine now.'

'Too dangerous and not right,' Melody answers crisply. 'You don't want to die, do you? You don't want to mess about with yourself and then find the pregnancy is still on and you give birth to a defective, do you? One woman I know had a child with half its face missing. Terrible. Besides, it's good to have your children young. They grow up with you. You enjoy them more.'

Depression wraps its arms around Daisy.

'I thought that's what you've always wanted, Carl and you married with a family,' her mother soothes, rubbing her daughter's back for comfort.

'Married because he wanted to – not because he had to. What kind of a start is that? It's not very romantic, is it? And everybody will talk.'

'Not in front of me, they won't,' Melody says stoutly. 'Lots of couples have their children soon after they marry. These things happen. Just think yourself fortunate that you won't end up in a mother-and-baby home with adoption on the cards.'

301

'Adoption?' Daisy repeats weakly.

'I wouldn't hear of it.' Melody draws herself up to her full, imposing height.

'It's not your choice,' Daisy protests, without much conviction.

Kit, in an eye-wounding shocking-pink nylon baby-doll nightie and dressing-gown, which barely covers her backside, is about to bring in the milk from Rose's newly scrubbed doorstep when she notices the float still parked outside – as is the milkman. He is in his late teens, hair in a teddy-boy quiff. Oblivious to the cold and her state of undress, she calls, 'Oi, mister, over here.'

The milkman brightens considerably when he sees her. 'Me?' he asks.

'Well, there isn't any other bugger in the street, is there? Do you fancy a cuppa?'

He is up the garden path quicker than it takes to smash a milk bottle. Not once in his nine-month stretch as a milkman has a customer propositioned him – an injustice since it was this particular perk that had first attracted him to the job.

'Nice place,' he says, wondering if he should get stuck in immediately. 'Where's your old man?' he asks cautiously.

'He's a bare-knuckle fighter and he's in the front room, reading the paper.' She moves to block the milkman's flight. 'Only joking,' she says. 'Has anyone told you you look like that bloke from the Yardbirds? How many sugars? Sit there,' she instructs, bringing him into the kitchen. 'How much do you make?' she asks him directly. 'Is it your milk float? Are you on commission? How

302

does it work, then?'

Taken aback, the young man sits down, dazzled by the transparency of Kit's attire and puzzled by her small-talk.

'Tell me how the whole thing works,' she demands again, paper and pencil in hand.

Baffled, the milkman sits down slowly at the kitchen table. 'Are you telling me you brought me in here to discuss my job prospects?'

'Not yours, mine.' Kit smiles brightly. 'I'm looking for an opportunity.'

While Lily is crossing London, Barry Taylor at Lawson's has been called before management, who demand better productivity and job restructuring. A company specialising in time-and-motion studies had spent two weeks at Lawson's six months earlier. Its recommendations will require every department to ratchet up the pace by a notch or several.

'"Enough, no more." That's what we heard our Barry said. They call it modernisation but it's bloody pressure for profits, that's all it is,' one man tells Doug, as the two of them, in wellington boots, splash through five inches of grey, bloody water in the sluice room where the fish are disembowelled.

Fifteen minutes later, another employee, a woman, in the dye room has the same story, more intricately embroidered. 'Barry told them where they can stick their modernisation plan, that's what I heard. He said that we'd all walk out if they pushed their luck, bloody right 'n' all. There wouldn't be a worker in the place.'

'Wouldn't there?' Doug says.

By the end of the afternoon, the modernisation plan is temporarily postponed. Management take Barry Taylor aside and tell him he's pushing his luck. It's done informally, so there is no written record.

Every Tuesday Carl Hicks has a stall in Cwmland in the car park of the Grand Metropolitan. It sells cut-price forty-fives. A mate, Michael 'Dicky' Hart, works for a company that supplies records for juke-boxes. After a certain number of plays, they're replaced. 'Used' records are supposed to be passed on to charitable organisations to be melted down and transformed into attractive vinyl vases for sale. Instead they find their way to Carl's stall, the profit split between him and Dicky, not always fairly. Daisy makes for the hotel car park in her lunch break.

'Can I talk to you?' she asks Carl, as he stands well wrapped-up against the cold, fag in gloved hand.

'You're doing it, ain't you?' he says cheerfully.

'In private,' she insists.

Carl makes a big show of looking up and down the street. 'Nobody in earshot. Any more private than this, sweetheart, and your mother would be banging on the door.'

'Carl, this is serious.'

He studies her face, stubs his cigarette out, takes her arm and steers her round to the back of a Morris Minor so he can keep an eye on his goods. Before he can open his mouth, Daisy bursts into tears. 'I'm in the club,' she sobs.

She has mentally rehearsed this scene all morning. In one version, Carl sweeps her up in his arms, covers her face with kisses, and says, 'I'm going to be a father. You are a clever girl. I'm so proud of you. I'll marry you today.'

In practise, the alternative scenario proves true. 'Oh, fuck,' says Carl. Then walks into the pub.

I come out of St Catherine's at eleven forty-three a.m. According to the original plan, I have to take a train to Coventry at some point soon for my second interview. A bus appears. On the front it says 'Regent Street'. Why would I want to go through the humiliation of a second interview when I have the whole of my life ahead of me as – a hairdresser, a housewife, a caller in a bingo hall? Life is rich in its choices. Who needs a university education?

I take a decision. I board the bus and turn my back on academia and my ability, one day, to pay back Rose's loan. I could, of course, return her the ten quid outstanding but, hell, if today's the day for failure, I might as well go the whole hog.

I might as well shop.

In Carnaby Street, the angel Gabriel stands outside a boutique called Lord John. He has blond hair parted in the middle, falling in waves down to his shoulders, a long droopy moustache, multi-striped hipster trousers, a patterned shirt and a khaki army greatcoat. I know he's Gabriel because he tells me so and he says he's in another place.

'Peace,' says Gabriel dreamily, showing me two fingers. 'Got any cash?'

I pull out a few coins. I'd imagined Carnaby

Street as big and bold and glamorous. Instead it's small and seedy and dirty, more like a third-rate carnival than a brave new world. What is intoxicating is the fizz that comes from the sheer numbers of young people of all shapes, sizes, colours and extremes. In Fairport, we're always a nuisance minority.

I move on and into another boutique, clouded in incense and soaked in patchouli oil with the Hollies booming out. The girl behind the counter wears two sets of false eyelashes; her hair is cropped at the back and geometrically cut longer at the front and it swings when she moves. She wears a sugar pink mini-dress with a chain belt, and a black and white PVC mac with large white plastic ear-rings, which dangle like a trio of counters from each lobe. She's so thin her knees resemble Adam's apples. I want to be her.

An hour later, I am her – or almost. I am having my hair cut by Gavin whose hips are the width of a ruler. He comes from Ellesmere Port and he calls everybody darling. He cuts my straggly shoulder-length hair into a crop at the back and a geometrical curtain at the front, smooth and shiny and swinging, just like the girl's in the shop. The cost is astronomic but it includes a cup of tea. I tip extravagantly and Gavin advises me to go to Kensington High Street. 'You remind me ever so much of my sister Phyllis,' he says, as he helps me into Penny's fur coat.

'What does she do?' I ask.

'Nothing much,' he replies. 'She's a housewife with twins. But, like you, she's a very smiley sort of person.'

I take the tube, depressed at the thought of being considered a smiley sort of person. A man sits next to me, and interrupts my thoughts. 'Like a cigarette?' I shake my head, slightly alarmed. He has very blue eyes, black curly hair and a slight tan. He's wearing a shirt that matches his eyes, jeans, a navy heavy-knit sweater and a donkey jacket with the collar turned up.

'Going somewhere?' he asks, in a faint Scottish accent.

'No.' I smile to hide my nervousness. I've heard about strangers in London, mad axemen all. 'I'm sitting on the tube all day as a way of passing the time.'

'Now, there's a biting tongue,' he says mildly. I reckon he's in his early twenties, an old man by my standards. He shifts in his seat slightly, eyes smiling. 'My place or yours?' he asks.

Annoyingly, I turn pink. My feet hurt again.

'I'm being serious,' he says. 'This is the decision that could change your life.'

Kit pops out and buys two meat and potato pies and two custard tarts from the bakery. She places the pies in the oven and waits for Rose to return from the launderette. The two have settled quickly into a routine. Rose works in the mornings, Kit's shift at the Contented Sole begins at five p.m. They overlap for any length of time only in the middle of the day. She takes a seat at the kitchen table, opens a notebook and resumes her calculations. She has a plan.

Rose hears the radio a hundred yards down the road. She likes having the younger woman in the house. Somehow Kit has wriggled free from all the don'ts and should-nots and nevers and does-exactly-as-she-pleases with no evident sign of guilt or the creak of a conscience. She also has curiosity, warmth and an appetite for risk that attracts Rose hugely.

'And what time do you call this?' Kit opens the back door, arms akimbo, rolling-pin in hand. Rose laughs. 'What do you reckon?' Kit asks, producing the pies from the oven. 'Do you think Lily will be on her way to her second interview by now?'

'Probably,' says Rose. 'Any tea coming up?'

'She'll do all right, won't she?'

'Of course.'

'She told me you'd given her the money.'

'Did she now? She was supposed to keep that secret.'

'What were you saving it for?'

Rose shrugs. 'I was going to take that milkman you've got your eye on to Majorca for a fortnight.'

Kit grimaces. 'Him? He's a piss-pot. He pretends he's sipping chocolate milk all day but you can't fool me. It's shot full of vodka. I had a swig. You know what's really nice,' she adds, spreading out her hands in front of her. 'What's nice is being in a house with just the three of us, you and me and Billy. We were eight. When Mam was alive we ate in shifts. I tried to keep the same routine going after she died but the older ones just stood around picking as if the house was a railway-station buffet. Mam would have gone mad if she'd seen us.'

Rose pushes her plate away, puts her elbows on the table and cups her face in her hands. She speaks gently, watching Kit intently. 'She must have been a lovely woman, your mam. Was it difficult for you, watching Sally move in?'

Kit takes the salt cellar and pours a small hill of salt on the table. She throws a pinch over her shoulder and draws patterns with her finger in the remainder. Rose stays silent, giving her time.

'You know what I feel about Sally and my dad?' she says eventually, her eyes troubled. 'I'm scared for both of them, really scared. We all are – even Harry who was only five when Mam died.'

'Scared? Whatever for? Scared of what?'

Kit sighs. 'Everyone on the outside looking in thought that my mam and dad got on well. The real truth is that they couldn't live without each other but they were bloody awful together. They fought, and when they weren't fighting we'd go for days with them not speaking. I think that's why we kids turned into a pack of jokers. If we could make either of them laugh that big bubble of anger would burst for a while. So that was us, day in, day out, fooling around, making light, acting daft.

'My dad was devastated when she went. He blamed himself. He thinks he may have caused the cancer that killed her. I told him not to be so bloody stupid. She was only forty-two. And all she'd ever done was have babies, laugh now and then – and fight.' A tear dents the small mound of salt on the table in front of Kit.

'That's enough to make some people very happy,' Rose suggests softly. Impetuously, she goes over and places her arms around the younger woman, briefly resting her chin on her head. As

Rose does so, she smells honeysuckle in Kit's hair and feels the unexpected heat from a flicker of fire deep within her. Alarmed, she moves away quickly and busies herself refilling the kettle. 'So why should that make you scared for your dad and Sally? Do you think he's going to thump her?'

Kit looks appalled. 'God, no, my dad wouldn't strike a soul. It's just that squabbling and pecking away is such a habit with him, I'm worried that that's the only way he knows how to behave with a woman. I didn't want the young ones to get fond of Sally and then she ups and leaves. She's young, she won't put up with it like my mam did.'

Rose places a fresh mug of tea in front of Kit. 'So why didn't you stay at home?'

'My dad said that with me around it was like my mam's ghost in the house, watching the pair of them.'

'Did he tell you to go?'

'No. He'd never do that. He didn't have to. I just knew it was for the best. Anyway, at the time it didn't seem such a bad idea. I honestly thought I'd marry Podge. He's a nice enough bloke but in thirty years' time we'd still be stuck in exactly the same relationship as we are now – give or take a few pimples. And I don't want that. I want something that goes somewhere. Do you know what I mean?'

'Yes. I think I do,' Rose answers.

Chapter Thirty-two

Biba's in Kensington Church Street is a converted butcher's shop, art deco, black and purple and gold. Clothes hang on a dozen or so coatstands. The assistants are Amazon skeletons in calf-length jersey dresses in raspberry and plum, eyes like marionettes'.

The tiny changing room is a lawn of discarded clothes. Bob Dylan's 'Like A Rolling Stone' is playing full blast. Conversation is pointless; semaphore rules. Everything I see, I want. Mash, the man I met on the tube, sits on a wall outside and waits. His name, he's told me, is Chris Nash, but he's always known as Mash. He's a medical student at St Thomas's – or so he says. He shares a flat with three friends in Palace Gardens Terrace, a few minutes' walk away. He's asked absolutely no questions of me. He said he'd been on his way to a couple of lectures but he'd changed his plans because he hated to see a bird in distress.

'I wasn't in distress,' I'd protested heatedly.

'You would've been if you'd missed the chance of meeting me,' he'd replied. So that's where we are now. Him outside, in the March winds, me inside, black Biba carrier bags in hand. A girl with long, silvery blonde hair and the features of a model casually helps herself to a couple of long-sleeved T-shirts and puts them in her bag, strung across her shoulder. She smiles at me as if we're in this together.

'Did you get what you wanted?' Mash asks, taking my hand when I emerge.

'Don't you mind shopping?' I ask, intrigued, since no boy in Fairport will be seen within a hundred yards of a retail outlet.

'Love it,' he says. 'I've got two older sisters and they spend more time in changing rooms than they do at home.'

Mash helps me to buy presents: a pair of goalie gloves for Billy, a burnt orange Indian scarf, decorated with tiny mirrors, for Rose, gardenia talcum powder for Mam, a pair of silver-plated cufflinks in the shape of Big Ben for Dad, Mary Quant tights for Daisy, Kit and Penny, each with a daisy embroidered on the ankle, and a sensible purse for Iris so she can continue to save for her wedding.

Then I remember Dulcie and Kath. 'Thank God, you don't come from a big family,' Mash says mildly. I buy Dulcie a Cat Stevens record, 'Matthew and Son', and a gruesome paperback for Kath. Rose's money is holding out well, and as there's no going back now, I extend my generosity to my newly acquired companion. 'What would you like?' I ask. 'It would've taken me twice as long without you.'

'What I'd like is this,' he says, and takes my face in his hands and kisses me gently on the lips. In comparison to Bryn, it's as if a fresh set of batteries have been inserted in my libido. 'What I'd like is to buy you a meal. I know a bistro just round the corner, open all day.'

The place is packed. It has a stripped-pine floor, bare tables, candles and, although it's

312

daylight outside, the feel of midnight about it. No one is over twenty-five and when the waitresses, long-legged like giraffes in aprons, take the order, they write it on a napkin and leave it on the table. Stupidly, I choose duck à l'orange. I have never eaten duck in my life. Mash watches me chase the bony breast in a jacket of fat around a plate of liquid marmalade. We drink white wine, which is too dry for me and makes me sleepy.

'Shouldn't you be studying or something?' I ask eventually. 'I should,' he says, pushing my geometrical swinging fringe back from my eyes. 'But I'm a situationist. Do you know about situationism?' I shake my head. 'We believe that we're all in danger of turning into robots, work, home, homework. We criticise modern consumer society for alienating people and turning their lives into a meaningless pursuit of commodities.'

'But I've just spent the last two hours shopping?'

'So you're not a situationist. I am.'

'But you said you enjoyed it too.'

'As a temporary diversion, not a way of life. At Christmas a couple of us dressed up as Father Christmas and went into Harrods and tried to give the shop's toys away to all the kids in the store.' He laughs ruefully. 'We'd only given five away when Security chucked us out.'

'What's all that got to do with me?'

'I'm just saying I don't believe in inflexible moral rules. For instance, you don't know me from Adam. I could be a rapist, a killer, a drug-dealing pimp who wants to put you on the streets once I've filled you up with heroin. I'm not any

313

of those. I'm an ordinary, decent bloke. I see you on the tube. I'm attracted to you. I have a girlfriend already, a steady girlfriend. Now, what am I going to do? Go to my lectures like a good boy? Pretend I never set eyes on you? Or do I take a chance – if only for a day? From the point of view of all sorts of people, what we're perhaps about to do is wrong. But if the end result is that we've had fun, given each other a bit of pleasure, made a tiny difference to our respective views of the world, then doesn't that have to be good?'

He smiles and calls for the bill. 'We'll split it,' I announce rashly.

'It's my dad's treat,' he insists, much to my relief. He puts his finger to my lips. 'Remember,' he says. 'You don't have to tell me anything – truth or lies. What we have is now. So, what's it to be? My place or the rest of your life?'

As we leave, I can't quite decide whether I've met an up-market version of bullshitting Pete, or a deep-thinking lover man. Either way, it's a good line: my place or the rest of your life?

Walking across the market square after work, Doug Tempest stops in front of Bunting's former site. Two months after the fire, fresh foundations have been laid and a large builder's hoarding announces the opening in May of a new self-service Co-operative Store.

The late afternoon holds a strong hint of spring. The hardware store owner already has his window festooned with plastic daffodils and fake Easter eggs. Doug looks again. A child in a blue coat skips across the square, chasing a hula-hoop.

A real child who brings no pain to his heart, no fears for a future forfeited by one act of baseness. 'Grandad!' calls a voice behind him. He turns to see Billy, running excitedly down Rydol Crescent towards him, arms outstretched. Doug catches him and swings him round and round and round, until the boy, giggling, begs for mercy.

'I'll race you to the house. If I get there first, you lose all the toffees I have in my pocket. If you get there first, I keep all the toffees in my pocket.' Billy bolts forward, then stops dead, realising he has been tricked.

'Catch!' Doug laughs, and throws him the paper bag. Together, hand in hand, they walk home.

'He can't come until later tonight.' Daisy lays the table for tea while her mother stirs several saucepans in the kitchen.

Melody emerges as her daughter sits down, tears never far away. 'Look, I know it probably feels like the worst thing that's ever happened,' Melody tells her gently, 'but in a few weeks, looking back, it won't appear nearly as bad. It might even be a blessing in disguise.'

'Heavily disguised,' Daisy comments wearily. She fiddles with the tablecloth. 'Mam, can I ask you something?' Melody nods. 'Did you ever – you know – before you got married? With Dad, I mean.'

Melody feigns horror. 'Whatever next? I wouldn't dream of telling you such a thing. That's private business. Anyway, things were different then.'

'What do you mean, different?'

'Just different.'

'What do you think our Lily'll be doing now?' Doug asks at tea, putting down his knife and fork and lighting a cigarette. 'Do you reckon she'll be all right finding her way around London? I thought she'd back out, change her mind at the last minute. She's done that before now. If something happens to her, I'll never forgive myself.'

'What if something happens to her that's nice?' Billy pipes up.

'I'll tan her hide,' Melody replies, in mock seriousness. 'If, that is, we ever find out. Eat up, Daisy,' she instructs. 'You need your strength.'

Chapter Thirty-three

Mash's flat consists of four large rooms with high ceilings, a small kitchen and access down a fire escape to a backyard, which Mash refers to as the Patio. The windows in Mash's room are breathtaking: floor-to-ceiling, leading out to two first-floor balconies, overlooking a communal garden.

Neatly stacked LPs provide a vinyl skirting-board along one wall. On the other walls he has posters of Jimi Hendrix, Che Guevara and an Indian god who has an elephant's trunk and several arms. A skeleton hangs from a clothes rail, dressed in a black lace brassière. The room also holds piles of books, a battered leather sofa, cushions and a mattress on the floor covered with a rumpled patchwork quilt. A pile of dirty washing is behind the door.

I stand on one side of his mattress, him on the other. I look at my watch. 'Don't go,' he says. 'I really like you.' The Punch and Judy show that has been playing inside my head, ever since I crossed the threshold, resumes trading blows: 'Go on, do it! You can't. Not with a stranger. Go on! No! Go on! No! Go on! No! It's rude, bad, wicked. Go on. No.'

'But who's going to find out?' says the puppet policeman.

Kath Morgan is devouring the details of the recent escape and recapture of Albert DeSalvo, the Boston Strangler, from a mental institution, an excuse for the media to detail his crimes once again.

Kit, slicing spuds into chips, watches her evident enjoyment with distaste. 'Kath, I hope you don't mind me asking, but why are you so interested in such gory stuff?' she asks. 'Why not go for love and romance and some enchanted evening, that kind of thing?'

Kath puts down her magazine. 'You learn a lot about human nature when crimes are committed. Not everyone is nice, you know. The Boston Strangler raped and murdered at least thirteen women.'

'You can learn about human nature in plenty of other ways as well,' Kit retorts robustly.

'No, you can't. Not with people the way they are. Without even realising they're doing it, they adjust a bit here, exaggerate something there, and before they know it, they've fashioned a whole new truth. Memories are just another word for story-telling. Everybody does it, some worse than others. I'm as bad as anyone,' Kath continues. 'I always say our mother left because my dad gave her no choice, he was that violent. But now I wonder. Perhaps, she left because she was fed up with the lot of us. Didn't want us. Never wanted us in the first place. Perhaps he used to thump hell out of her because she provoked him, tore him apart with jealousy. I wanted my mam to be the good thing in our lives. But maybe she wasn't. She never wrote, never sent a card. My dad told us she didn't care about us, and for all these years I've told myself he was lying. But perhaps he wasn't.' Kath wipes down the counter vigorously. 'But think about it,' she points the cloth at Kit, 'just suppose, one day, she'd turned up as a corpse. By the time the investigation was over, I would have had a lot of those questions answered, wouldn't I? See how it works?'

'Bloody hell!' Kit shivers. 'It's a pretty grim way to uncover a few family secrets, isn't it?'

Kath turns the sign on the chip shop door to 'Open'. 'That's why I'm interested in murder. It peels away all those layers of deception. It's what I imagine happens in an autopsy. Cut the body open and reveal what's always been there but not to the eye. Murder has that effect. A life is lost and everyone who's touched by it can't keep their secrets any more.

'A while back, there was a man called Peter Kurten, a German factory worker. His wife said he loved children, went to church, worked hard, he was a lovely man in the house. A friendly man. It turned out he was a sadist and a pervert. He'd killed and raped nine women and young children. The psychiatrists said he'd loved the sight of blood, the humiliation of his victims. He drew a sense of achievement from mutilation and murder. It was only by a fluke that he was caught. He could've gone on for years. He was a completely different person under the skin. And now he's in the history books for ever. And that's the other thing,' she adds, giving the younger woman a sideways glance, 'murder makes the ordinary famous.'

Kit stops peeling. She can feel the hairs on the back of her neck rising. 'That's horrible!' she bursts out. 'Are you saying it's worth killing somebody just to get your face in the paper? You wouldn't really knock someone off just to make your name, would you?'

Kath goes over to the sink and washes her hands. 'I've got enough on my conscience without adding murder,' she replies grimly. 'How about you?'

Our clothes lie in two piles on either side of the mattress. Suddenly, with the ease of a pole-vaulter, Mash flips himself on top of me. A second later I'm out of bed. Propelled by what? Self-preservation? Conscience? Or my mother's voice: *'You make your bed, you lie in it.'*

'Fuck!' says Mash. 'What's happening? What did I do wrong?'

'I'm sorry, I'm really sorry,' I say, struggling to dress. I expect him to be abusive and insulting

319

but he is neither. 'It's not you, it's me. I can't. I mean, I won't. It's not you, it's all sorts of other things ... I'm sorry.'

Mash sits up in bed, running his fingers through his hair. 'Christ,' he says. 'Is this your first time?'

'Of course it's not,' I insist, red-faced, only partly from trying to force my swollen and battered feet back into my shoes. 'It's not that at all. I just don't think this is...' I want to say 'right' but that wouldn't sound hip at all. 'It's not fair on my boyfriend, Bryn,' I improvise. 'It's disloyal.'

'Christ, man,' Mash smiles, 'you don't need to worry about that. Situationists believe–'

'I know, I know,' I interrupt. One political lecture a day is quite enough.

He jumps up, stark naked, easy with himself, and reaches for my hands. I try to keep my eyes on his face but it's difficult. 'You're right,' I admit. 'I haven't done it before. I don't want to get pregnant. I don't want to get gonorrhoea or syphilis. Above all, I don't want you to go and boast about it in the pub tonight.'

Mash looks at me incredulously. 'What kind of trip are you on? This is about pleasure, nothing else, no love, no ties, no commitment, just having fun in the way that men and women have had fun since time began. A journey to the astral plain. End of a satisfactory transaction. If it's really enjoyable, we come back for seconds, or thirds. No strings.'

Mash and Kit should get together, I think ruefully. Both can shed guilt as easily as a snake slips out of its skin. So why can't I? Why can't I be a girl who does, instead of one who doesn't?

'I'm not easy, you know,' I hear myself say wetly. In theory, the notion of a one-night – or, more precisely, a one-afternoon – stand seems exotic, exciting, grown-up. In practice, for some inexplicable reason, it suddenly seems quite threatening. Perhaps, deep down, what frightens me most is that once I start breaking the rules what will happen if I don't know how to stop?

Mash looks baffled. 'You look all cocky and confident and underneath, you're not that at all, are you? You don't really think I'm going to go down the pub and tell everyone? Don't be ridiculous. For a start, they won't have a clue who you are.'

'You'd be the first bloke I know who didn't. Even when they haven't, they say they have.'

'So what the hell have you got to lose?' Shivering, he wraps the quilt around himself and draws me down to the bed. 'You're a grown-up now. So long as you know why you do what you do, who gives a shit what anybody else thinks? What's the worst that can happen? That they talk about you? So bloody what?' Gently he kisses me and sighs. 'Goodbye, Lily Tempest,' he says. 'Come back when you're ready.'

Half-way to Euston station, I go back. I'm ready. And it is a long, long way from home.

'I'm sorry, I missed my connection.' I try to look contrite. I'd phoned to tell Bryn I was coming home a day early but then I missed the train I'd intended to catch. He must have been waiting for almost an hour. I'm sure that the loss of my virginity is emblazoned across my front and back in fluorescent capitals.

'So, how did it go?' Bryn eventually asks, a mile from Fairport. 'Do you think they'll give you a place?'

I shake my head. 'I wouldn't think so for a minute. I made a complete mess of the whole interview.'

'That means you're in,' Bryn replies glumly. 'Whenever you say you've been crap, it turns out the other way. At least Dad'll be pleased. He's asked if we'll give him a hand leafleting at the weekend. It's about Vietnam. I told him, "No other bastard bothers, so why should we?"'

'What did he say?'

'He said, "Because it matters."'

'I think he's right.'

'Bollocks,' Bryn comments cheerfully, unusually communicative. 'Of course it doesn't bloody matter. People want a bit of cash in their pocket, a telly in the front room and a fortnight's holiday where it doesn't rain. They don't give a flying toss about Vietnam. Or anywhere else that isn't here.'

'I care,' I say, partly because I'm miffed that he hasn't said anything about my new hair-do and partly because sexually experienced women can say what they like. 'I care very much about Vietnam. And so should you. It's about freedom and democracy and social justice – and imperialism.'

Bryn groans. 'Oh, Jesus,' he says, 'it's bad enough hearing it from my dad without you starting too. One day in London and you come back Miss Bloody Politics 1967. What's happened to you to get you so fired up?'

322

'Nothing at all,' I say.

Rydol Crescent is brightly lit but strangely silent: no sounds of arguments or television or radio or records. I let myself in, followed by Bryn. The family is in the back room, frozen in a tableau. Mum and Dad sit at the table. Iris is in front of the fire; on her lap is a half-completed letter, probably to Howard. Daisy, white-faced, stands next to a sulky Carl in front of the fire; both are staring at the flying ducks on the opposite wall, as if they expect one to flap its wings suddenly and make a break for the window.

'Who's died?' Bryn jokes.

'What's happened?' I ask. 'Are you all right, Daisy? What is it? What's the matter?'

Mam kisses me. 'You're back early. Why's that? How did you get on? Did it go well? We've got a little bit of a ... a little bit of a situation here. And we've come to a – well, a dead end, I suppose you might call it.'

'I'm pregnant,' Daisy announces flatly.

'Christ,' says Bryn.

'No, pal, it's mine. I'm going to be a father.' Carl almost sounds proud.

'It was only the once,' Daisy protests weakly.

'I've said I'll marry her,' Carl tells me, as if I've personally called him to account. 'She's been nagging me about that for ages, but now I've said I'll marry her and look after the kid, guess what? She doesn't want to know. Beats me. Do you understand women, Bryn, mate? Because I don't. I've told her straight, if it's not her now, it'll be some other bird later who's up the spout. So I might as well call it a day and do the deed

323

with Daisy.'

'Glad to see you haven't lost the romantic touch, then, Carl,' I say sharply, and reach for my sister's hand. 'Don't you want the baby, Daisy? You don't have to have it, do you?' Five pairs of eyes immediately stare at me.

'That's murder,' Carl says. 'My mam would go mad if she found out. She'd skin me alive, she would. Not that she'll be best pleased when she hears about this, anyway.'

'Daisy, what do you want to do?' I prompt my sister gently. 'You must have been really scared when you found out. Why didn't you tell one of us?'

'I don't know,' says Daisy, giving my hand a squeeze. 'I do want to marry him, Lily, but not like this. Not with a baby and no time on our own and that. That's not how I thought it would happen. I wanted Carl to say he loved me and propose because he wanted me. Not because he's got no choice. What sort of a start is that?'

'Same start as half the girls in my secondary modern,' Bryn offers cheerfully. 'And they're not doing so bad. Sandra Hughes is on her third and she's not even twenty-one yet. And her bloke's been inside for the past eighteen months. Ruddy miracle, that is...'

'It can work.' Mam speaks softly. 'If you want it to.'

'How about this?' Theatrically Carl goes down on one knee. 'Daisy Violet Tempest, will you marry me and be the mother of my children?'

Faces brighten. Daisy sobs, 'You don't understand anything, do you? None of you do. Leave

324

me alone. I hate you all.' And she flees from the room, runs upstairs and locks the bedroom door.

'Well, I'm buggered if I know if that's a yes or a no.' Carl cracks his knuckles, his confidence barely dented. 'New hairdo, Lil?'

'How much have you got left?' Rose asks her sister.

'Left, you say?' Lily repeats.

'Yes, the money I gave you. You can't have spent it all. How much have you got left? If you didn't go to the second interview, you must have loads still. When I said spend it, I meant on something bloody worthwhile – not shite presents.'

We sisters and Kit have gathered around Rose's kitchen table to discuss Daisy's dilemma. 'I don't care how much money there is, I want an abortion,' she repeats woodenly. 'Even if Carl never looks at me again, I want an abortion.'

'You told me the first time we met at your mam's that you wanted four children and you couldn't wait to get married,' Kit says, perplexed. 'What's changed?'

Daisy shrugs, tears never far away.

'How much money have you got, Lily?' Rose repeats, with increasing urgency. 'Let's see your purse.'

Lily swiftly moves across the kitchen and out of Rose's range. 'How much have I got left, you say?'

Rose jumps up now, furious. 'Bloody hell, don't tell me you've spent it all? I swear to God I'll bloody murder you if you have.'

Kit intervenes: 'Look, let's concentrate on one

problem at a time. If Lily's spent it, she's spent it. Daisy says she doesn't want this baby. She knows the risks – you know that if something goes wrong, you might never be able to have kids, don't you, Daisy? You're sure you understand that?'

Dumb with misery, Daisy nods. Kit gives her a hug. 'Right, well, I know a woman who'll do it. She's in Prestryn,' she says matter-of-factly, naming a town, a forty-five-minute drive away. 'She charges fifteen guineas and it takes about twenty minutes. The only problem is the cash.'

'You should be ashamed of yourself, Lily Tempest,' Rose interrupts. 'I thought you'd bring a bit back at least. Now look at the mess we're in.'

'I'm really sorry, I didn't mean to spend it. It just happened.'

'You're just like Mam,' Rose snaps. 'Spending money that's not yours on stuff that nobody wants.'

'Don't you dare say I'm like Mam. I am not. You've never been to London. You don't know what it's like. I am not like Mam. You take that back!'

Kit bangs her mug on the table. 'Will you two shut up? Look, can we each put in a quid?'

'I've spent my beauty-queen prize money but I've got three pounds saved in my Christmas club,' Daisy offers.

'Christmas club?' Kit repeats, impressed. 'But it's only March.'

'I like to plan ahead,' Daisy answers defensively. 'Well, usually I do.'

'I've got one pound fifteen shillings and a few coppers left, and she can have all my hotel money

326

on Saturday,' Lily volunteers in a quiet voice.
Rose throws her a dirty look. 'Chalkie's probably got a bit put by. I could–'
'I don't want anyone else to know,' Daisy breaks in, white-faced. 'What about Pete?' Iris suggests. 'He's got cash. Kath said he bought her a new outfit for the telly and told her he'd won money on the horses.
'Has he got cash?' Kit brightens. 'That's interesting to know.'
'He'd've spent it by now,' Lily says. 'And, besides, if we borrowed it off him, he'd expect the other in return. And I'm not volunteering.'
'We've got eight pounds fifteen shillings – we need another seven quid,' Rose calculates.
'I've got an idea,' Kit says.
'What are you going to do?' Daisy asks nervously.
'Hope luck is on our side,' Kit replies.

Iris sleeps, snoring, in a white face pack so it looks as if a dinner plate lies on her pillow. 'It's your turn,' Lily whispers.
'I can't get out of bed. I've got morning sickness,' Daisy protests.
'But it's the middle of the night.'
'It strikes at any time.'
Lily rolls out and tiptoes across the freezing linoleum. She gives Iris a shove hard enough to make her shift position and the snores ebb away. On the return journey, Lily stubs her toe on an Electrolux toaster, peeking out from under the bed. 'What do you think she sees in Howard?' she whispers to Daisy, as she slides in beside her,

teeth chattering, and rubs her back.

'A husband,' Daisy replies. A tear slides out of the corner of her eye. Any kindness, however small, brings on a watery response.

Lily leans on her elbow and peers at her sister in the gloom. 'You can always change your mind, keep the baby and marry Carl, you know,' she says. 'You don't have to get rid of it. I bet you'd be a really good mam.'

Daisy sits up, gives a howl, buries herself in her sister's arms, mumbling into her shoulder.

'What did you say?' Lily asks.

'I said ginger, it'll be born ginger,' Daisy sobs. 'It'll be born ginger and everybody will know.'

'Ginger?' Lily responds stupidly.

'It'll be ginger. And once I'd done it with him I had to do it with Carl, just in case. But as soon as Carl sees it, he'll know it's not his and so will everybody else. It'll be ginger and curly. Lily, I don't know what to do. What if this is the only chance I have to have a baby? What if the abortion goes wrong?'

They look instinctively at Iris, who snores soundly.

'Whose is it, then?' Lily asks.

'Don't you know? You introduced us.'

'Oh, God, it's not Pete's, is it?' Lily is horror-stricken.

'No. It's Daniel Bright.'

'Who?'

'Daniel Bright, Mr Big Ballad. Big Bastard more like. It's his. I got drunk and had sex with him and I can't remember a thing about it, except that he had the same smell as one of our boxes of

328

assorted biscuits. So I slept with Carl too, to cover myself.'

'But Daniel Bright is blond,' Lily points out pedantically.

'His other bits aren't.'

Lily giggles and even Daisy manages a smile. 'So what am I going to do?' she asks Lily.

'You could tell Carl the truth.'

'Are you crackers?'

'OK, you don't tell Carl, you have the baby and then you leave it to the neighbours. As soon as you wheel it out in the pram, they'll be full of how much like Carl he or she is. It happens all the time. Say it's a throwback to our ginger past.'

Daisy pulls the covers over her head. 'Oh, Lily, if God will make this all right, I swear I'll never have sex with another human being ever again in my whole life,' she whimpers. 'What am I going to do?'

'I honestly don't know,' Lily replies. And Daisy howls all the more because her sister usually has an answer for everything.

Two of the few skills Kit was taught at school were shorthand and typing. Now she types fast. She is using Don Wilson's typewriter in his empty study on Friday morning. 'Did you write this?' Penny asks.

'No, I didn't,' Kit replies, trying to prevent her reading over her shoulder. 'It's private, if you don't mind. I'm doing somebody a favour. They've written it in pencil and it needs to look a bit more professional. But it's a secret. Swear you won't tell anyone, Penny. Swear on my deathbed.'

Penny nods and pours herself a large glass of sherry.

'You want to knock off the sauce,' Kit admonishes her. 'Does it run in your family? If you drink in the day, you turn into an alcoholic.'

'I'm nerving myself.'

'What for?'

'Bulbie and I are having sex tonight.'

'How do you know?'

'Because I told him I would and I've always refused before. Dad's at a conference in York and Mummy's going too. You and Podge can stay the night, if you like.'

Kit shakes her head. 'No, thanks. We finished for good yesterday. I told him I was packing him in for his own sake. He deserves someone better. So, of course, he agreed. We're going to be friends.' Kit can't contain herself any longer: 'If I tell you something swear on your deathbed you won't tell a living soul? Daisy Tempest is up the spout.'

'No!'

'Yup. It's Carl's but she wants an abortion. You don't have a few bob you could contribute to it, do you? We're about seven quid short.'

Penny puts her glass down slowly. 'I'm really sorry. It's against my principles. I don't believe in the murder of the unborn child.'

'But you're not even Catholic. You're not even anything. I can't believe you're talking such a load of old bollocks, Oh, I get it,' Kit intuits. 'Your mother's pro-abortion so that automatically makes you against. Is that it? Do you really think it's right that kids of fifteen, sixteen, are packed off to some bloody horrible home with a lot of prune-faced cows telling them they should be ashamed of themselves only to hand over their baby to some jolly middle-class couple called Hugo and Annabel? Do you really think that's fair?' Kit is now shaking with rage. 'My mam did that and she always said she had a damn great hole where her child should've been – and she went on to have six more and we didn't fill the hole either. At least with abortion the decision is made, without lives being totally wrecked.'

'Except the baby that's killed, of course,' Penny retaliates, taken aback by the force of the normally easy-going Kit's passion.

'It's a foetus, not a baby. My mam called her baby Marlon, after Marlon Brando, and she said goodbye to him when he was five days old. The nuns took a picture of him and gave it to her. She kept it on the mantelpiece. She used to say that Marlon would find her one day. But he never did.'

Kit begins typing again, hitting the keys savagely. 'How do you know where to go to get one?' Penny asks. 'An abortion, I mean.'

'You'd be surprised the kind of things I know, Persephone Wilson.'

Penny drains her glass and reaches for a Toby jug on the sideboard. 'There's a couple of pounds in here. Take one. They'll never notice. But I'm still against it on principle,' she adds primly.

Kit rips the page out of the typewriter and reaches for her coat. 'Do me a favour, Penny Wilson,' she says tersely, 'grow up and make the most of what's been handed to you on a plate. Oh, and keep your bloody money. We'll manage without it, thanks very much.'

Chapter Thirty-four

Pete 'The Mercenary' Wells has had his teeth done – including a couple of gold crowns. Seeing himself smile on a television monitor prompted him to take action. Now when he visits his daughter, Hayley, at his mother-in-law's house, the toddler wails and refuses to stop. Marie, his estranged wife, is unimpressed. 'You've got another woman,' she says.

Without telling either Penny or Lily, on the grounds that they wouldn't understand her motives, Kit has made a visit to his house and, since she cannot resist her childhood training, she has taken a mop, brush and duster to it. The result is clean but Spartan. Once the rubbish is removed, there's not much else in the way of furnishings.

'What you need is a lodger,' she tells Pete. They quickly come to an agreement. Kit will alternate living with Rose when Chalkie is away and Pete when Chalkie is home for a small rent. 'That way nobody gets fed up with anybody.'

She also persuades her new part-time landlord to invest in a three-piece suite and a couple of rugs.

'He's not very hygienic, though, is he?' Lily says disapprovingly, when Kit eventually tells her about her new accommodation arrangements.

'He is when I'm around,' she replies firmly. 'He washes up quite well.'

'You're not…'

'Of course I will, but only when it suits,' Kit replies defiantly.

Kit refrains from asking Pete for a loan to help Daisy because she already has an alternative plan for which she will require some of his resources. She does, however, tell him that the girls are going on a day out and would like to borrow his battered white van, which bears the legend 'Willy Wonder Window Cleaners'. Since he has already gleaned that she may be generous with her favours when she is herself indulged, Pete agrees.

Four days after their original meeting, Kit has sufficient money to pay for the termination. She tells Daisy and the others that the woman has agreed to take half her payment now, half later. An appointment is made. On the agreed day Lily and Daisy leave the house as normal, to avoid raising suspicions. Lily changes out of her school uniform at Rose's. Then the three, Kit, Daisy and Lily, squeeze into the front seat of Pete's van. Attempts at making conversation are half-hearted. The radio fails to work.

'Is this place dirty? Do you think it'll be like the scene in *Alfie?*' Daisy asks nervously.

Kit is firm. 'You won't be in there long enough to notice. Will she?'

Lily nods in agreement but her doubts are multiplying by the minute. What if Daisy dies? What if she is rendered infertile? What if it's torture? What if the truth comes out and everybody blames her because she originally put Daniel Bright and Daisy together? Lily smiles at her sister as reassuringly as she can.

'How did Carl react when you told him?' Kit asks.

'I haven't told him,' Daisy replies, looking straight ahead. 'I'm not going to tell him. I'm going to marry him, then say I've had a miscarriage.'

Kit drives up and over the kerb, narrowly missing a lamp-post. 'God, Daisy, you're worse than me,' she says.

The house is in a cul-de-sac of newly built homes, each identical except for the different brightly painted doors and the gardens, barren of flowers but marked by curving garden paths, miniature wells and wrought-iron gates. Number four has a discreet sign on the wall, which reads, in gold paint on blue, 'Harold Wootton, Chiropodist', followed by a lot of letters.

'I'm not going anywhere near a man,' Daisy protests, sitting in the van. 'You never said it would be a man.'

'She's not,' Kit answers. 'Harold's her husband. He's got a part-time practice here, and one in Chester. She used to be a nurse but got struck off.'

'Terrific! Now you tell us,' Lily comments, her unease increasing.

'Well, the job of local abortionist is hardly going to attract anyone tip top, is it?' Kit says sarcastically. 'Anyway, she'll be out of business soon when it's legal.' Then she adds, in a softer tone, 'Are you sure you don't want to change your mind, Daisy?'

'I'm sure.'

'Right, you wait here,' Kit instructs. 'She's left me the address under the empty milk bottle. She never works at home.'

334

Ten minutes later, the van pulls up outside a butcher's shop. Daisy, Kit and Lily stare at the window, with its trays of bloodied chops, folded ox tongues and lumps of liver. 'I think I'm going to be sick,' Daisy says. A butcher's boy winks at them. 'Do you think he knows?' she asks tremulously. Nobody answers. Kit rings the bell on a door to the left of the shop. A woman appears instantly.

She seems ordinary, nondescript, a little watery-eyed. She wears a pale blue Crimplene dress with a beige cardigan and sensible shoes. Her hair is neatly permed. Both Lily and Daisy had assumed on the basis of a couple of films that all abortionists had a bottle in one hand and a fag hanging out of their mouth.

The woman speaks brusquely. 'I'll have the girl in question and one other, no more. There's a café down the road. Wait there half an hour – no longer because I'm busy today – then come back. Have you brought sanitary towels? Come with me.'

Lily and Daisy follow the woman up a steep flight of stairs. A strange muted sound, half sigh, half sob, escapes from Daisy's lips. Her face is ghostly white.

'Have you got the money?' the woman asks bluntly, when they reach the landing. Kit had handed Lily the envelope in the van and she in turn passes it on. To her surprise, the woman counts out the full sum, fifteen pounds and fifteen shillings. Under the naked bulb on the landing, Lily notices a greyness to the woman's skin and a slight tremble in her hands.

'In there.' She nods to one door. 'I'll be with you in a minute.'

335

The two girls go into a room that is chilly with no pretence of comfort. An elderly gas fire burns. A small rag rug provides the only carpet. Along one wall, under a framed 'Home Sweet Home' embroidery, there is a camp bed with two blankets. Next to it is a bucket and a pile of old towels that carry the same hospital mark. In one corner is a kitchen sink, a single gas ring and a kettle.

In the centre of the room is a large dining-room table, covered bizarrely with a gaudy plastic tablecloth patterned with maracas, Mexican hats and the legend, 'Welcome to Mexico!' Also on the table is a cushion, a bowl of soapy water, a rubber douche and the largest syringe either girl has ever seen. Daisy takes two steps forward and faints.

Kath Morgan, coat undone, face without makeup, runs down Rydol Crescent, uncaring that she is still in her slippers and with a pink curler in her hair. She charges into Woolworth's and runs as if the devil is nipping at her heels. Dulcie carefully lays out children's socks and knickers in neat lines, too absorbed in her work at first to hear the approaching maelstrom. 'Dulcieeee!' Kath screeches, and spots her prey at the other end of the shop.

Dulcie moves behind the counter, in the vain belief that Kath, an ordinary customer, will respect that this area is hallowed ground on which only Woolworth's personnel are allowed to tread. Kath darts in, showing no respect.

'What's the matter, Kath?' she asks. 'Are you all right?'

Kath, aware she has attracted a small crowd, whips the curler out of her hair and tucks it up her sleeve. 'Dulcie, I'm going to be on television. The letter came this morning. I'm going to be on television! The couple they chose instead of us have dropped out so we're going to be on telly. We're going to be on telly! *We're going to be on the telly!* On April the second! Oh, my Lord, can you believe it? On television. Me?'

'Just you?' Dulcie asks, happy for her sister.

'Don't be silly. Me and Pete, of course. It's a couples show. How can I do it on my own?'

Dulcie looks alarmed. 'But he said he didn't want–'

Kath interrupts, smiling, 'Oh, he'll do it all right. Pete will do it.'

'Open your legs. Come on, dear, the longer you take, the worse it'll be.' Lily holds Daisy's hand tightly and wonders why the nameless abortionist doesn't wear rubber gloves or a mask or a doctor's coat, anything to make the procedure look a bit more medical and a bit less like a mild distraction from bingo.

'I'd say you've left it late-ish. Tried anything yourself, lovey?'

Daisy looks at her blankly. 'Knitting needle? Slippery elm? Ex-lax? Snakeroot? Rue and parsley? Gin?'

Daisy shakes her head. The abortionist's face is without expression. 'If this doesn't work, come back within twenty-four hours,' the woman intones mechanically. 'You get two goes for your money. If it has worked, heavy bleeding should start very shortly. If the bleeding continues for more than a day and you have a fever, go to a Casualty department – do not go to your family doctor. Do not tell them what has happened. You won't need to, they'll know and they won't ask.'

'Is it going to hurt?' Daisy asks, in a small voice. 'No worse than period pains. Toby, shoo!' The woman's face softens noticeably. A black cat has jumped on the table and is dipping its paw playfully into the soapy water, chasing bubbles. 'Go on, you silly thing,' the woman orders. The black cat walks slowly across the table, taking its time, passing in front of Lily, its fur brushing Daisy's cheek.

'See?' says Daisy, trying to be brave. 'That means good luck for us both, Lily.'

'Now, young lady, I'd be grateful if you'd remove yourself to the landing.'

Lily does as she's told, the door closing firmly behind her. She waits, ear pressed up against the door. A radio is switched on in the room.

Even Tom Jones singing 'The Green Green Grass Of Home', at full volume, fails to drown Daisy's single never-ending scream.

Kath is certain her time has come. At home she reads the letter again. She is asked to telephone Granada immediately to indicate her acceptance or refusal of the request for her and her partner, Mr Peter Wells, to take part in a recording of *Double or Quit*. Ten minutes later, dressed and now carefully groomed, she finds Robert in his cabin in the car park.

'Robert,' says Kath, without bothering with the

niceties of a greeting. 'I want you to find Pete and bring him to our house, please. Now.'

Robert's eyes widen. He could swear that the woman is fizzing, like a glass of lemonade. Eyes popping, he wouldn't be surprised if a great big bubble burst out of her head, soaking the passers-by.

'Are you deaf as well as daft?' Kath demands.

'Pete's busy. He's on the quay helping Carl and a couple of fellows doing up a boat. You could go and see him down there. Are you all right?' Robert asks solicitously.

'All right? All right? Of course I'm all right,' Kath froths. 'Goodbye to all this,' she adds illogically, sweeping her arms around like a windmill.

'Goodbye,' Robert replies, ducking hastily.

'Out! Out!' shouts the woman at Lily, as she throws open the door and bursts into the room. Lily ignores her and runs over to Daisy, aware as she does so of the cat sitting on the mantelpiece like a Satanic voyeur. Daisy is doubled in two, screaming with pain, soapy water running down her bare legs.

'Is she dying? Is she going to be all right?' Lily asks. The woman dries her hands on a towel. Gently, Lily helps her sister to sit up.

'Now you're here, put an ST on her, then get her dressed and let her lie on the camp bed for fifteen minutes or so. She's bound to get belly ache.'

Daisy tries to help herself. She has forgotten to bring a sanitary belt, so Lily has to loop the pad through a scarf, making Daisy look like an overgrown baby in a nappy.

'The pain,' Daisy gasps. 'Oh, God, please let it stop. I'm sorry, I'm sorry, please let it stop…'

Precisely fifteen minutes later, the woman announces it is time to go. 'What if she can't get down the stairs?' Lily asks, aggression rising.

'If she falls,' the woman replies flatly, 'it'll probably help it on a bit. So long as she doesn't fall from the top, of course.'

Daisy and Lily slowly make it without mishap to the bottom step. The woman remains on the landing. 'Shut the door fast after you,' is all she says.

Kit leans against the van, eyes anxious behind her spectacles, hands reddened by the cold and the long wait, and the fact that her duster coat is too thin to offer protection. 'Mind your own bloody business, you nosy twat!' she shouts, giving two fingers to the butcher's boy who has stuck his head out of the door.

Lily could hug her, tiny, invincible Kit. Now she totters forward in her summer slingbacks and puts a protective arm around Daisy, who is bowed and in agony. As the two move forward, Lily sees with horror that the back of Daisy's corduroy coat bears a stain like a bright, red map of colonial Africa. She steps forward quickly to hide her sister from the prying eyes of the butcher's boy, takes off her own purple Biba coat and drapes it over Daisy's shoulders. 'Let's put you in the back of the van,' she suggests, trying to keep the panic out of her voice. 'You can lie down there.'

Kit opens the van doors to reveal a glimpse of Pete's various lives. A blanket has been thrown over sacking. A pair of black nylon knickers is discarded in one corner alongside a dozen

340

unopened bottles of Babycham, probably lifted from the hotel, a catering size tin of baked beans and a couple of dozen wrapped shirts bearing a Marks & Spencer label. 'Regular little love wagon, this,' Kit remarks. 'Lover boy thinks he can bed anyone with a Babycham and a tin of baked beans. They must fart all the way home.' She giggles, then stops as she looks at Daisy's face.

'I'm bleeding,' Daisy says, terrified. Daisy and Lily look down to see a thin trickle of blood snaking down the girl's bare leg.

'Let's take her to hospital now,' Lily insists, helping her sister into the van.

'Don't be ridiculous,' Kit snaps. 'She'll get into trouble. She'll be all right. Use one of the shirts. Go on, they're probably nicked in the first place. You stay with her in here. Take this, Daisy, good girl,' she says, giving her three aspirins and a swig from a miniature bottle of brandy. 'Give her until this evening. If it hasn't got easier then we'll do as you say. All right, pet?' she addresses Daisy again.

Daisy can barely focus, the spasms are so intense. 'I'm sorry, Lily,' she keeps repeating. 'I've spoiled your Biba coat. I'm sorry...'

Rose waits. Chalkie has phoned the launderette to say he'll be home the following afternoon, much earlier than expected. Billy is staying with his grandmother. Daisy has twenty-four hours to recover without questions being asked. Melody has been told that Daisy is going to Rose's after work and will spend the night with her sister. Kit and Lily carry Daisy in and up the stairs to the bedroom.

341

Silently, without conferring, the three women give her a bedbath, stopping whenever the pain is too intense. They change her into a nightdress and lay her on the bed on top of four towels. Daisy, delirious, falls in and out of sleep.

'How much blood can you lose before ... you know?' Lily asks. She and Rose instinctively turn to Kit for an answer.

'More than you'd think,' Kit says. 'Now, let's get a cup of tea and take turns to sit with her.'

The three troop downstairs. 'Even if they make it legal, I couldn't do it,' Rose says.

'Well, it won't be like that, will it?' Kit points out. 'It'll be like having your teeth out at the dentist. A sniff of gas and, hey presto, somebody'll be saying, "Hello, Mrs White, wakey-wakey and here's your bill."'

'What bill?' Lily questions. 'It'll be on the National Health.'

'Are you silly or what?' Kit challenges her, filling the kettle. 'I'll bet if you can't pay you'll have to wait so long you'll be able to see its bits with limbs and all–'

Rose puts her hands over her ears. 'Oh, God, stop it.'

Kit puts three mugs of tea on the table, takes another couple of miniature bottles of brandy from her handbag and pours a liberal amount into each. She downs the scalding hot drink, almost in one. Only now does Lily notice how much Kit's hands are shaking. 'Talking of paying,' Lily says, 'where did you get the money for the woman? She counted it out in front of us, fifteen pounds and fifteen shillings. You didn't ask Pete,

342

did you? Daisy'll go mad, if you have and–'

Before Kit can reply, there is the sound of a key in the back door. All three women stare at each other in alarm. 'It's Chalkie,' Rose says, panic-stricken. 'He's early. He must've driven all last night and parked up outside.'

'I've bolted it,' Kit confesses. 'I've bolted both doors. I didn't want anyone walking in.'

'Well, unbolt it, quick. It's his bloody house,' Rose demands. Kit rushes to do as she's told.

As she reaches the door, Daisy takes three steps into the room, her hair wet with perspiration, her face the colour of unbleached linen. Blood stains much of her nightdress. 'I want my mam,' she says. 'I want Mammy. Please get...' She looks down, with a series of long, low moans, gazing at what looks like a ruby red quivering jelly at her feet. 'My baby, is that my baby? Oh, please, don't let that be my baby...'

'Chalkie, quick!' Rose yells, through the door, at her husband on the other side, knowing only one event will deter him from trying to get into his own home. 'There's somebody trying to break into the lorry!'

Chapter Thirty-five

'I've told her no. Put myself out for what? So that madwoman can have her five minutes of fame? And if I go on now, I'm bound to be banged up.' Pete sponges up the remains of his egg and chips

343

and brown sauce with a rolled-up piece of white bread. He licks the goo covering his fingers with a furry tongue.

Robert gazes at his brother. 'But I think you'd be very good on television,' he says. 'Nobody from our family's ever been on the telly, have they?'

Pete picks his new teeth with a fingernail.

Robert persists, 'Mam would like to see you on the telly if she was here.'

Pete draws his chair closer to his brother's, bemusement in his eyes. 'If I said I might do this for you and Mam, take the risk,' he adds, swaggering, 'what would you reckon?'

'I'd be proud.'

'Well, I'll be buggered,' Pete says. 'You'd be proud of me? I tell you what. I've got a few problems to sort out first. I'll have to make sure Marie and Hayley have got a bob or two to get by, that sort of thing. Then I'll tell old Hatchet Face that I'll do it on one condition. That she lets you and Dulcie tie the knot. How about that?' Pete asks, pleased with his bit of bobbing and weaving.

'Tie the knot?' Robert answers, alarmed. 'Dulcie?'

Pete nods his head. 'Yes, get married, so you'll be a husband and Dulcie will be a wife. Wouldn't you like that, Robert, my old mate?'

His brother's face indicates that he's not at all sure that he would.

'She's quite pretty, isn't she?' Kit picks up the framed photograph on the bedroom mantelpiece. 'Was this your wedding day?'

Pete sits up in bed, overcoat on, smoking a fag.

344

'Was she pregnant?' Kit gazes at the slight figure, eyes like Bambi, in a matching dress and loose coat.

'I wouldn't have bloody married her, would I, if she weren't? Talk sense.'

'Do you miss her?'

'Nah. She was bloody hopeless in the house. I miss Hayley, though. She took after me. Knew what she wanted and didn't stop until she'd got it.'

'How old is she?'

'Two. I think. Chip off the old block.'

'How do you know she's yours?' Kit asks mischievously.

She watches as he considers the question, shoulders twitching as if preparing to fight off all comers on the issue of paternity. 'She better bloody well be mine – or there'll be hell to pay.'

'That's the thing, though. You'll never know. Not really. You blokes think you've got it just as you like it – but you shouldn't be quite so sure that what you hear and what you see are the truth.'

'So, what about you? Been round a bit, have you?' Pete asks casually, gazing at his cigarette to signal indifference.

'What do you mean?' Kit replies lightly. She pulls up her stocking and plucks a button off Pete's discarded shirt to fix it to her suspender belt. 'Do you mean, have I been saving myself for you? Or do you mean, am I not to be mentioned in the pub in case every other lad there says, "Me too"?'

'All mouth, you are,' Pete tells her amiably. 'You're all right, though, so I'm going to tell you straight. I'll be away for a bit soon.'

Kit shrugs, brushing her hair. 'Why should I care? What are you up to this time? Saving another African state for the white man, killing dozens with a single throw of your table-tennis bat? You and I should have a duel one day. I was dead good at table tennis in my youth-club days.'

Pete throws a pillow at her and misses. 'You need a good slap, you do,' he says. 'I'm doing this telly thing. Then I'm off for a bit. Shall I tell you why?'

'Not if it's a whopping big lie. I can make them up for myself, thank you very much.'

'No, I told you, I'm being dead straight.' Pete blows into his hands to warm them up. 'I did a little job. Well, a couple, actually. Down south. Me and a mate. They nabbed him but he's said nothing. A witness gave a description. Coppers are bloody hopeless but once I've been on the telly, sure as shit someone's going to offer their twopenceworth.' Pete gives Kit a quizzical look. 'You wouldn't tell anyone else what I just said, would you?'

'What did you just say? I can't remember. Your house is bloody freezing. You should get central heating. Podge's house is lovely. That's what I'm going to have one day, a nice house, centrally heated, a lilac bathroom, a bit–'

'Lilac? They don't make 'em lilac,' Pete interrupts.

'They do if you've got the money,' Kit replies. She waits while he disappears to put a shilling in the meter. When he comes back, he brings a two-bar electric fire with him. 'Talking of money,' she adds, 'you wouldn't do me a favour, would you? I've got a little business proposition. Something just for me?'

Pete's eyes narrow, on his guard.

'I'll pay it back.'

'Why should I do you a favour?' he asks curtly.

'Intimacies,' Kit replies. 'You know what that means? It was in a magazine. It means little things we have between us, nice things,' she adds, adjusting her skirt. 'Things I'll remember for a very long time.'

Pete frowns, taking a while to absorb the implications of what she has just said. He bunches his hands into fists, then cracks his knuckles. Kit retreats to the door warily. Then he laughs. 'You know what you are?' he says. 'You're a blackmailing tough old bird.'

'I'll take that as a compliment.' Kit smiles sweetly.

Carl is transformed. Pregnancy makes him protective. Every evening he calls in on his way home from work bearing chocolates or woollen booties or flowers for the mother-to-be. Melody also fusses constantly, making Daisy sandwiches and flasks of soup to take to work, and telling her to put her feet up as soon as she returns.

Daisy keeps her silence. The bleeding has slowed. Now the termination has ended her fear of delivering a carrot-coloured cuckoo in the marital nest, she has accepted Carl's proposal of marriage. Arrangements are proceeding for a register office wedding before the supposed bump shows.

347

'Why don't we go to Cwmland on Saturday and see if we can find you a nice outfit for the wedding? If it's a bit loose, nobody'll be able to tell,' her mother suggests.

'They know already,' Daisy replies flatly.

Melody ignores her. 'We've had a chat with Carl's mam and dad. I suggested a do here. There'll be a dozen or so. But Tanner insists on upstairs at Ravelli's. They've got a lovely function room and Mr Ravelli said he could lay on prawn cocktail, steak and a bit of a pudding. Tanner insists on paying. I did argue a bit but, frankly, it's a Godsend. I said I'll make the wedding cake, so it's all done and dusted. Pity, you can't have–'

'Mam,' Daisy interrupts, 'were you pregnant when you married Dad?'

Melody clears the table. 'What a thing to ask,' she says.

Lily reaches for her alarm clock. Twelve fifteen a.m. She turns, to find a space where Daisy should have been asleep. Addled, she tells herself she's probably staying at Carl's. Once marriage is on the horizon, some parental curfews are lifted. She hears the sound of a dustbin overturning in the backyard. Instantly she's out of bed. Undecided whether to rouse her father, she tiptoes down the stairs. 'Daisy, is that you?' she hisses in the dark.

Lily can see a figure silhouetted in the yard. She is about to turn on the light and scream for help when the face turns towards her.

'What the hell are you doing?' Lily asks, as her sister comes into the back room.

'Sleepwalking,' Daisy replies but she is not

348

addressing Lily. Instead she is staring straight over her shoulder. 'I was sleepwalking, I tell you.'

Melody, standing in the doorway, says nothing. She fetches the two-bar electric fire from the front room and switches it on. 'Sit down,' she instructs her daughters. She moves into the kitchen, puts the kettle on the hob, warming her hands on the steam coming from its spout, makes a pot of tea and returns to the table, bearing mugs. 'So,' she says, finally taking a seat herself, her face death-like from tiredness. 'What's going on? And don't tell me you sleepwalk, Daisy Tempest. What do you think I am? Daft?'

'What were you doing?' Lily asks, genuinely perplexed.

'I'll tell you what she was doing,' her mother answers, pushing her sleeves up to her elbows, as if preparing for a round of bareknuckle boxing. 'She was burying her unmentionables in the dustbin when she thought nobody was around. Now, I ask myself, how can a pregnant woman also be having her monthlies?'

'Unmentionables?' Lily says, puzzled, then understanding dawns. 'You mean sanitary towels.'

'Daisy?' Melody presses.

Daisy begins to pace up and down the small room, defiance on her face. 'You really want to know, Mam? I'll tell you. I got rid of it. It's gone. I thought when I got pregnant it would all be lovely. I'd look lovely. Carl would be pleased. But it's all wrong. And I'm glad I got rid of it. Anyway, there's nothing you can do about it now. It's done,' she adds aggressively.

'Are you all right?' Melody asks, reaching for

349

her daughter's hand. 'Are you going to tell Carl?'

Lily looks at her mother in surprise. 'What do you mean, is she going to tell Carl? Shouldn't that be "When are you going to tell Carl?"' Lily looks from her mother to her sister. 'I'll get Dad,' she says, rising to her feet. 'He'll talk sense to the two of you.'

'No.' Both women speak with one voice.

'If I tell Carl the truth,' Daisy stammers, her voice tearful, 'he'll never see me again and he'll tell everyone what happened and then nobody will want me. I'm nearly twenty, Mam, I can't have that. He doesn't have to know, does he? When we come back from the honeymoon, I'll tell him I had a miscarriage or something. He'll be all right.'

Melody puts her arms around Daisy and strokes her hair. 'You know what's best, love. And you, madam, you won't say a word, either way,' she adds, directing herself at Lily. 'Every family has its little mysteries.'

Lily shakes her head. 'And what's that supposed to mean? "Little mysteries"? You make it sound as if what Daisy's doing is a branch of bloody wizardry. If she cons that poor bastard into marrying her there's nothing mysterious about it. It's plain ordinary blackmail. It's a shot-gun wedding without any bullets, and that's not fair. It's disgusting.'

'I don't understand you,' she continues, a catch in her voice, only pride preventing her bursting into tears. 'Daisy's got herself pregnant and in one hell of a mess and you're sat there holding her hand, telling her nothing's wrong no matter what lies she tells. And I try as hard as I can to do as well as I can and I'm treated as if I've let the whole family down, just because I want a little bit more than you lot have ever had. I've got feelings too, you know, Mam. I need someone to put their arms around me too. And just once say, "Yes, you've done well. We're proud of you. We really are." Just once. That's not very much to ask, is it?'

Lily runs upstairs to the bedroom and slams the door hard. She throws open the window, and shouts to Mrs Hillyard, peering out of her bedroom window across the backyard, 'Go back to sleep, you nosy old cow!' She switches on the record-player and turns the volume up as far as it can go.

As Otis Redding blasts out, Lily whirls round and round like a dervish, leaping on to Iris's bed, jumping up and down, determined to hide her anger and disappointment and profound sense of rejection. Someone bangs on the wall from next door. Iris sits up with a start, spiky curlers making it look as if a sugar pink hedgehog has taken up residence on her head. 'Turn that racket off,' she shouts. 'It's the middle of the night. Have you gone mad? Do you have any idea how much noise you're making?' She climbs out of bed and makes for the record-player.

Lily jams a pillowcase over her head. Doug comes stumbling from the hall to see his two daughters playing a bizarre version of blindman's buff. One daughter is dancing furiously, while the other lurches around in the middle of the room, struggling to pull the pillowcase back over her curlers.

'Turn that ruddy row off, now,' Doug bellows. 'I've got to get to work in the morning. You'll wake the neighbours.'

'No, I will not turn it off!' Lily yells back, madness in her blood, jealousy pounding in her heart. 'It's my life and I'll live it as I want to. I'm sick to death of everyone telling me what I should and shouldn't be doing. From now on, I'm going to do what I want to do, when I want to do it. And I'll do it all at three o'clock in the morning if I bloody well want to, and sod the lot of you. See if I care!'

She yells again out of the open window, to a twitching curtain opposite. 'Mind your own bloody business, Mrs Hillyard!'

Suddenly Iris lurches against the record-player, bringing the song to a messy and premature end. She emerges, gasping and redfaced, from the pillowcase. 'Now look what you've made me do, Lily Tempest.'

Lily ignores her and advances on her father, determined to cause injury to her mother and furious with herself for needing her approval. 'Dad,' she says, a destructive glint in her eye, 'what makes you so sure that me and Daisy and Rose and Iris are your daughters? Maybe one of us isn't. Maybe there's quite a few little family mysteries about us lot that Mam has kept to herself.'

To her amazement, even as she speaks, her father begins to laugh and continues to laugh, so long and so hard, he has to sit down on the edge of Iris's bed.

Chapter Thirty-six

'I'm absolutely sure of it. It's big, it's beautiful, and with a little help from my friends and a tiny bit of cash from you, I shall be well on my way to my first million.' Kit, having ensured that she is wearing the shortest skirt in her wardrobe and her highest heels, smiles sweetly.

'This is it?' Pete asks bemused. 'This is the favour you want from me?'

She nods happily. 'It makes ever such a lot of sense. It's a service to lonely young housewives marooned on housing estates all over this county. They're not just lonely, they want something that shows they matter, that somebody really does care enough to put a smile back on their faces. And that person, indirectly, is you, Mr Killer Man.'

'I'm not a killer, I'm a dog of war,' Pete whispers, embarrassed. 'I'm a cold-hearted professional.'

'Whatever you say.' Kit shrugs, adjusting her headlamp glasses, the frames painted unsteadily in coral nail varnish to match her mohair jumper.

Its hundreds of tiny hairy tentacles remind Pete of one of those tropical plants he's seen on the telly whose leaves suddenly whip out and drag a fly to its death. He steps back and notices that she has a blob of nail varnish in the same colour in the middle of her left calf; blocking a ladder. He licks his lips. 'Here,' he says, tracing a route up her leg with a finger made shaky by his intake of alcohol the night before. 'You've got something running away with itself up here. And I can't say I blame it.'

Kit slaps his hand. 'So, are you going to cough?' she asks him bluntly. 'The bloke selling it wants a hundred and thirty-five nicker but he'll take a hundred from me because he likes me.'

'Let's have another look,' Pete grunts. 'My money doesn't come easy, you know.'

'Doesn't come easy?' Kit mocks gently. 'It can't be all that difficult holding up old ladies with a water-pistol. This,' she adds, before Pete can protest, 'is Vera.'

Vera is a dilapidated furniture-removal van, painted chocolate brown, big enough to take four stand-up pianos and a threepiece suite. 'She's thirty years old,' Kit says proudly. 'Only one owner.'

'My arse,' comments Pete curtly. 'More like forty and a couple of dozen prangs.'

Kit opens the van doors and climbs inside, making sure that she entertains Pete as she does so.

'Can you drive?' he asks.

'Course I can drive. I've been driving since I was thirteen, as soon as my feet could touch the pedals. Boss at the greengrocer paid for a couple of lessons and I passed my test first time. I worked when the van driver was sick, which was most Mondays. Do you know what I'm going to do in here?' she asks.

Pete bites back a crude comment and shakes his head.

'I'm going to turn it into a fruit-and-veg emporium. You can't get to the shops? Vera and me will bring it all right to your doorstep. I'll have a counter here, scales, special offers, tranny on in the background. It'll be just like a shop, except it'll be on wheels. No overheads. No nothing. Just me, a couple of gallons of petrol and a bit of stock. Invest in me, Pete, and we'll both be made.'

He shakes his head. 'Sorry, my old flower,' he says. 'I'm not pouring money down the drain, no matter how sweet it smells.'

'Your destiny lies in just one of my fingers,' she tells him confidently.

'What do you mean? Which finger?'

'This one,' Kit says, pointing. 'The one I use to dial the coppers and tell them what a wicked, wicked man you are, thieving and robbing.'

'So you've got a friend of a friend who thinks she isn't her dad's daughter?' Barry repeats gravely.

I nod. I'm convinced now that one of us sisters isn't Dad's. And it's probably me. 'Don't you think she should be told the truth?' I ask. 'Doesn't she have a right to know her own history? At least then she'd be able to make sense of all the little mannerisms and oddities and attitudes that make her seem so different from the rest of the family?'

Barry chuckles and begins to hunt around the garage until he eventually unearths the book for which he's been searching. 'This is what Johnson said.' He quotes: '"The value of every story depends upon it being true. A story is a picture of either an individual or of human nature in general; if it be false, it be nothing."'

'There! What did I tell you?' I say.

Barry shakes his head. 'I don't think he's right. At least, not all of the time. Sometimes, we have to show a little common sense and flexibility when it comes to those we love.'

'Let sleeping dogs lie?' I answer scornfully.

Barry shrugs. 'Secrets aren't only about malice and deception and selfishness. Often they're about survival. Ordinary people just trying to get by. Sometimes the truth should never be told. Then again, it might be a matter of choosing the right time. Deciding when that time is right is one helluva big decision for an individual to take. Still, if your friend of a friend insists on finding out the truth, tell her the evidence is probably right under her nose. Or, failing that, Somerset House has copies of birth and marriage certificates. But she probably knows that already. I've a–' Barry is interrupted by the doorbell. He comes back, followed, to my surprise, by Don Wilson. I didn't know they knew each other.

'So how did they go?' Don asks, taking off his coat and making himself at home. 'Your interviews?'

'Oh, fine. Quite well, I think.' I catch Barry's eye. Why lie? 'No, they didn't go quite well at all,' I correct myself irritably. 'They went very, very badly. I failed one and didn't bother to go to the second. I didn't see the point.' Don looks sympathetic, which makes me cringe. 'I've changed my mind about university anyway,' I say. 'I'll probably move to London. Get a job or something.'

Don shakes his head disapprovingly. 'Look, I've got a few contacts,' he offers. 'Let me see what I can do. Really, I'd like to.'

He walks over to the workbench. I'm about to tell him where he can keep his unwanted help but Barry gestures behind his back, so I shut up.

'How far have you got, then?' Don looks at Barry. 'Is this the rough draft?'

'How do you two know each other?' I ask.

Don folds his arms and leans against the table. 'I organised an anti-Vietnam meeting at the university, asked for a speaker and they sent a bloke from London with Barry as number two,' he replies. I notice he's flattening his vowels, more man-of-the-people. 'Bloody marvellous speaker he is too. We've had a few meetings since and now we're producing our own homegrown leaflet.'

Don picks up a couple of sheets of paper and begins to read. As he does so, a pink flush comes to his cheeks. 'What's this about? "From Protest to Resistance"?'

'Noam Chomsky's line,' Barry replies, clearly amused by his discomfiture. 'Or, to put it another way, sometimes intellectuals have to get up off their backsides and dirty their hands a little, confront the coppers, go in for a bit of the old direct action. CND, Aldermaston. But an old radical like you would know all about that.' He smiles. 'Salary, tenure, pension, you've got to lay it all down on the line, boyo.

'Read that, Lily,' he instructs. 'Out loud. Listen to this, Don. Bloody good stuff. Go ahead, girl.'

I do as I'm told. '"The picture of the world's greatest superpower killing or injuring a thousand non-combatants a week while trying to pound a tiny, backward nation into submission on an issue whose merits are hotly disputed is not a pretty one. Defence Secretary McNamara January 1967." That can't be right. A thousand people a week?'

'Probably more,' Don answers. 'Troop strength has increased this year to almost half a million.'

'Troop strength?' Barry stops pasting. 'I love that nice hygienic vocabulary. Do you know what that really means, Lily? Poor, ill-educated black and white kids conscripted to go and serve in a country they know bugger-all about, murdering the innocent as a way of stopping the big bad Communist wolf from gobbling up the so-called free world. Bollocks, is what I say. See that?' He points to a paperback under the leg of the table. 'Take that, read it, and then let's have a chat when you've done. Here, Don, write a couple of strong captions.'

While the two men work, I put on a record, the volume turned down low, John Lee Hooker singing 'High Priced Woman'. 'Make us a cup of tea, there's a sweetie,' Don demands, without looking up.

Bloody cheek! 'As Rosa Luxembourg once said,' I tell him, bridling, '"Down through the centuries, women have peered over men's shoulders to see how history is made."'

'Did she say that?' Don is impressed.

'Of course she bloody didn't.' Barry snorts. 'She's taking the piss, mate. I'll make the tea. Lily, you choose us a couple of pictures out of that lot. Napalmed kids, something strong and

358

straight to the heart. People think propaganda's all lies but they're wrong. The best is based on truth. Do you know why?'

I shake my head.

'Because it makes the blind see.'

Chapter Thirty-seven

Rose stops scrubbing and sits back on her haunches. She checks her watch, then remembers that Chalkie has agreed to collect Billy from school so she has no need to rush. She has spent the past three hours helping Kit to clean out the van. Strangely, now she has more time, she writes very little. Adversity suits her better, or perhaps, she tells herself, she is intimidated by the seriousness of her new setting: a whole desk to herself, a room of her own.

She has also begun to save again. The money, skimmed from housekeeping that Chalkie provides and her job at the launderette, is still secreted in the bottom of the birdcage, but this time it hangs in the cellar, a stuffed budgerigar swinging constantly in the dark, propelled by draughts.

'I'm a good earner, aren't I, Rose?' he'd asked her, earlier that day. 'I'm good at bringing money to the table.'

Chalkie has a routine when he's home. He goes out for a pint, watches the football, sees his mates, potters in the house. She had made love to him the night he'd come home and, for the first time, it had been like the early days. Except that Rose had had a woman in mind.

'You shall go to the ball, Cinders!' Kit shouts at Rose, jumping into the back of the van, holding a large baking potato in one hand. 'See this? I shall turn it into a marvellous coach. All wishes will come true, granted by me and my magic carrots,' she adds, flourishing a bunch in the air. 'I bought these at the greengrocers down the road just to get a feel for local prices. Bloody rip-off. Will my ladies be pleased to see me when I come knocking on their door! Here, I've brought you a flask of tea. You deserve it. It looks really smashing in here.'

Kit hands over her flask and, for a second, their fingers touch. Rose turns quickly and switches on the transistor radio. 'California Dreamin'' is playing, sung by the Mamas and the Papas. The two women join in, waltzing around the van, until the music comes to an end. Kit laughs, out of breath, 'I wish I was in LA. How about you? "Fairport Drizzlin" doesn't have quite the same ring.'

Rose smiles and leans against the side of the van. 'He's away tomorrow. Will you be coming back?' she says, careful to ensure her voice is neutral. 'Look at that. There's more cobwebs up in those corners than in Transylvania.'

An hour later Kit and Rose walk to the bus stop. Rose senses that, for some reason, Kit is nervous.

'There's something I've got to tell you,' Kit blurts out eventually. 'Don't be cross. Promise you won't be cross?'

'It depends,' Rose replies cautiously.

Kit pulls her into the newsagent's. 'Have you seen this?' She picks up a copy of a thick glossy magazine called *Nova*. Rose reads the cover: *'Yes, we're living in sin. No, we're not getting married. Why? It's out of date.'* Then she checks the price. 'Three shillings? If I want to know about living in sin, I can hear all about it in the launderette for free.'

Kit isn't listening. She's handing money over the counter. 'You've got two here. Do you want two?' the newsagent asks.

Kit nods, takes her change and follows Rose out of the shop. 'Take this,' she says abruptly, once they're in the street, handing one of the magazines to Rose. 'I'm really, really sorry, but I thought it was a good idea. I thought it would give you a bit of a boost and raise some money for Daisy's ... thingy. Except that when the cash comes, you've got to give it to Don Wilson. I borrowed it off him without telling him what it was for and–'

'What are you talking about?' Rose asks, exasperated, as she flicks through the magazine Kit has handed to her. It is a weekly called *Woman's Mirror*, a mix of news, fashion and short stories. Then, she stops dead and springs round towards the other woman. 'Kit, how could you? Oh, how could you?'

'Two smoked haddock and poached eggs and a side order of bread and butter, white, no crusts, please, love. And a pot of tea for two,' Veronica shouts through the hatch of the Olde Tudor Tea Rooms.

Melody busies herself but her mind is elsewhere. She senses calamity even though family life appears to have returned to relative normality. Doug has even resumed making his paper dogs, and a pub on the other side of Cwmland has given him a Thursday night booking. He'd applied to the new Co-op for the post of manager but he hadn't even received an acknowledgement. The building is taking shape on the market square, an upstart of chrome and glass in a line of drab shops. It looks more like a car showroom than the emporium of comestibles that Bunting's had once been. 'It'll be bright, brash, *American*,' Doug had said, in a way that made Melody visualise a new breed of robotic humans with motorised wheels for feet.

Now she watches as the two pieces of smoked haddock, the colour of Easter chicks, cook gently in the pan. The aroma fills the kitchen, calming her slightly. She reflects on Doug's growing closeness to his grandson, Billy. The only boy in the family, he is always keen to escape: fishing, making mischief, scooting over the hills and far away, out of the grasp of adults and their sometimes cruel and inexplicable ways.

'Why doesn't Mammy love Dad?' he'd asked Melody one afternoon, when he'd come to visit her at the tea rooms after school.

'Of course she does,' she'd replied, as she piled a scone with home-made blackcurrant jam and a dollop of cream. She gave it to him, knowing it wasn't comfort he required as much as an understanding she couldn't provide, of how and why grown-ups behave as peculiarly as they do.

'Women can't bring boys up alone,' Doug would say to Melody. She'd correct him gently: 'Women managed in the war, didn't they? Besides, he's not alone, he's got his dad. Chalkie's very good with Billy.' 'But he's not there all the time, is he?' Doug would insist. 'That's what a lad wants. He needs to know there's someone there for him all the time, keeping an eye out, telling him how to deal with the world in a way that women can't.'

Now a hand appears through the hatch waving a magazine and Veronica's voice breaks into Melody's thoughts. 'Well, who'd've thought it? Mabel's just dropped this in. I said you were bound to have a couple of dozen copies already. My, you are a dark horse. She'll be in the public library before you can say Mills and Boon. I bet you're dead chuffed.'

Melody takes the magazine, nonplussed, and passes out the two dishes of fish and a tray of tea and bread. 'Whoops, wait a minute, forgotten the parsley. I don't know what's the matter with me today.' She slips the garnish on the plates and Veronica whisks them away.

Then she sits down and flicks through the pages, unsure what she's looking for but anticipating that it will involve Lily and trouble. Towards the back of the magazine she finds the source of Veronica's excitement. 'The Day My Mother Left...' by Rose Tempest, winner of a third prize of ten guineas in a competition for articles on the theme of modern motherhood, '....its hardships, complexities and joy'.

The contributions of the first- and second-prize winners had also been published alongside the names and addresses of all three contestants.

Kit watches anxiously as Rose walks down the street, oblivious to passers-by, absorbed in what she's reading. 'Are you upset? Are you really angry?' Kit asks.

'Rose Tempest, nine Rydol Crescent,' Rose reads out loud. 'Bloody hell! Upset? Of course I'm upset.' She glares at the other woman. 'What did you do? Go sneaking around in my house when I wasn't there? Fishing about, on the hunt? I trusted you, Kit. You had no business reading my private stuff. Besides, this wasn't even finished. It was for Billy, it wasn't for – for the rest of the world.' She stops, aware that she's shouting and attracting the attention of a few passers-by.

Kit grabs the magazine from her. 'I knew you'd hate me. I knew it.'

Rose grabs it back. 'Hate you? Well, I'll tell you this for nothing, Kit Renshaw, you won't be looking in future, because you're never coming to my house again. Do you understand? You've got no standards, that's your trouble. You just do what you want to do, and damn everyone else. If I'd wanted you to see what I'd written I'd've shown you.'

Kit shuffles her feet and decides attack is the best form of defence. 'Of course it was finished. Of course it was for the rest of the world. Otherwise why had you put "by Rose Tempest"? You hadn't written "by Mam", had you? You're just scared of being judged. Well, there's not much point in bloody writing if you're never going to let anyone read it, is there?'

Rose frowns. 'Kit, I could kill you. I'm really, really bloody angry. I'll never forgive you – you do know that, don't you?' Kit nods, miserable.

The two walk on, Rose now reading the magazine again. Suddenly she hugs it to herself and gives a little skip. 'I can't believe it. I really can't believe it. Rose Tempest, nine Rydol Crescent. Rose Tempest, not Mrs Rose White. Just me: Rose Tempest.'

Kit cheers up a little. 'I gave your mam's address in case Chalkie objected, and the telephone number at the chip shop. They phoned the day after Daisy was seen to. They had thousands of entries,' she says. 'I knew if I asked you, you'd say no. You would've, wouldn't you? Said no? Anyway, the money's going to a good cause. Would you have said no?'

'Of course I'd've said no.' Rose rolls up the magazine and playfully whacks her round the head. 'Take this and this and this, and don't ever take liberties with my life again, Kit Renshaw, do you hear me?' This time, Rose is smiling.

Doug stubs out a cigarette and lights another. A headache makes him feel as if he's wearing a crash helmet several sizes too small. A cough unleashes several arrows of pain into his chest. He sings as he weaves the cardboard strips in and out on a dog's torso; one promised to a former customer at Bunting's. He's never worked to a commission before but perhaps, he tells himself, he can turn this into a little business. And try not to say goodbye to the pleasure it brings him.

The door of the shed opens and Melody says quietly, 'Come indoors, love. I've something to show you.'

Five minutes later, as he sits with a copy of the magazine open on the table in the back room, Lily comes in, leaving a trail of shoes, coat and umbrella from the front door. She dumps her school-bag on the table and looks over her father's shoulder. 'That's Rose!' she squawks. 'That's our Rose. That's bloody brilliant! Isn't it, Dad?'

Kath lays her outfit on the bed in preparation for the following day. Tomorrow, at six-thirty a.m., Pete will arrive by taxi, which will transport them to the station. Recording begins at two p.m. in Manchester at the studios of Granada Television, home of *Coronation Street*. At five minutes to five, she walks into the Contented Sole. Kit and the boss, Madge Hill, have strung up a banner in the window that reads, 'Good Luck, Kath! You'll Murder Them!!!!' Inside, a photographer and a reporter from the local paper wait to interview her. Kath is circumspect about her past, effusive about her knowledge of the mad and the murderous, and modest about her chances of winning. 'Just being selected is prize enough,' she says, and watches as the reporter, who admits to being unable to read back his shorthand, laboriously writes out her quote in longhand, polishing as he does so.

'I'm one in a million,' Kath reads from his notebook, as the reporter accepts a free bag of chips. For the first time in her life, she is on the record – even if they're not actually her words.

Chapter Thirty-eight

'Five copies, please,' Rose says, biting back the desire to shout at the newsagent, 'I'm in it! My name's in it! Page eighteen. It's me. Rose Tempest. A Published Person.' She rushes out of the door and runs up the street and into Rydol Crescent, oblivious, like a child, that her hair has fallen loose, her coat is undone. She throws open the front door and yells, 'Mam, Dad! Anyone home?'

When she reaches the back room, she stops at the threshold; Lily and her parents are seated at the table, a copy of the magazine in the centre. She reads delight mixed with a grain or two of envy on Lily's face. She cannot fathom what she sees in her parents' faces, except she knows, instinctively, that it is negative.

'What?' Rose asks, quick to anger. 'What's the matter? Now, what have I done wrong?'

Lily flings her arms around her sister. 'I knew you'd do it one day.' She turns to her parents. 'Go on, tell her,' she demands, holding tight to Rose's arm. 'Tell her how good it is that she's had something published.'

'I'm pleased for you, Rose.' Melody speaks quietly. 'I'm ever so pleased for you – but you shouldn't have done it. Not under your own name. Not with this address for anybody to see. Why didn't you say you were Rose White? Why Tempest?'

'I was writing long before I met Chalkie. Why should I put his name on what I've done? It's mine not his,' Rose replies fiercely, hurt and genuinely perplexed. 'Besides, I didn't have anything to do with it. Kit sent it in. And what's wrong with putting this address anyway? I come here every day, for God's sake.'

Lily examines her mother's face. 'Is it money you owe, is that it?'

Melody shakes her head.

Lily turns on her father. 'I get it. I understand what this is all about, Rose. It's him. He can't stand anyone else being in the limelight. If it's not him, Mr Dean Martin, taking a bow, then nobody else in the family can. How pathetic. How childish.'

Doug opens his mouth but Melody puts a hand on his arm. 'Leave it be,' she says. 'Just leave it be.'

Later, in bed, I wait for sleep which refuses to come. 'Leave it be,' my mother had said. Leave what be? Any normal person would be proud to see their daughter's story published but not my parents. Why not? If it isn't fear of the bailiffs and creditors, and if it isn't my dad's jealousy, what else makes them keep the curtains so tightly drawn on this family?

In the past, whenever Rose and I had carried out our sporadic hunts for evidence of Mam's debts, we'd only ever found bills. No lovers' letters, no clues to past misdemeanours. But then again, we'd only ever searched our mam's domestic empire, the kitchen and the back room. Perhaps it wasn't her secrets we should have been looking for.

I doze and wake and doze until, finally, in the early hours, I leave my bed and put on my dressing-gown. It is pitch black. Soft snores come from my mam and dad's room. I feel along the wall in the dark until I find the narrow, steep steps to the attic. As I climb the stairs, my face brushes against a row of our plastic-covered dresses, hanging from hooks like so many ghostly corpses.

The attic is icy. I switch on a small table-light, which throws unnerving shadows. An hour later I'm still hunting through boxes and suitcases and carrier bags, not even sure what it is that I'm seeking.

'Do it from behind.'

'What? You've got to be joking. I'm not doing anything kinky like that.'

'It's not kinky. It's normal. At least, it is in Liverpool. All right – well, then, you get on top.'

'Only if you promise not to be so quick.'

'What do you mean quick? Nobody's ever complained before.'

'Yes,' says Kit amiably. 'But how many have come back for more?'

Pete switches on the torch and studies his watch. 'Bloody hell,' he says. 'I've got to be up in a couple of hours.'

'You'll be fine,' Kit replies reassuringly.

Pete squeezes her affectionately. His new dentures have made him less aggressive, more mellow. Now if someone throws a glance in his direction, he assumes it's out of admiration, not distaste. 'Here, cuddle up and we'll get some kip.'

Kit snuggles into the bend of his body.

Soon both are asleep, locked together like pieces in a puzzle.

At five thirty a.m., in the winter dark, at the same time as Lily Tempest is foraging for family secrets, Pete wakes with a start. He gently disentangles himself from his bed companion, adjusting the covers so she remains warm. Two minutes later, he lets himself out of the back of Vera the van and finds himself whistling as he makes the long walk home.

I sit with my back to the attic wall facing a stack of my dad's LPs, which have travelled with us for years. Some are kept in the radio-gram in the front room downstairs, most are up here. Methodically, I pull record after record from its sleeve. Eventually in a Frankie Lame album, *Deuces Wild*, I find a slim battered leather folder.

Inside is a card, which says, 'If found please return to Douglas Tempest'. The address has been scribbled out and replaced three times. None is legible, only the changing dates: 1932, 1936, 1941. I unfold a cutting from a newspaper, dated July 1937, an obituary notice, announcing the death of Harold Tempest, aged 52, in Our Lady of the Cross Hospital, Northlake, Staffs, after a short illness. Funeral at Northlake Baptist Chapel, Waterloo Street, Staffs. I'm about to return the cutting when something makes me reread it. 'The deceased leaves two children.'

Doug, Kath and Dulcie makes three, not two. One of the few pieces of information that Dad has given us about our grandfather is that as soon as his wife had left him and the children, he had declared her dead, in his own eyes at least. Had Harold disowned one of his children as he had his wife? And, if so, which one and why?

The wallet also contains a number of photographs. One snap shows my mam and dad, in their twenties, on a sea-front leaning against a motorbike; a handsome couple. My dad stares gravely at the camera, so it must have been taken before he learned to smile and before he'd acquired the Dino quiff. Mam has her head back, laughing with delight. She is happy, her arm linked in his, looking like a woman who believes that, no matter what, with this man at her side she has a future.

Under the photograph, neatly folded, is our Rose's birth certificate. Name and surname of father, Douglas Harold Tempest. Occupation of father, salesman. Nothing untoward. Disappointingly, the same is true of my birth certificate and those of Daisy and Iris. I reach for a fragment torn from a newspaper. It announces the forthcoming marriage of my dad's parents, Elizabeth Tempest formerly Sedgewick, spinster, aged 18, to Harold Tempest, aged 31, a docker.

In a pocket of the wallet is Dulcie's birth certificate. Why is this here, and not in Kath's possession next door? When and where born, 6 June 1930, Rellington Lodge, Birmingham. Name, if any, Dulcie. Sex, girl. Name, surname and maiden name of mother, Katherine Tempest. Name and surname of father, N/K.

Name of father not known? Mother – sister – sister – mother? How can Kath be Dulcie's mother? She always says she was nine when Dulcie was born. I struggle to make sense of this information. If Kath is Dulcie's mother, then who is her father? What happened to the mysterious Mr Morgan? Or is he only a composite of all the men Kath has ever known and hated?

Poor Dulcie. Her mother, far from abandoning her as she has always believed, is with her and wants never to let her go.

Pete takes a quick swig from his hip flask and gives himself the once-over in his bedroom mirror. He's wearing a new suit, new black shoes and a thin shoestring tie from his teddy-boy days – his lucky tie. Even his underwear is clean. Time in Borstal taught him little except how to clean up well when the occasion merits. This morning, illuminated by the single electric lightbulb, he looks brand new, as if he's just slipped out of the packet, even if he says so himself – except, of course, for his drinker's eyes.

He picks up his wallet and keys and lets himself out, banging the door shut as he does so. 'I'll be five minutes,' he instructs the taxi driver, as they pull up outside Kath Morgan's house. She opens the door before he can knock and lets him in. 'OK,' Pete says, squaring his shoulders and doing away with any small-talk. 'I've thought about it a lot and I've got a proposition to make. You let Robert and Dulcie get hitched, in church with all the trimmings, or I turn around and go home now.'

'You can't do that,' Kath protests, eyes watering at the shock.

'I can and I will. Put it this way – even if we win, I lose, OK? I'm better off if my ugly mug isn't seen anywhere at all, never mind on the nation's bloody TV sets. I'm doing this for Robert. He wants me to go on the box, so I will. Then I'm lying low for a while. If you try and stop our two tying the knot, some very bad people will come looking for you. OK, missus?'

Outside, the taxi driver hoots loudly. Kath puts on her coat and moves towards the door.

'I take it that's a yes, then?' Pete says, pleased with himself.

Chapter Thirty-nine

'Three rolls of lino, lovely bright blue, you can have 'em for...' Carl pretends to count on his fingers. 'I'll give 'em to you for a very special price. Tell you what, if you promise to babysit now and then when the Big Fella arrives, I'll give you the lot for nowt. Is it a deal?'

Kit throws her arms around him and kisses him on both cheeks. 'I'll babysit for the rest of the year,' she offers, avoiding Daisy's eye. Early evening, and Vera the van has found a new home in the lock-up where Tanner keeps his stock for the market as well as his two lorries and a couple of old bangers that he and Carl are trying to restore to good health. The place is warm, well lit and noisy since two radios are tuned to Radio Caroline.

The word has been passed around that Kit

could do with a little help from her friends. Carl and his dad are messing about with the van's engine; Daisy, who is good at art, is at the top of a step-ladder providing fresh lettering in gold paint for the side of the van, now resprayed shocking pink. 'Kit Renshaw Inc. Fruit & Veg & Provisions', she inscribes, in careful lettering.

'You know what that'll mean?' Carl says. 'All your customers'll start calling you Mrs Ink.'

'I couldn't give a monkey's.' Kit smiles. 'So long as they pay their bills.'

She and Lily and Iris are trying to lay the linoleum. Much to Lily's annoyance, Kit is affecting such a degree of incompetence that even a blindfolded three-year-old could do better. Tanner watches, bemused. 'The trouble with you women is that you're all arse over tit,' he says. 'You three clear out and me and Carl'll do the rest. Otherwise you'll be here until next Christmas.'

'Thank God for that,' she whispers to Lily, a smug smile on her face. 'I thought he'd never take the bait.'

Carl has acquired a stack of good-quality wood from which Barry and Bryn are making shelves. Rose has written a leaflet describing Kit's door-to-door service and a list of prices, which Kit has handed out in the launderette and stuck through letterboxes, trudging around a couple of estates with Penny and Lily.

Penny brings a special gift. 'My mum and dad have said they'll lend you the money for the first year's tax and insurance,' she says, as she attempts to clear out the junk that has accumulated in the driver's cabin. 'You can pay them back later.'

374

'Lend, did you say?' Kit replies, a glint in her eye.

'Don't be daft, they've got plenty,' Penny chides, misreading her friend's response.

Kit whispers in Lily's ear, 'I think the least Mr Wilson can do is make a handsome donation – don't you?'

'Oh, for God's sake, let him off the hook,' Lily replies, simultaneously appalled and impressed by Kit's relentless dedication to self-interest.

'Someone's here to see you, Kit,' Daisy says, appearing around the back of the van. 'He's got something for you.'

A middle-aged man stands awkwardly by the lock-up doors. He wears a donkey jacket and a flat cap and carries a string bag. His face is lined but the features are strong and striking: Elvis Presley sideboards and a short-back-and-sides indicate a person who can't quite decide whether to hold on to his youth or relax into maturity

'Dad?' Kit says, as if she can't believe her eyes. 'What are you doing here? This is my dad,' she adds unnecessarily to everyone else. 'I haven't seen him for a little while.'

'I heard about what you were doing,' Trefor Renshaw replies gruffly, aware that he is the centre of attention. 'I thought this might come in handy.' He pulls a brown leather money-belt from the bag. 'Keep your notes safe, it will.'

Kit pushes her glasses up her nose and bites her bottom lip, unusually lost for words. Her father places the belt on the bonnet of the van and nods, then turns to go. Lily watches the yearning on his daughter's face. At the door, he stops, clears his throat, and turns to face Kit again. 'If you want, I mean you don't have to, like, but if you want, I'll come with you to market when you go. It'll be dark and that.'

She makes no response and Lily wants to kick her. Then, as if a spell has been broken, Kit clatters over in her high heels, but instead of throwing her arms around her father, as Lily expects, she politely taps him on the arm, as if this is the extent of the physical affection each allows the other. 'I'd like that, Dad. Thursday OK? I'll come and pick you up. Will Sally look after the kids?'

'She's gone,' her father replies. He gently touches his daughter's cheek, before walking out of the door.

'Are you all right?' Rose asks.

'Course, I am,' Kit replies defiantly. 'Why shouldn't I be?'

'Will you go back?' says Iris. 'I mean, go back to live with your dad?'

'Two months ago I would have gone back like a shot. But I've got Vera now. I'll make sure our kids are all right but now I want a little bit of freedom and a lot more money. Nothing wrong in that, is there?'

Daisy tuts theatrically. 'What you really want to do is find yourself a nice bloke, doesn't she, Carl?'

Lily puts her hands around her sister's throat playfully and pretends to throttle her.

'Mind the baby!' shouts Carl. And she lets her hands drop.

'You've got to tell him.'

'What's it to you?'

'You'll spend the rest of your life knowing that you got a man to marry you under false pretences.'

'I won't be the first. Besides, what he doesn't know can't harm him.'

'How can you look him in the face when he's obviously really pleased about the baby? How can you do that?'

'Easy. I remind myself of what his face would look like if the baby had popped out covered with ginger freckles.'

'Well, I promise you this, if you don't tell him before you turn up in the register office, I'll–'

'You'll what?' Daisy sits up suddenly in bed. Across the room Iris, as usual, is serenading herself with snores while her two sisters argue in whispers in the early morning.

'You'll have to tell him,' Lily insists again fiercely, also sitting up and pulling the blanket up to her chin.

'I will not. I know exactly what I'm doing. And I will not. And if you do breathe a word, I'll tell everybody that you've had it off with that Don Wilson.'

'That is not true!'

'It doesn't have to be true, does it, you silly cow? You say a word, Lily Tempest, and I promise you, I'll shred you to bits. You won't know where to put your face.'

'We'll see about that.' Her sister pulls the covers over her head.

'We'll see all right,' Daisy mutters, not at all sure that her sister will hold her tongue.

'Now, Kathleen and Pete, you've been a very sporting couple, tell me, what's it to be, double or quit?'

Kath is mesmerised by Hughie Green's pale blue blazer, blue and pink striped tie and his eyebrows, constantly on the move, like two worms on a trampoline.

'Larry, tell this lovely couple what they take home if they double and win...' The cardboard wall behind the comedian, sprayed with sequins, wobbles alarmingly.

Larry's deep baritone fills the studio as a cheap velvet curtain, in a corner of the set, begins to swing back, falters, then shifts again, helped by a young woman incongruously dressed in a full-length turquoise-satin evening dress, drop diamanté ear-rings and gloves to her elbows.

The curtain swings back to reveal another hostess, in a white swimming-costume, fake tan and sunglasses, reclining in one of a pair of deck-chairs, alongside a child's plastic paddling-pool.

'Here's everything you need for the alfresco lifestyle,' Larry's disembodied voice booms out. 'We will give you two lovely people not just the deck-chairs, not just a fantastic up-to-the-minute barbecue, not just an easily inflated paddling-pool, we will also give you – wait for it, folks, how generous can we be? We'll give you a week's holiday, all expenses paid, in Palma, Majorca.'

Pete winks at Kath. The two couples against whom they'd been pitched have proved easy meat. One couple opted for the Royal Family as their special subject; the other the career of Frank Sinatra. Kath and Pete so far have sixty pounds in the kitty. Pete had been very nervous at first, but had gradually relaxed. Kath had been at ease from the outset, as if her entire previous life had been a rehearsal for this one event.

She didn't care about the money or Majorca, or even that, when she glanced at herself on the monitors, she looked uncomfortably like a menacing Bette Davis: the best prize of all for Kath would be if this recording could last for ever. What has proved a surprise to her is the phoniness of the endeavour: tiny studio, cheap set, canned audience laughter. As a viewer, on the other side of the screen, it had all looked much more solid and splendid and *real*.

'All right, you lovely people, what's it to be? Are you going to quit while you're ahead, or take a risk and double your winnings and maybe, just maybe, you marvellous people will win a wonderful week on the beautiful island of Majorca?' One of Hughie Green's eyebrows bounces so high it disappears into his hairline.

Pete gives Kath's arm a squeeze. For a heart-stopping moment, she fears he's about to take the money and run. Then she hears him say loudly, 'Double, please, Hughie... And if we win, I'll keep the bird in the turquoise dress and Kath can have the rest.' Pete's growing bolder.

'Definitely double?' The compère milks the moment. 'If you win, you two gorgeous people will not only double the sixty pounds you have in the kitty already, and take home a holiday of a lifetime, you'll also return next week to play another round of Double or Quit.' His voice goes up several octaves. 'However, if you lose, my friends, you go home empty-handed. The choice is yours. But first, ladies and gentlemen, it's time to take a break. Don't go away, folks!'

'Robert! Robert, my old son, wake up! Christ! It's like raising the living dead. Robert!' Pete shakes his brother's shoulder even harder. Eventually he hears a groan. Robert sits up in bed, shielding his eyes from the light. Pete glances around the room. The last time he had been upstairs was when his mother had died. Someone has prettied it up since. The bed has a bright blue candlewick bedspread; a small rug is on the floor; doilies decorate the chest of drawers and there are ornaments on the mantelpiece. 'Here, mate, wake up. I've come to say goodbye. Here's forty quid. You ask that girl to marry you, and when she says yes, you take her to Majorca with these,' he instructs, handing over a gaudily decorated envelope.

'We won't want to go on our own,' Robert replies anxiously.

'No, well, you'd better ask Lily or Kath to go with you, then.' Robert's face clouds. 'Not Kath. . .Why can't you come?'

'I'm off for a bit. Till it quietens down.'

'Africa?' Robert says brightly.

Pete opens his mouth, tempted. Then, instead, opts for the truth.

'Nah, probably Ireland, this time. If anyone comes asking after me, tell 'em you don't know where I am and you don't want to know.'

'I don't want to know,' Robert repeats. Then his face crumples and his lip begins to quiver. 'Am I going to be all on my own?'

380

'You're not on your own,' Pete replies firmly. 'That's the whole point. If I get sent down again, you won't be on your own ever again. You've got a family now, mate. You've got the jackpot. You've got Dulcie and Lily and her lot. Even Marie'll come and see you, if only to slag me off. You've got lots of people around you now. And do you know why? Because you're bloody all right, that's why.'

Pete gives his brother a hug, holding him fast. 'Now, you tell Lily that you and Dulcie want to get married and I said it was all right and nobody can stop you. She'll know what to do. OK?'

Robert nods obediently. 'Pete,' he says, as his brother reaches the door. 'Will you come back and be my best man?'

Pete winks. 'Let's see how it goes.' He smiles, for once unwilling to make a promise that he may not be able to keep.

Daisy and Lily are summoned by their mother's shrieks, 'Oh, I say! Would you believe it? Doug! Doug!' Looking over the banisters, they see Kath, smiling like she's never smiled before and carrying two deck-chairs. 'She's won! Would you believe it! She's won!' Melody shouts up at them. 'When will we see it? What did you get? What's he like? Sixty quid each – oh, I say. Come in the back room. I bet you're starved.'

'Give the woman a brandy, Melody,' Doug instructs.

Unprotesting, Kath allows herself to be steered into the back room. The girls join her entourage. Doug gives his sister's arm a squeeze, as if testing for muscle. Lily had expected that the first time she set eyes on her aunt, since discovering her true relationship with Dulcie, she would look different. No longer would she be barren, bitter and childless. Instead, she'd be A Woman With A Past. But Kath looks like Kath, happier and more animated, but still Kath. Lily muses to herself, as she and the others admire the newly won deck-chairs, perhaps there is no Mr Morgan because Kath long ago polished him off. Perhaps that's what happened to Dulcie's dad.

'What are you looking at me like that for?' Kath asks, a smile taking the sting out of her words. 'Haven't you ever met anyone who's been on the telly before?'

'Did you drop Pete off?' Lily asks later, after the saga of *Double or Quit* has been repeated for the umpteenth time.

'Pete's telling the producer after this show goes out that due to pressing personal matters we won't be able to compete any further. By rights we should be going back next week.'

'Oh, Kath, what a shame!' Melody com-miserates. 'I bet you're hopping. Deprived you of your chance to shine some more. You could've become the queen of the quiz shows.'

Kath shakes her head. 'No, we made a deal,' she says firmly.

Daisy and Lily exchange glances.

'Doug, when she's on, shall we have a little family party?' Melody enthuses.

'Go on, then, Kath,' Lily interrupts her mother. 'Pete never does something for nothing. Tell us, what did you promise if he went on the box?'

Chapter Forty

'I'll remember this week for ever,' Kit says, polishing the front wing of Vera the van. 'I'll remember it because everybody came and gave me a hand and that means they've got to believe I can give this a go. I'll remember it because tomorrow my dad's coming with me to market. My dad! It's me and him together, but it's me who's the boss. My mam would love that.

'I'll remember it because I won't have to go into a crappy shop again with a boss who's got roving hands and sweaty armpits and who couldn't manage his way out of a Liverpool brothel unless his mother had a big piece of string tied round his waist to yank him home. I'm leaving all that behind, and whether this works or it doesn't I'm doing it for myself. Isn't that absolutely bloody brilliant?' Kit turns to us, her face alight with pleasure.

'Vera's a real work of art,' Penny says, carried away by the moment and a bottle of Bulmer's cider. 'The most beautiful creature to roll out of Tanner's lock-up unaided.'

The van's interior has been completely remodelled. It now holds three tiers of deep shelving for produce, a small counter, a boxed-off area for spuds, a till and scales. The lino has been laid, the paint is dry, the men have inspected her thoroughly and gone home, happy. 'It's all right,'

Tanner had said, as he'd left earlier. 'But I wouldn't let any girl of mine muck about like this.'

'That's because you don't like us to show you how it's done,' Kit had replied, wagging a finger cockily in his face.

'Don't you reckon you ought to wear an overall or something?' Penny asks now, as she fills our mugs with yet more cider. Kit shakes her head. No matter how dirty or daunting the task of renovation, Kit has continued to dress as if she's out on a Saturday night. Tight, short skirts, high heels. She owns seven pairs of spectacles, all National Health, all customised with what looks like the bottom of an elaborate aquarium. Bits of sea-shells, beads, lots of sparkle, stuck together with nail varnish. Life's weird. If anyone had introduced me to Kit, I'd've thought she and I had nothing in common. I see now she's special. She's looking for a way out too.

We've agreed to spend the night in Tanner's lock-up with Kit, who is off to market at five thirty in the morning. We've eaten Cornish pasties, warmed on the stove, drunk too much cider, and sung our way through our usual repertoire of songs – 'Respect', 'Shake!', 'Chapel Of Love', 'Cathy's Clown'. Penny uses a pair of pliers as a microphone, Kit plays drums on an empty petrol can, I syncopate with a teaspoon on an empty milk bottle.

Later, we loll on the beaten-up sofa as the paraffin stove pumps out toxic warmth; we're exhausted from the day's graft. Not for the first time, I mull over the revelation that Kath is

Dulcie's mother and restrain myself yet again from sharing the news with the others. It's hard – the shock factor alone makes it tempting – but the thought of what it might do to Dulcie if she's not properly prepared (and how do you properly prepare someone for turning their life inside out?) keeps me silent. More pleasurably, I run through in my head the encounter with Mash, my situationist. Kit would approve but not Penny so I've kept him to myself, too. Perhaps, if I ever pay off my debts, I'll make a return trip to London. Then again, I'm a Tempest and, as a family, we never go back.

I'm so lost in my thoughts, it takes a while to register that somebody is wailing noisily. It's Penny. Drunk, she is sobbing into a pile of Kit's virginal potato sacks, waiting to be filled tomorrow for the very first time. 'I want to be like you two,' Penny wails. 'I want to know what I'm doing, where I'm going, what it's all about. Sometimes I can't wait to go away, go to university, feel free,' more wailing, 'then I think, What if I'm lonely and I don't like anybody there and they don't like me? What if Bulbie won't wait and finds somebody else? And after I've got my degree, what happens then? Everybody in our house keeps on and on about getting a qualification but what do I do with the bloody thing once I've got it? Tell me that! What do I do for the rest of my life?'

Kit and I look at each other blankly, which makes Penny howl even more energetically. Kit puts her arms around her and I hand her one of Tanner's rags to blot her tears. Penny chokes, then shifts up a gear. 'You're so lucky. I wish I was

you two. You know what you want. You can do
things. You're funny and all that. I haven't a clue
about anything. Except that I hate myself even
more than I hate my mum and dad. And I don't
know ... I don't know ... I just don't know...'

'All right, babe,' Kit replies reassuringly. 'We
get the picture, you really don't know. But we
don't know either. We just look as if we do.'

'This might make you feel better,' I volunteer.
'As far as chances go, I'm stuffed. Well, temporarily stuffed. The letter came this morning.
Rejected. I mucked up my interview. So that's
that. No university place for me. But I'll tell you
this for nothing, I'm not hanging around here. As
soon as A levels are over, I'm off.'

Penny is visibly cheered by the downturn in my
future. 'Doing what?'

'Learning how to fly.'

'What can I do for you, lovey?' Kit beams at the
pensioner who has climbed on board to inspect
her goods the next morning.

'You need chimes, like the ice-cream van. That's
what you need,' the elderly woman comments. 'Is
it fresh?' she asks, adjusting her hairnet.

'Can't get fresher,' Kit promises, blowing into
her gloves to keep her hands warm.

'Only usually if I buy something and it goes off
I bring it back. But there's nowhere to bring it
back to with you, is there? What with you moving
about and all. I mean, if I want to bring it back,
what do I do? Stand in the road for a week until
you drive by?'

A couple of younger women have also

appeared, purses in hand, now with amusement on their faces.

'I'll be here twice a week, Mondays and Thursdays, without fail. It's just like going to the shops except the shop comes to you,' Kit explains patiently.

'Do you give Green Shield stamps?' the elderly woman persists.

''Fraid not, but I will deliver to your door, if you like. You give me the order and I'll leave it on the doorstep, rain or shine.'

'That doesn't suit me, I like to be out and about. I'm seventy-six, you know.'

'Marvellous, too, if I may say so,' Kit replies.

'Where's the boss, then?' the woman asks.

'That's me.' Kit smiles. 'I'm the boss.'

'Well, you should've said that at the beginning. I like to see a girl making her own way,' she says approvingly. 'I'll have a couple of carrots, one onion, three tomatoes and two potatoes, for baking, not too large, mind. And you can make that a regular order, love.'

'I could kiss you, darling.' Kit chuckles as she makes her first transaction.

On Tuesday evening, at seven thirty p.m., Kath and Pete's appearance on *Double or Quit* is broadcast to the nation. Kath, however, is missing. She only arrives at Doug's house and a full family turnout during the commercial break. 'Got caught up,' she explains. The truth is that she has sneaked down to Rediffusion and, on a street deserted apart from a couple of lads larking about, she has watched herself replicated a dozen times on the

387

bank of screens, dizzy with delight.

Nineteen minutes later it's all over, to whistles and claps. 'A week in Majorca, how lovely. Let's see the tickets, go on, Kath.' Melody hands around a plate of warm sausage rolls. 'I've never seen an air ticket in my life. What a pity you couldn't go back. You might have found yourself jetting all over the world.'

Robert clears his throat. 'She hasn't got the tickets. I've got them. Pete gave them to me before he went away. He gave me money to buy Lily a ticket too. He wants the three of us to go away together. Isn't that right, missus?' he addresses Kath anxiously. 'He wants me to ask Dulcie something and–'

'Stop talking daft, man,' Kath cuts him off curtly.

On Friday morning, two men arrive on Kath's doorstep. They wear identical black coats with velvet collars and leather gloves. One is very blond with a broken nose, the other is black and carries more bulk.

'Can I help you?' she asks frostily.

'Excuse me, madam,' one says, in a thick Birmingham accent. 'We're looking for your friend.'

'My friend?'

'Mr Peter Wells, your partner on the television. We represent solicitors in Edgbaston. A relative of his has died, and he has come into a windfall.' The blond male speaks persuasively. 'We've written to him several times at his address but with no response. We wondered if you might know his present whereabouts?'

'Solicitors, you say?'

'Solicitors,' the two men repeat firmly.

'Do you have a card or identification or something?'

Both men produce wallets from which business cards are extracted. 'I'm Paul Wood and my colleague here is Gary Peters. We're employed by Burns, Templeton and Archer. Give Mr Archer a call, if it puts your mind at rest.'

Lacking a telephone, Kath shakes her head. She thaws slightly. What she sees before her are potential allies who could scupper Pete's plans for Robert and Dulcie. 'Come in and let me see if I can help.' She smiles. 'I know he said he was going away for a while ... on business.'

Before she can so much as offer a cup of tea, the pair are over the threshold and already sitting stiffly in the deck-chairs, now on display in her best parlour, like a couple of waxwork figures marooned on a pier.

Chapter Forty-one

At Lawson's, Doug soon learns that the personnel manager stays in his office most of the time, shuffling paper and holding interviews. His task is to fill the never-ending vacancies. A proportion of the younger men hand in their cards at the slightest upset since, for their age group at least, jobs are plentiful. Many move round a constant circuit, Lawson's, the iron works, labouring in the summer months, then back again to the fish factory. Doug has been given the post of production controller, part of whose task is to try to staunch this costly flow of labour out of the front door.

'I never had this problem with the last fella who did your job,' grumbles a blue-rinsed woman, sorting the cod for size.

'No,' smiles Doug, with a wink. 'That's why I'm here and he's gone.'

He jokes and chivvies and calms, his own relaxed style defusing the dozens of tiny crises that regularly arise. Conditions in the factory are always bad. The floor is permanently awash with icy water, the women who sort the fish wear wellington boots and several pairs of socks, then stand in buckets of hot water in an attempt to keep the chilblains at bay. They stay put because the money is the best that's going, and friendship counts.

Early on this Friday morning, a new young lad, working alongside Bryn Taylor dipping fish into vats of dye, asks for rubber gloves. 'Look, laddie,' responds the foreman on the line, 'by the time you've finished working here, you'll be so bloody tough, you'll have hairs on your chest like sticks of rhubarb. Get on with it, or get out.'

Doug persuades the freshly trained lad not to take the second option. In the afternoon, the senior production manager, a university graduate in his mid-twenties and a cause of constant friction in the weeks since his arrival from head office in Runcorn, orders a team to lay out fish for packing opposite the freezer door. His reasoning is that this is a more economic use of the factory floor. Except that each time the freezer door opens an Arctic gale blows.

'Can't we shift to somewhere warmer?' Alf Jenkins, an employee for over twenty years, asks.

'If you're not happy,' the manager instructs curtly, 'pick up your cards.'

Instead Alf picks up a filleting knife and waves it dangerously close to the manager's cheek. Slowly, coolly, he slices the palm of his own hand and allows the blood to drip across the neat lines of white fillets, turning some a delicate shell pink. Then he turns to his workmates gathered around. 'See what that bastard did? He sliced me with the knife. I've a good mind to have you bloody prosecuted. I could do you in court. You all saw it, didn't you?'

Several of the men nod in agreement. Alf turns to Doug for affirmation too, but he turns and walks away. As he does so, he hears Alf challenge the manager again. 'So, what's it to be? A day in court with half a dozen witnesses, sonny? Or do we get our way?'

Fifteen minutes later Alf and his team are relocated. Later, at the factory gate, Alf salutes Doug mockingly with his bandaged hand.

'All right, laughing boy?' Then, as he walks past, he whispers, 'So now we know whose side you're on, cunt.'

'Police are bloody hopeless, if you ask me. Must be someone the lad knew. It's weeks now.' The newsagent hands Doug his change, gossiping about the decision to scale down the hunt for the missing boy, Daniel Andrews. 'He'll be one of

391

those they never find. You mark my words.'

A second voice interrupts Doug's thoughts. 'Heard your Daisy's in the register office tomorrow.' He knows who the owner of the voice is even before he turns around. 'Hello, Dougie, how are you keeping? Long time, no see. Perhaps I'll pop down to the pub and watch you singing. Going well, is it?'

Betty Procter, ungarlanded by small children, holds an evening newspaper. Doug notices that she is wearing a violet jumper, which matches her eyes. She smells of something sweet and soft and comforting. If the events of that day hadn't consisted of one small act of unkindness after another, he would probably have exchanged a greeting and left. Instead he waits for her to make her purchases and tells her, as they leave the shop together, 'I'll be walking along the Fairport road in an hour.'

Melody, Iris and Daisy take this Friday off. Lily refuses to acknowledge that Daisy's wedding is twenty-four hours away. Instead she goes to school, as usual, stepping into the Reformation and Francis Bacon and *King Lear,* then stepping out of it again, when the day is done, education as a tablet to be swallowed daily, during school hours only. She writes an essay in the lunch-break, telling herself that it's unlikely anyone in the Tempest household will have thoughts on the degree to which Luther's constipation influenced his break with the Catholic Church.

Now, late afternoon, the house in Rydol Crescent vibrates with female activity. Daisy has taken over the kitchen for her ablutions. Pans boil on the stove while the tin bath, so far, contains only a couple of inches of water. Howard, home on a long weekend especially for the wedding, holds an elaborate pink hat decorated with crushed and battered-looking feathers while Iris attempts to fluff them out, employing a hairdryer. 'I told the woman in the shop they looked a bit funny,' she keeps repeating. 'It's all your fault, Howard, you made me buy it.'

'Yes, dear,' he replies meekly.

'Wearing your blazer tomorrow, are you, Howard, or your uniform?' Lily asks cheekily.

'Take no notice,' Iris tells him. 'She's ignorant, that's what she is. For your information, he's wearing his uniform. And very smart he looks in it too.'

Melody is carefully pressing Doug's wedding suit, wheeled out only for matrimonial occasions. Already hanging on the back of the door is her own lilac ensemble, a rare personal purchase acquired via a catalogue. Alongside it is the pink bouclé wool suit that Daisy plans to wear with a navy blouse, shoes and hat.

'Nip down to the shops and fetch us a pair of nylons, there's a love,' Melody asks Lily. 'Best to have a spare pair, just in case.' She gives her youngest daughter a sideways glance. 'Are you sure you're not going to come to the wedding? I've pressed that suit you bought for the interviews, just in case. Come up lovely, it has.'

'Don't even talk about it,' Lily replies crossly, taking the money her mother offers and banging the door behind her.

'Why wouldn't she want to go to her sister's wedding?' Howard asks innocently. 'Is it her monthlies?'

'Oh, don't be so wet,' Iris snaps, exasperated.

Daisy goes to bed at eight, as if, as a married woman, she will never again accrue enough hours of sleep. Before retiring, having exfoliated and bleached every hair on her body, she issues instructions to the assembled company. 'Wake me up at seven, Mam, and–'

'Breakfast in bed,' Melody interrupts. 'A couple of nice soft-boiled eggs, toast and honey, thinly cut white bread and butter, fresh pot of tea, lovely–'

'Hairdresser's at nine a.m. Car arrives here at noon. Register office. Ravelli's straight after. Party at the railwaymen's club starts at seven – Bryn's lot are definitely going to play because Carl's dad has already promised a fiver if they turn up sober and another fiver if they stay that way. And Dad'll sing, won't he, Mam?'

'Do you think you can stop him?' Melody smiles.

Daisy ignores Lily's display of disinterest. 'Then a taxi's booked to take us to the station for the nine o'clock train. You lot can drink on.'

'And it's happy ever after, is it?' Lily asks sarcastically.

'It will be as long as you stay away,' Daisy retorts.

Iris stands up abruptly. 'Come on, Howard, let's go for a drink,' she commands, aware that these undercurrents are bound to suck her into a family row unless she removes herself.

'I want to watch *The Man from U.N.C.L.E.* and

then I'm going to Carl's stag night. I don't want to go out now,' her fiancé protests.

'Oh, yes, you do,' Iris insists, handing him his coat.

Doug uses Carl's stag night as the reason to leave the house early. The road is dark, the early-spring air warm. Very few cars and lorries pass. In the past, when he had an assignation, the terms were clear – or so he told himself. No real harm done, pleasure all round. Take what you can, a mutual pact. Melody has always known he wouldn't, he couldn't leave: he owes her too much.

An articulated lorry, its bulk hidden by the night, drives towards him, lights on full. Doug is temporarily blinded. Once he is able to focus again, it is to see the boy dancing on the verge, in and out of the shadows, jumping up and down in the ditch that borders the field. Shirt hanging out of his trousers, socks around his ankles, twirling and leaping with the manic energy that only the young can exhibit. Suddenly the small figure jumps high, then darts across the road. Doug follows, running hard, arms outstretched. 'No...' From a very long way away, he hears a scream.

Betty Procter always goes to bingo on a Friday night. Tonight she leaves the older ones in charge of the little ones, since her husband is late home. She announces she'll be back before ten. Initially when Doug Tempest had suggested they meet, the temptation to continue making mischief had been acute. She could have knocked on his door and suggested that Melody come with her on a little drive, a rendezvous with her husband. Or she might have dropped a hint to one of his girls. But her original appetite for revenge has grown cold. So he had rejected her, she'd admonished herself, worse things occur. Although, admittedly, not often to her. And now he'd apparently changed his mind. These things happen.

If Betty was honest with herself, since misfortune had seen Doug Tempest demoted from shop manager to factory hand, from Sunday-night entertainer to Monday-night stop-gap, her interest in him had waned. She has a standard to maintain. Why had she agreed to meet him tonight? More to the point, why had he asked when she could see no desire in his eyes?

As she drives through Fairport's deserted market square, a thought briefly crosses Betty's mind. What if Doug Tempest has arranged the meeting only to tip off the old man and leave her to explain why she's driving in the opposite direction to bingo with a ton of slap on her face and a half-bottle of whisky in her bag?

Five minutes past Taff's, the café, Betty glances in the mirror to check that she has no lipstick on her teeth. Preoccupied, she hears the screech of brakes before she sees the articulated lorry a hundred yards ahead. As she watches, it almost topples, then swerves and curves surprisingly gracefully, like a snake slithering across the road. Eventually, it screeches to a stop, inches from the ditch that runs parallel to the road, its front wheels overhanging precariously.

Betty pulls over. The driver revs up his engine, making the wheels spin, sending dirt and grit flying, as he tries and fails several times to get sufficient grip to reverse back on to the road. Instinct makes her run round to the front of the vehicle where she sees what the driver cannot. A dazed Doug Tempest is sprawled in the ditch. She bangs on the door of the cab furiously, then discards her high heels and endeavours to pull him clear.

'Where the bloody hell did you two come from?' the driver asks, jumping down from his cab. 'I could've sworn what I saw was a fox. It ran right in front of me. I swerved to avoid it, and next thing I know I'm all over the place. Is he OK? Bloody hell, you don't reckon he tried to top himself, do you?'

Doug Tempest, a graze on his cheek, twigs and brambles stuck to his coat, slowly sits up. 'I must've slipped as I ran,' he says, his eyes growing clearer. 'Where's the boy? I saw the boy...' His words fade away. The driver, satisfied that no damage has been done, is now inspecting the state of his lorry, muttering obscenities.

'What boy, Doug? There is no boy,' Betty Procter says. She guides him to her car. 'Let's go quick before he gets nasty,' she says, gesturing with her head at the lorry. 'Neither of us are where we should be, are we, love? Still, that's nothing new,' she adds, with a smile. She opens the passenger door.

'That's what I wanted to ask you tonight,' Doug says. He stoops a little until his face is so close to hers he can see the dozens of tiny lines around her mouth where her lipstick has bled, and he can smell the onion gravy she must have had for tea. 'Is there something I've done to someone close to you, Betty?' he probes. 'Is that it? Is it something in the past that I've done to someone you love? What is it? Tell me.'

She opens her handbag and passes him her half-bottle of whisky, alarmed by this man without a smile and paranoia in his tone. 'Don't be so bloody daft,' she replies lightly. 'We enjoyed ourselves. That's all. Don't worry yourself. I told your wife that you hadn't touched me. So I'm not all bad, am I?'

Later, after she has dropped him off on the edge of town, she parks the car outside the bingo hall and sits there for several minutes, lost in thought. What, she wonders, has Doug Tempest done that haunts him still?

Chapter Forty-two

Early Saturday morning, the day of her sister's wedding, Lily walks along the path that skirts Coronation Park, overlooking the sea. She is alone except for the gulls who swoop and dive, attracted to the toast in her hand. The sky is a brilliant turquoise blue. Crocuses and daffodils stud the steep banks that lead down to the beach. It is the season of beginnings, and for that reason alone Lily jumps high into the air, yelling like a child, hurling her toast up into the flock of birds.

She had left a sleeping house, she returns to mayhem. The Beatles are singing 'Penny Lane' on the radio in the kitchen, and 'I Wanna Hold Your Hand' on the radio in the back room where her father sits, polishing his shoes. Her mother is frying bacon in the kitchen. The girl from the flower shop is in the front room, laying out on the coffee-table single carnations wrapped in tinfoil for button-holes. 'Good job it's a bit parky in here,' she says. 'They'll last longer. Are you a bridesmaid?'

Lily is suddenly swept by a wave of nostalgia. As if the scene is already a memory, and she has long since moved on. She shakes her head.

'Won't you change your mind and come, love?' Melody asks, emerging from the kitchen to offer the florist a bacon butty. 'Your dad can't understand why you won't. I've told him, it's only a silly falling-out. Daisy will be ever so disappointed. I know she will.'

Upstairs, outside the bedroom door, Lily hears sobbing. She opens it to find Iris and Daisy huddled on the double bed – but as they turn towards her, it is Iris's face that is streaked with tears, not Daisy's. 'Whatever's the matter? What's happened?'

'Howard's dumped her,' Daisy explains. 'He got drunk at Carl's do, came back here and told her he couldn't go through with it.'

'The bastard,' Lily replies loyally. 'Has he got somebody else?'

'He's giving me up for God,' Iris sobs. 'He's got a calling. He wants to join the church, become a vicar, and he doesn't think I'll make a very good vicar's wife. I knew there was something wrong. I knew it but I thought we could sort it out. Oh, I'm so ashamed! What will everybody say? They'll

399

think it's all my fault. I'll become a nun, that's what I'll do. I'll join a convent.'

Daisy and Lily struggle to control themselves but fail miserably, collapsing in a heap of giggles, their animosity towards each other melting.

Melody is attracted by the noise. 'I always thought you were too good for him,' she says stoutly, when told. 'Plenty more where he came from. And to think of all those Sunday dinners he had in my house.' She takes her weeping daughter back downstairs.

Alone with Daisy, Lily can hold her secret no longer. 'If I tell you something,' she says, 'you promise you won't say a word? I mean, really promise. If you do tell, I swear I'll tell Carl about ... you know.'

Daisy, intrigued and eager to accept a truce, nods in agreement. She watches as Lily pulls out a drawer and retrieves a piece of paper taped to the back. She hands the document to her sister.

'Bloody hell!' Daisy says. 'How did you get hold of this? What will you do? I don't believe it. Kath can't be Dulcie's mum... So who's the dad? Have you told Kath you know?'

Lily shakes her head. 'I don't know what I'll do. Maybe I'll do nothing. It's made me see Kath differently. She's still a weird bloodthirsty old cow but it must've been really hard for her having Dulcie. She could only have been in her teens. That's part of the reason why she doesn't want Dulcie getting married. It's not just that she's scared of being left alone. It's not even that she thinks Dulcie will breed like a rabbit...'

'Well, what else is there?' Daisy looks blank.

'Can't you see? It's also because of the birth certificate. Dulcie would have to see her birth certificate. She'd know then, wouldn't she? Even our Dulcie would start asking questions.' Lily takes the document from her sister and returns it to its hiding-place. 'See, Daisy?' she says triumphantly. 'Secrets don't belong to anyone. They have a life of their own. They do what they want to, when they want to. This one's been kept for nearly forty years – but just by chance...'

Her sister turns on her fiercely. 'Not by bloody chance. Don't make it seem you've had nothing to do with it. As usual you've stuck your nose where it's not wanted and now what's going to happen? You'll have your blessed truth, all right, but everybody's lives will be turned upside down when they're fine as they are.'

Lily hits back. 'Fine as they are? Dulcie believes her mother left her. Do you know what that does to somebody? To believe they weren't good enough to make their mam stay? All her life Dulcie has felt grateful to Kath for taking care of her beyond what a sister's supposed to do. Do you really think that's right?'

Daisy is unimpressed. 'You know as well as I do Kath could've put Dulcie in a home and forgotten all about her. All right, she's made a mess and a muddle but she's done the best she knew how. That's how real people live, Lily Tempest, not like those daft people in all those books and plays you read. We know what's right and what's wrong and we struggle because we want to be good, but we also want to find love and–We struggle...' Daisy's bottom lip begins to tremble. She adds, in a far

401

softer tone, 'Like I am now...'

'Tell Carl.' Lily grabs her sister by the shoulders.

'I can't.' Daisy holds her hands over her ears. 'I can't. And I bet you never grow up enough to understand the reasons why.'

Two hours later the women, dressed in flimsy pastels and too much makeup, stand to avoid creasing their outfits, and wait self-consciously in the back room, occasionally taking peeks at themselves in the mirror over the mantelpiece. Doug and Chalkie hang about outside the front door in their best suits, chain-smoking, while Billy hops on and off the pavement excitedly. A Rover, supplied by Tanner Hicks, is parked outside, decorated with white satin ribbons. Only the bride-to-be is absent.

Daisy has gone AWOL. She has been missing for almost an hour, failing to return on schedule from the hairdresser's. 'Do you think she's done something silly?' Kath suggests, a gleam in her eye.

Melody ignores her and issues instructions: 'Lily, you get dressed, you're coming to the wedding whether you like it or not – and then pop down to the salon to see if she said where she was going. Iris, pull yourself together and nip to the phone-box. Call Carl's house, see if she's there. And ask your dad on your way out to go down to the quay. Maybe she fancied a bit of a walk to calm her nerves.'

Her daughters are about to scatter to carry out her orders when Chalkie puts his head round the door. 'It's OK,' he says. 'She's coming up the road.'

'Is she all in one piece?' Kath asks.

'I've told him,' Daisy says to Lily, her eyes filling with tears, as the two sit side by side on the bed. 'Well, I've told him about the abortion. I didn't say anything about the father of the baby.'

'And?'

'And I think his exact words were "Drop fucking dead." I think that's what he said.' Daisy swallows hard, steeling herself, aware that if she weeps now there will be no stopping.

'He's not coming?' Lily asks inanely. 'So why are we all going? Oh, I'm so sorry, Daisy.'

'You were right. I couldn't have gone ahead without telling him, not really. I thought he'd never trust me again if he found out. Well, he has found out, and I was right, he won't ever trust me again. He won't even see me again. So now,' she adds bitterly, 'there'll be not one, not two, but three of us on the shelf, like a set of fat little Toby jugs, stuck for the rest of our lives.'

'That's not true,' Lily protests. 'Are you sure you don't want to tell people the whole thing is off?'

'Why should I? Let him face the music for not turning up.'

'But it's going to be so humiliating.'

'What's the alternative, Miss Know-It-All? To go downstairs and tell everyone I tried to get him to marry me under false pretences? That I've had an abortion? That I'm glad I did? That I'm, well, I'm recovered and I'm glad? Is that what you think I should tell everyone? At least this way it's the same old boring story. Boy does a bolt.'

Lily squeezes her sister's hand. 'I promise you'll

403

never be alone as long as I'm around,' she says.

'Look, I'm depressed enough already,' Daisy replies, 'don't make me feel any worse.'

The décor of the register office in Cwmland is clearly designed as punishment for those who have dared to turn their back on the Church. Brown lino on the floor, brown straight-backed chairs, brown desk and a vase of plastic lilies-of-the-valley so caked in grey dust they look like relics from Pompeii. The registrar is brusque. He keeps glancing at his watch.

'It's the traffic,' my dad says. 'Give it a couple more minutes, there's a good lad, Hugh.'

Hugh West used to be one of my dad's customers at Bunting's. He'd give him a couple of slices over the quarter. Now it's time for the favour to be repaid.

'Five minutes and no more,' Mr West concedes. 'Then I'll have to press on.'

I watch the clock above the registrar's head as it ticks slowly through one minute, then another. Daisy, several chairs along, is stony-faced, staring ahead. My mother keeps dabbing her eyes. Dad slips his arm through Daisy's, gives her a wink and holds her hand fast. A tear trickles down my sister's cheek, partially hidden by the short veil on her bright pink hat.

I sit there chastising myself. If Daisy hadn't won the contest, she wouldn't have met Bright, she wouldn't have got pregnant, she wouldn't have slept with Carl, she wouldn't have had an abortion and she definitely wouldn't be waiting in a register office, knowing that it's bye-bye bridegroom. It's all my fault.

'Ladies and gentlemen,' Hugh West says, genuine concern written on his face, 'I'm so very sorry. Perhaps we can reschedule our gathering when the situation becomes a little clearer. Doug...'

'We're here,' Tanner Hicks says, standing at the door. The assembled group exhales as one. 'We're all here. Go on, son.'

Carl walks towards the registrar's desk as if he's heading for the guillotine, his jaw set, his eyes the colour of a grey winter sea.

Half-way through the reception at Ravelli's, when the speeches are done, alcohol is flowing and the noise level is deafening, Carl finally whispers a few words into the ear of his new wife. To onlookers, they might be sweet nothings. 'I don't want to talk about this again. Ever,' he tells her. 'And I want us to have a baby before the year's out. You took one away without asking, now you'll give me another. Right?'

Daisy nods, optimism flowing back, helped by a couple of sherries and several glasses of sweet white wine. 'You love me, don't you, Carl? You must do – otherwise you wouldn't have turned up, would you? You didn't have to come...' She shuts her eyes and purses her lips, in preparation for a kiss of reconciliation. 'I love you, I really do...' She opens them again to see Carl ordering himself a pint at the bar. He'll get over it, she tells herself, the hope inherited from her mother strong in her heart.

An hour before the evening celebrations begin,

the Berries, led by Bryn, arrive at the railway-men's club to set up their instruments, accompanied by their women. Kit is no longer officially a girlfriend but comes anyway. She wears a lime-green, pink, purple and turquoise Pucci-patterned mini-skirt and a lime-green sleeveless polo-neck jumper. Her shoes are slingbacks, also lime green, while gigantic hoop ear-rings, large enough to accommodate a couple of parrots, swing from her ears.

Penny is in an empire-line dress with see-through chiffon sleeves. She has her hair tied back, flattened over her ears in what's supposed to be a Mod style, but it makes her look like Jane Eyre. I'm wearing a black and white op-art shift with white nylons and black patent shoes and lots of white eye shadow. I also have Robert and Dulcie in tow.

While the group carry out a sound-check, Dulcie and I and the others dance to records in a still empty hall. Two strangers come in. I know they're foreign to the area because one is black, and the only black faces that Fairport ever sees are on the television. They are reasonably good-looking, probably in their late twenties, sharply dressed and, bizarrely, they both hold instrument cases – or maybe they're tommy guns.

'Kath's friends,' Dulcie reports. 'They're looking for Pete to give him some money. They think you or Kit or Robert will know where he is. Kath told them to come tonight and join in. They play trumpets in their spare time.'

'*They* want to give *him* some money?' I repeat. The two men come over and make their introductions, Gary and Paul. I decline their offer of a drink. As the Berries warm up with a very loud version of 'Poison Ivy', Gary bellows at me, unconvincingly, 'Pete's inherited some money from an aunt in Worthing. We're trying to give him the good news.' His colleague nods vigorously.

'What's her address?'

Gary looks at me sharply. 'See, this is how it works,' he says, cracking his knuckles. 'You give us a little piece of information and we give you a little piece of information. And everybody's happy.'

'Except Pete.'

'Now, why would you say that?' Paul, the blond-haired man fences.

'I don't think you want to give him money. I think he's got money that you think is yours. Nobody in Pete's entire life has ever given him cash. No offence, but I don't believe a word you two are saying.'

The two men glance at each other. 'Fair enough,' says Paul. 'I'll come clean. Marie is my cousin. When she left, Pete promised he'd send her money regularly and he's fallen behind. She saw him on the telly and asked me if I'd come and have a chat. No rough stuff, just a pleasant request. He's not at home, so we thought you might know where he's gone... Think of little Hayley,' he adds.

I obviously don't look convinced because he reaches for his wallet and takes out a photograph. It's Marie and Pete at the register office. Gary and Paul are next to them, among a group of five or six middle-aged couples.

'I'm Paul's mate,' Gary says, as if I've demanded how he was invited to the wedding too. 'We're session musicians and we play brass in a group – tour American bases, that kind of stuff. Tamla Motown. R&B. We thought we'd ask your lads if we could join in for a couple of numbers – maybe later. Perhaps one of them would know where Pete's fetched up.'

He smiles broadly.

By nine thirty p.m., after Mr and Mrs Carl Hicks have made their departure for a week's honeymoon in Great Yarmouth, the Berries are playing to a packed hall. Half-way through 'Route 66' there is a crackle, a flash, and then silence. 'Fuck,' Podge says, the word echoing around the room to whistles and slow handclaps. Mick, Podge and Bryn go into a small huddle, backs to the audience, fiddling with the equipment.

Harry Jones, Bulbie's uncle, who manages the club, officiously bustles on to the stage. 'Give the lads a couple of minutes, ladies and gentlemen, please.' Penny and I have sat listening to Kit all evening, charting the vegetable-eating habits of every cul-de-sac, avenue and street on her patch. 'Windsor Drive aren't at all keen on bananas, but show 'em spring greens and they just can't get enough. Ran out I did. And it was only half past two...' We've drunk several gin and oranges to numb the pain.

The catcalls and stamping of feet thankfully stop her monologue and draw us to the hall where we weave our way to the front. 'Microphones are OK,' a harassed Bulbie says to Bryn, 'it's the speakers that are buggered. I'll go to Dave's and see if we can borrow some of his gear. It'll only take fifteen minutes – if he's in,' he adds glumly.

'Right,' Kit says, giving me an almighty shove forward. 'You're on. Come on, Penny. Straighten up, for God's sake.'

While we gawp, she steps boldly on to the stage, waving at the crowd as if she's been a professional entertainer for years, ignoring the glares of the Berries.

'Belt up!' she shouts cheerily to the audience. 'Ladies and gentlemen, first a commercial. If any of you wants lovely ripe fruit and the freshest of veg delivered to your door, I'm the woman for you. Come and see me afterwards.'

'I wouldn't mind a bite of one of your cherries!' someone shouts from the back. Kit ignores him and beckons to me and Penny again. We are both stuck to the spot, paralysed by the awfulness of what is about to happen.

'She wouldn't,' squeaks Penny.

'She has,' I say.

'Ladies and gentlemen,' Kit continues, giving a wiggle, 'as the Berries are facing a temporary inconvenience, I have great pleasure in bringing to you straight from a long-running engagement in Las Vegas ... the Gooseberries!'

Out of the corner of my eye, I see that my dad has also made his way to the front, as if he expects to be called to fill the entertainment gap. He winks and indicates with his head, encouraging me on to the stage but not before I've noticed how disappointment has deepened the lines on his face. Then Kit has me by the hand and is yanking me towards her.

The audience breaks into cheers. 'Please,' Kit

commands, 'I want you to be very, very quiet because we're going to sing a *capella*, which, for all you ignorant sods, means that we won't have any backing,' she explains. Then she turns to Podge, who has vacated his seat behind the drums. 'Sit!' she commands, clearly in her element. 'We'll need you in a minute.'

'Go on, "Chapel of Love",' Kit hisses at me. 'Give us the key.' Penny, filled with good spirits, all from a bottle, is beginning to enjoy the attention. A lad to her left wolf-whistles and she blows him a kiss. I click my fingers to provide the beat and, shakily at first but with increasing bravado, we sing the song, mostly in tune. As soon as Kit opens her mouth, with her deep, deep voice like a southern American bullfrog, the hall erupts.

Bryn and Mick stop and stare. The audience yell for more. For the second song I sit at the piano, while Podge, ignoring the disapproving looks of his fellow group members, joins in on drums. We enthusiastically belt through 'Long Tall Sally' and the Kinks' 'You Really Got Me'. Gary and Paul have made their way to the front and Kit beckons them on stage too, drunkenly demanding that they play 'O Mein Papa'. Gary declines politely. 'What's it to be then, girl?' he asks me.

We rip through 'Shake!' and 'My Girl' and 'Knock On Wood'. Then I start playing 'I've Been Loving You Too Long (To Stop Now)'. I've had more than one too many drinks, so my inhibitions have long ago dissolved.

Penny and Kit, spectacles constantly slipping down her nose in the excitement, sing in

410

harmony as backing singers while Podge plays on drums as he's never been allowed to play before, taking risks he's probably only ever tried out previously in his bedroom.

As I sing the last note, I search for my dad in the crowd, but he's already slipped away.

'Why didn't you tell me you could sing like that?' Bryn asks accusingly, a little later, in the bar, in which, this being a special occasion, us girls are permitted tonight.

'You never asked and, besides, we were only messing about. It's not serious. People thought we were brilliant only because we weren't supposed to be doing it.' Something in his tone, as if he owned me, makes me bristle. 'Mind you, I reckon we could make a career out of it. What do you think, girls?'

'Sorry, Lily.' Penny looks at me uncertainly, unsure whether I'm serious. 'I'm going to Oxford, I think. Or perhaps not,' she adds, turning expectantly to a sulking Bulbie, who looks the other way.

'Count me out, my darling.' Kit smiles happily. 'I know how to make my first million and it certainly isn't going to come from exercising my tonsils on some draughty stage in Scunthorpe, thank you very much.'

'So that just leaves me,' I say, slightly the worse for wear and high on adrenaline. 'I shall plot a course on my own. No boyfriends, no ties, no nothing... I've had a little proposition and, thinking about it, I don't see why I shouldn't say yes.'

'What do you mean, a proposition?' I hear Bryn ask but I'm already weaving my way between the

411

tables in search of Gary and Paul. I find them upstairs, looking down at the talent, or lack of it, on the dance-floor below.

'So, have you made up your mind?' Gary asks. 'Our lot have been looking for a singer for a couple of months now. You do the audition, and if you sing like you did tonight you'll be in. We've got a tour starts October. American bases in Germany, then Holland, Denmark and Sweden, eight weeks. Chas, who runs the band, was big in the Scandinavian top ten a couple of years ago. We've got a summer gig too, Brighton. Three times a week, July to September...'

'Germany in October? You mean going abroad in October?' I try to sound casual but I'm sure my face gives me away.

'Germany, yes. October follows September, comes before November, that's what I'm talking about.' Gary smiles. 'They give you a contract. You sign. You turn up. You get plenty of experience singing with one of the best grown-up bands in the land. And there's me and Paul to look after you. What have you got to lose?'

It's ironic. The one ambition I've had for as long as I can remember has been not to become a singer, not to follow in my dad's shoes and risk ending up a pub crooner who fights every night to be heard. Then again, perhaps, every job, however highflown its title, has its monotonous routines, its frustrated opportunities, its scaled-down aspirations. What's so special about going to university, after all? Nobody else in the family has ever had much of an education, and they've all got by. Sort of. Looking at Gary and Paul, another idea begins

412

to germinate.

'I know what you're thinking,' Paul says. 'You're thinking dosh. What's it pay?'

I shake my head. 'I'll tell you what I'm really thinking. I'm wondering if either of you two know how I can get hold of a fake birth certificate, one that's good enough to pass for real. And how much it might cost. And whether I could pay that off in a couple of weeks gigging in Brighton if I get the job.'

Paul opens his mouth to answer when Kit arrives. 'So what's this about you paying good cash to get hold of Pete Wells?' she asks, her eyes glistening behind her glasses.

'Kit, you wouldn't,' I protest, knowing that she can, and will.

Chapter Forty-three

Three days after Daisy's wedding, Barry Taylor is summoned to the production manager's office at Lawson's – and sacked. The official reason is his alleged repeated obstruction of the management's attempts to modernise the factory floor. Barry subsequently explains to the workers, in an emergency meeting, that the unofficial reason is that Lawson's intends to impose a wage freeze for a year, effectively making a cut in every wage packet, as well as demanding an increased rate of production. 'They are squeezing the working man because this Labour government encourages

413

them to!' Barry thunders to the factory floor.

He explains the options. They can all resign – but in such large numbers only some will find jobs elsewhere – they can accept the management's decision, or they can strike. The vote is almost unanimous. Everybody out. Mid-morning, a crowd duly troops across the road to the pub. The pattern in the past has been that such action is followed by negotiations, management compromise, and everybody back in, often within hours, spirits high, fuelled by a brief dose of excitement in an otherwise mundane routine. This time it's different.

First, the management refuses to hold talks. Second, two men and five women refuse to strike. After several hours of unpleasantness, this number is reduced to one – Doug Tempest. Barry attempts to talk him out of his decision but he is adamant. In spite of the cussing, jostling and barracking every morning and afternoon over the next three days when he crosses the picket line, he is clear where his duty lies: to continue to put money on the family table.

On the fourth day, Barry suggests to Lily that she try to talk to her father. Now she stands in the doorway of the shed, watching him at work on his dogs. 'Are you going to come in?' he asks, without looking up. He lights a cigarette and looks at her quizzically through the smoke.

'I've got something to tell you, Dad,' she says. 'I'm not going to college. I'm going to try for a job as a singer. I've got an audition in Liverpool. I'll be able to send some money home.'

If she's seeking approval, her father offers none.

All he does is nod. Lily seethes at his lack of generosity and her own hunger for his attention. She is tempted to yell and scream and walk out in frustration. Instead she tries to wound him verbally. 'About the factory–' she begins.

Doug interrupts her: 'Before you say anything, let me tell you this. Barry keeps talking about solidarity, but the way I see it it's not solidarity, it's stupidity. Sooner or later the modernisation will happen. No use in pretending otherwise. Barry believes he can hold back change. He has to believe that. But, deep down, he knows.'

Lily shakes her head. 'Why are you so bloody defeatist, Dad? Does that mean everyone just sits back and accepts that it can't get better than this? I thought you were a fighter?'

Doug chuckles. 'Do you know what I've only ever really wanted? To prove that I was worth something – and to live a decent life. Your generation is after other things – a big house, holidays abroad, a better three-piece suite than the next-door neighbour, a new car, a larger telly. It's all about things, lots and lots of things. Not people, not the commitments we make and the promises we should keep. It's just things. In the end, it's family that counts most. That's why I go in every day. I have mouths to feed, obligations to fulfil, a duty to–'

'Everyone on strike has mouths to feed,' she challenges. 'You're not the only one who cares about his family. They all do. Barry does. That's why they're out, to try and make sure they have a future. To show that if they stand together the bosses will learn that they can't be trampled on.'

Doug puts up his hands as if to fend off her arguments. 'OK, OK, we all have obligations. I'm fulfilling mine in a different way. Tell me this, is Barry really helping that lot on the picket line to face up to the future? Is he honestly?'

'Honestly? Honestly, you say?' Lily is aware she's shouting. 'How can you, of all people, talk about honesty? Never mind the women and the little deceits, what about your bloody big whoppers? I found Dulcie's birth certificate,' she adds bluntly. 'You've let that happen. Where was your sense of duty to Dulcie? Tell me that. How do you think she'll feel if she finds out? How could Kath not have acted like her mother all these years? How could she do that? And you have the nerve to talk about honesty?'

Doug's face is ashen. 'Kath did what she thought was right in the circumstances. She wasn't just an unmarried mother – the shame would have ruined Dulcie's life as well as Kath's. What are you going to do?'

'Tell,' his daughter replies. 'What else can I do?'

'Dear Matthew'. Kath writes the words very carefully. She has taken a long time to decide on the appropriate stationery. Basildon Bond blue seemed too unimaginative, pale pink decorated with spring flowers too flirty. She'd taken a real fancy to notepaper in lavender, only to have it pointed out to her, as she handed over her money, that it was imbued with the scent of violets – much too suggestive of the boudoir. Finally, she'd opted for unlined cream.

Dear Matthew,

Thank you for taking the trouble to contact me. I realise your time must be severely constrained, so I appreciate your words all the more. I have to confess, I have never received a fan letter before. Thank you, too, for your suggestion that I am a natural performer. I would very much like to appear again on television but, due to unforeseen circumstances, that is no longer possible. Still, I realise that I'm one of those rare people, who has been fortunate enough to have a dream come true...

Then Kath stops and rereads her admirer's letter. He has had no agonising over the style of stationery. Prisoner No. 59301 has sent his missive on regulation prison paper. He informs Kath that he has served the first year of a three-year sentence for the manslaughter of his wife.

I don't know what came over me (he explains). She mocked the new suit I'd bought for a family wedding, and other aspects of my personality, then informed me in a brutal fashion that she was leaving me for another man. Next thing I knew, the brass lamp wasn't where it should be.

Sadly, we had never been blessed with children. We had been relatively happy for a number of years, and I'd be the first to say that she had been an excellent wife. I am writing to you because I share your interest in bygone crimes. I was very much hoping that, if you didn't mind communicating with an incarcerated person, we might become pen-pals?

Yours very sincerely,

Matthew James.

PS I have been very honest with you in the hope that, this way, we may go forward unencumbered.

Kath picks up her pen and begins writing again:

After much thought, I have decided that I would like to communicate with you, at least for a probationary period. I have checked with the prison authorities. Sadly they have refused permission for you to have the two issues of Illustrated Crime I'd intended to send you.

Yours etc.

Kathleen Morgan

'Kath?'

She gives a start, then quickly covers her letters with a leather-bound copy of the *Radio Times*.

'Could I talk to you, please?'

'Whatever's the matter? You look as white as a sheet,' Kath says, pulling out a chair from the back-room table.

'Is Dulcie at work?' Lily checks.

Kath nods. Without speaking, the younger woman takes the birth certificate out of her pocket, unfolds it and lays it flat on the table before her aunt.

Her aunt gets up slowly, then sits down again. She picks up the certificate with shaking hands and turns to Lily with a look of such profound anguish that the girl's heart lurches. Panic briefly takes hold – what if Kath *dies* or something, right here, right now?

418

To stave off her aunt's possible demise, Lily pulls out a second birth certificate, in which Dulcie's father and mother are detailed as Harold and Elizabeth Tempest. She lays that before Kath too. Her aunt reads it, realisation dawning. 'You're not going to tell her?' she asks, a catch in her voice. 'Does this mean you're not going to tell her? Who else knows? How did you find this? Oh, my God, what am I going to do?'

'Of course I won't say a word,' Lily promises, growing more and more alarmed. 'You're the only one who can do that.'

'Where did you get these?' Kath repeats, more composed, picking up the two documents.

'It doesn't matter. Look, Kath, you know what this means, don't you? It means that Robert and Dulcie can marry without any upset.'

'What if someone checks?' Kath asks. 'What if they go back to Somerset House? You'll be done for forgery or something.'

'Nobody's going to check. People believe what they see. You should know that better than anyone. Are you all right?' Lily asks, realising even as she speaks how ridiculously inadequate the words sound.

Her aunt nods. Then her face caves in. 'I don't want to be on my own, Lily,' she says, her face distorted by loss. 'I can't bear to be on my own.'

The moon is full, a lustrous large silver marble, caught as if mid-roll across the navy blue sky. Down the side of the cinema is Snog Alley where couples, propped up against the brick wall, have a pre-film session or make another attempt at whatever they failed to achieve in the back row. On a night normally reserved for hair-washing duties, Penny has agreed to accompany her mother to the pictures. *A Man For All Seasons* is guaranteed to have a full house since whatever is on is seen. They are late.

'You know what Alexandra Kollontai said, don't you, darling?' Adele scrabbles around in her bag for her purse. 'The development of capitalism has placed a triple burden on women. They are workers, maintainers of the household and they care for the children. Only socialism is going to ease the burden of domestic drudgery and...'

Having heard it all before, Penny glances down the alley. What she sees is the back of her father's black mohair three-quarter-length coat around which is wrapped a pair of arms dressed in a bright red mac. The female feet she can see between her father's legs are wearing a pair of white stilettos. Immediately Penny thinks of Kit. It couldn't be her, could it? *Kit?*

Quickly Penny pushes her mother in the direction of the ticket office but a mix of incredulity and revulsion at her father's behaviour with her *best friend* propels her to take a second look. The girl, giggling, breaks free, pulling her enthusiastic lover round with her, revealing her face and his. As she does so, Penny stands transfixed. Then she throws back her head and howls at the moon.

Lily, Kit and Penny sit with Rose around her kitchen table to give Penny support in a time of crisis.

In recounting her tale, she has omitted to voice her first reaction that she thought her father was snogging Kit. That, the girls would never believe.

'What a bastard! What an absolute rotten bastard. I bet that completely ruined the film for you, didn't it, you poor thing?' says Kit.

'Christ, sometimes I really think there's a bit missing with you,' Penny says exasperated. 'You don't honestly think I'd sit through a film when that's happened, the most seismic event in my entire life, do you?

'What's worse is that at first I really thought it was my dad,' she continues. 'But I just knew he's not the type to mess about like that. He wouldn't dream of playing around behind Mummy's back. I just know he wouldn't.'

Kit gets up noisily to make more tea. 'Then when he turned round and I realised it was Bulbie! BULBIE! Can you believe it? *My Bulbie* with a fifteen-year-old slapper. I could've killed him. I could've killed her. I could've killed myself.'

Kit returns to the table and dispenses mugs of tea. 'None of us thought he was up to much anyway,' she says, oblivious to the signals she is being given by the others. 'I mean, he's never got anything to say for himself, has he? He's the kind of bloke who thinks with his willy and, given its size, no wonder he's so bloody clueless.'

'How dare you?' Penny yells, jumping to her feet. 'You're talking about the man I love! And how would you know about the size of his – anything? How would you?'

'Imagination, that's all. I've got a wonderful imagination,' Kit replies, deadpan.

Chapter Forty-four

After work, Doug Tempest wipes the spit off his coat and pretends not to notice the exodus of passengers from the top deck of the bus as soon as he sits down. He gets off at the market square and walks, collar up, hands in pockets. Since crossing the picket line that morning, Doug has methodically sung every song on *The Very Best of Dino,* in the right order, in his head, one lyric after the other, beginning again and again.

He is about to cross the market square, considering whether he should perform an encore, when he is distracted by what sounds like a muffled scream. It comes from the direction of the disused railway station. He walks into the car park and, hearing nothing more, is about to resume his journey when he hears a noise, as if someone is kicking desperately against a locked door. It takes him only a couple of minutes to run through the decrepit ticket office and on to Platform One, now covered with weeds, graffiti and litter.

Again, there is the sound of kicking, this time from the defunct waiting room. Several of its frosted windows have long ago been smashed and crudely boarded up. 'Hi!' Doug shouts. 'Are you OK? Is anyone there?'

At first, the door refuses to yield to his pushing. Then, suddenly, it opens wide. Two hands reach out and grip him by the shoulders. Doug sees something coming towards him at a ferocious speed. Next second, he experiences a pain so prolonged and searing it's as if his entire body is moving through a bacon slicer, neatly carving nerves, organs, muscles into thin slivers of living pulp.

Dazed and in shock, Doug puts his hand to his nose, and it comes away bright red with small, delicate shards of cartilage, like bleached splinters of wood. He blows a bubble of blood from what's left of his nostril. He tries to steady himself and focus. He sees, in the dark, three bulky shadows, moving constantly, like malevolent stormclouds scudding across the sky. One is carrying what looks like the leg of a chair. A small voice in the back of his head says, No more smiles, for you, then, Dougie, my lad!

A boot kicks him hard between the legs, and he doubles up, vomiting bile. As he does so, blows from fists and boots rain down on his head and back, haphazardly, as if those throwing the punches are determined to give their all before their collective nerve runs out. He tries to run forward to tackle the first pair of legs, but a fountain of blood spurts from his mouth, making it hard to breathe.

'Jesus!' a voice says, as a crimson arc spews from his mouth and splatters the boots of his attacker. Out of the corner of his eye, he catches sight of a faded and torn poster. A plump cartoon sailor is skipping along a pier. 'Welcome to Sunny Skegness!' the poster reads, and Doug could swear that the sailor gives him a wink. Then, he sees no more because the weapon, made of wood and nails, is driven hard against the side of his head, tearing his ear and opening up a jagged wound. He knows that because when he puts his fingers to his face, instead of touching his cheek, what they feel reminds him of uncooked liver.

Under the sailor's smiling gaze, Doug Tempest slides away.

Kath steadfastly shovels portions of chips into greaseproof bags and stacks them up in the heated cabinet, ready for the early-evening rush. On the other side of the counter stands a radiant Dulcie with Robert and Lily.

'Tell her, then,' Dulcie nervously instructs Lily.

'I've got customers to serve, you know.' Kath nods at a bemused woman with hair tightly coiled around rollers, partly hidden by a headscarf.

'Don't mind me,' she says. 'You go ahead and sort yourselves out.'

Robert takes hold of Dulcie's hand and tells the unknown woman ponderously, 'We're getting married in August. She's going to be my wife.' Then he takes a step back, as if he expects Kath to attack him with the vinegar bottle.

The customer looks slightly taken aback. 'Well, congratulations, pet. I don't see why you two don't stand as good a chance as anybody else of making it work. Let's face it, it shouldn't take all that much upstairs to learn how to rub along together, should it?'

Kath's lips tighten.

The woman continues enthusiastically, 'Is it going to be a white wedding? I love a nice white wedding with all the trimmings. Something old, something new, bridesmaids, flowers, wedding bells, confetti... Can't beat a good wedding.'

Dulcie, Robert and Lily turn expectantly to Kath. 'I hate white weddings,' she snaps. 'I really hate them. A waste of money.' She catches Lily's eye and sighs. 'Let's just wait and see.'

Robert makes his way round to Kath's side of the counter. 'Mrs Morgan,' he says timidly, 'thank you.'

'Do you think Penny's going to be all right?' Lily asks Kit, in Tanner's lock-up, as they load the van with fresh produce for the following day.

Kit stops polishing apples. 'You never really thought she'd marry him, did you? Deep down, she wants to do exactly what Mammy and Daddy say. For all we know, Daddy probably engineered the whole trick. Gave Bulbie the coat, encouraged him to chat up the bird, fixed for Penny and her mam to go to the pictures...'

'Christ, you are the most devious-minded person I've ever met.'

Kit shrugs. 'People think that a few white lies, a bit of shagging around, is bad and sinful and disgusting, but do you know what the greatest crime of all is, and it's not even included in the Ten Commandments?'

Lily shakes her head and helps herself to an orange. 'It's trying to make other people do what you want them to do. Don't do as I do, do as I say. Well, stuff bloody that.'

Kit stabs her finger into a rotten orange, and waggles it in defiance. '"Thou shalt not control", that's what Moses should've had written on his tablet. If he'd started with that, he wouldn't have

425

needed all the other stuff about adultery, and honouring your mother and your father and what-not. Most of that is just kicking back at someone who's got their hands around your throat and is squeezing hard because you won't do exactly what they think is right for you. My dad tried to do it to my mam, Penny's parents try to do it to her,' she continues, warming to her theme. 'My view is, forget whatever anybody else tells you about what is right or wrong, truth or lies, good or bad behaviour. It doesn't mean you don't have morals. It means you don't have their morals. Treat others as you would wish to be treated.'

Lily pretends to choke on a piece of orange. 'Well, you certainly don't do that.'

Kit gives a broad smile. 'I would if it was more fun.'

Melody cuts and carves and flours and fries and boils and batters until the kitchen resembles a steam room and her entire body is glowing with the heat and the effort. Doug is late. He's usually in before her, fire lit, radio on, evening newspaper read, and into his shed until she shouts that tea is on the table. At six thirty she takes the steak and kidney pudding out of the oven. It is in a round white bowl. Small puddles of brown gravy have broken through the suet crust, giving a piebald effect. Carefully she circles the dish with a knife, loosening the crust. The released aroma is rich and comforting. The dish is hot, very hot, so Melody is glad of the gloves that protect her fingers.

She puts on her coat and scarf and tells Iris, mournfully watching television, that if her father appears to tell him she has popped out. 'Where are you going with the steak and kidney?' Iris asks.

'Can't stop,' Melody answers.

Several minutes later, she walks into the railwaymen's club, the favourite haunt of many of Lawson's employees who live in Fairport. Barry Taylor, seeking respite from the picket line, is at the bar, along with three fellow strikers. He has a glass of lemonade in his hand. 'Evening, Melody,' he greets her. His companions turn their backs.

The woman, unsmiling, straight-backed, tall and formidable, walks up to the men whose faces she can no longer see. 'Whatever has happened to my Dougie, I know you're all to blame,' she says, her voice flinty with anger. 'Help yourselves, boys,' she adds – and, holding fast to the dish, she throws its contents in the direction of the men. The meat and gravy bomb, encased in suet, flies with deadly accuracy and hits the man nearest to her squarely on the nape of his neck, exploding lumps of meat, kidneys and scalding hot gravy in all directions.

'Holy Mary,' screams the man, as the results of Melody's cooking slide down his back.

'What the bloody hell?' says his colleague, splattered brown.

'That'll do you a power of good, boys,' Melody says grimly, then walks out, coat swirling around her like a cloak of vengeance, pudding basin in hand.

It is dark by the time Doug Tempest regains consciousness. He knows that his face is a mess, because his features no longer follow a familiar terrain when he tries delicately to touch them.

427

Whoever attacked him has also broken a couple of ribs. A piercing pain in the area of his kidneys tells him where his attackers' boots have aimed.

'Cowards, bloody cowards,' he tells himself, steeling himself to stand. He groans as he puts weight on his left foot. He cannot see but he guesses that the ankle is broken or sprained. Slowly, he begins to hop. Several hops out of the waiting room, each one jogging lacerated flesh and a badly bruised body.

What propels him forward, ironically, is the raw raging anger that he has spent years struggling to contain: his father's anger. Hop, hop, I'll kill the bastards. Hop, hop, I'll give no bugger the pleasure of finishing me off. Hop, hop. Hop, hop, hop, hop. Doug's anger dissolves as he becomes aware that hopping alongside him, hopping in time, is the child, not mocking him, not goading him, not reminding him of that which he'd most like to forget but willing him on, *meaning him no harm.*

Hop, hop. Tears course down the man's cheeks, not from pain but from gratitude for this, the first sign that one day he might finally reach the end of his path of penance.

Chapter Forty-five

Lily and Kit have almost completed loading the van when someone bangs on the door of the lock-up. 'Lily!' a voice shouts. 'It's Barry.' He comes in, accompanied by Tanner Hicks, their faces grave.

'It's your dad,' Barry says immediately. 'He's in hospital.'

Lily looks at him blankly, uncomprehending. Barry shakes his head miserably. 'It was nothing to do with me, Lily love. I'm very, very sorry. If I find out who did it, I promise you, I'll make them pay.'

'What? Is he dead? Have they killed my dad?' Lily panics, her voice rising in fear. 'What have they done?' she screams at the two men.

Tanner intervenes. 'He's been battered quite badly. He was found collapsed in the station car park. He's—'

Lily turns on Barry in a fury. 'You had nothing to do with it? How can you say that? You've egged on the stupid bastards. My dad is as entitled to his beliefs as you are without getting his head bashed in. You've got a nerve to tell me about the bloody sins of the police state. You—'

Instinctively Barry puts his arms out to comfort her.

'No, don't touch me,' she shouts. 'I don't want to see you or your pamphlets or your bloody records or your politics or your propaganda and posters ever again. Do you hear me?'

Barry opens his mouth to speak, his face convulsed with emotion, but he fails to find the words.

Iris, in curlers, sits at the table in the back room at Rydol Crescent. Her broken heart is mending with impressive speed. Her attention is now focused on finding a replacement for Howard as rapidly as possible. 'This time make sure he's an atheist,' Lily advises, watching her sister pluck her eyebrows using their dad's shaving mirror.

'Not on your life,' Iris says. 'No more religion for me. Next time I'm definitely going for someone who doesn't believe in God.'

'Iris, even you can't be that thick,' Daisy says. She is newly returned from honeymoon and now living with her in-laws until a council house comes up. 'Why didn't anyone tell me?' she adds crossly. 'I'm swanning around in the freezing spring on honeymoon, and my dad's lying in a bed wrapped in so many bandages he looks like a mummy. What if he'd died? What if he'd died and the moment he died it turned out I was going round and round on the ferris wheel, laughing my head off, having a really good time? I mean, that can't be right, can it? How do you think I would've felt for the rest of my life? "And where were you when your father passed away?"

'"Having a whale of a time, eating candy-floss, thank you very much." How would that've made me look?'

Melody puts two mugs of tea and a couple of sausage sandwiches in front of her and Carl. The bread is saturated with fat and HP sauce. Carl grunts as he helps himself, slurping his tea with greasy lips. 'Look, love,' Melody coaxes, 'your dad told us not to spoil your fun. He had a rough twenty-four hours with a lot of internal bleeding but he's on the mend now. We've taken it in turns to visit. Lily's popping in from school this afternoon, so you can go this evening if you'd like. He's got a few broken ribs and a busted ankle, his nose is a mess, his cheek'll have a scar and they broke all the fingers on one hand. Apart from that, he'll be as right as rain – if the hospital food doesn't kill him.' She smiles brightly.

'God, Mam, is there nothing that wipes the smile off your face?' Lily asks irritably.

'Do they know the bastards who did it?' Carl mumbles, his mouth full. 'I'll get a few of the lads together and we'll soon sort 'em out.'

Melody shakes her head. 'No, don't do that, pet. It'll only make matters worse. Barry's asking around. He'll find out, but I can't see that he's going to turn his own crew in, is he now?'

'What's Dad going to do? He can't go back to Lawson's, can he?' Daisy asks.

Her mother shrugs resignedly. 'He says he will. He says nobody's going to scare him off. Anyway, when the management heard what had happened, they issued a joint statement with the union expressing regret, and it looks as if Barry'll get his job back, but they're going ahead with the wage freeze–'

Lily butts in drily, 'So that's a victory all round, is it – except for our dad?'

Carl wipes his hands on his trousers. 'I couldn't be arsed to work for anyone else. It suits me, just me and my dad.'

'Not everybody can do that, though, can they?' Daisy says.

Melody intervenes before a row brews: she collects the empty mugs and plates and asks Carl, 'So, how's married life suiting you?'

He winks. 'Too soon to tell. But dinner on the table, shirts nicely ironed and Friday night with the lads, that's what I'm looking forward to – and a baby called Noel, sooner rather than later. Isn't that right, girl?'

'I'll have a pound of bananas, no rotten ones, mind. I know your sort, here today and gone tomorrow, buying rotten fruit and selling it for twice the price.'

Kit, in the rear of the van, laughs with delight as she recognises the voice. 'Rose, what are you doing out here?'

In the periods when Chalkie is home, as now, Rose misses the younger girl. She misses her ebullience and the mix of her perfumes – Imperial Leather, hair lacquer, deodorant – that leave a sensory trail in the house for a long time after she has left. Rose wants to tell Kit this, and much more besides, but today, as always, she tells her something else instead. 'I'm being published,' she says shyly. 'A whole short story. And paid two guineas. It's another women's magazine, so I've come to say thank you. If you hadn't done what you did, I'd never have tried. Never in a million years.' She falls silent, embarrassed.

Kit jumps down from the back of the van, and screams her approval, causing curtains to twitch in the road where the van is parked. Calmer, she pushes back a strand of hair from Rose's eye, and the woman's heart gives a thud so loud, she swears it is heard in Coronation Park.

'Are you going to leave Chalkie one day?' Kit asks quietly.

'That's what I used to dream about,' Rose admits. 'Everything was his fault. So everything would get better once I left him behind – and – and Billy too. I was going to go one day, without telling anyone, and never come back. I was going

432

to abandon my son, I told myself, for the very best of reasons. So I wouldn't spend his childhood punishing him for what he made me give up...'

'And now?'

'Now, I don't know any more. I thought that we were set in stone. But it's changing, little by little, like fresh skin growing over a wound. Chalkie is trying ... and then there's Billy ... I can write. I can stay. I can try, can't I?'

'Tell you what,' the younger woman offers, 'once I'm out and about on my travels, you can come and visit me, for holidays, wherever I am. How about that?'

Rose reddens. 'Are you leaving?' she asks, trying to keep her voice normal. 'You never said that. I thought this was going well. What about the money you owe?'

'Whoa!' Kit laughs. 'Not yet, but maybe next year. I'll pay off my debts, save a bit, then go off and see the world. Penny's always saying money isn't everything – but, then, she can afford to. And maybe she's right. So perhaps I'll just take off. There's nothing to keep me here, really, is there?'

'No,' says Rose. 'I don't suppose there is.'

Miss Edna Baxter, a highly gifted English teacher, twenty-eight going on forty, skirt at mid-calf, sensible cardigan, lace-up shoes, thick stockings, walks into the upper sixth of my comprehensive. She has told us often that she regards the Sexual Revolution as a concoction of the media (sleaze), the pharmaceutical companies (drugs), the Jewish garment industry (short skirts) and dirty old men (newspaper editors). The aim of this so-called revolution is not to liberate the young, according to Miss Baxter, it is to enslave generations to come to the deification of the trivial. Pop music is poison.

She cannot for the life of her see how such a revolution can provide fun, cerebral satisfaction or, most important of all, security for her gender. What she implies when she's addressing us is that no sexual experience, no matter how earth-shattering, is sufficient compensation for the loss of the most valuable asset a woman possesses: her reputation.

We have pointed out to her that the revolution has already arrived in our school. Mr Ted Innes, the music teacher, and Mrs Valerie Guy, who instructs girls in domestic science, have recently had their activities described in seven paragraphs in the *News of the World:* 'Sir Caught Fiddling With Somebody Else's Dumplings'.

I'm sitting on my desk, chatting to Hilary Sanders, when Miss Baxter walks in. 'Could you do something about your hemline, please, Lily?' she says scathingly. 'This is an educational establishment, not a peep-show.'

'Miss Baxter, Hilary and I were just talking about *The Duchess of Malfi,*' I lie. 'We were wondering why we haven't discussed one of the main themes of the play.'

Miss Baxter always gives the blackboard an energetic clean when she knows a trap is being set. Now she practically disappears in a cloud of chalk dust. 'What precisely do you mean by that?'

'Well, we know it's about what happens when a woman refuses to abide by the social code of the

434

day. We know that it shows the consequences of deception. We know it's a portrait of madness and even black humour. But why haven't we discussed the passion?'

Several of the boys snigger. 'The what?' says Miss Baxter.

'The passion.' I try to sound earnest. 'The Duchess falls for her steward even though he's her servant and the whole of society will react in shock and horror. I mean, that has to be a profoundly passionate love, doesn't it, Miss? Or do you think there's a contemporary resonance, and the Duchess is just a contrary woman – like many women of today – who goes against the grain to challenge the establishment, no matter what the cost?'

Miss Baxter arranges the books, her pencils and her spectacle case neatly on the desk, then folds her hands, crosses her ankles and finally says, 'A very interesting set of questions, Lily. What's your view?'

That is a clever move. What I have to avoid is an intelligent answer or everyone else in the class will mock. Not that I care – much. 'Well, the romantic in me–' I'm interrupted by squeals and whistles from the others. 'Well, I think it's perhaps a bit of both. But the romantic in me wants to believe that sometimes passion is so overwhelming, the certainty that you have found your soulmate is so strong, that you step outside society's conventions. You say, "Stuff what everybody else thinks, this is what's good for us." I think the ability to risk so much for love has to be one of the strongest and most radical forces in society. You fight to defend your own so you fight to defend the values that those actions incorporate. So, individual acts of defiance – like the Duchess marrying whom she chooses – link up to become a major drive for change.' I pause, aware I've gone too far, so I try to lower the tone. 'Or do you think she just fancied him literally to death, Miss?'

Miss Baxter ignores the hoots and shouts from the class. She looks over her glasses at me. This signals trouble. 'What I think, Lily Tempest,' she says, 'is that no matter how long it takes, or how difficult and humiliating and frustrating the route might be, you should resist all temptations to find your calling in a hairdressing salon and proceed to university. What you've got is too good to go to waste. That's what I think.'

'Too late for that, Miss,' I say.

I spot Bryn's car parked a hundred yards from the school gates. We haven't spoken since the wedding and, officially, we are no longer 'courting'. Frankly, I'm relieved. Now I dither, unsure whether to head off in the opposite direction or say hello casually and walk on.

'All right?' he asks, sticking his head out of the driver's window.

'Not bad.'

'How's your dad?'

'It'll take a while but he's on the mend. He's going back to work. Tell that to the bullies who did him over.'

'I think they just meant to scare him.'

'It would have been less painful if they'd just said, "Boo!"'

Bryn shrugs. 'If the men don't stick up for

436

themselves, the bosses will have them doing women's work.'

'And about time too.'

'Are you getting in or what?' he asks, embarrassed by the attention we're attracting.

'You can give me a lift to the hospital, if you like,' I concede.

Bryn busies himself driving. Eventually, he says, 'What do you reckon, then?'

'About what?'

'About us getting back together. We can get engaged, if you like,' he adds casually. He runs his hand through his hair and checks himself in the mirror. 'My dad says we're too young but I know what I'm doing. He's not right about everything.'

I slide down in the seat trying to work out the kindest way to say no.

'You and I could do all right, couldn't we?' Bryn asks, a yearning in his voice that takes me by surprise. It can't be love, so perhaps it's loneliness. 'You talk too much – but I even miss that.' He sounds surprised.

I'm about to speak when I realise he's turning into his road.

'I know you don't want to talk to him but Dad says he's got something important to tell you. It won't take a minute. I'll drive you to the hospital after, if you like.'

I stand in the middle of Barry's garage, refusing to take a seat. 'Come on, Lily, let's shake and be friends,' he says.

'It wouldn't be fair. Not after what your lot did to my dad.'

'What you said about your dad being entitled to his own beliefs is right,' he says, as he makes himself a cup of tea. 'But it's when lots of individuals hold the same beliefs that, sometimes, things happen.'

'That doesn't give anyone the right to use violence, though, does it? Anyway, I've got to go.'

Barry persists: 'I remember when I first became a union official, I was on a sub-committee. Two of the six were wife-beaters, another just couldn't stay off the booze, even though he had three children at home in need of the money he was pouring down his throat. Three out of six. But, as far as I was concerned, it was their politics that mattered. They spouted the right line about class and social justice and equality. But your dad's right. That's the easy bit, isn't it? Words. It's not what you say but what you do that counts for more. Always.

'Beware of men with big mouths who posture and piss on their own families in the name of a greater cause, is my advice, Lily. You may listen to what they say but judge them only by their deeds.' Barry smiles wryly. 'Now, I don't doubt you're about to judge me, but will you tell your dad that we found out who did him over? The three lads – no, wait, listen,' he adds, as I head towards the door. The urgency in his voice makes me stop. 'The three lads weren't from Lawson's. I promise you they weren't. They weren't even from Fairport. They say that your dad beat up one of them in a pub just after Christmas. They wanted to settle the score and went a bit too far. They were drunk. The police are charging them with GBH.'

438

'Why should I believe you?' I ask, aware that I preferred the previous truth because that made my dad a maverick hero.

'Because they've admitted it,' he replies simply. I can tell by the look on his face that he knows my thoughts.

Annoyed, I ask aggressively, 'I bet if those lads had been strikers from your lot, you wouldn't have told the police, would you?'

Barry pauses. 'The honest answer is no. But I would've made sure that they made some restitution.'

'That's very Biblical of you,' I say sarcastically. 'Judge, jury and enforcer of penalties. Whoever the police have got are lying anyway. My dad has never had a fight in a pub in his life. He's never had a fight. Never.'

Barry shrugs. 'If he does come back to Lawson's, he's in for a rough ride. The blokes will send him to Coventry. There's nothing I can do about that. Here,' he adds, 'give him these, please.'

Barry hands me a battered carrier bag. 'It's a couple of Dean Martin albums, American imports – can't get 'em here. Can't stand the man myself, but still... I checked up. Your dad never joined the union. He said he wouldn't. I've had scabs in the past who sign up to the union when it suits and turn their backs on it when it doesn't. Your dad's not like that. He's a contrary bastard but I admire a man with principles, even if they're not my principles. But I'll still do everything in my power to keep him out of the factory. Tell him that as well.'

I refuse to take the records and ignore Barry's

439

proffered hand. 'He doesn't want anything from you,' I say, and head for the door. 'Lily,' Barry calls out, 'don't stay around here. Go.'

'I'm off to Manchester for an audition,' I blurt out. 'I might sign up with a group. Go on the road. They do a bit of rhythm 'n' blues, a lot of soul and stuff. Not authentic, of course,' I add, with a small smile. 'Most of 'em come from Borehamwood.'

'So, you really have given university the elbow?' Barry asks, his voice neutral.

'You know how it is, things happen. Anyway, it's more like it's given me up. Stupid to even think about it, really. Maybe later...'

'Maybe.'

I make for the door, aware that there is an awkwardness between us now. 'I've still got a couple of books of yours on Vietnam,' I say.

'Have you read them?'

'Of course I've read them.'

'Well, you'd better pick up another couple the next time you come by,' he suggests hesitantly. He holds out his hand to me again. 'Shake?' he asks.

This time, I do.

Chapter Forty-six

Churchill is a men's ward. As I walk down it, looking for my father, I pass complexions in colours I'd never imagined possible – chrome yellow, translucent blue. I smile at each person, not wishing to intrude on privacy but not wishing to appear uncaring either.

At the far end of the room, Dad is sitting up in bed, heavily bandaged, talking to a woman. As I watch, she turns and makes for the exit nearest to her. She wears black patent-leather high heels, a smart pale green two-piece; she carries a light-weight coat over her arm and a small weekend case. Rose is right. My dad just can't stop himself – even in here, even wrapped up like a lost parcel.

'Lily, that's a nice surprise,' he says, anxiety in his eyes. I slip a packet of Player's under his sheets, as requested but show my anger. 'Who is she, Dad? You swore you wouldn't. You promised. You know you promised.'

'Who is who?'

'Dad, you promised. You promised faithfully...'

On impulse, not waiting to hear his lies, I turn and run, following in the woman's footsteps. A small crowd is waiting at the lift so I race down four flights of stairs. On the ground floor there are two entrances: one leads to the car park, the other is for the use of ambulances only but also provides a short-cut for pedestrians to the bus stop at the hospital's main gates. Would she have a car? No woman around here owns a car, not unless she's posh or has dosh. Then again, she might have gone to the cafeteria or the hospital shop or the public phone-box or the lavatory.

The doors to my left open automatically, as an elderly woman is carried in on a stretcher. Hand of fate, I tell myself, and run out of the still open doors, adrenaline and fury speeding me on. Find this woman. Let her know that Doug 'Dino'

Tempest isn't footloose and fancy-free, he's a dad, he's my dad, he's a husband, he's a fool who can't grow up. Tell her that she's kidding herself if she thinks that she'll have him all to herself, serenading her in years to come.

I reach the car park, mentally composing the conversation I'll have, once she's caught and confronted and shamed. Then I see her, a hand on the boot of a dark blue Austin Healey, one foot bare, as she shakes her shoe.

She wears gloves and her hair is styled like Jackie Kennedy's. And there is something else about the woman that is particularly striking: she could be my mother's double.

If, over the years, anybody had asked Doug Tempest how he would react should a part of his past introduce itself to his present, he would probably have given a variety of responses: panic, relief, alarm, fear, dread. Instead, now, there is nothing. Gradually that is replaced by a strengthening of the hope that he first experienced dragging himself out of the railway-station waiting room. Once the confessions are heard, the truth reinterpreted, the memories adjusted like a tailor updates a jacket, tweaking a lapel, narrowing the waist, perhaps then...

'Excuse me, Nurse, sorry to bother you,' Doug gives one of his best smiles, 'would you be so kind as to wheel the phone over to me, please, when you've got a moment?'

'Got enough coppers?' the nurse asks, returning his smile and bending over him to straighten his sheets. He nods. She wheels the trolley to his

442

bedside. He phones Melody at work. Veronica answers and huffs and puffs and talks of being rushed off her feet, when the background silence indicates that afternoon business is poor, as usual.

'Hello, sweetheart, is something wrong?' Melody asks. For a few seconds, Doug can't bring himself to answer. He is suddenly overwhelmed by her unwavering conviction throughout the years that he is a man worth loving.

'I'm lucky to have you,' he whispers.

'Oh, don't be so daft.' Melody laughs. Then, she adds, her instinct strong, 'What's happened?'

'I think it's over,' he replies simply.

'Excuse me,' my voice is almost drowned by a car that has pulled up close by, its radio blasting out pop music, 'excuse me... Would you mind telling me, are you Doug Tempest's girlfriend?'

'Why? Who are you?' the woman replies coldly in an accent I can't place.

'Are you his girlfriend?' I repeat, now feeling foolish. 'I saw you with him.'

'I'm not his girlfriend,' the woman interrupts firmly. 'I'm his wife. I'm Mrs Douglas Tempest.'

Through one of the glass walls of the small partitioned area in which we now sit, the smokers' room, at the end of the ward, I can see a middle-aged man whose body is anchored to various machines by numerous tubes and wires. He looks exactly like I feel: a fly caught in a spider's web. 'Lung cancer,' my dad says, lighting up another cigarette. My mother had explained to the nurses that a small family crisis needed to be resolved

443

and, if possible, we required somewhere private to talk. As a result four of us are now in this glass box with a sign reading 'Do Not Disturb' on the door, watched by at least a dozen patients.

Mrs Douglas Tempest and the other Mrs Douglas Tempest sit opposite my dad, who is in a wheelchair. I stand by the door. If I sit that makes me part of this conspiracy and I am not, since I know nothing. It's as if I've been trying to finish a particularly difficult jigsaw puzzle, only to discover, now the pieces are in place, a completely different and darker picture.

I try to keep the tremble out of my voice. 'So, basically, what you're saying is that we're all bastards. I'm a bastard and so are Daisy, Iris and Rose?'

Dad puts his head into his hands. Mum's eyes fill with tears and that only adds to my alarm. Smiles I can cope with – but not her tears. 'I'm so sorry, love,' she says. 'It wasn't what we wanted.'

'What about all that stuff you churn out all the time about never letting a bloke touch you? What about that? It didn't stop you, did it? It most certainly did not. But I saw our birth certificates. You'll be–'

'Lily,' my dad tries to break in, 'you're talking to your mother as if it's all her fault. It's not her, it's me ... and–'

I turn on him. 'She's the one who's spun the lies. What about all that stuff about your wedding day and the lodging-house and your trousers being all that was left? What about all those stories you told us? Those stories meant something to me. They were about us, our past, our family. And now I find that they were fairytales and lies. Lies, lies, lies. How could you? How could you, Mum? Now I don't know what's real and what's not.'

'Lily, Lily, listen.' My mam tries to soothe me, as the other woman watches, impassive. 'We changed your names and mine by deed poll to your dad's. I've never talked about our wedding, honestly I haven't. I've never called your dad my husband ... never. I tried as best I could to avoid any more deceit–'

'Christ!' I shout, then look down the ward to see a line of faces turned in our direction, completely absorbed. As if on a timer, each immediately turns and looks straight ahead.

'Cup of tea, anyone?' Without knocking, a woman in a blue overall comes into the room backwards, pulling a tea-trolley. 'No biscuits for you, Mr Tempest. Or do you fancy something sweet today?' She winks, apparently oblivious to the atmosphere. Silently, we accept our drinks and wait for the woman to leave.

As soon as she goes, Mam speaks to my dad's wife. 'I've always wanted to ask you this, Renee, I know you owe Doug nothing but did you ever think what taking his money week in week out would do to his family? He struggled and struggled to keep up the payments and, I admit it, I spent so you couldn't have it – sometimes I spent and spent and spent and, if I'm honest, the only pleasure it brought me was that it meant the money wasn't yours. Then, when the debts became too much, we'd up and run. Did you know that, Renee? Did you know that happened?

'Each time I'd hope he'd use that as an excuse

445

to disappear from your life, stop the maintenance. You wouldn't have known where we were. But no. We scrimped and scraped for you – always living with the worry that one day, some day, you'd turn up on our doorstep and tell the girls, tell the world that we'd been living in sin. Well, it wasn't sin, to me, it was never a sin.

'Do you hear me? It was love, Renee, love. I want Lily to understand that. Love matters more than anything in the world. Your dad could've walked away from us at any time but he never did. How long were you married, Renee, two, three years? And is that really supposed to be a debt that a man carries for life?'

As she speaks my mam seems physically to grow in stature. Anger suits her. 'All the time, Doug was trying to find the one idea that would work. The business that would finally produce enough cash to buy you off – and never once did you think to say, "Enough is enough. You've paid your dues."'

Her voice is steady but her shaking hands cause her tea to spill into the saucer. 'Now you've turned up here – for what? To up the price? I don't care what Doug says, Renee, it's got to stop, do you hear me? There is no more. We're done. We're done with the lying and the running. Our kids are old enough now to fend for themselves. We'll have to learn to live with what they think of us. As for what anybody–'

'I want a divorce,' the woman says, in a low, controlled voice. To my surprise, I'm suddenly sorry for this stranger who, for years, like an invisible boxer, has been in the ring with my family, landing so many hard punches. Yet her eyes, the way she sits now, tell of some deep and terrible hurt. Or perhaps that's just the Duchess of Malfi talking to me.

'You want a divorce?' my dad repeats disbelievingly. 'You want a divorce?'

'That's why I came. Every week, the money's come to my post-office box. I know why you never included an address. You were right, at least at the beginning. I would've done anything to cause you a fraction of the pain that I've experienced for years and years. But it's been different for a little while now. That's why I had to find you.'

'Was it Rose's name and address in the magazine? I knew you'd see it. I just knew,' my dad says, his face haggard.

'Who's Rose? What magazine?' The woman looks puzzled.

'Was it our Kath on the telly?' I ask, curiosity roused.

My dad interrupts, 'Renee's never met Kath.'

The woman gives a small smile. 'The last couple of years, I've had a bit of money. I've subscribed to a cuttings service. I knew, sooner or later, you'd be in the news. You couldn't resist it. So I asked the service to send me every news story that featured a Tempest. I was sure that, no matter what, you'd never give up your name. Not your father's name,' she adds slyly. 'Every two or three months I'm sent a bundle of stories. You'd be surprised how many Tempests there are but not that many with a face like Dean Martin's,' she adds drily. 'Thank God for local newspapers. They print names and addresses at the drop of a hat – the largest turnip, first prize in the flower show, a regular singing spot in a local pub, stick on the name and address.'

'Was it Bunting's fire?' I ask.

The woman shakes her head. 'I saw that later. It was this.' She reaches into her handbag and pulls out a half-page torn from the *Cwmland Weekly News,* a newspaper that never reaches our house. Cwmland might be the town next door, but as far as Fairport people are concerned, it's a foreign country. The newspaper clipping shows a photograph of Daisy, smiling broadly. She holds a large box of assorted biscuits and gazes up at Daniel Bright. The caption underneath describes her as the daughter of Doug and Melody Tempest of 9 Rydol Crescent, Fairport. Not for the first time, this is all my fault.

'That's how I found you. I didn't want to call on you at Rydol Crescent so I asked the local news-agent if he knew where you worked. The men on the picket line told me what had happened.'

Silence falls. Everyone sits lost in their own thoughts, pondering the ramifications of what has been said. All my life I'd believed my dad was frightened by success, running away as soon as it seemed possible. All my life I'd seen my mam as a ridiculous spendthrift, obsessed with my father, miring us in debt. Now, like a fresh pattern revealed at the twist of a kaleidoscope, how they have behaved takes on a very different meaning. Call me self-centred, but that still doesn't diminish my sense of betrayal. Nor does it dilute my rage that their choices have turned my sisters and me into a bunch of nomads, probably incurably addicted to rootlessness.

My dad wakes as if from a sleep. 'You said, "It's been different for a little while now." What do you mean? What's different, Renee?'

The woman looks guarded. 'You made me do the unforgivable,' she says, 'but I've finally come to realise that in never letting go I'm destroying myself, not you. I don't want your money any more. I've met someone. We want to get married. How you live with your conscience from now on, Doug, is your business. My solicitor will send you the divorce papers. Unless, that is, you object.' She gives a strange little laugh and stands up. 'Pleased to meet you,' she says mechanically to me, as if we've bumped into each other in the Co-op. Then she's gone.

Three of us sit stunned, as if each of us is waiting for a cue so we can rejoin the play that is the rest of our lives.

Chapter Forty-seven

If a long-held secret is divulged to you, you possess an awesome, almost magical power over others who are also affected but who remain unknowing. I'm now a co-conspirator. Do I stay dumb and shore up a mythical family history? Or, as I've already learned with Kath, do I speak out, change the past and therefore – perhaps frighteningly – affect the present too?

My mam and I sit in the bleak, thinly populated

hospital canteen, nursing grey coffee, with a slick left by the cup's previous contents, and a sickly-looking cake. 'I don't think I can do that,' I finally say. 'It wouldn't be right. You have to tell the others.'

'You do what you think is best, love,' my mam says, giving my hand a squeeze, but her face belies her words. 'Go on then, ask me what you like,' she suggests wearily.

'But how will I know if you're telling the truth?'

'You'll have to trust me.'

'None of us can do that ever again. How can we?' I answer bitterly, suddenly aware of the extent of my confusion and bewilderment. 'I'll never be like you two. Never,' I hiss.

Mam stares at her coffee. 'Listen, love, and then decide,' she says. 'I met your dad when I was eighteen and he was twenty-four. He was separated from Renee, had been for several months. They were together for three years and he was away off and on for fifteen months of that – that's how it was in the war. Your dad also spent six months in a military prison. He'd got into a fight and the other lad received a terrible beating. Your dad has ... had a terrible temper. That's where he learned to make the dogs. In prison.'

'You said he'd learned to make them in hospital.'

'He did. Prison hospital. That's the joke about the dog on the shelf. The one he calls Scrubs. Wormwood Scrubs. It was the first dog he ever made. They told him he had a creative streak. Making them used to calm him down ... sometimes. One minute there'd be flat calm seas, not even a ripple, next minute he'd rage, thrash, snap and snarl, like something horrible that's come up from the deep and suddenly smelt blood.'

I look at her disbelievingly. 'Weren't you scared?'

She touches my cheek. 'Twice I was very, very frightened. I...'

'Did he hit you?'

She shakes her head. 'No, he smashed a chair, punched the wall with his fist until it bled. The second time I told him that if he ever did it again, I'd leave.'

'And?'

'We had Rose, and I was pregnant with Iris. He did it again. I never knew what triggered it. I did as I said I would. I left him. I took Rose and I left him. I got a job in a factory and put Rose with Martha, a Polish woman in the same road, while I was at work. She had two kids of her own. Your dad tracked me down, begged me to come back. I made him wait until Iris was three months old. I wanted him to understand that I loved him. I wanted our children to have a father. But I would never, ever live in a house ruled by fear and violence.

'Your dad's learned to be a lovely man to me, Lily, he understands me. He's taken the trouble to find out what makes me content. You'd be surprised how many couples – men and women – never bother to do that. It's all "how is she going to make me happy?" Your dad has learned that's not the question that matters.'

'What about his women?' I ask bluntly, trying to inflict a flesh wound. 'What about when he's

451

telling stupid old birds what he should be telling you? Spending your money on them? Using time with them when he should've been with us?'

Mam sighs. 'It's his gift of the gab they like and that comes cheap enough. Every man needs time to himself. Some go fishing, some play darts. Your dad, not very often, but more than once or twice...' she glances at my face, heavy now with scepticism '... every once in a while, he would, will, spend a couple of hours with a woman. He–'

'I can't believe that you knew and put up with it. Have you ever asked him to stop?' I ask curtly. 'Have you ever said, "Stop doing it now or I go"? You did it over him being a bully. Why not this? Why allow yourself to be so humiliated? Have you no self-respect? What kind of message does that send to us when we see our mother allowing herself to be used as number-fourteen wife in the bloody harem?'

'Look, Lily,' Mam rallies, 'I devour people – haven't you, of all people, noticed?' she adds drily. 'I never want to let them go. I smother them. Yes, it hurts. Of course it hurts. That's why he tries to make sure I never find out. He tries, but I've always known anyway.'

'Aren't you frightened that one day he'll meet somebody and never come back?'

'Why would he do that? He's lucky to have me. He's always known that. Anyway, if he did go, I'd survive.'

'But why can't he just be normal? When I live with someone, if I thought he'd been unfaithful, even once, that would be it. It's wrong, wrong, wrong.'

452

'Wrong?' Mam says the word reflectively. 'If I asked your dad a direct question, "Douglas, have you been with another woman tonight?" he'd answer truthfully. I didn't ask, he didn't see the need to tell me.'

'So if you're all so honest, why pretend you're married?'

'We wanted to get married but Doug's wife wouldn't agree to a divorce. He agreed to pay her maintenance and he thought that, with time, she'd change her mind. But she never did. Once you girls came along, I told you, I changed my name by deed poll. We didn't have a choice.

'People could be very, very nasty... I didn't want any of you to go through that.'

'Does Kath know?'

Mam shrugs. 'I don't know. We've never spoken about it. The first time we met, I'd already changed my name. Kath had her own difficulties. She'd left home with Dulcie and was taking jobs as a housekeeper, but it was hard. Some people didn't want a child like Dulcie in their house ... so she got paid very little and worked terribly long hours. The first time I met her she had a job just outside Glasgow.'

'Do you know who Dulcie's dad is?'

'What? Are you determined to drag every skeleton out until the cupboard is bare? Yes. I do know. I found out when I was trying to work out why your dad had such a dark side to him... I thought something had happened to him in the war.

'And?'

'He got a couple of medals but he hates to talk about it. He'd dragged one friend clear and went

453

back for a second. It was hand-to-hand fighting.' She stops and cups my face in her hands. 'It seems strange. You're the one who's found out. Perhaps it's fate, perhaps somebody's decided that you're the one who needs to know.'

I pull away, prickling. 'It's not about needing to know, is it? It's about the truth. The truth matters, Mam. You've lived so long without it, you've forgotten that.' A growing sense of unease has begun to overtake all my other conflicted emotions.

'Did Dad do something terrible?' I ask, winded, as if someone has hit me hard in the stomach. 'Did he? That woman said, "You made me do the unforgivable." What did she mean? Did they have any children? Did Dad make her get rid of a baby? What did she mean, Mam? Did he kill her child? Their child? What happened, Mam? What really happened?'

'A lot of soldiers did terrible things in the war,' Melody replies. 'He told me that it was strange, all the violence his father had inflicted on him, the constant beatings, the name-calling, that's what came together in the war. He was ashamed that it was called "courage". He says when he fought, sometimes the man he was attacking was little more than a kid himself but what Doug would see was his dad. It was his dad, over and over again. So he made them pay... But people change... You have to believe that, Lily love, people change. They can and do make amends... That's all I know about your dad.'

She has that look that says, 'no more', so I change tack. 'Had Dad or Kath ever tried to find their mother?'

'They wouldn't know where to begin. Kath always believed that their dad had killed their mam. That she'd never leave her children willingly. I think Kath told herself that because she couldn't bear to face the alternative ... but who knows? Once their dad died, so did the chance of discovering where she'd gone because he knew what had happened to her but he wouldn't tell... He treated his kiddies brutally.'

I sit stunned, trying to absorb what I've been told. 'They were all alone with him and nobody tried to help? Nobody did anything?'

'Nobody wanted to know,' Melody says gently. 'From the outside, they were just an ordinary family, like every other family...'

'Why didn't Kath stay with the man who made her pregnant? Was he married?'

I can see Mam choosing her words carefully. 'This is Kath's secret, not mine, but I'm telling you now because I'm worried that if I don't you'll ferret around and cause even more upset. I want you to promise that, no matter who you decide to tell about your dad and me, you will keep Kath's secret. Do you promise?'

'I swear on my life.'

Mam takes a deep breath. 'Kath was raped by her father,' she says. 'She was fourteen years of age. He had interfered with her. Doug came home unexpectedly and found them. Kath was crying and terrified and her dad had his trousers round his ankles with a belt in his hand. Doug beat him so badly he thought he'd killed him. Kath was put in a home for unmarried mothers but she refused to name the child's father. If she had, her dad would have gone to prison.

'Her dad insisted that the child be adopted. It's wrong that, isn't it? The rapist having the right to decide?'

'What did Kath do?'

'She ran away. She took Dulcie and she walked out of the home. Doug was waiting for her. He had a tiny bit saved and he bought two single tickets to Bridlington. They'd been there once as kids when their mother was around. She got a job as a lady's companion, looking after an old biddy, and Dulcie went into a nursery.

'She looked after herself and a baby at fourteen?'

'I think the old lady was really good to her – used to give her bits and pieces for the baby. She had to say she was Dulcie's sister because they could've put her in a home for wayward girls. Then, she gradually knocked off a few years from her age and told Dulcie she was nine when she was born. That's how the fibbing began. It was part shame, part survival. Everyone kept telling Kath to put Dulcie away but she wouldn't. Nobody would've thought the worse of her for abandoning Dulcie but she didn't. However spiky she may be, Lily, she's a good woman. And there's another thing...'

Mam shifts in her seat, uncomfortable with the consequences of what she's about to say. 'She's always been tough on Dulcie because of her father ... if you know what I mean.'

I'm puzzled, then realisation dawns. 'What? That the child will be horrible like him? She believes people are born bad? Oh, that's ridiculous. We're all part of the same family tree – what are we going

456

to do? Start lopping off all the branches we don't like, render ourselves barren? What does that make me and Daisy and Rose and Iris? What?'

'It makes you good girls,' Mam says firmly. 'Underneath, you're a lovely person, Lily.'

Underneath? I look into my mother's eyes, and where before I'd seen a woman of irritatingly simple satisfactions and annoyingly blind optimism, content to live in a suffocatingly tiny world in which the decision of greatest import is when to start boiling the spuds, now I have a glimpse of her strengths and the power of her self-belief and the complexities that love brings to the most ordinary lives. But I'm still not sure I like her.

Chapter Forty-eight

Don Wilson wears a pale green polo-neck, a dark brown corduroy jacket and camel-coloured slacks. He helps himself to toast and marmalade. 'Hello, darling,' he greets his wife, as she comes through the door on the opposite side of the kitchen. He puckers his lips and kisses the air. Behind Adele, is a woman in her early thirties, Linda Westman. 'Sleep all right, Linda?' Don asks cheerily.

Adele glowers at him as if he has just performed an act of gross insensitivity.

'Toast, Linda? A boiled egg, perhaps.' Don is undeterred. 'Got to keep your strength up.'

'Don, do shut up,' his wife demands, exasperated. 'Eating's the last thing on Linda's mind.

Talk sense.'

'Actually, I'd quite like a boiled egg,' the woman says, taking a seat at the table. Penny switches on the radio. Dinah Washington's voice fills the room, singing 'What A Diff'rence A Day Makes'. Linda promptly and spectacularly bursts into tears, her voice ululating with increasing volume.

'God,' Penny says.

'Turn that bloody radio off,' Adele snaps. 'Don't you know anything? It's their song.'

'*Was* our song.' Linda stops sobbing briefly. 'Was our song. Not any more. Not now he's run off with that cow, bitch, whore.'

'Linda, it can't have been all Norman's fault,' Adele suggests slyly.

'Oh, fuck off!' Linda shouts. 'Of course she's to bloody blame. Norman wouldn't look at anyone without my permission. And now he's gone.' More sobs.

Don pats the woman's back in an ineffectual attempt at comfort. 'The complete and utter bastard,' he says, a gleam of envy in his eyes.

Later, when the two women have left to visit a solicitor, he tidies up the kitchen while Penny finishes some homework. 'How about the boyfriend?' he asks his daughter gingerly.

'Bulbie. He's a prat,' Penny replies curtly. 'God knows what I saw in him. He was outside Woolie's yesterday and I had to stop myself vomiting on the spot. It's odd, really, because I could've sworn he was the love of my life...'

'Well, we all make mistakes.' Her father looks at his watch. 'How's Lily? I heard about her father... Difficult political position to take up – a Tory

458

among the comrades.'

'He's not a Tory – he just thinks union bosses are as bad as every other boss and–'

'No lectures. It's too early in the morning. Has Lily heard anything yet?' Don asks casually, pulling on his coat.

'About what?'

'About university.'

'She's not bothered about that any more. She's virtually signed up to sing in a group. They're not famous, just a jobbing lot. She says she'll probably end up singing Peggy Lee songs on cruise ships. She's off straight after A levels and perhaps I'll go along too as her roadie or dresser or groupie or something.'

'That's a good idea,' her father replies absent-mindedly.

'Vladimir Komorov, aged forty, the Soviet cosmonaut, was killed yesterday when his Soyuz spacecraft crashed to earth after coming out of orbit. A Kremlin commission will investigate the tragedy, the world's first space-flight disaster. All forty-seven American astronauts have signed a telegram of symp–'

Daisy reaches over and switches off the television news. 'One of the good things about being a nobody who never goes anywhere is that nothing ever happens,' she says cheerily, opening a box of chocolates that someone has left for her father as a get-well present. 'Is that the time?' she adds, glancing at the clock on the mantelpiece. 'I've got to fly.'

'What? Does Carl expect dinner on the table or

459

there'll be hell to pay?' I ask sarcastically.

'No, he doesn't – but I like to do it,' she replies defensively, flushing. 'I've packed in my job so I should make sure the house is nice and he's got something to eat when he comes home. What's wrong with that?' She throws a cushion at me. 'I can't help it if nobody wants you, can I?' she taunts. 'Are you getting back with Bryn?' She looks at herself in the mirror over the mantelpiece, apparently reasonably pleased with the image reflected back: the good wife.

'Pam Jackson from the caravan site is up the duff,' Daisy chats. 'He's been promising to get married since the day they met. The only women who fall for that line, if you ask me, are thickos and slappers.'

Bored, irritated and fed up with the fodder that fills my sister's mind, I nod in the direction of the clock. 'I forgot to tell you,' I lie. 'That's twenty minutes slow. Carl will be standing at the door with a rolling-pin, yelling for his din-dins.'

'Cow!'

She runs for the door, grabbing her coat. Then she stops. 'You said you wanted to tell me something?'

'It's nothing.' I wave her off. 'Nothing matters.'

After she's gone, I sit in my dad's shed. I light the paraffin stove because it's cold in spite of the early-spring weather. Strips of cardboard are laid out on the workbench, alongside a half-completed dog, a stack of empty cigarette packets and an overflowing ashtray. The smell of tobacco still hangs in the air. They say that one human

460

year is equivalent to seven dog years. So, in the hundreds of dog days since Christmas, our family has moved and shifted and changed, and, strangely, also stayed the same.

Daisy has married; Iris hasn't; Dulcie may yet see her dream come true and be powdered with confetti; Kath has had her five minutes of fame; Rose is A Published Author; and I've cocked up on several fronts.

I'm still in the back row of history but at least I'll have a small chance of dancing in the aisles if I spend six months on the road with eight sweaty men. I've also discovered that I do have something in common with my three sisters: we were all born on the wrong side of the sheets. My mam has followed her heart, and I admire her for that – but what else has she concealed, especially about the dark side of my dad? What did he make Renee do that she considered unforgivable?

I switch on my dad's old tape-recorder. Dean Martin's soft toffee voice has a spooky effect, as if he's in the room. In a corner of the hut is a stack of old biscuit tins. I poke about. The first two hold junk – balls of string, screwdrivers, fuse wires. The third contains a stash of newspaper cuttings. Heart thudding, I unfold the first handful. Each details the disappearance of a young boy, Daniel Andrews, a little boy who went missing not long after Christmas. I sift through, faster and faster. They detail the search, the arrest and release of a suspect, the parents' heartbreak and, last week, a press statement that said police were scaling down their investigation.

'Have you found what you're looking for?' my

dad asks, standing in the doorway. He is white-faced and on crutches. What strikes me immediately is that there is no smile on his face.

Afraid, I grab the tin and run out of the door, down Rydol Crescent, to the quay and Coronation Park. I promise myself that I will never trust another human being ever again. I will never trust my judgement of anyone again, ever. If you don't know your own parents, how can you know anyone?

My dad, the smiling survivor – is he really capable of killing? Capable of killing a child? Did he strike out in temper? Or perhaps he was in a car with Betty Procter. Does that explain her hold over him? Perhaps they knocked the boy down by accident. I know my dad, he couldn't do that. But in reality, I tell myself, as I fly through the park, I know next to nothing about my dad. The past never stays quiet. It always hits back. I'd told Daisy that. Now I know it's true.

At the cricket pavilion, in the park, I sit on a bench and empty the tin. I arrange the newspaper cuttings chronologically. The dates coincide. The night my father was supposed to be at the pub, the night that Bunting's burned, was the day the boy went missing – only twenty or so miles from Fairport.

Had Renee covered up for a previous crime? Had he paid her all these years not because he ought to but because he must? To buy her silence? How much does my mother know? Only once have I seen his temper. He hit Rose so hard, when I was four or five, that she knocked her head against the table corner, and a bump the

462

size of a duck's egg appeared on her forehead.

'It was an accident,' my dad had said again and again, white-faced. 'It was an accident. Things happen.' It was also the only time I can remember my mother truly, ferociously angry with my dad. 'Never touch the girls again,' she'd said. And he hadn't. But what had he done outside the home?

Things happen.

Barry had said he respected my dad as a man of principle. Could he have been conned too? Barry, who took pride in his ability to spot the fake, the unauthentic? My mother swims into view, plate of sandwiches in one hand, cup of tea in the other. 'I like the Duchess of Malfi,' she'd said. 'She does what her heart tells her to do no matter what society says. That's brave.' Brave? Or mad?

I return the cuttings to the tin. I have absolutely no idea what to do. Least of all, how to shake off the fear that somehow everything that's happened is my fault. I am to blame. I am bad. I am my father's daughter.

Chapter Forty-nine

Eventually I go home. But first I collect Daisy and Rose and haul Iris out of the Bible reading group, which she has recently joined. 'It's life and death,' I say.

'Isn't it always?' Iris replies, rolling her eyes. But they all agree to come with me. We four walk along the quay. Iris links arms with Daisy and

Rose links arms with me, as if she senses how troubled I am.

We pass Kath, in the Contented Sole, who waves. We skirt Woolworth's and cross the square. Daisy whittles on about Carl's supper and how lovely the new Co-op is looking.

'What's in the tin?' Rose asks me.

I don't trust my voice to answer.

A bizarre sight greets us in the back room of Rydol Crescent. Dad is sitting at the table. Scrubs, the dog, is in front of him. Mam is handing him a pair of scissors. 'What's this?' says Rose. 'Ritual sacrifice?'

'Sit down, girls,' Mam instructs. 'Your father's got something to say. Are you all right, love?' she asks me.

Dad remains dumb. He plunges the scissors into the dog's back, then begins to snip away. Snip, snip, snip. He puts the scissors down and takes a small passport-size photograph from the dog's belly. I draw in my breath sharply. I can see it's a photograph of a boy, grey shorts, curly hair like Dad's, frowning at the camera.

'Is he dead?' I say, before I can stop myself. 'Did you do something terrible to him, Dad?'

Kit wearily locks up the van for the night. Business is building nicely. After a few mishaps, she has learned to order reasonably accurately but she needs a permanent roof over her head and a garage for the van: Tanner Hicks wants to reclaim his space.

As she shifts a crate of apples, a swede rolls across the floor from the other side of the lock-up towards her. 'Hello, is anybody there?' she whispers, her voice cracking. 'My dad's on his way. He'll be here any minute.'

Another swede rolls across the floor. Kit drops the crate, opens her mouth wide and screams and screams. 'Christ almighty, girl.' Pete scrambles from behind a pile of Tanner's stock. 'I only meant it as a joke. Are you all right?'

'Oh, you stupid, stupid fool.' Kit hits his arm in pretend anger. 'What a bloody silly stunt to pull.' She smiles, but moves swiftly as Pete reaches out for her. 'Two fellas are after you, say you owe them something. They've gone back now but they didn't look too happy.'

'Gary and Paul? They wouldn't hurt me. They like me too much,' Pete swaggers. 'How's business?'

Kit pulls out ten single pound notes. 'Here, take this, I can pay the rest soon, too.' To her disappointment, Pete takes the notes. 'How do you know those two? They played brass with us at Daisy's wedding, and they were brilliant.'

'Paul is Marie's cousin. She wants a divorce. She's met a fella and, for some bloody silly reason, she thought because I wasn't around that I was trying to avoid her.'

Kit looks at him quizzically. 'That's not what Paul told Lily. He said they wanted money from you for Marie. Why is it, Pete Wells, that every event in your life has at least half a dozen versions? How do I know whether what you've just said is the gospel truth or a pack of lies?'

Pete grins.

'What's brought you back this time?' Kit asks.

'Robert's getting married but you knew that anyway. In August. The four girls are going to be dressed in lemon sherbet, like lollipops, and Billy will be pageboy.'

'And Kath?'

Kit shrugs. 'She seems sort of OK about it. She's still as bloodthirsty as ever, but since she's been in the local paper she's a bit less prickly. She's got a couple of pen-pals. Are you staying?'

Pete shakes his head. 'Just called by for a night in with you. It's still not safe round here. I've got things to do. Clients to talk to.'

'Clients?' Kit says sceptically. 'In Africa, I expect?'

'All round the world, babe. You know me.'

Later, Pete tells Kit the truth. He is due in court shortly and expects to be sent down for several months for possession of stolen goods. 'Is that why you've been playing Cupid? So Robert isn't left on his own?' Kit asks.

'Look at me,' he says. 'Do I look that soft?'

'Who is he?' Rose asks quietly, holding the photograph of the boy. 'Is he yours, Dad?'

'Can I talk to them first, love?' Mam turns to Dad. He nods. He looks drawn and dulled and trapped.

'Your father and I aren't married. We....'

Iris slumps forward theatrically on to the kitchen table. 'Not married? Not married? Oh, my God, that makes me a... That means I'm illegitimate. Oh, my God, how can I show my face in the chapel again?'

Daisy feeds off her sister's panic. 'Does that

mean I'm not married to Carl? Does that make me a bigamist or something? Why didn't you tell us? How could you do that to us?'

Rose and I say nothing. Mam gets up and puts her hands on Dad's shoulders, as if she's trying to transmit some energy into him. 'We wanted to get married but Dad's wife wouldn't divorce him. Now she will. We did what we thought was best for all of you. When your name was in the magazine, Rose love, we weren't cross with you. We were proud, very proud. But we thought that it meant she'd be able to find us. She'd make a fuss and it would all come out... I'm sorry.'

'The boy in the photo, Dad,' Rose says, her voice tense. 'What about the boy?'

I empty the contents of the biscuit tin on to the table. 'And what about this boy too, Dad? What happened to Daniel Andrews?'

My dad's hands shake when he lights his cigarette. He takes an age to speak. 'I first met Renee, the woman I married, when I was eighteen. She was a couple of years older. She lived near the barracks and I used to see her around. We courted for a couple of months until I was posted away. She wrote for a few weeks but then the letters stopped coming. War's like that.

'Two years later I was in England on leave. I had nowhere much to go. I was lonely, I suppose. On impulse, I decided to travel down and pay her a visit. If she'd married or had a bloke, I'd say hello and goodbye. That was the plan. She was still living with her mum and dad. She was playing in the garden with a toddler. This boy.' He holds up the photograph. 'His name was

Michael. Straight away she said he was mine. She said she thought I'd been killed. She wasn't next-of-kin. She wouldn't have been told if I'd died.

'The boy was a good little chap. When I looked at him, I thought I could see myself. He didn't smile much, like me. I was happy. I'd always wanted to be part of a proper family, one without cruelty, and now I'd got one ready-made.

'We were married with a special licence. It seemed the right thing to do. We rented a flat, and whenever I was away I'd send her money, dead regular. I was proud: I was a father. Each time I came home on leave, it was a bit difficult between us but then we'd settle down all right. But the more time I spent with the little lad, the more certain I became that he wasn't mine. She wouldn't have it. She swore she'd fallen for him the first month we met.

'When the boy was four or so, I was having a drink in a pub and a soldier came up to me. He was a little bit drunk. He didn't have to tell me, but he wanted to anyway. Pride, I suppose. I knew anyway, just by looking at him. I knew he was Michael's father.

'He was looking for a fight – or that's what I told myself at the time. Now, I don't know... I'm ashamed to say that I beat him near to death. As far as I was concerned, he was a robber and a thief. He'd taken my dreams, my family from me.

'Only later did I think that maybe she'd been stringing us both along, living off the money we both sent. I found out he was married. Already had three kids of his own. Perhaps he'd come to warn me off... I just don't know any more...' Dad puts his head in his hands. We sit frozen, shocked, as if his body has cleaved open, like the prickly skin of a chestnut, and something strange and diabolical has been revealed within.

'Witnesses said I'd been provoked, so I only got six months. It was wartime.

'She visited me a couple of times in prison. I told her I didn't want to see her. She sent me a letter saying she would make it up to me. Make it all better.'

'What did she do?' Daisy asks in a whisper.

Dad's voice is almost inaudible. 'I came out and went to the flat to pick up my stuff. She was waiting. She'd sent the boy away. She'd put Michael in a home. Told them she couldn't cope any more. She told him she'd be back for him after tea. Poor little so-and-so must've waited for days, months...

'She said that I'd more or less told her it was him or me. I don't think I ever did. I know I never did. But perhaps ... I don't know ... I had a terrible, terrible temper. I must have scared that poor boy witless a few times, but I never laid a hand on him... I've gone over the time I was with her again and again, but I can't remember ever saying, "Put the boy away..."'

None of us moves. Daisy is looking sympathetic.

Iris is dabbing her eyes, as if she's attending the funeral of her own reputation. 'See, Dad? See how one lie leads to another?' she lectures. '"Thou shalt not lie", that's what it says in the–'

'Oh, piss off, Iris,' Rose snaps, exasperated.

'Did you try to find him?' Daisy asks. 'Have you ever looked for Michael?'

Dad nods. 'Renee wouldn't tell me anything.

469

And nobody else would either, since he wasn't mine to find. In a way, though, he's never left me. For years I've seen him out of the corner of my eye, or across the street, or in the dark of a room. Sometimes he's laughing, sometimes he's mocking me, sometimes he's just standing with a certain look he used to have on his face when he knew I had to go back to barracks. A ghost of a boy.' He gives a hollow laugh, which dissolves into coughing. 'I suppose that's why it's hard for me to let any of you go, no matter how grown-up you've become.' He looks at me. 'That and the fact that I still think university is a bloody waste of time.' He smiles weakly.

'Why didn't you just tell us everything when we were old enough to understand?' Daisy challenges.

'And now you know, do you understand – do you really?' he says gently.

'How long did you and the woman stay together after Michael had gone?' Iris's voice wavers.

'Only for a few months. Sometimes we were angry, mostly there was this terrible sadness. I just couldn't make sense of it. Eventually I left. I kept Michael's photograph. I opened up Scrubs and put him inside. I didn't want his photograph to become just another snapshot in a stack; just another picture on the page of an album...

'What about Daniel Andrews?' I ask tersely. 'What about this boy, this year?'

Mam squeezes my arm, and I pull away, angry with the smashed mirror that was once our family history. Odd pieces are still recognisable, but so much is now distorted and discordant.

'Listen, Lily,' she says, 'he hasn't harmed the

470

child. He does it every time a child goes missing, he keeps the bits from the newspapers. I've tried to make him stop. It's almost as if he's punishing himself over and over again–'

'Michael wasn't mine,' Dad interrupts, 'but I'd known him on and off for almost two years. He was a good boy. Then there was the suddenness of his going. The memory of all the things I should have said and didn't...'

'So why have you paid her maintenance all these years?' Rose asks abruptly.

'I left her. I owed it to her. She forfeited her son and I was the cause.'

'Oh, bollocks.' Rose moves away from the table, as if to illustrate the distance between herself and our dad. 'She milked you for money and did what she wanted to do. Unless, of course, you did say, "It's me or him." Did you, Dad?'

'Rose, how can you be so horrible?' Daisy breaks in. 'She loved Dad, she must have loved Dad, and he didn't... well, he didn't... it's so sad. It's so sad, for everyone ... that poor little Michael...'

'It could've been the best thing that happened to him,' Rose answers back robustly. 'He wasn't Dad's flesh and blood, was he?... He might have gone to a family who cared, a family with books and ideas and...' Her voice peters out as she becomes aware of the implications of what she is saying.

Silence follows. Eventually Mam gets up. 'How about a nice cup of tea?' she suggests, her terrible brightness returned. 'By the way, there's a letter come for you, Lily. Let's hope it's good news. We could do with a bit of cheering up.'

Chapter Fifty

Local newspapers should have a section for this particular rite of passage. Births, marriages, deaths – and what? Revelations? Strangely, over the next several days, no one in the family mentions any of what has emerged. It's as if we need to bury what we've been told until we have each recovered enough either to make personal sense of it or remould it into a more manageable 'truth'. Only the matrimonially obsessed Iris can't shut up. She refuses to speak to my father on account of his transgressions but doesn't stop yakking to Mam. She's realised that while she may no longer be arranging her own nuptials with Howard, she can now wallow in organising a wedding for our mother. I'm too busy for reflection or recriminations. The exit door has suddenly opened wide.

The letter that had arrived for me offers a second chance. The interview that I had failed to attend at Warwick University has been rescheduled. Dr Jack Spurling, head of the history department, is looking forward to meeting me, if I am inclined to attend. I call round to see Penny. Her father is in his den, looking pleased with himself. But then again, he always looks pleased with himself. 'Excuse me, Mr Wilson, Don ... do you know Jack Spurling?'

'Yes, Lily,' he says, smirking. 'As a matter of fact I do. He's a good friend of mine.'

472

'Oh,' I reply. 'I just wondered.'
He looks disappointed.

At the end of April I have a successful audition in Manchester. I am offered a job in Brighton for the summer, working with Gary and Paul and the Blues Makers for seven pounds a week. Once I leave, however often I come back, I'll never belong again. Exile is painful. I'll have to discover whether the freedom it also brings is worth what I forfeit. Either way I have no choice. If I stay I suffocate.

My dad also plans changes. His former boss, Mrs Bunting, knows one of the directors of Whitman's breweries. When the post of manager of the Duck and Fox falls vacant, she puts in a good word and he charms his way into the job. Mam is going to do the cooking. To celebrate, they announce their engagement in the local paper. Veronica in the tea shop almost has a heart-attack; the gossip is never-ending but, of course, nobody says a word, not to our faces.

Daisy reveals that she is pregnant. She'll miss her husband's deadline by two months since the baby will be born in February. She seems happy. The day before my university interview, my dad asks to talk to me. On the stool in his shed, the *Daily Express* has a front-page story about Daniel Andrews. A boy's skeleton – believed to be Daniel's – has been found 102 days after his disappearance, in woodland thirteen miles from his home. It is unlikely that the cause of death will ever be established.

'It's the never knowing,' my dad says. 'That's what gets to me about Michael. The never knowing. The pain that Daniel's poor family have endured is nothing to what lies ahead. The never knowing. Why them? Why their little boy?' A muscle jumps in his cheek. Angrily he rips out the page, crumples it up and throws it in a wastepaper basket, already full with all his discarded cuttings.

I make us tea. As I hand him the mug, I can see that he has lost weight, his face is slightly scarred, but otherwise he is spruce again: a good-looking man. He says he's had the results of his medical for the publican's job, and they reveal what he'd already suspected. He has lung cancer. We are in the dog days of death. He says that he's telling me because I am leaving. A few months ago, I would have seen that as emotional blackmail. Now I prefer to believe that it's because he wants us to have a chance to make amends.

My dad asks me – always the conspirator – not to tell the others. 'I'm proud of you Lily,' he says, for the first time in my life, and I can see how he struggles with the words. 'I don't agree with this decision to go to university, but I'm proud of you and each of my girls.'

I try not to cry. He takes me in his arms. 'I've been a very lucky man,' he says, without irony. 'I never thought I'd learn what it means to be loved. But I have.'

'I'm still going, Dad,' I say, hating myself for acting so selfishly.

'I know,' he says.

On the day of my interview, Kit insists on taking a day off and drives me to Coventry in Vera the van. We travel for seven hours. It would have only taken four on the train. But she insisted that that's what friends are for. She waits in the university car park, and does a bit of business, flogging fruit and veg, until someone official tells her she needs a licence. A couple of students successfully protest at this barbaric intervention by the police state. In solidarity with the people, Kit gives away a whole load of bananas that are on the point of going soft anyway. So everyone is happy.

Professor Jack Spurling's office is in a prefabricated building marooned in a sea of mud. The entire university consists of prefabs. No danger of being spiked by dreaming spires here. He has silverwhite hair and wears a black leather jacket, black slacks and a black shirt. He sits in a very large black leather chair, which he periodically swings round, whizzing past sentences. 'Interesting, yup,' he says, at every second word I speak. 'Interesting, yup. Tell me more.'

Frankly, after the first ten minutes, there isn't much more to tell. This time I'm not nearly so nervous, partly because the setting reflects how I feel, put-together and shambolic.

Dr Spurling can't find my personal file, so he improvises from memory. 'Interesting, yup. I see you come from a comprehensive... quite a few schools you've been to, in fact... Tell me more. And your father? Blue collar? White? What? History, aah, history. Now, tell me, why history? Tell me, come on, tell me...

'Interesting ... yup ... and your point is...' Professor Spurling says, bouncing up and down in his chair, running his fingers through his hair, looking at my legs, before I've opened my mouth.

'The point is, I'm less interested in traditional history, the record of the politics of power,' I say. 'I want to be the kind of historian who looks for the forgotten voices, the oral testimonies of people who don't think they're important enough or who can't read or write, or who find themselves stuck in the back row of history when all the action appears to be going on in a totally different place. Their voices are as authentic and have as much a part to play as any diary of a lord chancellor or...' I'm beginning to run out of steam as, for the umpteenth time, Dr Spurling's face goes spinning past in a blur. I struggle on: 'I think you can learn as much from the blues singers in the Delta belt as–'

'Two Bs,' Jack Spurling says, suddenly braking and writing furiously.

'Pardon?'

'Two Bs – see you in October.'

See you in October. I shout the words like some mad, delirious woman as I career down the path towards the car park. Kit is standing, waiting, a bunch of bananas in each hand. She waves and, uncaring, I take a short-cut, ploughing straight across the dug-up field, towards her, sinking ankle deep in mud. 'Two Bs,' I yell at her uncomprehending face. 'Two Bs.'

She laughs because I'm laughing. I grab her and we do an impromptu polka around the car park, scattering bananas. 'I'm in! I'm in! Two Bs, two Bs, I'm in...'

'Two Bs. Is that all they've asked for?' says a tall, thin boy with a posh accent, wearing a corduroy jacket and checked shirt. 'They want three As from me. That's not fair.'

'Isn't it?' Kit retorts. 'Don't you know? Things are different now.'

The publishers hope that this book has given you enjoyable reading. Large Print Books are especially designed to be as easy to see and hold as possible. If you wish a complete list of our books please ask at your local library or write directly to:

Magna Large Print Books
Magna House, Long Preston,
Skipton, North Yorkshire.
BD23 4ND

This Large Print Book for the partially sighted, who cannot read normal print, is published under the auspices of

THE ULVERSCROFT FOUNDATION